Alex Palmer is a Canberra-based novelist who took up writing full time when she was made redundant from the Australian Public Service. With *Blood Redemption*, she won the Ned Kelly Award for best first crime novel, and shared the Sisters in Crime Davitt Award for best crime novel by a woman with Gabrielle Lord. *The Tattooed Man* won the 2008 Canberra Critics Cricle Award.

Books by Alex Palmer

Blood Redemption
The Tattooed Man
The Labyrinth of Drowning

THE LABYRINTH OF DROWNING

ALEX PALMER

To Tara & weegie at 13th
Street

Alex Palmer

■ HarperCollins*Publi*

Author's Note

All events, places and individuals depicted in this novel are wholly fictional. Any resemblance to any actual event, place or individual, whether existing or historical, is purely coincidental and unintentional.

HarperCollins*Publishers*

First published in Australia in 2009
by HarperCollins*Publishers* Australia Pty Limited
ABN 36 009 913 517
www.harpercollins.com.au

HarperCollins*Publishers*
25 Ryde Road, Pymble, Sydney, NSW 2073, Australia
31 View Road, Glenfield, Auckland 0627, New Zealand
1–A, Hamilton House, Connaught Place, New Delhi – 110 001, India
77–85 Fulham Palace Road, London, W6 8JB, United Kingdom
2 Bloor Street East, 20th floor, Toronto, Ontario M4W 1A8, Canada
10 East 53rd Street, New York NY 10022, USA

National Library of Australia Cataloguing-in-Publication data:

Palmer, Alex, 1952– .
  Labyrinth of drowning / Alex Palmer.
  ISBN: 978 0 7322 8574 6 (pbk.)
  Murder–Investigation–Fiction.
  Sydney (N.S.W.)–Fiction
A823.4

Cover design by Natalie Winter
Cover image by Shutterstock
Typeset in 11/15 Sabon by Kirby Jones
Printed and bound in Australia by Griffin Press
The Book Ivory used by HarperCollins*Publishers* is a natural,
product made from wood grown in sustainable forests. The manufacturing
conform to the environmental regulations in the country of origin, Finland.

5 4   10 11 12

For Maggie Shapley

Nobody knows himself
Goya, *Los Caprichos*, Number 6.

1

If I had wings, I could fly away. Grace Riordan improvised the lyric and the music in her head, infinitely sad. More often there's no way out, she thought. The Thai woman, the one with no name, had only gone so far. From the Villawood Immigration Detention Centre in the southwest of the city to the dry soil and sandstone rocks of northern Sydney's Ku-ring-gai Chase National Park. Under trees that gave off the sharp, antiseptic smell of eucalyptus, she lay with the back of her head broken open against the ground. The floodlights set up by the police cast a monochrome glare over the woman and the surrounding bushland.

Grace was used to death; it was part of the work she did in law enforcement. But sometimes you met with something that brought you to a stop; where the reality was too powerful for you to brush it aside. The woman's dress, flimsy and girlish, was partly torn away, the fabric thickened with blood. The torn pieces clung to her, held in place by the belt left around her waist, seeming strangely obscene. Not only the back of her head but also her legs and arms, which were small, almost delicate, had been smashed. Her face and torso were covered with the marks of the beating she must have thought would never stop, not while she was living. Someone had broken this woman down piece by piece until she might not have been human and then left her here for someone to find. Seeing her was like walking into a glass wall.

The woman's eyes were still open. Grace met the blank gaze. She stood up, her hand bunched as a fist at her mouth for a few seconds. She had to take photographs, it was standard operating procedure.

'Where are her shoes?' she asked.

'Who knows? But she must have run quite a distance. Her feet are in bad shape.'

The man who answered her, the local command's senior detective sergeant, was stocky with a black, pencil-thin beard. Mark Borghini. She hadn't heard of him before.

'Who found her?'

'A married couple who live about a kilometre away in North Turramurra, out with their kids for a night-time walk. They heard something crashing through the bush. The wife thought it was a dog. Then they found her.' He looked down at the body. 'They probably disturbed the killer. I think she was beaten and assaulted somewhere else and tried to make a run for it.'

The pathologist arrived, Kenneth McMichael, his technicians following him like acolytes.

'My God,' he said, kneeling and studying the dead woman's head. 'Who did this?' His huge frame dwarfed the small corpse.

'Any idea of the weapon?' Borghini asked.

'Something very hard and heavy. That's what it usually takes to smash the back of the head.' McMichael was renowned for his withering sarcasm.

'Thanks, mate. I could have worked that out for myself.' Borghini stepped away from the woman's broken body, turning his back.

McMichael was frowning. 'Someone's given her a real beating. Not enough to kill but savage. You two have got your work cut out for you here. I often think you get to deal with the nicest people.'

Fist to skin. The sound, the shock. Dead-sounding when it connected. Crack, smack, instantaneous, so harsh. It was their strength — you should be able to stop them but you couldn't. The thought: I'm going to die. Grace had not died. Her assailant had raped her.

'Has she been sexually assaulted?' she asked.

Something in her voice made both Borghini and McMichael turn to look at her.

'You'll have to wait for the autopsy to know the extent,' McMichael said. 'But there is one thing.' He had a swab in his hand, which he brushed around and inside the woman's mouth. 'She was made to kneel before she died. I think this will be semen.'

'Fucking arsehole,' Borghini muttered.

My face was like that once, Grace thought. But that wasn't the worst of it. The man who had beaten and raped her then carved a slow and careful cut into her neck. It was still there as a scar, a thin thread from her chin to her breastbone, a cut as much in her mind as in her body. Remember me, he'd said. Because I love you.

Past the pathologist's shoulder, Grace could still see the woman's face. Her dead eyes had taken hold of her. *We wouldn't let you go home and I told you we would protect you. And here you are.*

Grace had met the woman a few days earlier, sent to interview her by her boss, Clive Smith. He'd watched her closely as he gave her the brief, a strange edge to his voice.

'You've read the alert,' he said. 'A Thai woman, with very little English, twenty-eight, physically very small. Possibly brought to and held in Australia against her will. In other words, she fits the profile for Jirawan Sanders. I want you to interview her. Most of all, I want you to gauge her reaction to her present situation. Try to get a take on what kind of person she is. Is she susceptible to pressure? Can she be bought? When you've done that, I'll make a judgement where we take this.'

'If there's an alert, why don't we have a photograph of her?' Grace asked.

'You'll have to take it from me that there's none available.'

'My information on this detainee is that she's refused to identify herself except to say she's Thai and she wants to go home. Assuming that she is Jirawan Sanders, I'd like to know why you've given me a direct order not to mention that name under any circumstances.' Grace was careful to keep her voice even. She didn't want Clive to know he was getting to her.

Clive smiled a little arrogantly. He was always smooth. He'd been given the job as director of operations at Orion while she was away on maternity leave, making him directly her superior — an unpleasant surprise waiting for her when she came back to her position as a field operative with the ultra-secretive intelligence-gathering organisation where she'd worked for the last five years.

Orion was run directly by the federal government and answered to no one but the attorney-general and the cabinet. Grace could quote its brief in her sleep: the investigation and extirpation of externally generated threats that could endanger the Commonwealth's fabric and the lives of its citizens. Turned into action, this commonly meant that Orion undertook covert operations to counter the possibility of either terrorist activity or international criminal networks damaging the nation. It had draconian powers of surveillance, detention and arrest, which were often discussed in the media by worried commentators. Grace had taken a job here because she had thought she could make a difference, that she could do this work without damaging innocent bystanders. She had standards; she was here to save lives, not to coerce people or wrongly convict them. She wasn't so certain about Clive's motives.

'That name has to stay classified under all circumstances,' he was saying. 'As to the operation, it's my policy only to give operatives as much information as they need to do their work.'

'I believe I need to know more,' she replied, looking him in the eye. 'This alert is listed as a code one. That means there's an automatic stop on this detainee's deportation for as long as we're interested in her. That's going to lead to questions and I have to be able to field them. Besides that, there wasn't any information given about why we're interested in this Jirawan Sanders in the first place, or why it's so urgent we find her. Given she's Thai, presumably Sanders is her married name. Where's her husband? What's his involvement in this? If my interview with this detainee is going to be useful, don't I at least need some basic biographical information?'

Clive smiled at her again. He was somewhere in his mid-fifties, with well-preserved features and an unshakeable sense of calm.

This calm was genuine ice and it repulsed her. Emotion was only useful when it was being manipulated, something he did with finesse. Even the way he told everyone to call him by his first name seemed a pretence at openness. She shouldn't let her feelings affect her judgement so much. He came with the territory; by necessity it was a cold-blooded profession. But her dislike was too deep. Whether he had another life, any kind of lover, a partner perhaps, even children, she didn't know and didn't want to know.

'You know how to think,' he said, patronisingly, as if she had passed a test.

'That's why I'm here, isn't it?' she replied, manufacturing a professional smile of her own.

'Then you don't need to keep talking to me. There's nothing you've raised in this meeting that you shouldn't be able to handle. Go and see her. Then come back and tell me how she reacts. I think this discussion has gone on long enough.'

Clive wasn't someone you argued with for too long. She'd left his office quickly and made her way to the Villawood Immigration Detention Centre, where the woman was being held as an illegal immigrant. She'd been picked up in the city on George Street outside the concourse to Wynyard railway station at midnight four days ago, with no identification and only the clothes she'd been wearing. She'd refused to cooperate with the police, and they'd sent her to Villawood, not knowing what else to do.

Four people had been present for the interview: the Thai woman; Grace; the interpreter; and a Department of Immigration official, Jon Kidd. He was the officer in charge of the woman's case, and senior enough to have the necessary security clearance to deal with Orion. A short man, he was expensively and meticulously dressed, his leather shoes brushed to an almost mirror finish.

The Thai woman was tiny. Eye to eye, the first quality Grace saw in her was fear. It sat on her delicate frame as if it would break her. After that first terrified glance, she refused to look at Grace or the interpreter again, her eyes sliding sickly to the door, begging for a way out. Too often, like the reflex action of someone trapped, she looked at Kidd and then away, as if she was even more frightened of him. He didn't meet her eye but instead stared at Grace.

'Tell her not to be so afraid,' Grace said. 'We can give her protection if she needs it.'

The reply was brief tears, almost laughter.

'There's no such thing,' the interpreter translated awkwardly, clearly embarrassed. 'You can't help me.'

'I thought we were here for a meaningful interview,' Kidd said sarcastically. 'Why are you telling her things like that?'

'This woman is terrified.'

'I can see that. Ask your questions and go. Clearly you're frightening her.'

'I would have said she's just as much frightened of you.'

'She has no reason to be. We want to deport her, which is what she wants as well. You're just getting in the way,' Kidd said. 'Finish and let her go.'

'I want a name.'

'Nothing,' the interpreter said. 'She has no name.'

'That's not true. We all have a name.'

'Not her. She's wiped it out.'

'Then I'll find a way to give it back to her.'

Grace was shocked at herself. She was a professional; she didn't say things like that. But by then the woman was weeping continuously and the words weren't translated.

'For God's sake, finish it,' Kidd said. 'Let her go back to Thailand. That's all you can do for her.'

Impossible, Grace thought. The machinery has started; it'll grind us all down.

'That's the one thing I can't do now,' she said, maintaining composure. 'You must know that. Ask her one more time to talk to me.'

'She can't,' the interpreter said.

'This is going to be all your fault,' Kidd said ferociously in Grace's ear after they'd left the room.

'What are you talking about?' she demanded.

He looked at her with eyes bright with anger and accusation. 'Whatever happens next … it'll be your fault. Goodbye.'

Grace had carried the woman's fear back to Clive. Fear and secrecy were poisons she couldn't cure alone.

'Terrified,' she'd said. 'Absolutely terrified. She's acting like she expects to be murdered at any moment. And there's something else — Kidd, the immigration officer. I think we should check him out. Given the way he acted today and some of the things he said to me, I'd question his motives. Apart from that, this woman acted as if she felt in danger from him.'

Clive stared at her for some moments. 'That had better not be a wild accusation,' he said.

'I don't make those calls lightly.'

'Then get her out of there,' he replied. 'Now.'

But someone else had got there first. The information came through from Kidd himself: in the hour after Grace and the interpreter had left Villawood, the Thai woman had escaped while on her way to a medical appointment. Her whereabouts were unknown. Listening, Grace had to wonder if he was involved in any way. No one could get out of Villawood without help. But she had no grounds for putting the question directly to him, or not yet. Then, some thirty-six hours later, at 1:45 am, she got the phone call she'd been dreading.

I saw her before and after death, and now here on this cold, hard bed. It was several days later. Behind the glass partition at the morgue, Grace was watching the autopsy.

'Subject has a very neat Caesarean scar,' McMichael announced. 'Very well done. She's had at least one child at some stage. All right, let's get started.'

Under the pathologist's knife the most intrinsic of intrusions took place. It was the dead woman's final nakedness. With scalp removed and skull opened, the body peeled back breastbone to pelvic bone, the Thai woman ceased to be human and became a series of parts. Jon Kidd was standing next to Grace; he drew in his breath sharply, swore, then walked out.

'Get after him. We need him,' Borghini said to his offsider, who left the viewing area immediately. He turned to Grace. 'I thought he was her case manager. Didn't he ask to be here?'

'He's not used to seeing the dead,' Grace replied. 'They get killed somewhere else.'

She caught her breath; her façade had almost cracked as well. Every morning before going to work, she coiled up her long dark hair to sit at the back of her head, then put on her make-up, pale foundation that turned her face into the china mask of a heroine from an ancient Japanese drama. Her work clothes made up the rest of her armour. It wasn't an impenetrable disguise but it was usually enough to get her through. But she hadn't known this woman had had a child.

Grace had that same scar. Just eighteen months ago her daughter Ellie had been brought into the world in that same way when, after Grace had been in labour for twelve hours, the baby's heartbeat had dropped alarmingly. Paul Harrigan, her partner, carried in his wallet a photograph he had taken just after they'd first put the baby into her arms. Her hair was dark and messy against the white pillow, her face exhausted. Her long eyelashes brushed towards her cheeks as she looked down at Ellie, whom she seemed to be holding almost too tightly, the baby's head resting on the crook of her arm. Ellie's sparse hair clung in wet lines against her large and delicate head and her tiny crooked fingers were almost translucent.

There was no damp, newly breathing child or clean white sheets for this unknown woman on her metal bed. For the first time in her career, Grace was caught between two powerful emotions: fury at what had happened and the feeling that she might cry for the woman on the table.

'What do we have here?' McMichael said. 'I think it's a wedding ring.' He held up the proverbial gold band in a pair of tweezers.

'Mate,' Borghini said, 'we need that ring. Bag it up.'

'She swallowed it,' Grace said, shocked. 'She wasn't going to let her murderer take it away from her.'

The pathologist heard her over the intercom. 'Thank you, Mrs Harrigan,' he said furiously. 'How else was it going to get into her oesophagus? She barely got it down. It must have hurt.'

'She was brave then, wasn't she? And for your information, my surname is still Riordan.'

For once silenced, McMichael went back to work. He didn't speak again until he'd finished the autopsy.

'Definite signs of sexual contact but not necessarily actual physical sexual assault,' he said. 'Terrified into compliance presumably. As expected, the swab revealed semen in the mouth. As for the weapon, some kind of hammer, possibly the back of an axe head. Whoever your murderer is, he's clearly an evil bastard.'

'One wedding ring.' Borghini dropped the bag onto the meeting room table.

Grace picked it up. Inside was a thickish, eighteen-carat gold ring engraved with *P&J 4ever* against a background of two intertwined hearts. J for Jirawan.

'Where did that come from?' Jon Kidd asked.

'Out of her gut,' Grace replied, deliberately brutal. 'She swallowed it, probably just before she was murdered.'

He stared at her, glassy-eyed with shock.

'Did she have it with her in Villawood?' Borghini asked.

'No. How do we know it's hers?'

'Why else would she swallow it?' Grace asked, watching him closely.

'That ring is departmental property,' Kidd said. 'We have an obligation to return it to its rightful owners, which are this woman's relatives. I need to take it back with me.'

'No. In this case, this ring is evidence. It stays with the police.'

Kidd looked flustered. 'That's their decision, isn't it?' he said in a shaky voice.

'Yeah, and like Grace says, it stays with us,' Borghini said. 'Now, we have a name. Coco. She was a sex worker at a brothel called Life's Pleasures in Parramatta. A client rang the hotline. We've already interviewed him. You're seeing him this afternoon, aren't you?' He spoke to Grace.

'Yes, after I get back.'

'Has anyone else rung in?' Kidd asked.

'Not yet.'

'Then how do you know this information is accurate?'

'That's what we're going to find out,' Borghini said. 'We're raiding the brothel tonight.'

'You should have cleared it with the department before you made those plans. We need to be involved.'

Grace hadn't taken her eyes off Kidd throughout the exchange. Why be so obstructionist, she wondered. Why try to take possession of the ring? Surely Immigration wouldn't be bothered with finding its so-called owners, whoever they may be.

'No, we don't have to clear it with you,' Borghini said. 'This is a murder inquiry and we're going in. Grace will be there. You're welcome to come along as well. Now, I want some information. Coco, so-called, how did she get out of Villawood?'

Borghini was looking at Kidd with barely concealed contempt. In reply, Kidd opened his briefcase, an expensive leather item with combination locks. He took out two thick wads of paper, each secured with a bulldog clip. Grace accepted hers and began to flick through it.

'You can thank my regional head for those — Coco's file. That will tell you everything you need to know.' He was staring at Grace, his expression accusing. 'Orion rang the department and insisted I bring them. Presumably you don't realise we have other things to do besides your photocopying.'

'We've only got one interest in this,' Grace replied, glancing up from the mass of paper. 'Finding out who killed her. I'd be very surprised if you didn't have the same aim.'

She watched the sudden jerk of fear in his face and again wondered whose side he was on.

'Mate,' Borghini pushed his wad of paper to the side, 'I don't have time for this bumf right now. Tell me the story.'

Kidd was staring at the table. He was white and shaking.

'Coco, so-called,' he said. 'She refused to give us a name, she had a file number. All she wanted was to go home as soon as possible. She —'

He stopped, dropped his head into his hands.

'Are you all right?' Grace asked.

He looked up, sweat edging his hair. Without warning, he shot fury at her. 'But then Orion turned up and made it very clear that wasn't going to happen. Now she's dead. In my opinion, you as good as killed her!'

'Hey, hey. Watch it!' Borghini said.

'What did you say?' The anger in Grace's voice was like a whiplash.

'If you'd just let her go home …' He stopped.

'Are you telling us she wouldn't have been murdered if we had done that?' Grace said. 'Why? What do you know that we don't?'

'I'm just saying what the outcome is. I don't see why I have to put up with —'

Like a man not in control of himself, he jerked to his feet and reached towards his briefcase as if to walk out of the room. He looked at each of them in turn with something close to panic on his face.

'Sit down,' Grace said, by now calmer. He stared at her. 'I don't want to call your department head and tell her you've just accused me of being responsible for Coco's death. Or that you walked out on this meeting. Sit down.'

He sat.

'You owe Grace an apology, mate,' Borghini said.

'I haven't dealt with a situation like this before. I'm sorry. Believe me, I realise it's not true.'

Oddly, he sounded as if he meant it, if only for those moments. Panic had given way to exhaustion.

'Your apology's accepted. We'll say that's finished with,' Grace replied, her voice distant, under control.

'All right, Jon. You chill out, we'll move on,' Borghini said, glancing from Grace to Kidd. 'How did she get out?'

'All detainees have to have extensive medical checks. That procedure's been outsourced — government policy. The medical practice we use is at Parramatta. She and her guard were getting out of the car at the clinic when she made a run for it. There was a white Holden waiting nearby that picked her up. She'd been given a phone card at Villawood, which she'd used. Obviously she'd arranged this escape beforehand.'

Borghini's offsider was a senior detective constable called Joe McBride, an older man with a lined face and a sprinkle of dandruff on his shoulders. He snorted sarcastically. Kidd gave him an angry glance.

'We'll trace those calls,' Borghini said. 'But that's pretty sloppy work by whoever was guarding her.'

11

'A guard and a driver were involved. Both women. Their details are on file. They were deemed negligent in their duty and stood down immediately. Their contracts have since been terminated.'

Grace found this document, close to the top of the mass of paper. An Arleen McKenzie, the driver, and a Sophie Jovanov, the guard. They lived locally to Villawood: Arleen in Fairfield and Sophie in Canley Heights. Both were in their thirties. Sophie was married with children; Arleen single.

'What are you doing to protect these women from the media?' she asked. 'This is a hot news item. It was all over the airways when Coco's body was found.'

'On termination of their contracts they were required to sign a confidentiality agreement,' Kidd said. 'If they speak to the media, with or without a financial inducement, they will be sued and forfeit any money they may have been paid.'

'You blokes mean business,' McBride muttered.

'We'll need to speak to these women ourselves,' Grace replied. 'I'm not expecting anything to get in the way of that.'

'You can talk to them as much as you like. I'll doubt they'll say anything that's not already in the statement on file.'

Why? Did you write it for them? Perhaps her eyes said this. Kidd looked away and this time did stand and move away from the table.

'Parramatta Police Station at six tonight,' Borghini said. 'See you then.'

Kidd nodded and walked out without speaking.

'Ran from the guard and was picked up by a white Holden. What fucking bullshit!' McBride said.

'When we talk to those women, we can ask them what really happened,' Grace said, gathering her things together, also readying to leave.

'Yeah. Like who paid them and how much.'

'Put it on the list of things to do. This is getting murkier by the minute,' Borghini said. Then to Grace: 'We'll see you at six tonight. How's the boss?'

Always, she was asked this question. Two years after he had left the police service, ex-Commander Paul Harrigan was still 'the boss' to almost all the police officers she met in her work. After eighteen years in the service, his name carried weight. More than one hopeful had taken her aside to ask if there was any chance Harrigan could give them the reference that would guarantee their next promotion.

'He's fine,' she said. 'Very busy. He has a lot of work.'

'Does he like being a consultant? If he'd stayed on, he'd probably be Commissioner Harrigan by now. That's what everybody was expecting.'

Borghini was watching her with a calculating look, but not one that seemed to want anything so self-serving as a reference. It was more like he was trying to find something out. Grace could have told him that Harrigan made far more money as a consultant than he ever had as a policeman, but it wasn't Borghini's business.

'I don't think he regrets it,' she said neutrally.

'You'd hope not. Why did he walk away? He never really told anyone.'

This was the other question people always asked her. Why had Harrigan gone when the top job was in his grasp? Fantastic rumours and conspiracy theories abounded, including the widely circulated gossip that Grace herself had forced him to quit as a condition of their relationship. The fact as he had told her was simple: it's my life and I've had enough. But no one, not the police nor the media, wanted to believe anything so straightforward.

'He's said why,' Grace replied. 'I don't have anything to add.'

She was about to stand up when McBride spoke.

'What's he been doing at Darlo Court House all week watching Chris Newell go down for murder?'

At the sound of this name, fear went through Grace to the pit of her stomach. Then she got to her feet.

'That's his work and it's confidential. See you this evening.'

'I hear he's publishing a book. *Justice Under the Law*.' Borghini's statement stopped her at the door.

'He is. It's due out soon. You can buy it and read it if you want. See you later.'

'Yeah. See you.'

She made a grateful exit from the building and began the drive to the nondescript building in Mascot that housed Orion's offices.

In the flow of traffic, her mind returned to the dissection room, to the marks on Jirawan's body that had reminded her of the marks that had once covered hers. Chris Newell, now in the dock at Darlinghurst Court House, had been the one who had put them there, and then raped her, fifteen years ago when she was just nineteen.

When she'd heard that Newell, already in gaol for armed robbery, had been charged with the murder of a fellow prisoner, her first thought had been that this time he'd managed to kill someone. McBride had been spot-on: Harrigan *was* at Darlo Court House to see Newell go down for murder. After that first nightmarish attack, Newell had stalked and threatened her on and off through the years since. The worst incident had been not long before she met Harrigan. She'd come home late from a party to find him waiting for her in the car park of her apartment block. He had thrown petrol over her and tried to light it. The lighter failed, she ran for her life. The next day, she got hold of a gun to protect herself. Swore that if she saw him again, she wouldn't hesitate. Not long afterwards, he'd gone down for armed robbery. He'd almost served that sentence and had been due for release within a few months. If he was convicted for murder, he would be out of her life for another twenty years, perhaps forever.

People assumed Grace did the work she did because of her father's influence. Discipline, upholding the law. A duty to serve and protect. Her father was an army officer who had fought in the Vietnam War and been awarded the Military Cross, later retiring as a brigadier. These days, he worked as hard for peace as he had ever done for war. There was some truth in the theory — she had lived with her father's ideals throughout her life — but when she looked in the mirror and saw her scar, she knew it was this thin thread that drove her. She felt it as a mental thing, a mark in her consciousness as well as on her body. No one should go through what I went through. A simple sentence that carried too much weight.

2

Courtrooms always reminded Paul Harrigan of those miniature mazes into which scientific researchers drove rats against their will. The squared layout with the judge staring directly at the dock and the accused. The witness stand located beside the judge's high seat, trapping the witness in a vice between the judge and both sets of lawyers. And then the jury side-on in their box, supposedly disinterested assessors instead of disparate individuals who might be confused, bored, or ruled by prejudice. Whatever a courtroom's vintage, it gave him a sense of claustrophobia to be inside one. Today he was seated in the public gallery at Darlinghurst Court House, where the age of the courtroom gave it a sense of harsh ritual that some modern ones didn't immediately have. At least, not until the verdict was read out and the sentence handed down, with the usual outcome of leaving everyone involved feeling cheated.

There were too few people in the public gallery for Harrigan to go unnoticed. His tall figure with its dark-fair hair was too easy to spot. Already a journalist had waylaid him to ask what he was doing there, then dropped the snippet into the gossip column on the back page of the *Sydney Morning Herald*. As sharp-minded as she was, the journalist hadn't guessed that Harrigan was there for Grace.

Grace had never told him the full story of how she'd got her scar, but she'd said enough for him to put the facts together. Ever since she'd told him about Newell stalking her and throwing petrol over her, he'd made sure he always knew exactly where the man was and what he was doing. Called in favours so that Newell's request for parole was kept at the back of the queue. Grace would have said she could protect herself. True or not, there was no way he could have sat back and left her to worry about it alone. He had lost too much in his past life to let anything like this remain out of his control, not for someone he cared for as much as he did her. His life had become a gift, made up of a happiness he had never expected to achieve. No one was going to wreck it. What he wanted was for Newell to get the maximum, preferably to spend the rest of his life in gaol. But that was up to the lawyers and the judge and finally the jury, not him.

The prosecution had noticed him in the public gallery as well; he had seen them comment to each other. Whether the defence lawyer, Joel Griffin, knew he was watching, Harrigan couldn't tell. He hoped not. Chris Newell's barrister was the last person he wanted to talk to. As to whether Newell knew who he was, he didn't care about that either. All Harrigan wanted was for him to go down, but the way his barrister was defending him, maybe he wouldn't.

Once a factotum for organised crime boss Sam Nguyen, Newell had been a useful if minor player in the drug distribution business, until he'd been gaoled for armed robbery five years ago. When he was charged with murder, it had been implied in the tabloids that he'd beaten his cell mate to death on the orders of his former boss, innuendo Nguyen had stridently rejected, going so far as to threaten to sue, and earning himself a few more headlines into the bargain. Harrigan had dismissed the story from the start. According to his intelligence, Nguyen had cut his ties with Newell way back when he was gaoled for robbery.

Harrigan had heard of Joel Griffin before this trial but didn't know much about him. He seemed to be a middling Sydney criminal lawyer with no flamboyant habits and who did nothing to attract attention to himself. His practice was irregular at best. There were years when he hadn't worked at all. When his name did appear in the court records, it was on low-key cases where he represented the foot soldiers or lower-level lieutenants of various criminal organisations. Most of the time, he won these cases. When he'd taken on Newell's defence, people had said he had no chance; the prosecution's case was unassailable; he and his client would get eaten alive.

Harrigan had soon decided the opposite. Griffin was giving a performance many other more highly paid and better-known barristers would have envied. He dealt with the prosecution witnesses clinically, pitilessly destroying their credibility and chipping away at the crown's supposedly rock-solid case. He represented the victim for what he was: a man with a history as violent as Newell's. More than once, he had outmanoeuvred the prosecution on points of law. Griffin was well on his way to constructing a convincing argument that Newell had acted in self-defence, that the victim's death had been the consequence of a series of wild punches thrown in desperation instead of a sustained and brutal beating. Best of all, he had the right judge. Justice Marian O'Connor was scrupulously fair, concerned with the niceties of the law and always leaned towards the benefit of the doubt.

Harrigan would have been worried if there hadn't been one other person in the courtroom determined to convict the accused — Newell himself. His fair curled hair and good-looking face made him appear less dangerous and damaged than he was, but Harrigan had dealt with men like Newell throughout his years on the job. Their violence was always waiting on a hair trigger. Violence like the kind that was erupting now, with Newell beginning to shout at the prosecution witness, another prisoner who looked like he wanted to be almost anywhere else.

'You fucking liar. Who paid you to get up there and talk that fucking shit? I'll get you, you cunt!'

He exploded in the dock, fists flying, wrestling with the guards who pounced on him.

'Take him down,' the judge ordered. 'Mr Griffin, you can tell your client he is looking at charges of contempt of court at the least. I have to say, his behaviour today is of a piece with his behaviour throughout. As his counsel, you should advise him that treating these proceedings with this degree of contempt does his case no good at all. Court is adjourned until tomorrow.'

The judge's advice said it all. Griffin might not win the case, but he was skilled enough to get his client a reduced sentence for manslaughter. Newell, on the other hand, was inviting the jury to convict him for cold-blooded murder.

Griffin took the lecture in his stride. He got to his feet with a slight bow. 'I thank Your Honour for her advice and I will convey it to my client at the first opportunity,' he said coolly before gathering up his papers.

Harrigan was on his way out of the building when an attendant stopped him and handed him Griffin's card. *Please wait for me at the main entrance,* Griffin had written on the back. *I want to talk to you.*

He'd been noticed after all. Harrigan felt an unpleasant spark of dread. Newell was connected to matters too private and sensitive for him to meet his defence counsel without wondering what might be in the man's mind. Who knew what had passed between them as client and barrister? If any of Grace's past history with Newell was ever made public, she would find it devastating. Supposedly Griffin would be bound by client confidentiality, but if so, why ask to see him?

Shortly afterwards, Griffin appeared in the foyer.

'Joel Griffin,' he said. 'We haven't met before but I've heard about you. Hi.'

'Paul Harrigan. What can I do for you?'

They shook hands as they introduced themselves. Griffin had a disconcertingly weak grip; as if the touch of someone else's hand was distasteful to him. His clothes were of good quality and had a tailored look, appearing more pricey than a part-time, cut-rate barrister should have been able to afford. A small badge was pinned to his lapel: Gromit, the dog from the Aardman Wallace and Gromit animations, who reads *Engineering for Dogs* while saving his accident-prone owner from disaster. Griffin saw Harrigan looking at it.

'I'm a fan,' he said. 'What about you?'

'Yeah, they make me laugh.'

Face to face, Griffin was more impressive than in the courtroom.

In his early forties, he was solidly built and his colouring was unusual: very pale skin, black hair and blue eyes. He was tall enough to look Harrigan in the eye and did so almost unblinkingly.

'Would you mind walking out with me while we talk?' he said. 'I need to get a taxi on Oxford Street.'

'Not a problem. I was going that way myself,' Harrigan replied.

'You're a consultant these days,' Griffin said.

'That's right. I advise individuals and companies how to manage their security and also how to control their legal affairs. It's all on my website.'

It would have been more accurate for Harrigan to say he advised people on how to protect themselves from both the law and the police. This was a definition he kept to himself.

'I've checked your website.' Griffin spoke without sociability. 'You've done work for any number of people. State and federal governments, private companies. Important companies, some very large ones. You're a solicitor. It even says you're proficient in Indonesian. You must make a lot of money.'

Harrigan ignored the jibe. Bizarrely, there seemed to be almost a touch of envy in Griffin's tone. 'I spent some time in Indonesia a number of years ago when I was on secondment with the Australian Federal Police. I learned the language while I was there. Why?'

'That's a lot of firepower for someone who's interested in this trial,' Griffin said. 'You've been here every day so far. Is there someone you're advising who's asked you to watch this case so closely?'

'Let me ask you a question first. You must know who your client is and the kind of people this case is connecting you to. Are you representing Newell on your own or are your services being paid for by someone else? And do those people want to know why I'm here?'

Griffin laughed. 'No, Sam Nguyen's not paying me. In fact, everyone from Chris's past is running for cover as fast as they can. I don't think he realises how alone he is. But you've got connections of your own, to the police obviously. Maybe they're at work here.'

You have done your homework, Harrigan thought.

'Does this mean you're doing this case pro bono?' he asked.

Griffin hesitated before replying. 'Yes, I am.'

'Then you can ignore the fact that I'm here. It's got nothing to do with anyone.'

Griffin didn't like the rebuff. There was a slight flush in his face when he spoke again.

'There's another side to you that's not on your website,' he said. 'There's any number of newspaper articles out there. Years of dealing with Sydney's crime bosses while people asked what your connections to those bosses really were.'

'Exactly what they should have been. Straight as a ruler. Is that something you want to discuss in court?'

'You're the man who didn't want to be Police Commissioner. That's not something everyone can boast about. And then there's your partner as well.'

'She's got nothing to do with this. You'd be a fool to think she did.'

'One thing I'm not is a fool,' Griffin said.

'Then don't talk like one, mate,' Harrigan replied calmly.

Griffin looked at him, his expression as if the shutters had come down. There might have been nothing in his mind. They had reached Oxford Street and were standing just outside the court house's dark-honey sandstone gateway. Harrigan again asked himself how much this man might know. If Griffin thought he had a case for blackmail, he would tell him soon enough. Maybe it was time to take the offensive.

'I've checked you out too,' he said. 'You don't have a high profile. No one knows much about you at all. There are times in the past when you might as well have been living in Greenland. Why did you take Newell on, particularly pro bono? Did you think there was something in this for you?'

'I thought he needed good representation. There's a lot of interesting information in Chris's head. Some of it's pretty scrambled but you can usually sort out what's true and what's not.'

'You'd want to be very careful with anything he told you,' Harrigan replied, a man offering friendly advice. 'Given the people he mixes with, you'd probably end up putting your head in a noose. The best thing you could do is keep it to yourself.'

'I've seen pictures of your partner online,' Griffin said. 'You and her together. She's a very attractive woman. But she's got a scar. You can just see it in the pictures. It runs from here to here.' He touched his chin and then the top of his breastbone. 'It must have been a nasty cut.'

Harrigan took a step forward, close enough to Griffin to have taken hold of him by the collar if he'd wanted to. He pointed a finger in his face. 'You involve yourself in my affairs and you'll be picking up the pieces for a long time afterwards. You remember that and you mind your own business as of now. Because I've got nothing for you. Not now, not ever.'

'You care about her, don't you? Why else would you be here? Even if you haven't married her. And there's your daughter. You'd care about her too, wouldn't you?'

Harrigan dropped his voice. 'You're one step away, mate. Say another word ...'

Griffin moved back. He smiled and put on a pair of wrap-around sunglasses. Now Harrigan was looking at his own reflection.

'You want to know what's in it for me? Chris is my client and I'm defending him. Simple as that. It's a pity he won't cooperate with me. If he did, he might be out of gaol before the end of the year. But there he is right now. On his way back to Long Bay.'

Harrigan turned. Two unmarked police cars had appeared in convoy at the intersection of Oxford Street and Darlinghurst Road. The first was an escort car; the second carried Newell sitting between two plain-clothes officers. They were waiting to turn left onto Oxford.

'What are they doing here? Why didn't they ask for a van to take Newell back?' Harrigan said.

Griffin made no reply.

As the cars made the turn, two motorbikes came roaring alongside them. The riders shot first into the cars' tyres then into the cars themselves before slaloming out of the way. The cars slewed dangerously. A heavy four-wheel-drive broke through the lights and rammed into the car carrying Newell, smashing it halfway onto the pavement, causing the passers-by to run. The escort car had skewed to a stop at a dangerous angle across the road, blocking both lanes.

One motorbike rider had shot into the escort car while the second fired at people around the scene, keeping them at bay. Pedestrians hit the footpath. Harrigan dragged Griffin to the ground. Bullets echoed around them.

The driver of the four-wheel-drive got out and shot into the prisoner's car, smashing the glass. He was wearing a balaclava. 'Open it!' he yelled at the driver. The back door on the intact side was opened and the gunman shot the driver at point-blank range. One of the guards, clearly wounded, was pushed out onto the road, Newell tumbling after him. Dragging some kind of cutter out of his pocket, the gunman cut the handcuffs that joined the two men together.

Then it was all over. The driver of the four-wheel-drive and Newell were on the back of the two motorbikes, roaring out of sight.

Harrigan and Griffin got to their feet. Griffin's sunglasses had been knocked off in the fall and had landed some distance away on the footpath. He went and got them before brushing himself down. He touched his lapel. 'I've lost my badge.' His face and voice were calm. 'Pow! Pow! Pow! Pow!' he said, sounding almost like a schoolboy. 'Trigger-happy people. They really like using their guns.' He matched his words with the feigned action of shooting at the people lying on the road.

'Are you okay, mate?' Harrigan asked, wondering if the reaction might be shock.

'I'm fine. There's my badge.' He bent down and picked it up. 'The pin's broken.'

'Wait here for the police,' Harrigan said. 'They'll want your statement.'

Griffin looked at Harrigan. His eyes showed no emotion. 'Don't call me mate,' he said.

'Aren't you worried about your client?'

'Why should I be? You'd have to say his troubles are over.'

Harrigan would have said they were just starting but he didn't have time to talk to Griffin any longer. He ran to the scene through the chaos of stopped traffic. Passers-by were getting shakily to their feet. When he reached the prisoner's car, he saw the driver clearly dead, one guard lying seriously wounded on the road and the other bleeding and unconscious in the back. There was another dead man at the wheel of the escort car, while his partner was sprawled on the road, wounded and bleeding, unable to move.

A man shouted over the ruckus. 'I'm from St Vincent's, we've got help coming. Stay calm.'

'I'm a doctor,' a woman called and hurried to the wounded man lying on the road by the escort car.

Harrigan returned to the prisoner's car to help the two wounded men there. 'We need another doctor over here and quickly,' he yelled back. Around him, car horns rose to a blaring cacophony. On what should have been a quiet autumn day in Sydney, all hell had broken loose.

3

Grace sat facing a largish man at a small table in the bright room; a video camera was recording their meeting. There were no windows in the room; its brightness came from the overhead lights and the bare white walls and floor. The man was reading over the fine print on a form he had just filled in. He looked up at Grace; she smiled professionally.

'If you're happy to agree to all this, Doug,' she said, 'I need you to sign here and here.'

He half-smiled in return, with a touch of embarrassed egotism at finding himself the centre of attention. 'Will I really go to gaol if I tell anyone I've been here or even that I know this place exists?'

The sound of their voices was sharp in the bright clarity of the room. He wore light-sensitive glasses which seemed to have become fixed in a permanent, very pale blue colour, giving him the look of someone wearing sunglasses unnecessarily.

'Do you want anyone to know what we're going to discuss here?' she asked in reply.

He shook his head. He had heavy features and looked older than his thirty-nine years. The form said he was a married man with three children, and that his wife was a part-time commerce teacher at the local Catholic high school. He worked as a middle-ranking public servant for the state government. A family without much spare cash after the mortgage, car and private school fees had been paid. The last person who'd want his wife to know he regularly visited a brothel called Life's Pleasures.

'I'm only here because Coco's dead,' he said. He didn't look at Grace. 'She had to be illegal. When you went and saw her, she'd freeze up. The last time I saw her, she was curled up on the bed, really tense. I walked out. I asked Lynette if I could see one of the other girls instead. It just wasn't fun.'

'Who's Lynette?' Grace said.

'The receptionist. She said I could swap if I wanted to. I didn't have to pay again.'

'Was there any other reason you thought Coco might have been illegal?'

'Her English wasn't very good. I thought if you were here legally, you'd have to have some English. And she was new. She started just a couple of months ago.'

'Why did you keep seeing her?' Grace prodded gently.

'No one's going to know?'

'No,' she said. 'Passing on this information would be a criminal offence.'

The reassurance seemed to help. He held his hands together on the table, looking ahead. His face went red.

'You didn't have to wear a condom,' he said.

'I don't think you told the police that,' Grace said quietly.

'I didn't trust them to keep their mouths shut.'

Orion had given him a paper-thin sense of safety where he could reveal himself. His sense of guilt must have weighed on him every night before he went to sleep.

'Were there any other workers you didn't have to wear a condom for?' Grace asked.

'No. Not that I knew about anyway.'

'You weren't worried about your health? Or your wife's?'

'Marie said Coco had regular health checks. Me and my wife don't have sex that often. She doesn't seem to like it much.' His voice was flat.

'Who's Marie?'

'*Miss* Marie Li. The manageress.' He drew quotation marks in the air. 'She hasn't been there that long. She's mainly decorative. Lynette's the one who makes things happen.'

'Except in this case,' Grace said.

'Lynette said Coco wasn't anything to do with her. I should always talk to Marie about her.'

'How did you hear about Coco in the first place?'

His face was still red. 'It was on the net. They've got a website. *Ask Marie for something special.* I thought I'd see what it was.'

'How often do you visit?'

'Once a fortnight. I build up my flexitime at work and go before I come home.'

'How do you pay?'

'Cash.'

Doesn't your wife notice the money? She must know.

'What sort of an establishment is it?'

'Well run. It's got a lot of girls, a spa. It's private.'

'Private?'

'You don't have to walk in off the street. You'd know what I mean if you went there.'

'Were there any other workers there from overseas?'

'Oh yeah. I'll tell you what, they're beautiful girls. I know men who go there just for them. There's an African girl — she's out of this world. But you have to pay extra, a lot extra. Coco and the other girls, you didn't.' He looked away, his heavy body seeming to be weighed down. 'Is that it? I should get back to work.'

'One last question. Did Coco ever wear any jewellery when you saw her?'

'She didn't wear anything.'

'No rings?'

'Nope.'

She glanced at his left hand. He was wearing his wedding ring. Did he take it off before he visited? Not a question to ask.

'Thank you, Doug. That's all. You will have to wait until the transcript's printed out because you have to read and sign it as an accurate record. But that won't take very long.'

'My family's not going to hear about this?'

Grace shook her head. 'No. That's a promise. Shall I get Carol outside to get you a coffee?'

'Yeah. White, one sugar.'

'It's on its way.'

Grace left quickly. She had another meeting, in a room much deeper into the centre of the building, where Clive was waiting for her. She'd already sent him a brief summary of her morning's work.

In contrast to the noise outside — the aircraft flying overhead and the daily clamour of the city's traffic — this room had a quietness that ate sound. Again there were no windows but this time the lights were muted. Grace sat down without speaking a greeting. The table was often bare; its function was to serve as a barrier between them, something to lean on. Today Clive had brought a folder with him; this meant he had plans of his own.

'What did our informant have to say?' he asked.

'A bit more than he told the police. You didn't have to wear a condom when you had sex with Coco. The brothel put out a teaser on the net for clients. Which means our informant also surfs the net.'

'We're not interested in his tastes. Are there any other workers there with that same job description?'

'He didn't know about them if there were.'

'Is this man telling the truth?'

'Oh, I think so. It's cost him a lot to come forward. He's the perfect informant for us. All he wants is complete secrecy, particularly from his family.'

'His wife really doesn't know?'

'Of course she knows,' Grace replied briskly. 'She probably knows down to the last cent what he spends. And whatever he says, he probably knows exactly how much she's prepared to tolerate. It's the lack of a condom she won't know about, and that's what he doesn't want her to find out. He'd be in the family court the next day.'

Clive smiled with scorn and turned his attention to her interim report.

'It's interesting what you have to say about Kidd from this morning's meeting.'

'There's a possibility of corruption here,' she said. 'If Kidd was involved in this woman's escape in any way, that's a weakness we need to identify.'

Clive was looking at her distantly. He had a red-covered document in his hand. 'Is it only that? I'd say you haven't forgiven him for saying you were responsible for Coco's death. In the meantime, read that. When she supposedly escaped, I decided we should follow your judgement and have a good look at this Mr Kidd. That's what the finance people came up with.'

His comment had caught her off guard, wounding her a little. She flicked open the dossier on Jon Kidd. A single man in his late forties and a long-term employee with the Department of Immigration, based at their Parramatta offices. Once a wealthy man, his financial records indicated a constant and substantial drain of money over the last three years, including the sale of shares and investments, culminating in a 100 per cent mortgage on his house in Mosman, where he lived with his mother. There was also a large personal loan with his car, a Mercedes, as surety. Previously he had been a regular visitor to Thailand and Cambodia and, until recently, a generous donor to orphanages in Bangkok and Phnom Penh. Those trips had stopped in recent months, presumably due to a lack of funds.

'Looking at his travel records, he mainly preferred the Cambodian orphanage,' Clive said, 'but he still spent time in Thailand.'

'What did he do with these children from the orphanages?' Grace said. 'Take them away on holiday with him? Whatever it was, he doesn't do it now. He's almost bankrupt. He's being blackmailed.'

'Bled dry,' Clive agreed. 'I've directed our IT people to trace his computer traffic and, if they can, to hack into his own computer. I've also put out a "don't touch" order on him just in case any other agency knows about his existence. The Thai woman's escape was interesting. An act of desperation if ever I saw one, and Kidd was the person best placed to make it happen. I want to know if he is in fact responsible and what's behind it.'

'Does this mean we've decided once and for all that Coco is Jirawan Sanders, as the initials on her wedding ring would suggest?'

He leaned over the table towards her. Grace sat upright, preventing herself from drawing back. 'Did you at any time tell Jon Kidd or the police that we were seeking a woman of that name?'

'No, of course I didn't.'

'Then this is for you.' He pushed a photograph across the table. It was sourced from Interpol and labelled as top secret. The Thai woman, Coco, was sitting at a table somewhere shyly smiling for the camera. The name underneath the image was Jirawan Sanders.

'You had a photograph after all,' Grace said in a neutral voice. 'Why didn't we just take her out of there? And why couldn't you tell me you knew who she was?'

'I had no reason to believe she wouldn't be safe in Villawood. I didn't want to broadcast just how interested we were.' He smiled again. 'This is the first significant job I've given you. I had no way of knowing I could trust you. I wanted you to prove that I could.'

'I've worked for Orion for five years. You had no basis for assuming that I couldn't be trusted with classified information.'

'I wanted to know if you were competent. It's turned out you are.'

Grace sat for a few moments not trusting herself to speak. *You as good as killed her.* Kidd had said that to her. Orion, via Clive, had as good as killed Jirawan Sanders by looking to finesse for advantage instead of acting in the most straightforward way. In that moment, it became crucial to Grace that she saw this through and found whoever had murdered the Thai woman.

'Can we call her Jirawan in that case?' she asked, her voice calm.

'If you think that's necessary. What I want you to do at the brothel tonight is to see if you can confirm our informant's information. See if there's anyone there who might have acted as this woman's gaoler. And watch Kidd. See what he does. Does he know or is he known to anyone there? Any detail you can pick up. We're already monitoring his phone calls.'

'What's our relationship with the police on this?' she asked. 'So far, they're running it as a murder investigation with me as an observer. Are we going to bring them into this operation? They must be wondering why we're still in there.'

'Not just yet. If we're watching Kidd, I don't want them getting in the way. Right now, I want to know how you're feeling about this job. My judgement is you're emotionally involved.'

'No, it's just another a job.'

'No, it's not. Not this time.'

He looked at her silently. The tension in the room made her sit rigidly in her chair. She hated it here where there was no place to hide. Things said in this room could be as intimate as those said between her and Paul but without the warmth or the connection. Clive knew almost as much about her as Paul did. The biographies of all his officers were secured on his hard drive, variables that might affect someone's work.

'You're not the woman I was expecting to meet when you came back from maternity leave,' he said finally. 'From everything I've heard about you, I'd say you lost a skin or two in that time. Your personal life has taken a lot of hours recently, which I've accommodated at our inconvenience. In this profession, your work comes first. But I'm still going to keep you on this operation.'

'What made you decide that?' she asked, managing to keep her anger out of her voice.

'Let's assume Kidd is corrupt and being blackmailed. His security clearance means he knows you're an agent with Orion. If the person who has him on a string also knows you're from Orion, they might come looking for you. Let's find out.'

'Wouldn't it be more likely they'd give me as wide a berth as possible?'

'Think of that escape. A desperate act. Wouldn't they want to try and find out exactly what we know?'

'I'm the bait, you mean. For what? I still have no information on what this operation's really about or who or what the target is.'

'When you need to know, you'll be told. I don't think that time has come yet. But I can tell you this is a very significant operation. Being involved in this way would be quite a feather in your cap.' He tossed this cliché at her as if it were a hook.

'How much danger would that scenario put me in?' she asked.

'You'd have full backup. My judgement is you're still professional enough to deal with it.'

'Is this a direction from you?' she asked. 'And if it is, is there any agreement to support it? Normally when this kind of arrangement is made, there's a written agreement and a set of directions on how to proceed.'

'That's a refusal.'

'No, it's a request for clear, written directions.'

'Then we'll see what happens first. In the meantime, you stay assigned to this operation under my direction.'

Again, he opened his folder. This time, he spread out a series of photographs. Jirawan in the Ku-ring-gai Chase National Park. Photographs Grace had taken herself.

'There's something else I think we should discuss,' Grace said, keeping her irritation under control. 'Given this woman is Jirawan Sanders, what about her husband? Is he missing? Or is he dead?'

Clive looked up from the photographs. 'He's dead. Peter Sanders. He was an Australian who ran an import–export business in Bangkok, which is where he met this woman. That's the last piece of information I'm going to give you right now.'

'She has a child somewhere. If both parents are dead, shouldn't we find out where this child is, or at least ask someone to locate him or her?'

'Whatever's happened to that child, it's not our responsibility.'

It's our first responsibility! Grace wanted to shout, but choked back the words. She couldn't risk losing this job.

Finally Clive gathered up the pictures and put them away. 'The man who did this —'

'Man?' she interrupted.

'Apart from the evidence of sexual assault, do you think a woman would have the physical strength to do this?'

'A woman could watch. She could administer a beating.'

'Yes, she could. But whoever did this likes to kill. That's my opinion. Report to me tomorrow about tonight's raid. One other thing. Have you heard the news in the last hour?'

'No. I haven't had time.'

'You should go and listen to it.'

'Why?'

'Chris Newell was snatched as he left court today in a very bloody affair. Two people are dead and several badly wounded. We both know about Newell's connection to you. If he turns up on your radar, I need to know.'

'I'm going to make a personal call. Excuse me,' Grace said, and left the room immediately.

At Orion, personal calls were only tolerated under very unusual circumstances and had to be made on your own phone. Walking at speed down the hallway to her office, Grace rang Harrigan with a shaking hand. She was desperate to talk to him, but nothing would have made her call in front of Clive.

The phone was answered almost at once. 'Harrigan.'

She breathed relief. 'It's me. Are you all right? What's happened?'

'I'm okay, babe. I don't have a scratch on me, which is more than you can say for some of the people here. It's bad. Two men shot dead. It happened in front of me.'

'You're okay?'

'I'm handling it. It's like being back on the job again.'

'Someone did that for Newell? Why?'

'Don't ask me. He's not worth anything like this. I can't talk to you now — I've got people who want me this end. What time will you be home tonight?'

'Late. There's an op going on. I don't know when I'll get back.'

'We'll talk about it then. You take care.'

'Where's Ellie?'

'She's fine. She's at Kidz Corner. I'll pick her up the same time I always do. She won't know anything's happened. Okay? I'll see you.'

'Yeah.'

'Take care, babe.'

'You too.'

Babe. A name he had given her this last year or so. At first, it had seemed so unlike him it had startled her. One of those small pieces of intimacy between them she could still be surprised by.

She thought about Clive's comment on her personal life. She wasn't the only one who had changed. Since Clive had arrived,

Orion had changed as well. To an agency already obsessed with secrecy, he'd brought new levels of paranoia. People worked in compartments; no one was allowed to know what the next person was doing. It had reached a level where operatives didn't share even the most trivial pieces of information. People muttered that this was Clive's way of making sure there was no one to challenge him. Grace agreed with this opinion; it was the oldest tactic in the world. But aside from that was his attitude to her. He was always trying to get under her skin, to play games with her feelings. She wondered if she was imagining it, but there seemed to be a touch of obsession in his treatment of her, as if he couldn't leave her alone.

Even today, he'd sat on the news about Newell throughout their meeting, a meeting he had deliberately drawn out. Perhaps it was his way of getting rid of her; he had driven out other operatives since he'd arrived. Whatever his ultimate aim, he'd succeeded in putting the question in her mind. Did she want to do this kind of work any longer?

At the heart of Grace's life there were cracks, events that marked the time before and after happiness. She had grown up in New Guinea where her father had been a defence attaché at the Australian High Commission. Her life had been spent happily between boarding school in Brisbane and time with her family, including her brother, Nicky, to whom she was still very close. Her childhood lived in her memory as time spent in a magical place. In her mind she could still see the landscapes she had grown up in, all of which had an intense beauty. But when she was fourteen, her mother had died in a little less than twenty-four hours from a rare form of cerebral malaria. Grace had once believed that nothing in her life could match that heartbreak, not even if her father or her brother died. She knew now that losing either Paul or Ellie would be as bad.

Her father had ceased to be Brigadier Kep Riordan with the High Commission in Port Moresby and had come back to Australia to raise his two children as best he could, on the Central Coast of New South Wales, where he'd been born. There Grace ran wild, falling in with a group of older kids who stole cars and took them for joy rides. She remembered one night shouting at the driver to go faster and faster, so much so that she'd spooked him. She'd been scouring away the emotional pain, almost killing herself in the process. It was only her father's efforts that had kept her out of the children's courts.

Finally, barely sixteen, she had left school and home for Sydney and found herself singing in pubs when she was too young to drink in them. From there, she started singing for a group called Wasted Daze, a name she thought suited her. They were a group of young men who were as lost as she was. They'd toured the east coast of Australia, always heading north, camping out on beaches, too poor to do much more than buy beer and takeaway food. Grace had liked the life. She liked the open road with no destination at the end of it, just the vanishing point on the horizon. The immediate impression of each day had become a good enough substitute for happiness.

Then Chris Newell walked into their lives. It wasn't so unusual; they seemed to pick up stray people as they drove around in their rusting Kombi van. They were in northern Queensland by then, playing at the local pubs in a district where the main industry was growing sugar cane. Occasionally they met Newell socially; he always had dope to sell. Then one day the owner of a pub where they'd played refused to pay them; Newell told the man he'd better if he knew what was good for him. He paid with a bonus. After this, Newell offered to manage them as far as it went. They accepted the offer, but they were all, including Grace, too naïve and casual in the way they did things.

She and Newell became an item, not for very long, a couple of months at most. By the end of this short time it was clear to everyone that Newell was a controller who liked tormenting people. They'd also discovered he was a serious dealer, not just someone who could get a bit of marihuana for his friends. No one wanted anything to do with the kind of people he was bringing into their lives. Grace decided she'd had enough. The idyll was broken, real life had asserted itself. She'd discovered she didn't want to be a singer after all. She didn't have the gift for performance; she didn't want to stand up there and put her emotions on display in her music. Then there was Newell, who was beginning to frighten her;

he was possessive and had a short fuse. Already he'd started shouting at her. He hadn't hit her but she began to realise that he could and one day he would.

The band split in a series of angry arguments; she packed her bags and left for Sydney. Newell followed her although not immediately. Someone had dobbed him in to the police; not her, probably another member of the band. Newell didn't care; he thought she'd done it and he'd come after her.

In that space of time when Newell had beaten and raped her, Grace had thought that she would die. In the aftermath, she'd thought she might do so anyway, in her own way.

She had refused to go to the police. She was too frightened of Newell to testify against him in court. Nothing would shift her on this, and she hid the extent of her injuries from her family, knowing that if her father ever found out what had happened to her, nothing would have stopped him going after Newell. It was only years later that she'd told him and her brother everything that had happened to her. As well as being angry, they'd been hurt that she'd shut them out. It was the fear, she'd told them; she had never felt anything like that fear. Her father understood fear; he had fought in Vietnam. He spoke about it then to his daughter and son; the first time he'd spoken to anyone about it since he'd come home from the war. It became a point of understanding between them, something that allowed all three of them to reach some kind of resolution about the past.

In those bad times after Newell, Grace had drunk herself into insensibility, but even as an alcoholic she was unsuccessful. Her family had been there, they had helped her. Her brother had protected her, come and taken her away from parties, poured the booze down the sink, taken her to hospital when she fell and cut herself, helped her through detox. When she was in recovery, her father had taught her to shoot, telling her it would restore her hand–eye coordination. 'You should only ever shoot at a target,' he'd said. 'Never at people.' She never drank now but she was still a very good shot.

She had taken herself to university, studied criminology, and, before Orion, had worked briefly for the police. Unexpectedly met

Paul Harrigan and found herself where she was now.

When Grace had first joined Orion five years ago, she had still been an angry young woman. If asked, she would have said her heart was dead and she was glad it was. At times her anger drove her to take risks, just as she had done at fourteen, speeding in cars badly controlled by adolescent drivers. Saying to death, come and get me if you can. These days she was careful. Now she asked herself: what happens to my daughter if something happens to me? This anxiety was one of the sharpest feelings she'd ever had. These days, she felt everything too much.

Quit, Harrigan had said to her more than once. If Orion's not what you want any more, quit. If you want to, why not just walk away? Because she wasn't a quitter. I don't like being driven out, she thought, not by someone like Clive. If he thought she was an easy target, he would find out differently.

She had a name now for the woman she'd met in Villawood. It was a step towards sending her home to her relatives, possibly parents who could see her properly put to rest. Who could tell her child what had happened to his or her mother. Grace had more significant things than Clive to think about. However much she'd changed, she still had work to do; important work. Finding the person who could murder Jirawan so savagely and then just walk away.

4

The sign *Life's Pleasures* glittered above the lintel of the door in thin multicoloured neon letters, while the bulbs illuminating the stairs inside cast an inviting glow onto the footpath. To Grace, it seemed an offer impossible to refuse in this drab semi-business district of downtown Parramatta, a landscape of warehouses, video stores, cash converters and takeaway food chains.

A police car was already stationed on the street outside. She followed the rest of the convoy to an area at the back of the four-storeyed building where there was room to park in a largish courtyard. A line of cars was parked along one side, presumably belonging to the sex workers and their clients. 'Get their regos,' Borghini said to one of his people.

The private entrance Doug had mentioned, a badly lit doorway, led to a flight of stairs next to a service elevator. A short climb took them to the brothel's open doorway on the first floor. As soon as they walked in, two men waiting in deep armchairs rose to their feet and melted out of the entrance like smoke. They would have disappeared downstairs at speed if they hadn't been stopped by the police and asked for their names and addresses.

Borghini had organised the raid well — a straightforward exercise without histrionics. He presented his warrant card and the legal papers at the reception desk and sent his people to search the premises in an orderly way. Kidd, last through the doorway, stood in the background, watching. Already the receptionist, an older woman with a solid build, dyed blonde hair and wearing a fashionable off-the-shoulder red number, was on the phone.

'I'm just ringing Marie,' she said with a professional smile. 'She has a flat on the top floor, she's there now. I'm sure she'll be down in a moment.'

'We know where she lives,' Borghini replied. 'I've already sent some people upstairs to talk to her. But go ahead. You can tell her I'll be up to see her as soon as I've sorted things out down here.'

Officers moved along the hallways knocking on doors, announcing themselves. 'We have reason to believe there may be illegal immigrants working on these premises,' they repeated with each knock. 'Could you come out to the reception desk now with your personal identification ready, please? Thank you.'

Clients began to appear in the hallways in various states of dress. Their IDs checked, they disappeared with the same speed as the men in the reception area earlier. Once out of the rooms, the workers sat in a communal kitchen, smoking and occasionally chatting. Some looked nervous but most seemed bored or irritated as they presented their IDs to the various officers on demand and were interviewed. Grace looked them over but saw no sign of the exotic workers Doug had described earlier that day. So far everybody was just another citizen.

It wasn't the look of the brothel — much of which had an air of the suburban, of polyester chic — but its size that interested Grace. Whoever owned it was on to a good thing, and whoever had set it up in the first place had had money to invest. So far, that side of the business had proved to be a maze. Both Orion and the police investigation had identified the owner as a company, Santos Associates. Attempts to track down that company's office holders had led nowhere. Calls to their phone numbers went unanswered, and when the company's premises were visited no one was there. The brothel's accounts were handled by a company called Stamfords, who actually did exist and whose people were being interviewed. They had confirmed one fact: all the money Life's Pleasures made was automatically transferred offshore.

The brothel itself was large enough for Jirawan to have been hidden away in one room while business went on as normal in the rest of the place. Each room had a theme, a colour, a fantasy for whatever taste. The erotic paintings had the commercial look of pneumatic sex, while the mirrors on the walls and ceilings made her wonder why people so enjoyed watching themselves.

At the end of one corridor there was a fire door. Grace opened it to see the landing of a bleak, cement fire stair. She opened the door of the room closest to the exit. It was a little more spare than the others she'd seen, but it was serviceable and could be locked. It held a faint smell of air freshener gone stale. Grace climbed the fire stairs to the fourth floor. The fire door opened onto what seemed to be a private hallway laid with a length of red carpet. Not far from the fire exit a uniformed police officer stood outside an open doorway. Miss Marie Li's apartment, with a direct line to the most discreet room in the brothel. Grace decided it was time to introduce herself.

She walked into a room where someone had let their imagination take a different turn altogether from the pay-as-you-go fantasy downstairs. It was softer, a place where all negativities were expelled. Close the door behind you and you left the grey Parramatta streets below for some much more romantic place. Even so it had a fake quality, a chinoiserie such as you might find in a 1930s Hollywood film set where the action was supposedly situated in the exotic colonial Far East. The Art Deco furnishings, the drapes in period prints, the light fittings, the potted palms, the decorated screens, even the wallpaper, were a loving recreation of the time; elegant, richly coloured and luxurious.

The room was filled with a sweet, fresh, but still almost overpowering odour. On the tables roundabout stood vases of cut flowers: red, white, lilac and yellow roses, deep blue irises, lilies. An ornate sideboard was covered with an array of orchids in heavy gilded metal pots. The flowers bloomed in every shade of colour merging to deeply variegated textures, one patterned almost like leopard skin. Downstairs, the clients paid by the half-hour to the hour; here the fantasy could go on for as long as anyone wanted.

A smaller room off the main lounge had been set up for entertainment and was dominated by a large, flat screen. There were shelves of DVDs: silent and 1930s films, Hollywood musicals — *Chicago*, *Singing in the Rain* and *Camelot*. Along one wall were framed photographs of famous former love goddesses: Jean Harlow, Greta Garbo, Marlene Dietrich, Marilyn Monroe: their dresses and their blonde hair shimmering under lights. A photograph of the actor Gong Li, exquisite in a gold cheongsam, hung alongside them. Grace saw a DVD of one of her films, *Shanghai Triad*, sitting on the top of the DVD player.

The sudden and pervasive smell of cigarette smoke caught her attention. She moved towards the kitchen, a room with gleaming stainless-steel fittings and pale granite bench tops. There were signs of interrupted food preparation on one of the benches: an array of dishes usually found on a yum cha menu and a bottle of vintage Pol Roger champagne in an ice bucket with two champagne flutes beside it. Borghini was sitting with Marie Li at the table, a uniformed policewoman with them. The rest of his team were searching the apartment. Jon Kidd was already there, leaning against the bench and watching everything.

Marie was smoking quickly, a packet of cigarettes and a gold lighter close to her hand. There was no ingrained smell of stale cigarette smoke in the flat; if there had been, it would have disturbed the ambience, the smell of the flowers. If Marie lit up at other times, she must have had to go outside. No more than in her early twenties, she was stylishly attractive with a resemblance to Gong Li herself. Her eyebrows were finely curved, her mouth shaped full with red lipstick. Iridescent red tints in her black hair matched her rose-coloured fingernails. Her hands were shaking badly and she seemed unable to sit completely still.

'Who's this?' she asked, her face showing more confusion and fear than anger.

Borghini gave the standard reply to that question. 'Grace Riordan, one of my officers. I've already shown Marie a photograph of Coco and told her she's dead,' he said to Grace. 'I've also told her we have information that she was a worker here. She denies that. She also says she's never met the brothel's owners and doesn't know who they are.'

'Lynette handles all that kind of thing,' Marie said. 'She deals with the accountants. I'm the hostess. That's all I do.'

'You're the manager,' Borghini said.

'The hostess,' she replied sharply. 'It might be called manager but it really means hostess. I make people feel at ease. I'm better at that than Lynette.'

Grace sat down. Marie lit a cigarette from the end of the one she was just finishing. Jirawan's photograph, taken at the Villawood Immigration Detention Centre, lay on the table.

'Where did you get this information about this girl?' Marie asked. 'Whoever it was, they must have been mistaken. I don't know her. She's never worked here.'

'Our informant knew your receptionist's name,' Borghini said.

'Maybe he's been a customer here. He might have a grudge against us.'

'So if I go downstairs and ask Lynette about Coco, what's she going to tell me?'

'That she's never seen her here and she's never heard of her.'

'And the workers?'

'The same!' Marie's voice had an edge of panic. 'She was never here. I don't know why you keep asking me. Where did this information come from? What was this informant's name?' She spoke with a modified Australian accent, giving her speech a strained, artificial, up-market gloss.

'That information is confidential,' Borghini said.

'We don't even know who's accusing us. That doesn't seem very fair.'

'Who were you expecting tonight? You got the champagne out for someone.'

'That's none of your business!' She almost shrieked this, theatrically.

'I think you'll find it is,' Borghini replied. 'Whoever he is, he hasn't turned up.'

'My private life is my affair. It's got nothing to do with this.'

Grace's gaze went past Marie to a plain-clothes officer heading towards them from the hallway that presumably led to the bedrooms. He whispered in Borghini's ear.

'Okay,' Borghini said. 'If you don't mind, Marie, we'll just stop there for the moment. There's a room in your flat I want to have a look at.'

She stubbed out her cigarette. 'I don't have anything to hide. This is my home and I don't like you being here but I don't have anything to hide. Which room is it?'

'The one beside the linen cupboard.'

'There's nothing to see in there. I'll show you.'

Marie rose to her feet. She was slender, and wearing a red silk cheongsam set off by very high stiletto heels. Kidd fell into step behind her. They all followed her down the hallway past the main bedroom — a large room furnished with a king-size bed and soft rugs, including one that seemed to be a genuine tiger's skin. The windows were covered with heavy drapes. They stopped outside another door.

'Is this the room you're interested in?' she said. 'I can't see why.'

Furnished with a single bed, it was small and spare and lacking the gaudy luxury of the rest of the flat. There was no window and the door had a lock on the outside.

'Why do you need a lock on this door?' Borghini asked. 'Do you lock anyone in here?'

'No, of course I don't. That lock was here when I moved into this place. I don't use this room. Go inside and look at it if you want to. It's not such a terrible place. It has heating and an en suite.'

Grace stepped into the room. The surfaces seemed free of dust and there was the same faint smell of artificial air freshener as in the room downstairs. There would be nothing in here, not even a hair. A place with no exit, except to another room downstairs which also had no way out. She returned to the hallway.

'It's very clean for a room you never use,' she said to Marie. 'Have you cleaned it recently? It smells of air freshener.'

'I like things clean.'

Grace glanced at Borghini. He was standing back a little, watching; a slight nod said she should go on.

'You like things clean?' she said. 'Is this a maid's room? A place for someone who cooks and cleans for you?'

'I do my own cooking. I like to cook.'

'Then who does your cleaning? Whoever slept in there?'

'No one slept in there.'

'Then who cleaned it last and when? It must have been recently. You can smell the air freshener. Why do you need to clean and put air freshener into a room no one uses?'

'I don't know. I ...' Marie stopped, not knowing what to say.

Another of Borghini's people appeared in the hallway. 'Something else you need to see,' she said to him quietly.

In the main bedroom, an ornate Chinese cabinet stood open on the dressing table. Beside it was a shiny, silver-edged mirror, a razor blade with a silver edge matching the mirror's and a thin silver straw, similarly decorated. The silverwork was delicately, intricately made.

'We found those in the cabinet,' the officer said.

'Are these yours?' Borghini asked Marie.

'No. I don't know what they are.'

'If they're not yours, can you tell me how they might have got here?'

She shook her head dumbly. She had tears in her eyes.

'Perhaps someone put them there. A visitor who didn't like me. I don't know.'

'We found this as well,' one of the other plain-clothes officers said. He was holding a black silk pouch peeled open to reveal several broken lumps of cocaine in a plastic bag. It looked like a stash kept for personal use.

Grace glanced around the room once more. On the dressing table were vases of white roses mixed with smaller flowers, dark blue in colour. A silk and lace negligee lay thrown over a chair, waiting for someone to slip it on. The negligee was for two to enjoy; the cocaine seemed to be only for one. And not Marie.

'Marie, why don't you take a seat back out in the kitchen?' Borghini said. 'We'll keep looking through here and then we'll need to ask you some more questions. I'm afraid we'll be keeping you for a while yet. Maybe you'd like to have a cup of coffee while you're waiting. We'll get to you as soon as we can.'

'Can I call someone? I want to call someone.'

'Who do you want to call?'

'In these circumstances, who do you think?' Kidd said. It was the first time he'd spoken. 'Your family. A lawyer.'

'I'll call my brother,' Marie said. 'Can I do that?'

Grace wasn't certain who she was asking.

'You can do that if you want to,' Borghini told her. 'But I'm going to ask you not to leave the premises. If you go and sit down now and make your call, we'll keep searching in here. I'll send someone to look after you.'

Marie turned to leave the room. She bumped against the uniformed policewoman as if she hadn't seen her, then glanced around confused. She saw Kidd and looked away. The policewoman guided her out.

'I think that might be it for me tonight,' Grace said. 'This isn't my field.'

'No problem.' Borghini dredged up a smile, presumably pleased to have her out from under his feet. 'Why don't you give me a call tomorrow? I'll let you know how we finished up here and what we're going to do next.'

'I'll do that, thanks.'

Passing the kitchen, she saw Marie sitting at the table, crying while she tried to call a number on her phone. The policewoman sat with her, watching. Kidd, following Grace, went back to his place leaning against the bench. Grace guessed he wanted to listen to whatever Marie Li was going to say on the phone. Ignoring Clive's instructions to watch him, she walked out of the flat, feeling his eyes on her back.

Downstairs in the reception area, some of the workers were readying to leave. The police had finished their questioning. There was a low buzz of conversation. Lynette, the receptionist, was sitting at the desk flicking half-heartedly through a magazine. Grace went over to her.

'Lynette,' she said. 'Is that who you are?'

'I've already told the police that. Who are you?'

'Grace Riordan. I'm with the police.'

Lynette looked up at her, polite but ungiving. She was older than

Grace had thought, at least fifty. They were interrupted by a chorus of 'Night, Lynette,' as the workers left, moving in a small group past the reception desk.

'You take care out there,' Lynette called back, watching the women out the door before turning back to Grace. 'What do you want? I've already given you people all my details.'

'You look like a professional to me,' Grace said. 'You've been in this business a lot longer than Marie Li, haven't you? You were doing this when she was in nappies. Now she's your boss. Do you like that situation? Or do you have to do things you'd normally never do under any other circumstances?'

The woman said nothing, only stared. Grace saw the same fear in her eyes that she'd seen in Marie Li's.

'Take this,' she said and offered a card that had nothing on it but a phone number.

'What is it?'

'A contact number. Put it away out of sight.'

The card disappeared into Lynette's bag. 'I thought you were with the police.'

'I want to show you something. This is Coco after we found her.'

Grace slid a photograph across the desk: Coco lying in the scrub in the Ku-ring-gai Chase National Park.

'Oh, Christ.' Lynette closed her eyes and covered her mouth.

Grace picked up the photograph and put it back in her bag. 'I want to know who did that to her. Who is she, and where did she come from?'

Lynette still had her eyes closed. She shook her head.

'I've never seen her before.'

'Yes, you have. Don't think anyone believes you when you say that. And don't think this is going to go away. We're going to keep coming back and we're going to keep asking questions. You're going to be asked to come in for questioning and that questioning is going to go on for hours. We're going to talk to all your workers. Some of them will have seen something. Besides that,' Grace said, 'you saw Coco in that picture. Think about the people who did that. How do you know they won't see you as a weak link? And if they do, what are they going to do about it?

Do you want to trust them? Or do you want us to offer you some protection?'

'I can't talk to you here,' Lynette said, barely audibly.

'But she was here.'

The woman had folded her arms close about herself and was staring down into her lap. Very faintly, she nodded.

'If you want to talk to me in complete privacy, with a promise of complete confidentiality, you can ring that number any time you like. No one has to know you've called me. Just ask for me by my first name. If you're a witness, we may be able to get you immunity. If you need protection, we'll arrange it.'

The woman looked up, shaking her head, her mouth slightly open. Her make-up seemed old and her eyes were moist as if she might cry. At that moment, Kidd walked into the reception area and came up to the desk.

'What are you two talking about?'

'I want to know if Lynette has a book with her workers' photographs,' Grace replied. 'So far she's been telling me to mind my own business.'

Lynette placed a leather-bound photograph album on the desk.

'Everyone in there is legal,' she said. 'Have a look.'

Grace flicked through, finding the workers Doug had described. A number of Asian women and one African, all very lovely, none of whom had been at work tonight.

'Satisfied?' Lynette asked.

'You have some very attractive workers. I'm sure they bring in the clients.'

'That's what we do here — bring in clients.'

'But not tonight. You had customers waiting.'

'I was expecting a quiet night. I care about my ladies' welfare and I make sure they have adequate time off.'

'Then I'll say good night,' Grace said.

She walked out, giving Kidd and Lynette one last backward glance. Lynette was staring into the distance. It was impossible to say if she knew Kidd or not. He was looking after Grace, angry, suspicious. *Go on, follow me. Prove you're what I think you are.*

In the courtyard, only one car remained of the workers' vehicles, an old yellow Toyota Corolla. It didn't look like the kind of car Grace would have expected Marie Li to drive and she guessed it to be Lynette's. She took a quick note of the registration number and went to her own car, which was parked at a distance from the building. She didn't start the engine but looked back, waiting. This side of the building was in darkness; all the house lights looked out onto the front street. There was only the white gleam of the fluorescent tube over the back door. Suddenly Kidd stepped out. He looked around but didn't seem able to see her in the dark. Then his phone rang. He answered it, turned and walked back inside. The door closed and she could no longer see him. She waited a few minutes longer to see if he would come back. She was about to ring in for a registration check on the Corolla when Lynette, wearing a leather jacket over her dress and with her bag in hand, came running out and went to the car, yanking the door open. Grace watched her start it and then drive away at speed.

She gave a quick glance at the back door to see if Kidd was following, then drove after her. Out on the road, she called in to the Orion control centre with the details of Lynette's car's make and registration.

'Owned by a Jacqueline Ryan,' the operative said. 'Her address is the Royal Hotel on Victoria Road, West Ryde. She must be a long-term resident. Do you need backup?'

Grace felt the pressure of her firearm against her ribcage, just under her arm.

'Not yet. I think we need to pick this woman up. Can you log that as an urgent request, please?'

'Just a minute. There's a call coming through to you. Do you want to take it?'

'Yes. Log the number and put it through, thanks.'

'Is that Grace?' the caller said.

'Yes. Go ahead, Lynette.'

'I will talk to you but only if it's tonight. Like now. As soon as you can.'

'Where do you want to do that?'

'Do you know the Royal Hotel? It's on Victoria Road. Can you meet me in the bistro?'

'I'll be there as soon as I can. Does that suit you?'

'I'll be waiting. I want this over and done with.'

Grace didn't doubt it. The woman's voice was shaking with fear. As soon as she'd cut the connection, Grace was back at the control centre.

'Did you get that?' she asked.

'We did.'

'I'll report in when I've seen her. I think we'll still need to pick her up but I'll confirm that after I've talked to her.'

'We'll be waiting.'

Grace hadn't been to the Royal Hotel before but it was easy enough to find. A renovated brick building, it had the look of a popular local watering hole with several bars, gaming and a restaurant. The sign said it offered long-stay budget accommodation. Was this all Lynette could afford? Or was she saving her money for a rainy day?

She was in the bistro, drinking a glass of white wine. This late on a week night, there were few diners at the tables. Grace bought a mineral water and went to join her. Lynette looked tired, and the jacket robbed her of whatever glamour she'd had in the brothel.

'I know it's not that warm but do you want to go outside?' she said. 'That way I can smoke.'

'Sure.'

'Don't you drink?'

'Not when I'm working,' Grace replied, this being the easiest explanation.

'What about a cigarette?'

A former smoker, Grace mentally gritted her teeth. 'No, I don't smoke,' she said.

'You're healthy.'

Lynette bought a half-carafe of house white and they went outside. The beer garden was empty. Lynette lit her cigarette with relief. Grace smelled the smoke and was glad she'd said no.

'How did you get away tonight?' she asked.

'I rang what's-her-features upstairs and told her she could close up, I was going home. She screamed at me! Said she had the police there and she couldn't do it. I said she'd just have to cope. I won't have a job as of now but it doesn't matter. I've had enough. As soon as I can book one, I'm getting on a flight to Perth.'

'Why Perth?'

'My son's in Western Australia, working up north with Woodside Petroleum. He's been asking me to come out and see him for a while. I will now. With a bit of luck, I might be able to get some work over there. There's a lot of single men working up there besides him. Someone must need a receptionist somewhere.'

'Some details, Lynette. What's your real name?'

'Jacqueline Ryan. Before you ask, yes, I live here. It's cheap. I've got money but I don't spend it if I can help it. When I quit the business, I'll buy my dream home.'

'Who owns the brothel?' Grace asked.

'Don't have a clue and I don't care. I deal with the accountants. Stamfords. They're in Parramatta. They do everything. If you want to know more, go talk to them.'

'Marie's new, isn't she? Where did she come from?'

'Stamfords.' Lynette blew out smoke. 'They rang one day and said she was on her way. She was the boss and I had to do what she said. Fine. Why should I give a shit? Look, I don't ask anybody any questions. In this business, you don't.'

No, you just did what you were told by a hysterical girl half your age without a murmur, Grace thought. The same way you took on an illegal and unwilling sex worker without batting an eyelid. Whatever's in the pay packet must be good.

'Coco,' Grace said, pushing along. 'When did she arrive and did she come alone?'

Lynette shook her head over her glass. 'No. She turned up with Marie, about two months ago now. When I heard she was dead, I didn't know what to think. I honestly don't know anything about that.'

'Marie brought her down by the fire stairs,' Grace said without pity. 'You handled the bookings.'

'I did not handle the bookings. Whatever that nasty little cow says, she did it all.' Lynette took another mouthful of wine. 'Cheap white,' she said with a grimace.

49

Grace could guess what it tasted like. Alcohol was a caustic poison moving at the edge of the blood, twisting your mind into such a disfigured shape you couldn't recognise yourself. Others could drink; she could not.

'What about the other workers? Didn't they know she was there?'

'That's what I used to say to *her*! They had to see her taking the customers down there. She just laughed at me.'

'How did the customers find out about Coco?'

Lynette looked at her sharply. 'You know, don't you? No condoms if you didn't want to. On the fucking net!'

'Yes, I know about that. How did you deal with it?' Grace asked. 'Normally you'd never do that, right?'

Lynette wouldn't meet her eye. 'There's plenty of men who don't want that. They like the protection themselves. I couldn't help her. I wasn't the boss any more.'

'It can't be good business to do something like that. Didn't Marie know that?'

This time Lynette did look at her. 'Anything that gives the clients what they want is good business. There's a fair few arseholes out there, you know.'

'Who put it on the net?'

'Marie. It said *Ask Marie.*'

Marie was the front. Possibly even the sucker. The one pushed out there to do the dirty work. From Lynette's description, she'd got a kick out of it.

'Marie isn't a big woman,' Grace said. 'How did she control Coco?'

'She had someone to help her. Some guy, I don't know who he was. He used to bring her down and take her up.'

'Can you describe him?'

'I hardly ever saw him. He was a big guy, black hair, Italian probably. Head like a bullet. Never washed. You could smell him before you saw him. I stayed out of his way.'

'Did you ever talk to Coco? Find out anything about her while she was there?' Grace asked.

'She didn't speak enough English. One thing though — I'd give her a break sometimes when there was no one else around. I couldn't let her go, but I'd let her out of that room and get her a cup of tea and something to eat in the kitchen. She wanted to use a phone one day. She kept pointing to my mobile. She was crying so I let her use it. I think she called Peter, whoever he was.'

'Peter. That's all?'

'That's all I could understand. But I do know that whatever that call was about, it made her happy. That's when she started to jack up.'

'What did she do?'

'When the men came into the room, she'd be curled up in a heap. Sometimes she'd be in the corner on the floor. She wouldn't move, wouldn't even look at them. If they wanted sex, they'd have to force it. Look, the place we run — a lot of our clientele is suburban dads. This is their break. They want someone to give them a good time. Marie would leave the clients there, and often enough they'd come back to me and say they didn't want that. It wasn't what they'd paid for. Then Marie started getting angry with Coco because she wouldn't cooperate. One day, madam dragged me down there and told me to sort her out. What was I supposed to do? Coco was wrapped up like this tight little ball. You could see her shaking. I lost it. I shouted at that little bitch for once. I said, you can't fucking do this! It's creating too many bad vibes. That shut her up. Anyway, after that Coco disappeared.'

'Disappeared?'

'She wasn't there any more. That was maybe three weeks ago. I never saw her again. Then a bunch of cleaners turned up and went through that room like a dose of salts. Marie came and saw me. She had that look in her eye. She hadn't forgiven me for swearing at her. If I told anyone about Coco, I was going to regret it, she said. She meant it, too.'

Easy enough, once the brothel was closed, to take someone down in the service elevator and out the back door to a waiting car, Grace thought. But where to from there?

'Were you expecting us tonight?' she asked.

Lynette shook her head.

'You were, weren't you? Someone called. When? Early? Late? And what about your workers?' Grace asked. 'Quite a few of them weren't there tonight. You had customers waiting. Did you call them or did someone else?'

Lynette refilled her glass. 'It was just a normal night.'

Someone had called, Grace felt certain of it. But too late to stop Marie making preparations to meet her lover, who instead had sent along his watchdog, Kidd, to keep an eye on her. Not much of an exchange for her.

'Who's Marie's boyfriend?'

'I wouldn't have a clue. I've never seen him and I don't want to.'

'Was there anyone there tonight that you recognised? Anyone you'd seen before?'

'In your mob?' She grinned. 'No, no clients. None that I recognised anyway.'

'It was your more exotic workers who didn't turn up tonight, wasn't it? The Asian and African workers.'

Lynette shrugged, waving Grace away with one hand.

'Does Marie look after them as well?' she persisted.

'No. She didn't have anything to do with them. I handled the bookings and the money, that's all.'

'Do those workers cost more?'

'What do you think?'

'And do they get paid more as well?'

'Of course they do.'

'You'd know that, wouldn't you? If you look after them,' Grace said, watching the sudden panic in the woman's eyes. 'Let's assume they're not getting paid as much as they should. Where does the money go? Do you split it with the owners?'

Lynette put down her glass. 'That's it from me. Good night.'

'Walk away from here and I'll have you arrested.'

Lynette, half on her feet, slumped back into her chair, tired and frightened. Her make-up seemed to be slipping away.

'How can you have me arrested?'

'There's plenty in what you've told me tonight. Harbouring an illegal immigrant for starters. Deprivation of liberty. Now let's do this the easy way. You answer my questions. You get looked after.'

'What do you think I can tell you? I'm just front of house. That's all.'

'How much do these workers get paid?'

Lynette looked away. 'They don't.'

'You take the money.'

'I take a percentage. Do you know how old I am? I'm fifty-three. If I don't get some money together, what I am going to live on ten years from now? The fucking old-age pension?'

Grace ignored this. 'Why are these workers doing this? There must be something in it for them. Is it a visa? For them or their families?'

'I don't know what the deal is. Some of them have other jobs as well, I'm pretty certain about that. They come in, they work a set number of shifts each week, they go home. I handle it. That's all.'

'Do you know Jon Kidd? The man who was at the reception desk when I left.'

'That little shortie? I've never seen him before. And that's a fact. I never have.'

'Who brings these workers in to meet you?'

'They come themselves.' Lynette took a mouthful of wine. 'They say they're here to work for Amelie. I know what that means and I look after them from then on. The money they make gets recorded separately against their names. I send it off to the accountants. They deal with it and then I get my bit at the end of the month. In cash.'

'They just front up out of the blue? You don't know they're coming.'

'All right. I get a note from the accountant. It comes in a sealed envelope. If they don't front, I have to send a letter back saying so.'

Someone tells them they'd better be there if they know what's good for them, Grace thought. And if they don't or won't listen to that advice, what happens then?

'Do they always turn up?'

'Yeah,' Lynette said. 'Except one. That was just a month ago. Another African girl. I had her picture. She was a stunner.'

'Do you still have the picture?'

'No, I sent it back when she didn't turn up.'

'What was her name?'

'I wasn't given a name. I don't get names for any of them and I don't ask. We settle on a working name when they get there.'

'What happened to the one who didn't turn up?'

'I don't know and I didn't ask.'

'Why didn't Marie handle these workers?'

'Because she doesn't know her arse from her elbow.'

'But you do. You've been in this business for years. How long have you been working at Life's Pleasures? Has this been going on all the time you've been there?'

'All my fucking life, it feels like. Three years.' Lynette had stood up. She was crying. 'Yes, it's been going on the whole time. I got paid for it, didn't I? You can have me arrested now. I don't give a shit. I'm walking away. I need to get some sleep.'

'One last question. Did Coco have a wedding ring when she was with you?'

'Is that a joke? What would she do with that?'

And she was gone, leaving behind an empty glass and carafe and a full ashtray.

Grace walked out to her car, passing a man a distance away from her on his way in. She glanced at him but he was heading for the bar. In her car, she rang the control centre.

'Did you get that conversation?'

'We did,' the operative replied. 'What's the request now?'

'We need to pick her up for questioning ASAP. Her movements need to be monitored and Clive needs to be notified as well. We should pick her up before tomorrow morning at the latest if we can. We also need to notify the police. Can you forward them a transcript of everything that was said tonight? And we need to check Jacqueline Ryan's mobile phone records for any calls to Thailand.'

'Will do,' the operative said. 'I'll send that request for a team through now.'

'Thanks. I'm off duty. You can close my wire down. Call me if you need me.'

'Okay.'

Grace was tired and it was late. She hadn't seen Ellie that evening and by now she would be in bed, hopefully asleep. She felt jaded; she didn't like badgering worn-out, middle-aged women in desperate circumstances, it made her feel grubby. When she got home she would wash off her make-up and become herself. But wasn't this who she was, with or without the pancake? The hard-faced operative? Orion had extraordinary powers. Those powers were hers to exercise even if they broke people's lives apart. This was the tightrope she had to walk: find the killers without doing too much damage to herself or anyone else.

She began the drive home, to Harrigan's Victorian terrace in Birchgrove. His haunted house, she called it; ghosts from his past lived in every room. He had told her to change it as much as she wanted — repaint it, redecorate, whatever she liked. Make it her own. She was working on it, room by room.

It was only after she'd crossed the Gladesville Bridge that she began to wonder if she was being followed. A single light as if from a motorbike seemed to be always at the same distance behind her. Then the light grew closer — a small, agile bike, the kind that slips easily in and out of the traffic. Was it Newell? It couldn't be. Every police officer in New South Wales would be looking for him. Even he wouldn't be so mad as to show himself in public right now. And how could he know where she was?

Her mind kept her driving under control but it didn't stop her fear from growing. The bike came closer; it seemed to be letting her know it was there. She turned on her phone and rang the Orion control centre.

'I'm fairly certain I'm being followed,' she said. 'A bike, small. I can't see any registration and I've got no description of the rider.'

'Where from?'

'I first noticed it coming over the Gladesville Bridge. I'm on Victoria Road coming up to Darling Street where I'm turning left. It's accelerating, coming up beside me, swerving in close.'

'Take evasive action now.'

'It's gone,' she said.

Suddenly the road was clear. The rider had swerved in dangerously towards her car, then sped past her through the orange light at the intersection of Victoria Road and Darling Street. She hoped her voice hadn't sounded panicky; it seemed as if it had.

'Are you there?' the operative asked.

'Yes. I don't know what that was about. Whether it was someone's idea of a joke or if someone was following me from my op. Can you report it? And make my request for a team to pick up Jacqueline Ryan urgent. Just in case they were following me all the way from Parramatta.'

'Will do.'

She hung up. She was shaky, tired.

When she turned off Darling Street and was on her way down the hill, she noticed a car behind her. It was still with her when she reached Snails Bay. As she was backing down the steep driveway of her house, the car passed her, turning into Wharf Road. It was a red Saab, a car she'd often seen speeding up the street. She turned off the ignition and sat looking around her. Everything was peaceful. Maybe no one was out there and she could just relax.

Could she tell Paul what had just happened or was it work? No, it was work. Another secret between them. At least she was home, she thought, looking at the lighted windows with relief.

5

In the silence of the house, Harrigan, standing by Ellie's open doorway, could hear only the quiet breathing of his daughter while she slept. If Grace were home, she'd have put on some music; the jazz she loved so much, singers and musicians he'd never heard of before he met her. She sang their daughter to sleep in her own soft, slightly throaty voice. Other than in the shower, it was almost the only time she sang these days. He liked her voice and wished she would sing more. 'One day I'll join a choir,' she'd told him. 'Whatever you want,' he'd replied, wanting her to be happy, even now not quite able to believe that she could be happy with him.

When she wasn't here, he preferred silence. Tonight, after what he'd seen just a few hours ago, this silence mixed with the sound of Ellie's breathing gave him a sense of cleanness. He had fed and bathed Ellie, settled her to bed and read her to sleep. She had curled up on the pillow with the promise that her mother would be there in the morning. Each of these things worked against the pictures in his mind of the dead and wounded men he had seen that day. He was yet to find out if the memory would reassert itself like some malignant intrusion.

It wasn't as if he hadn't seen that kind of thing before. Often enough when he'd been with the police, he'd looked cold-bloodedly at the dead, dealt in a detached way with the living, and then worked as hard as he could to find who'd done the killing.

Throughout, other people did the grieving. He'd hoped he had left all that behind. He had come home this afternoon with a sense of sickness that was new to him.

Downstairs, he poured himself a whisky. Grace didn't drink and because of that he didn't drink much himself. Tonight he needed alcohol to ease his thoughts. He went upstairs again and into his study, a plain room at the back of the house that looked down onto his long, narrow strip of land to Snails Bay on the inner harbour. This was where he collected his thoughts, where he worked. Joel Griffin had left almost as bad a taste in Harrigan's mouth as the killings he'd witnessed. What did Griffin know about either Grace or him? And what did he need to do about it?

He googled Griffin's name and waited to see if anything new might come up from the last time he'd gone searching. There was one fact he hadn't thought much about before: Griffin hadn't qualified in Australia. He'd got his degree at the University of London seventeen years ago and been admitted to the bar in Australia when he had returned to the country in the mid-1990s. Qualifications gained overseas were too convenient to Harrigan's mind. Maybe they were genuine, maybe they weren't. But if his qualifications were fake, Griffin, as a fraud, was better at his work than any number of lawyers Harrigan knew to be genuine. At best, this fragment of information only proved where he had been seventeen years ago and when he had come back to Australia.

The information he couldn't find was also interesting. Griffin was a lone wolf, listed as an individual only, not connected to any particular legal firm. Unlike some other practitioners, there was no photograph attached to his contact details. This wasn't so very unusual, but it fitted the man's elusiveness. Harrigan phoned the number given for Griffin's office and was answered by a recorded message, the kind preinstalled on any readily available answering machine. There was nothing to identify that you were leaving a message for Joel Griffin, barrister. He hung up without leaving his details.

After a moment's thought, he googled again — not Griffin, but himself and Grace. On a few occasions their photographs had made it to the gossip columns of various media websites. Grace called it her fifteen seconds of virtual fame. Harrigan studied the photographs one after the other. On none was her scar visible.

He heard her car outside and went down to the kitchen, relieved that she was home. Despite the lateness of the hour he had waited for her before eating, caught in his own thoughts and occupied with his daughter's needs. Then Grace was there in the doorway, smiling. As he always did, he touched her face and then kissed her. He knew the real face under the make-up, the feel of her skin, her mouth. He knew her, the emotions she kept hidden, her body, better than anyone.

'How are you?' she asked.

'I'm okay. It's nothing I haven't dealt with before. We need to talk about it.'

'I'll get changed and put my gun away. Is Ellie asleep?'

'Yeah.'

'Maybe I won't look in on her. I might wake her up.'

'The door's open. You can look in.'

When she came back downstairs, the transformation was complete. The real woman had appeared. Her long dark hair was out on her shoulders, her make-up was gone. The drab pants suit had been changed for jeans, a yellow T-shirt and socks. She curled up cross-legged on a chair.

'Put your gun away?' he asked.

Both he and Grace had an unbreakable rule that they never wore their firearms in their daughter's presence, even if they were concealed. Harrigan had a licence for a firearm for his personal safety and kept a handgun and ammunition in a safe in his study. Grace, whose work allowed her to keep her gun with her at all times, locked hers in there as well when she was home.

'It's where little children's hands can't get to it. I did look in on her. She's fast asleep. She's got your hair. It's so beautiful. When we cut it, I'm going to keep some.'

Harrigan put the meal on the table — food Grace had cooked on her days off, his interest in kitchen matters reaching no further than setting the microwave and turning it on.

'Newell, babe,' he said. 'Is he going to turn up here?'

Could Newell really be so mad? The fear was like living in shadows where you couldn't distinguish real from false. Had it been him on her tail tonight? It depressed her that she couldn't talk to Harrigan about it.

'It'd be lunacy,' she said instead. 'Every police officer in New South Wales must be out there looking for him. He won't be able to show his face anywhere. How did it happen?'

'It was a setup. Someone must have been paid to make sure Chris Newell was there at that time and they could get to him. If that includes either of the drivers, they're both dead now. They can't tell anyone anything. I was talking to Joel Griffin when it happened.'

'Why him?'

'He wanted to see me. He knows about you and Newell, babe. He knows about your scar and how you got it. He was trying to blackmail me. Kept fishing to see what I was prepared to give him.'

Grace looked as if she'd been punched in the stomach. She put down her fork, covered her face for a few seconds.

'Oh, God,' she said.

'It hasn't happened yet.'

He reached over and took her hand. She held on to him, squeezing hard, then let go.

'What did you tell him?' she asked.

'That he could go jump. If he tried anything funny, he'd regret it.'

She picked up her fork again. The mood had changed. He couldn't remember the last time he'd seen her so angry.

'He can put it all over the front page of the *Telegraph* if he wants to. I wouldn't give him the time of day.'

'We're giving him nothing,' Harrigan said. 'What's he going to do? If he puts it out there, he's in breach of client confidence. What's that going to do for his reputation? If he does, I'll go after him through the Bar Council.'

'If it does get out, it'll affect me at work. Clive won't like it.'

'Are you going to tell him about it?'

'No,' she said eventually. 'He might take me off what I'm working on and I don't want that. I don't have to tell him everything. My life's my own.'

'How was it today?'

She shrugged, frowning. Her work was beginning to affect her, he thought. Grace, at ease, put other people at their ease, laughed and made him laugh. The woman who liked to dress up and go out and enjoy herself was another self to the one who dressed so plainly for work. When she was under pressure, she changed; she put on a hard, excluding shell. He knew that Newell was partly to blame for that cold barrier being there, but that didn't help things. He didn't want her to become like that again, the way she had been when he'd first met her. He wanted her light-hearted and full of sparkle again, the way she had been these last few years.

'It was okay,' she said. 'I think I achieved something so that was good. Do you know a Mark Borghini? He's my contact with the police. He asked about you.'

'Mark? Yeah, I know him. He's not exactly Mr Tactful but he's good value. That's good for you, babe. You can rely on him. What did he want to know?'

'Just how you were.'

He waited but she seemed to have nothing else to say. He let the subject pass. Knowing Mark Borghini was her contact made him feel better about the work she was doing.

'This escape — it's madness,' she said. 'The police are going to find whoever's behind it, sooner rather than later because they'll put everything they've got into it. And when they do, those people will end up dead.'

'It's suicide,' Harrigan agreed. 'Makes no sense to me at all. Whatever's going on, we don't want anything to do with it. Or Griffin. He's a strange fish. He told me he was representing Newell pro bono.'

'Why?'

'As far as I can tell, for the information in Newell's head. Maybe that's how Griffin makes his money. Extortion.'

'It won't work with us,' Grace said.

'No way.' There was a pause. 'You're tired, babe.'

'Yeah. Let's go to bed.'

As they were clearing up, their home phone rang: a private unlisted number they gave out only to friends and family. Grace glanced at Harrigan.

'For you?' she asked.

'I don't know who it could be at this time of night.'

'Could be Nicky, I suppose. He can call this late.'

Her brother ran a restaurant on the Central Coast and sometimes rang at the end of his working day to chat to her. She picked up the phone, putting it on speakerphone.

'Hi there,' she said, cautiously.

A woman began to laugh, softly and maliciously. 'Grace,' she said and laughed again.

Grace turned off the speakerphone but left the line open, then picked up her work mobile and called the Orion control centre. 'I have an anonymous call on my home phone right now. The caller said my first name, then began to laugh.' She glanced at the phone. 'They've just hung up. Can you trace that call and log the time and date, please? Thank you.'

'Why do you think that call's related to your work?' Harrigan asked when she'd finished.

'I don't know for sure. But I was followed home from my op tonight.' She took a breath, knowing this simple confidence was breaking the rules. 'All the way to Darling Street by someone who wanted me to know they were there. Whoever they were, they were trying to frighten me.'

'Are you supposed to tell me that?' he asked.

'No.'

'Was it Newell?'

'No, I don't think so. He couldn't know I'd be there at that time.'

Harrigan reflected that he often didn't know where she was or what she was doing either.

'Is that what this operation is?' he asked. 'Dangerous?'

'Maybe.'

'You should have told me, babe. I need to know if you're in danger. It's not just me. There's Ellie as well.'

'I know that. I never stop thinking about it. Since Clive's been there, it's been impossible,' she said. 'You can't tell anyone the simplest thing.'

'He's a control freak. Forget him. It's late.'

They went to bed and, in defiance of the phone call, made love. Grace's thought was that she needed this to feel human, needed the comfort. Just to let the physical pleasure cleanse her of what had happened that day and bring her back to herself. She felt the warmth of his body and was never more at ease with herself.

Harrigan thought of this as his fundamental territory; something he had that no one else could touch. If everything else was gone, this exclusiveness would still exist between them. This closeness was a refuge for them both, somewhere they needed no disguises and where no one could threaten either of them. The room, like the house, was their own world, safe, inviolable. Later, he lightly traced out her face.

'You're lovely,' he said. 'You have a face like the Madonna.'

'And what kind of face does she have?'

'Like yours. Clean. Dark, beautiful eyes.'

'She's more peaceful than me, she must be. I'm not a peaceful person.'

'I just want you the way you are,' Harrigan replied.

Harrigan woke in the early morning feeling a deep sense of unease. He couldn't go back to sleep; the phone call had jangled him too much. By the radio clock, it was 3:15 am. After a while he got up, pulled on his tracksuit and went to check the house. First, he looked in on Ellie. Her long, dark-fair hair was tousled over the pillow. She turned over just after he looked through the open doorway but kept on sleeping. Very quietly he shut the door in case she should wake and hear him moving around. He stood in the darkness of the hallway, thinking.

His house was secure; his history with the police made that essential. He had a drawerful of death threats against him and his family, some more lurid than others. It wasn't only criminals who wanted him harmed or dead; there were police, some still serving and some not, who had scores to settle with him. There were bars on his windows, security doors on all the entrances, and an alarm system installed. There was a number to ring at police headquarters if he or his family needed protection. His car was always parked in the single locked brick garage, the only one there was room for on his block. Grace's car was kept behind the locked gate at the front of the house. The wall that ran between his garden and Birchgrove Park was higher than he would have liked but he had no choice. Maybe one day, when people were dead or had worn out their passions, these locks and bars could go, but not now.

He went downstairs and checked the doors, front and back, including those that led out onto the deck. The old exotic trees that had been planted in the backyard decades ago were beginning to die. Soon they would need to be replaced. Their mostly bare branches were black against the pale glow of the city lights in the night sky. In this partial light, he saw two possums, mother and offspring, sitting on the rail of the deck, silhouettes against the lighter shadows. Suddenly they were gone. Harrigan tensed, waiting, but saw no one.

Throughout much of his life, on and off, Harrigan had lived in this house. Originally, it had been an inheritance from his aunt when he was fifteen, held in trust until he was of age. A single, church-obsessed woman, she had left it to him as an insult to his father, her brother, whom she'd hated. It had been left to her by an uncle, who'd also disapproved of his father, adding to the depth of the bitterness between them. Family loathings had given him an enviable address. The Harrigans had lived on the Balmain peninsula for several generations but, other than the uncle, they had never owned a house. His father had been a wharfie who had drunk and gambled too much and, until they had come here, Harrigan had grown up in rented accommodation near White Bay.

The house wasn't only his home. It was memory and experience, each room reminding him of the events, some of them violent, that had shaped his life.

Harrigan had another child from a long-ago marriage, Toby, who was disabled with cerebral palsy and had always had to live in care. His mother had abandoned both him and Harrigan almost as soon as he'd been born and then disappeared from their lives. Now Toby was a twenty-year-old university student studying pure mathematics. His body kept him in a wheelchair but his mind ranged freely. Harrigan had built the room in which he now stood — during the day, a large, light-filled space — for his son, combining the two smaller rooms that had once been here. It was a place for Toby to come in his chair and feel at home. But he had not only been creating a space for his son. Harrigan had been expunging the past, in its place building something he valued, something that had meaning for him. Once these walls had been painted a drab green. One night, when he was eighteen, he had seen his mother's blood splashed all over that green paint, when his father had fatally shot her in the face.

Jim Harrigan had supplemented his income on the wharves by petty thievery, and from there moved into more dangerous company dealing in heroin. One night he had brought home a gun he'd been told to hide. Harrigan remembered hearing his parents arguing furiously over the gun before being sickened by the sound of the shot. He remembered — could not forget — his mother lying against the wall with no face. His father said she'd grabbed at the gun. Maybe she had, but those words had no meaning for him. 'Kill me,' Jim Harrigan said to his son. Blinded by rage, his hands shaking, Harrigan fired wildly, almost unaware that he had, but only wounded his father. 'That won't do it. Try again,' Jim Harrigan demanded. But Harrigan couldn't shoot for a second time, and the memory stayed with him as a marker between what he could and couldn't do. No events could have torn a hole in his life so powerfully. No one would ever harm anyone he cared about like that again.

He went upstairs and, giving up on the possibility of sleep, went into his study. Despite his unease, a deep reluctance prevented him from taking his gun out of the safe with his daughter sleeping just down the hall.

He sat down at his desk in the dark. A little to the side stood a picture of Grace seated on a blanket in Birchgrove Park, with Ellie, dressed in a white froth of baby clothes, cuddled in her arms. She was laughing and saying to her daughter, 'Wave to the camera.' He remembered the day when, to her shock, Grace had found out she was pregnant. They had set up house together but not married; they had never once talked about marriage. It might have been the memory of his first marriage, or his parents' savage arguments, that prevented Harrigan from suggesting it. He rejected the possibility at a deeper level than he brought into his conscious mind. His only experiences of marriage had been destructive.

Maybe Grace understood this about him and that was why she never spoke of it herself. He left the subject alone for fear of breaking the balance between them, the easy way they accepted each other. But he still remembered sitting with her and his daughter on the blanket that day and thinking that whatever they might do, he'd never leave either of them. Toby's photograph stood next to Grace and Ellie's, taken the day he had received his final examination results, which he was holding in his one good hand. All three were so much a part of his life he could not imagine himself existing without them.

Perhaps he had been too caught in his night thoughts, looking inwards, something habitual to him. Staring into the dark, he saw the figure in his back garden, a man, solid against the lighter city darkness, moving away from a camphor laurel towards the wall between his garden and Birchgrove Park.

Harrigan was at his safe almost immediately and had his gun out. Moving as silently as possible, he went into the spare bedroom at the front of the house. Snatching the keys out of the drawer there, he unlocked the double doors onto the veranda and stepped outside. He heard a car starting on the street but had no intention of running outside after it, possibly straight into a bullet. He leaned over the balcony and saw it in the streetlight — a white Toyota Camry speeding up the street. It was too far away to get the numberplate. Then it was gone.

When he came out of the room, he saw Grace standing by Ellie's door, listening. She put a finger to her lips. 'She's still asleep,' she mouthed. He nodded and took his gun back to the safe. Silently they both went back to bed.

'She didn't wake up,' she said softly. 'What happened? I woke up and you weren't here. Why did you have your gun out?'

'I couldn't sleep. I went and sat in my study. Then I saw someone standing in the back garden watching the house. I don't know how long they'd been there. That car got away too quickly. Someone else must have been driving.'

'Was it Newell?' she asked.

'It was hard to see who it was. I would have said he was too tall for Newell but I can't be sure. Someone's telling us they can get to us.'

'Are you going to tell the police?'

'Maybe. Maybe not.'

'Why not?'

'Because on that amount of information, my old work mates won't be able to find him any better than I can. I'll ask around. See if anyone's been talking about coming after me.'

'We don't need this,' she said.

'No one can get in here. And if they do, they'll be sorry they bothered.'

'At least Ellie didn't wake up. She doesn't have to know about this.'

They slept patchily until Ellie woke them in the morning and got them out of bed. While Grace bathed and dressed her, Harrigan checked the back garden. There had been some rain recently and the ground was softish. There were signs where the intruder had climbed over the wall into the garden, and partial footprints pressed into the ground. But the soles of nondescript mass market shoes were leads to nothing. Looking back up at the house, Harrigan saw the intruder had had a clear view of his study. It was possible he could have seen the darker outline of Harrigan's figure through the tall window when he had sat down at his desk. If so, then he'd been making certain Harrigan knew he was there.

He took photographs of the intruder's traces and went inside to make the morning coffee. It was just perking when Ellie ran into the kitchen and demanded to be picked up.

'Hello, princess,' he said, hoisting her up. 'How are you? You sleep well? Yeah.'

'You spoil her,' Grace said, following after and smiling. 'Calling her princess all the time.'

'It won't do her any harm. She'll grow out of it.'

'Breakfast. Come on, chicken. You're hungry, aren't you?'

Soon, his daughter was in her highchair with her mouth smeared with mashed banana. Harrigan had to laugh. If only his troops could see him now, not as the boss no one intelligent dared to put offside but as Harrigan the family man. Grace's work aside, life had never been so sweet. Now he could feel a poison eating away at that sweetness. Outside, it was still dangerous; survival could be balanced on the thinnest edge, the way it always had been. But whatever happened, no one was getting into his house to do any of them any harm. Today, he was going to take his gun out, check it, clean it and make sure it was in good working order. He had too much at stake to stay unarmed.

'I'll take Ellie up to Kidz Corner if you like,' Grace said. 'I can do it on my way to work. What are you going to do today?'

'Since I don't have to be in court, I'll make a few calls. I've got some digging to do. If I have time, I'll go and see Toby this afternoon. I'll take Ellie.'

When he had been with the police and saw sights like the one he'd seen yesterday, he had gone to see his son to recover. Being with Toby connected him to what mattered.

'She'll like that,' Grace said, and picked her daughter out of her highchair. 'Come on, sweetie. We'll clean you up and then we'll go, okay?'

Her phone rang. Harrigan picked it up for her. 'Clive,' he said.

She set Ellie on the floor and, taking the phone, walked out of the room. Not long afterwards, she was back.

'Something's happened,' she said. 'I've got to go now. Can you …?'

'Yeah, I'll look after things. When will you be back?'

'I don't know. I think I'm in for a long day.'

She was frowning. Probably she didn't know how disturbed she looked.

'Take care, babe,' he said.

'Always do. You too.'

Harrigan and Ellie waved her goodbye at the door.

'Gone,' his little daughter said.

'Don't worry, princess. She'll be back. Let's get ready. We have to go as well.'

Ellie's childcare centre was near Birchgrove Primary School, far enough from the house to be a useful walk. Harrigan carried her on his back in her harness. When they were almost there, she started to tug playfully at his hair. 'Take it easy, princess,' he said with a grin. 'That's me on the other end.' She giggled and he turned his head to look up at her. Then, with a feeling like a cold tap on the shoulder, he turned completely and saw a white Toyota Camry with tinted windows edging along the street not far past the corner behind them. It was the same car from last night; it hadn't been there just moments ago.

Harrigan was carrying his daughter but he also wanted the car's numberplate and began walking back quickly to get it. Immediately the Camry backed out the way it had come and drove at speed up the cross street. By the time he reached the corner, it was out of sight, vanished in the narrow tree-lined streets and laneways.

His next thought was to get Ellie where she would be safe. Kidz Corner was close, too close if they were being stalked. The converted duplex offered its clients security and privacy and had its own discreet security officer. Numbers of the children who went there were the sons and daughters of the very rich or the actors and writers who lived along the deepwater frontage of Louisa Road. Harrigan was none of these things but, like them, he wanted his child protected.

As soon as he'd set Ellie down to play, he went to see the owner, Kate, a big, capable woman, in her office. She knew his history and had still offered Ellie a place. It was another reason he was prepared to pay the hefty fees to make sure his daughter was safe.

'Have you noticed a white Toyota Camry hanging around here lately?' he asked. 'Not the most noticeable of cars, I know.'

'We always keep an eye out for that sort of thing. Yes, we have, several times now. We thought it might be paparazzi. Why?'

'I don't think it's paparazzi. It may have been stalking me and Ellie here. I scared it off. Can you get me the rego if it comes back?'

She grinned, opened her diary and handed him a piece of paper. 'We only offer the best service here. Mac got that the last time it turned up. He was watching it on the CCTV. If it turned up again, we were going to call the police. What do you want us to do?'

Harrigan had contacts among his former work colleagues who had offered him protection should he need it. He was careful about calling in the favour, not wanting to wear out his credit. This situation was different.

'I'll ring them myself when I get home. I'll get them to call you and work out a time to come over and talk to you and Mac.'

'Not a problem. I'll be waiting.'

Harrigan left, looking at the high brick walls at the front of the centre, the secure gate, the intercom watched by CCTV where you announced yourself when you collected your child. It was a long way from the freedoms of his own childhood when he had roamed the Balmain peninsula at will. All his mother had asked of him was that he be home in time for tea. But the world had changed; the tough, poor, working-class suburb he had been born into over forty years ago no longer existed. His life had no resemblance to the life his parents had lived. The area, on the harbour and close to the city, with its nineteenth-century terraced houses and mansions, was so completely gentrified they would not have felt at home here.

Someone was letting him know they were out there, they could get to him. They knew his home phone number, his daughter's childcare centre. They were prepared to get into his garden, to make him think his house might be insecure. And maybe, somehow, they might even have been the ones following Grace last night. Someone who liked to play mind games. Among his old inemies, that didn't narrow the field very much. He would make inquiries, contact old informants. See what they could tell him. He had always relied on himself. Too often, other people let you down when it mattered most.

Whatever you're trying to do to us, whoever you are, don't think it'll be easy. Don't think you'll get anywhere near us. With this promise to whoever was stalking him, he went home.

6

Grace thought it strange that the bright Sydney sunlight should seem so full of shadows. Clive's phone call had broken the pleasure of the morning, the respite with her family before she started work. 'There's a dead woman waiting for you. Jacqueline Ryan.' A sentence spoken as if it were a blunt instrument. He'd sent a team to the Royal Hotel to pick Ryan up but they'd arrived too late. She was already dead from a gunshot wound.

'Why do I need to go?' she'd asked him. 'Presumably the team can give you all the information you want. What can I add to it?'

'I want your judgement on the scene. Borghini's there. He's waiting for you. He wants to talk to you about your meeting with her. You'd better get going.'

You want me to see it. You want to shock me. Because you think I'm emotionally involved? Is that it? She crossed the white concrete arc of the Gladesville Bridge over the Parramatta River, the water glistening in the sun, going over the same ground as the night before. Boats in the nearby marina were moored in rows like white, lozenge-shaped seeds in a pod; the green of surrounding suburbs edged the water.

By now Paul would be walking their daughter to her childcare centre. There was no one she trusted more than him. They should be safe enough; just as all three of them were safe enough inside the

71

house. But when people threatened you from outside, sanctuaries became like prisons; places where you were locked inside your head. Her mind rejected the possibility that the man watching their house last night was Newell. It was too soon, if nothing else. Wouldn't the people who had sprung him see it as too dangerous for him to show himself? But fear ran in parallel with her reasoning. Newell was a ghost in her head. He was her own fear, never exorcised; a fear that was waiting its time, reasserting its control over its rightful territory, the way it was now.

There was no time for these kinds of thoughts. She was working. She couldn't guess Clive's motives but she could protect herself. When she drove into the hotel's car park, filled with police cars, she was in role. She was no longer the woman who'd wanted to cry for Jirawan. From here on in, she would be hard-faced. Lynette was going to be just a body. Not the edgy, tired, trapped woman from last night — a woman caught in something bigger than she was — but someone who'd ceased to be, who wasn't able to feel. *If I see it any other way, I won't be able to deal with it. I'll break down.* Maybe that was what Clive wanted: for her to break. She couldn't let it happen.

Dropping this shutter in her mind, detaching herself from the possibility of human emotion, she got out of her car and looked for Borghini. He was standing with a group of police, still dressed in the clothes he had worn the night before and drinking a cup of takeaway coffee. Seeing her, he walked over.

'Morning,' he said, blinking. 'Your boss told me you were on your way. Hope you got a good night's sleep.'

He was clearly angry with her. She ignored the bait. 'Good morning. Where is she?'

'In her room. The pathologist is with her. You went and questioned her last night without letting me know or even clearing it with me.'

'I don't have to clear anything with you. I've already asked my people to forward you the transcript. I'm not keeping you in the dark.'

'Do we have a team here? Or do you just go and do what you want, when you want?'

'There wasn't time for teamwork last night. If I hadn't spoken to her, she'd still be dead and we wouldn't have the information we have now.'

'Do you know who found her?' he asked. 'Your people. What were they doing here? Taking her into custody? Did they search the place? Take away something we don't know about? Is anyone going to tell me about that?'

'If anything like that happened, you'll be advised. Now I have to see the body. Let's get on with it.'

'What Orion wants, Orion gets. Come on. Scissorhands is waiting for you.'

Lynette's room was cordoned off behind the blue police ribbons. It was the last unit on the ground floor of a double-storeyed row of motel rooms. Numbers of the other residents were standing on the upstairs veranda watching. The door to Lynette's unit was open. McMichael and his technicians were at work inside but stopped when Grace appeared. The big man got to his feet, irritated at being interrupted.

'I hope you're going to make this quick,' he said. 'We've got work to do.'

'So do I,' she replied. 'Do we have a time of death?'

'Before midnight. I'm not prepared to be more precise at this stage. She wasn't carrying a stopwatch.'

'Did she die quickly?'

'Instantaneously. I doubt she knew what hit her.'

'Small mercies in that case,' Grace said, looking at him with an angry glint in her eye.

'If you want to put it that way.'

Lynette was slumped with her back against the wall near the door, shot in the head, the grubby white paint stained behind her. She was dressed exactly as she had been when Grace had seen her last night. The room had been perfunctorily searched. Lynette's bag was open, its contents scattered around her. A bottle of wine, still with its cork in place, lay smashed on the floor in the middle of the room. There was more broken glass on the table. On the bed was an open suitcase, a few clothes tossed into it.

'Did she take that bottle to her attacker?' Grace asked.

'We think so,' Borghini said. 'It looks like she was packing when someone walked in the door. She tried to whack him with a bottle of chardonnay. He managed to get out of the way and shoot her. Fun and games,' he added grimly.

'Didn't anyone hear anything?' she asked. 'What about her next-door neighbour? This room doesn't exactly look soundproof.'

'Apparently, it wasn't unusual for her to have company. He heard banging sometime around ten, thought it was business as usual, knocked on the wall and everything went quiet. He didn't notice anything else, he was watching TV. He said he might have heard a thud after he knocked on the wall. That could have been from a silencer.'

Lynette's eyes were open. On impact, the terror she had felt had been obliterated; death had been brutal and immediate. Whoever had done this, they'd seen her face looking at them immediately before they fired. It hadn't mattered to them. Killing was just another job. Grace was caught in the woman's vacant stare, and, despite her determination to stay detached, went cold with the unexpected horror that someone could do this so easily.

'Satisfied?' the pathologist asked.

Perhaps there was something in the way she looked at him that made even the feared McMichael step backward.

'I've seen what I need to see,' she replied, keeping a grip on herself, unexpectedly feeling the prick of tears at the back of her eyes. She walked out.

Outside, she spoke to Borghini. 'She was heading for the door. Running for her life, not getting there.'

'I don't think this was a planned killing,' he said. 'Or at best it wasn't supposed to happen here. Whoever shot her fired on the kneejerk. Let me tell you something. Lynette phoned Marie Li before she left the brothel and told her she had to close up, she was going home. After that Madam chucked a wobbly. Too much of a wobbly even for her. Did this Lynette have something important in her possession? It'd be one good reason why she's dead.'

'If she did, she didn't give it to me. Where was Kidd when all this was going on?'

'He was there to see Marie Li losing it. After that, he went to make some phone calls. Then he left. Why? Does this mean there's something else you haven't told me?'

'What you get told is in the hands of my boss.' Grace looked back at the unit. Nothing was more sordid than violent death. 'Did she die because I talked to her, because the brothel was raided or was she going to die anyway?'

'The way things are shaping up,' Borghini said, 'she was going to die anyway.'

'Then maybe Marie Li is in danger too.'

'The thought had crossed my mind. Do you know who she really is? Narelle Wong of Chipping Norton. Her brother came and bailed her in the small hours of this morning. Let's hope her family's not in danger as well.'

In the meeting room at Orion, Clive handed Grace a manila envelope.

'From the hotel's strongbox, put there by Jacqueline Ryan,' he said. 'Our people recovered it early this morning.'

Grace took out a Thai passport in the name of Jirawan Sanders. Jirawan's smiling photograph was on the details page. Stamped inside the passport was a permanent resident's visa for Australia.

'P&J. Peter and Jirawan forever,' she said. 'If her husband's dead, the Peter she wanted to contact could have been a son. Which means he might be okay one way or the other. Immigration didn't have the right to deport her. Did Kidd know that?'

'When it's the right time, we'll ask him. But that passport is a valuable item. And right now, someone's missing it.'

'Whoever really owns the brothel,' Grace replied. 'They didn't trust Marie, the same way they didn't trust her with the foreign workers. Her role is strictly limited by the look of it.'

'To what?'

'A convenient gaoler. A fantasy for someone to visit. One they've spent a lot of money on. They even changed her name.'

'Who are these exotic workers? Are they illegal?'

'Not necessarily. I think they'll be foreign women newly settled in Australia or possibly on bridging visas. But maybe getting a resident's visa depends on them working at Life's Pleasures. That's where Kidd comes in. He'd see a lot of applications. Maybe he's the talent spotter. He's senior enough to slow down or speed up the process or maybe just make it impossible to get other family members over here. Maybe all he has to do is make the threat.'

'The initial judgement of our finance people is that Life's Pleasures, while turning a very tidy profit of its own, is principally a money-laundering business,' Clive said. 'The sums involved are very substantial and it all gets moved offshore. That's curious psychology, wouldn't you agree?'

'What do you mean?'

'However much those women are making for that brothel by working for nothing, it's still small beer compared to the money it's really turning over. Why do it?'

'That probably means we're dealing with someone who likes to exercise control over other people for the sake of it,' Grace said. The same way you do, she added in the silence of her thoughts.

'Maybe that person can be goaded,' Clive replied. 'Lynette had the key to the strongbox in her jacket pocket. The search our killer carried out was pretty basic. Probably he just wanted to get out of there. But did she tell him she'd given this passport to the last person she spoke to, which is you?'

'We can't know what she said.'

'No, and no one can know the truth, including her killers. They only know they don't have this passport. It's feasible you've stolen it. You had the opportunity.' Clive was watching her closely. 'Exactly what are you prepared to do?'

'What does that mean?'

'A sting. What if you offer this passport for sale back to both Marie Li and Kidd and see who bites?'

'Are you telling me it's no longer necessary we keep Jirawan's name secret?' she asked. She felt an intense snap of anger. After all that fuss and with Jirawan dead.

'I'm saying we need a new strategy. What's your answer?'

'Why would I want to do a thing like that in the first place?'

He opened a manila folder and placed three slender identical documents on the table in front of her.

'You're badly paid. Or not enough for you anyway. You're bored.

Now your partner's not a top cop any more, he's just not interesting enough. You don't like motherhood, it bores you too. There's no excitement in your life and not enough money to make it happen. You're thinking about having an affair, if you can just find someone.'

'That's all in here, is it?' she asked.

'Yes. The written agreement and clear directions you wanted,' he said. 'Read it. Tell me what you think.'

'Before we go anywhere, I'm definitely not thinking of having an affair with anyone.'

'It's an option you don't have to follow if you don't want to. You've got the face to make that scenario work. But no organisation has the power to direct one of its operatives to act in that way. We all know that.'

'Good,' she said, and picked up the documents, looked through them. 'This is detailed. You didn't prepare this sting overnight.'

'I've been thinking about the possibilities ever since Jirawan Sanders was found dead. Her murder means our target is almost certainly in Australia.'

'You still haven't said who or what that is.'

'That document says I will brief you in full when the time comes. And there's something else. There's a wild card at work here.'

He had a nakedly manipulative look on his face.

'What?' she asked.

'These people following you, phoning you last night. Who might they be? Do you think it's Newell?'

'Newell couldn't have known where I was last night. Harrigan has a lot of enemies. It's more likely to be one of them.' She never referred to Harrigan by his first name in front of Clive.

'What about the people behind these two women's murders? As you've said, how could anyone know where you were last night unless they were following you from Parramatta? If they've identified you, then they're already interested in you. If you go seeking them, they may well want to deal.'

'We can't know that.'

'No. But it's a possibility.'

One that put her in even greater danger. She didn't say this; she didn't want him to think the possibilities frightened her.

Clive opened his folder and took out two photographs, placing them next to each other like playing cards. Jirawan lying in Ku-ring-gai Chase National Park; Lynette as she'd been found in her hotel room.

'Take these pictures with you,' he said. 'When you're reading that agreement, keep them on the desk in front of you.'

Rather than argue, Grace gathered them up.

'Who do I talk to first?'

'*When* you've read and signed the agreement, you talk to this Marie Li or Narelle Wong or whatever her name is. Then you call on Kidd.'

'Do I tell Harrigan?'

'That's all in there,' Clive said a little sharply. 'I told you to read it. If you sign the agreement, then I'll want to speak to your partner about the operation myself. Don't worry, you'll be there when I do. If you don't want me to do that, I'll take you off the job now.'

She pulled back a little from the abruptness with which he spoke.

'Are we sharing any of this with the police?' she asked.

'I've decided we are, at least with Borghini. He'll know about the role you're playing but no one else will. I'll brief his senior command myself on what they need to know. You were a sworn police officer once. You can appear to be seconded back while this operation is going on. But the proviso is this. Both you and Borghini take your directions from me and no one else.'

'Borghini probably won't like that.'

'He can take it or leave it,' Clive said. 'The question is, will you?'

'I'll let you know this afternoon,' she replied and walked out.

Give Clive his due, he had set it out in detail. There was nothing in these pieces of paper to trap her; it was the reverse, the details were comprehensive. Despite that, the job was both dangerous and secretive, even by Orion's standards. The worst aspect of her work had always been its loneliness. This agreement isolated her further.

On her desk, she had a photograph of Paul holding Ellie at her naming ceremony. She remembered thinking at the time, how had she got here? How had she managed to achieve so much just by blundering around the way she always did? The photograph held a world, one that mattered to her more than anything. Clive's agreement cut her off from that world and left her isolated in another one. The two photographs he had given her lay on the desk; they showed her exactly what she was walking into. They were openings into some other kind of darkness, a place that had nothing to do with the life she lived outside her work. Clive might say that he meant them to make her think twice about what she was taking on. But really he knew her well enough to realise they would have the opposite effect.

She looked at the picture of Paul and Ellie again and the anxiety came back. What happens to my daughter if something happens to me? But it was there on paper: backup, safety, an opt-out clause if she couldn't handle it. Orion was careful with its operatives' safety. Her own experience had demonstrated that to her. She would have to step away from both Paul and Ellie in her mind. If she didn't, the focus she needed, the cold-bloodedness, would not be there. If she once wavered in her intent, not only would she be in danger but she could put the operation at risk and other people who were involved as well.

Clive was asking a lot of her and it angered her to think he probably realised just how much this would cost her. And, regardless of the detail in this document, the real aim of the operation was being hidden from her. All she was being offered was a briefing sometime in the future. In other words, she was being asked to fly blind; she was being used. But she wanted this person, these people, whoever they were, as much as he did. This was her agenda and it was just as important as whatever Clive might have planned. No one was safe when people like this were out there, including the people who meant most to her. She picked up her pen and signed the documents.

7

Back home in Birchgrove, Harrigan rang his old mate and former 2IC, Trevor Gabriel. He and Trev had worked together for years.

'Got your info, boss. I've just emailed it to you,' Trevor said. 'That car is owned by a Craig Wells, forty-three, who lives in Lakemba. Unit by the looks of it. No criminal record. Not even a parking ticket.'

'Is there a picture?'

'Glasses, fair complexion, brown hair and beard, brown eyes. A short arse — 170 centimetres.'

'Why is that name familiar?'

'Yeah, it rings a bell with me as well. I'll look into it and get back to you. I'll send a body over to Kidz Corner for you today. Do you want me to send a couple of people around to watch your house as well? I can find them.'

'No, mate. I just want to make sure my daughter's safe. You need everyone for the Oxford Street shootings right now. How are the men who got shot?'

'One's still critical, the others are stable.'

'Any word?' Harrigan asked.

'Nothing. Everyone's singing the same tune — they had nothing to do with it.'

'Someone will crack.'

'We'll be ready when they do. See you, boss. Give us a call if you need any help, okay?'

'Will do.'

Harrigan hung up with a sense of betrayal of his former 2IC. But he knew that if he mentioned even the faintest possibility that Newell might have been last night's intruder, he would lose control of the situation. The police would crawl all over any lead that might help them solve the massacre on Oxford Street and his own investigations would be taken out of his hands. Harrigan wanted control. Keeping the details to himself was the best way to get it.

Before he left, he put on his shoulder holster and his gun. Then he was on his way across the packed suburbs of the Sydney basin, through a landscape of red-brick and fibro houses, concreted creeks, home units, scraps of bushland and parks, coming close to the geographical heart of the city in the southwest. Another world, just a drive away. A few more rocks to turn over and see what might be underneath. Something slimy probably. Just a normal day really.

The block of units looked ordinary: a white-rendered building with square, deep-set brown wooden balconies, all a little worse for wear. At the back of the building ran the suburban train line between Wiley Park and Lakemba stations. A row of big bins, various numbers painted on their sides, stood on the footpath. It was garbage collection day. There was no grass, just a cement forecourt. The main door opened to Harrigan's push. He stepped into a brick hallway with a cement floor. There was no name attached to the unit he was seeking. He walked upstairs and knocked on the door.

At first he heard nothing, then the sound of quiet movement inside. He waited. He was about to knock again when the door was opened by a tall African man, possibly in his sixties.

'Can I help you?' he asked in accented English.

'I was looking for a Craig Wells,' Harrigan said.

'Are you with the police?'

'No, I'm a consultant. This is my card.'

The man took it and studied it for a few moments.

'Why are you looking for this man here?' he asked.

'His car is registered to this address. I'm trying to get in touch with him.'

The man's expression was troubled, frowning. Another glance at Harrigan, a weighing up of actions.

'Will you come in?'

'Thanks.'

Harrigan stepped into a small, plainly furnished living room, where his host offered him a chair. No one else was present. Then the man opened the door to another room and went inside. Harrigan caught a glimpse of a kitchen where an older woman was seated at a table peeling vegetables while another woman, perhaps in her thirties, was standing by the bench. Both were wearing what seemed to be traditional dress. He heard soft voices from behind the door and then the man came out again, shutting the door behind him.

'Mr Paul Harrigan,' he said. 'May I keep this card?'

'Please do. And you are … ?'

'Mohammed Hasan Ibrahim. This person you're looking for, he's used this address to register his car?'

'Yes.'

'Why do you want to find him?'

'There's no reason for you to be concerned by this, Mr Ibrahim,' Harrigan said. 'If this man has used a false address, it's not going to affect you.'

'I would like to judge the consequences of the situation for myself,' Ibrahim replied. 'Can you tell me why you want to find this person?'

The voice was educated, the English meticulous. Mohammed Ibrahim's face was thinned out, the bones accentuated. His hair was whitening. His look was one of deeply felt caution, distrust just held at bay. Someone who had learned the hard way to be wary of whatever life was going to throw at you next because who knew what it would destroy or kill.

The kitchen door opened and the younger woman appeared carrying a tray with two cups of coffee and a plate of dates. She had covered her head. She served them both and then left the room, closing the door behind her.

'Please,' Ibrahim said, gesturing to the small plate of dates.

The dates were sweet; the coffee spiced with cinnamon and ginger.

'Thank you,' Harrigan said. 'To answer your question, I've had a car stalking me and my daughter. I was able to get the registration number. This was the address.'

'You didn't go to the police.'

'I'm an ex-policeman. I prefer to handle my own affairs.'

Ibrahim had placed Harrigan's card on the arm of the chair he sat in. He picked it up and looked at it. 'What kind of consultant are you?'

'I assist people in assessing their security needs and their legal affairs. I'm a qualified solicitor. I'm a guide, if you like. People who deal with the police and the courts often need one.'

Ibrahim looked at the card again, and this time put it in his pocket.

'I thought you might have come here to give me some information about my niece,' he said. 'She's been missing for a number of weeks now. I can't convince the police that we're very worried for her safety. They seem to think she must have gone off with someone but I'm very sure that's not the case.'

'I'm afraid that's not why I'm here. It was simply to see if this man had lived here.'

'I don't like this coincidence,' Ibrahim said. 'We are from Somalia. My niece has been trying to get her brother into Australia for several years now. He's in a refugee camp in Kenya. She contacts him there as often as she can. She is always ringing or writing to the Department of Immigration, trying to get some kind of visa for him. All of this has stopped. She would not have done that of her own free will. Getting him here is the object of her life. Now you're here asking after an unknown man. I have to ask myself what this means.'

'This man has never lived here?'

'Not while we have been here, which is over two years now.'

'I'm sorry I can't help you,' Harrigan said. 'What is your niece's name?'

'Nadifa Hasan Ibrahim. You haven't found this man here. Will you keep looking for him?'

'Yes,' Harrigan replied, knowing the request that was to come.

'If you should find out anything about my niece, I would like to know.'

'If I do find anything, I'll be in touch. I give you my word on that. Are you able to tell me something about her?'

Ibrahim got to his feet and went to a cabinet, where he took out a photograph. He passed it to Harrigan almost reluctantly.

'When I was growing up, women always covered their heads whenever they went out. She's a young woman, of course, and everything is done differently here. This is a photograph a friend took. She used to work at Westmead Hospital. Then one day we discovered she'd left her job. Her aunt asked her why and she told us that she'd changed her mind. She asked to be reinstated and they agreed. Then she disappeared. She was not at her work, she didn't come home. We're very concerned.'

The photograph showed a serious-looking young woman of about twenty-four, tall, slender and very beautiful.

'If you want me to keep an eye out for your niece, I may need this photograph,' Harrigan said.

Ibrahim nodded wordlessly.

'Would you be prepared to give me some information?' Harrigan asked. 'If I give you my word that I won't involve or mention you in any way, would you tell me who the managing agent for this block of units is?'

Ibrahim looked at him for a few moments.

'If you would wait,' he said, and went into the kitchen, returning with a fridge magnet in his hand. 'This is our agent. He leaves these magnets in our mailbox for us. It would be more useful if he fixed the plumbing when we asked him to. Please take it if you want.'

Four Square Real Estate, Haldon Street, Lakemba. A private agency, not a franchise. Harrigan finished his coffee.

'I can promise you won't be troubled by anyone, Mr Ibrahim, and if I find anything about your niece, I'll be in touch,' he said. 'Thank you for your time.'

Ibrahim rose to his feet. 'It was an honour to have you as our guest,' he said formally, and saw him to the door.

In most meetings like this, Harrigan had rarely been treated with the kind of courtesy he had received today. Despite this, the chances that he would find any information concerning Ibrahim's niece were slim to say the least. Grimly, the ex-policeman in him said she was probably already dead and most likely Ibrahim thought that too. He drove to Haldon Street to see where the next step might take him.

Four Square Real Estate was a single, narrow shopfront in the main commercial precinct of Lakemba, almost invisible with its dark window. Harrigan cruised past it, then parked off the street on the other side of the road. He was about to cross over when the door to the agency opened and an old foe stepped out: Tony Ponticelli junior, a middle-aged man in a sharp suit, slipping on a pair of sunglasses. Harrigan stopped where he was but Tony junior didn't seem to have seen him. He walked to a red Ferrari parked just up the street, and drove off.

To put it mildly, Four Square's presentation to the world was low-key. *Property Managers*, *Rental Properties*, said the sign on the brown-painted window. Even so, there was no display of properties for sale or rent. Harrigan went inside. A drab-looking woman sat at the desk. What are you doing in here? her eyes said.

'Is the manager in?' he asked.

'No. Why do you want to see him?'

Harrigan looked around. The reception area was a small space, cheaply furnished. Everything he saw suggested that anyone who walked in here on the off chance would be told to go away. To his right was a door which he guessed led to the manager's office.

'What's his name?' he asked.

'What's yours?' she replied as the door opened.

'Gail, get this info written up, would you — fuck!'

'Eddie Grippo,' Harrigan said. 'I heard you were out. This is where you've come to rest, is it?'

The short man in the doorway looked sick. The papers he was carrying dangled from his hand.

'Paul Harrigan. What the fuck are you doing here?'

'I think we should have a little chat, mate.'

Gail's hand was hovering over the phone.

'Leave it,' Eddie said, and when she hesitated, shouted, 'Leave it! For fuck's sake! *Don't*!'

'You want to do your job,' Harrigan said to her, 'keep your mouth shut. You didn't see me.'

Her face went blank and she went back to whatever she'd been doing.

Eddie's office was as run-down as the rest of the shop, with a dead pot plant in one corner. He had put on weight since Harrigan had last seen him, his girth nudging the desk. In gaol some prisoners made sure they stayed fit, they worked at it like men possessed. Eddie hadn't. All that muscle had gone to fat. Age was catching up with him the same way it was catching up with everyone, all the way to the hair on his head, which, unlike the rest of him, was thinner.

'What do you want, Harrigan? Why should I give you the time of day? You're nobody now.'

'Look at you,' Harrigan replied, unmoved. 'You're old. You couldn't take on anyone any more. You want people to forget you, don't you? So here you are in this shithole, keeping your head down. I can think of a lot of people who'd want to know where you are right now. In gaol you had people watching your arse. Out here you've got no one. You might open the door one day and find someone else besides me waiting for you. What was Tony Ponticelli junior doing here? I just saw him leave.'

'The whole fucking thing's legitimate, for fuck's sake.'

'Keep talking, mate. You make me laugh.'

'It's the property. All we do is manage the family property. That's it.'

'What was Tony junior doing here?'

'Don't you know? You don't, do you? You're out of the loop.' Eddie grinned. 'Tony senior's got fucking Alzheimer's. Word is he's getting loonier every day. Tony junior runs the business now.'

Harrigan knew the business all too well: extortion, enforcement, murder. The Ponticellis were the people to hire if you wanted anything like that done. They provided, with gusto. Once they'd been into anything — sex, drugs, any kind of contraband, corrupt property developments, shadier business deals, blackmail. Anything that could turn a dollar, which they had also done very successfully. Once, they'd probably had a higher turnover and owned more assets than some well-known companies. But the operations Harrigan had run had cut them down to size. He had gaoled their lieutenants, like Eddie, along with Tony senior's brother, and seen others get shot in gang wars. After that, they had never recovered their territory. There was no such thing as a vacuum in the crime world. Other gangs, other nationalities, newer to the scene, had moved in.

Harrigan's own involvement with the Ponticellis had teetered a little too close at times. There were one or two personal matters between him and Tony senior, which were another good reason for the old man to hate his guts, even more perhaps than for destroying his empire.

'Tony junior doesn't give a shit about you, mate,' Harrigan said. 'You're not his man. You're his dad's. He's doing you a favour, isn't he?'

'They need someone,' Eddie muttered.

'But it doesn't have to be you. You're a favour to his dad, aren't you? Cause Tony junior any trouble and you can sleep in the street. You can give me some information. Is Tony senior thinking he might settle a few scores with me before he carks it?'

'Why? Are you frightened?'

The old Eddie was coming out. Behind that soft expanse of stomach was the same hard man, the one who got a kick out of taking a knife to other people. He still had that look, the one that said he didn't care if you died in front of him just so long as he had the pleasure of doing it. All that poison was still in his head.

'If you think I'm frightened of you, mate, take me on and see who walks away at the end. It won't be you. You didn't answer my question.'

'If he is, he hasn't told me,' Eddie said. 'I haven't heard anything.'

'The white building near the railway line between Wiley Park and Lakemba. It's a block of units. Tell me about it.'

'Fairview Mansions,' Eddie said.

'I didn't see any sign.'

'It fell down. That's not family property. It belongs to someone else.'

'So what are you doing with it?'

'Fucked if I know. It's just on the books, isn't it?'

'Who owns it?' Harrigan asked.

'Fuck,' Eddie muttered and turned to an ancient-looking computer. 'Shillingworth Trust. I don't know who they are. According to this fucking thing, that's all we have of theirs.'

'Give me the contact details,' Harrigan said.

'I don't fucking have them. I was told: fucking rent it out, collect the rent, put it in a bank account. Any expenses I take them out of a float. I don't see anyone! I don't want to. Why should I?'

'Renting out a building like that isn't just fixing broken taps,' Harrigan said. 'Who do you contact when something happens the owners have to know about?'

'I fucking don't contact anyone. I've been told it goes back through the family.'

'Do you know the name Craig Wells?'

'No. Fucking never heard it before.'

'Don't cross me, mate,' Harrigan said. 'That would be a really stupid thing to do. Now, you and your woman friend out there, or whatever she is, didn't see me here today. And if I want information from you, you give it to me. You keep your ear to the ground, you pick up what's going on and you get back to me. Because I want to know if anyone's coming after me or my family. And if I don't hear, it won't just be me that comes knocking.'

'Jesus,' Eddie said. 'What the fuck do you want from me? You want me to end up dead? The family hates you. You know that. They just want to piss on your grave.'

'That pleasure's going to be mine, mate,' Harrigan replied.

He got to his feet and walked out. He glanced at Gail at the desk but she was doing what she'd been told and not seeing him. Then he was gone, glad to get out of there.

Knowing that Tony Ponticelli senior had Alzheimer's was a handy piece of information. It was hardly a surprise: Tony must have been in his late eighties. Harrigan wished he'd known before he'd talked to Eddie, but why should anyone have told him? He wasn't Commander Harrigan any more. He no longer had intelligence reports across his desk, nor could he put people on the street when it suited him. Not for the first time, he saw the paradox in his situation. He had left the police to make his life his own; but the past kept following him while he had the handicap of only his own resources to rely on. One day he wanted to see the end of it.

He was about to start his car when his phone rang.

'Boss,' Trevor said, 'some info for you. Craig Wells. Remember when the special homicide branch had a team dealing with the cold cases?'

'Wells was one of them,' Harrigan said. 'I remember. One of the detectives from the original investigation came to see the team.'

'That's right. The records are in the archives. I've given Naomi a bell. She's got a chair waiting for you whenever you want to go and have a look.'

'I'll do that now. Thanks.'

It was only a short drive to the police archives from where he was. Naomi, the archivist, was a substantially built middle-aged woman whom had he sweet-talked often enough when he'd been a serving police officer. She placed the square box of files in front of him with a disapproving look on her face.

'I hope I don't get into trouble doing this for you,' she grumbled. 'You're lucky it's still here. It's listed to go to the State Archives in the next transfer.'

'I'm grateful,' he replied with a smile.

She went back to her desk. Perhaps she was lonely here in this isolated, climate-controlled shed that wasn't much more than a staging post for records either doomed to the furnaces or awaiting perpetual incarceration in the Archives Office of New South Wales.

He opened the box and went through the records with the proficiency of a man who knows what he's looking for. Memory came back as he searched. It had been a murder from the early '80s, before the use of DNA testing. It had come to his cold-case team because one of the original detectives had been unable to shake off his doubts about it. On the face of it, it had been a straightforward murder–suicide. Craig Wells, then eighteen, had murdered his mother, Janice, in their rented Concord home and afterwards set fire to her car with the both of them in it, on the edge of the cliffs near Stanwell Park early one Sunday morning. The car had exploded and both bodies had been burnt past recognition. It seemed a hard way to commit suicide.

When, the next day, the police had gone to the Wellses' home in Concord, it was all too clearly the scene of a murder. The living room was drenched in blood and there were bone pieces on the carpet, later identified as parts of a skull. A sheet had been torn from Janice's unmade bed and presumably used to wrap and move her body to the car. The neighbours said they had seen Craig arriving home at about ten o'clock on the Saturday morning. He hadn't been home for some days and no one knew where he'd been. No one had seen or heard anything of either Janice or Craig after that. The closest neighbour, an elderly man, said he had heard a car — he assumed Janice's — leaving the house sometime between eight and nine that night.

Neighbours told the police that the Wellses had lived in the house for the last six years. It seemed it was just the next in a series of cheap houses they'd rented over the years. Relations between mother and son were known to be rocky. When they had first arrived, they were often heard shouting at each other. During all those years, no one had once seen Craig's father. Janice drank heavily and had a string of lovers, some of whom stayed for a while and some who didn't. Occasionally they were violent to her. Sometimes the police were called; at other times Janice was seen at the local shops with bruises on her face. She had worked as a receptionist at a local panel-beating business and had little money. When she died, she'd had no assets, her credit cards were in arrears and there was only a small amount of money in her bank account. Unkindly, her neighbours had called her a whinger: a woman who was always complaining how everyone had let her down. Craig never spoke to anyone.

Both victims were identified through their teeth and the pathologist was also able to establish that Janice had died as the result of a blow to the head. Mother and son had consulted a dentist only relatively recently. Craig's records dated from when he was fifteen, his mother's from only a few months ago. He'd gone to a busy city practice, while she'd gone to a much more up-market surgery in the northern suburbs, where they'd never seen her before or since. The treatment had been expensive and she'd paid cash. Where she'd got the money, no one knew.

Craig's dentist had seen him several times but it turned out there were no pictures of him to help in the identification. A search of the Concord house had found photographs of Janice but none of her son. The dentist was a busy woman. Her general description of her patient fitted with the one they got from the neighbours but it wasn't conclusive. In the house, there seemed to be very little that could have belonged to Craig and few signs he'd actually lived there. The forensic team hadn't checked the house for fingerprints because there was nothing to compare them with.

There had been an inquest where, on the basis of probabilities, the coroner had ruled that Craig Wells had murdered his mother and then committed suicide. The small remains of both mother and son had been further cremated and the ashes scattered. Once the inquest had been completed, the few personal possessions left were either thrown away or given to charity. Both Janice and Craig Wells might never have existed.

The detective who had brought his worries to Harrigan some nine years ago now had doubted this outcome from the start. It had started with a simple detail he'd heard when he'd first gone to the crime scene. A resident had seen the car burning on the cliff and called the police. On its way there, the patrol car had passed a bike rider with a pillion passenger coming towards them and heading north. It seemed to the detective they must have seen the fire. Why hadn't they stopped? He would have liked to ask them the question but there was no way to find them. And why choose this location to burn the car? To draw attention to it? Why not just drive it over the cliff? Another detail was that Craig had left the house in Concord between eight and nine in the evening but hadn't set fire to the car until one in the morning. What had he been doing in the meantime?

A plea through the media brought mixed results. The bike riders didn't come forward but a man called Andrew Spence did. A real estate agent, he had been Janice's latest lover. He had been in the kitchen, making himself a cup of coffee before leaving, when Craig had walked in that Saturday morning. He was adamant that Craig was empty-handed. Janice had still been in bed. Spence had heard about this eighteen-year-old boy but hadn't met him before. The way Craig had looked at him was so disturbing that Spence had left without drinking his coffee. He hadn't even said goodbye to Janice who he'd intended to see at least once or twice more. This led to another question. Where was the murder weapon? There'd been no sign of one in the house. If you were going to commit suicide, why bother to conceal it afterwards?

The detective checked with the local high school. Craig's record there was of a troubled, withdrawn boy who'd made no real friends and whose academic record was a list of failures. He'd left when he was fifteen. Again, there were no photographs. Craig hadn't liked having his picture taken and it was known he'd go out of his way to avoid it. The year he left school he'd gone to a holiday camp for underprivileged children called Camp Sunshine, run by a private charity. The detective checked with the charity but discovered it had been wound up just recently.

It turned out that Craig had attended only once. The charity forwarded the youth worker's case notes, which the detective had briefly summarised in his report. Craig was described as a disturbed and disturbing boy. In one serious incident, another boy had woken at night to find him standing over his bed menacing him with a hammer. When the lights had come on, Craig had been unable to stop laughing. The incident was all the more troubling because another of the boys in the dormitory had seen his mother attacked by his father with an iron bar, almost killing her. This boy had told Craig about the incident, which had apparently given him the idea for his joke (as he called it) in the first place. After this, Craig had been sent home. Again, there were no photographs.

According to the neighbours, once Craig had left school, he had spent very little time at home. When he had turned up, he was better dressed than they remembered him being in the past. No one had any idea what he'd been doing with himself. When asked, Janice had brushed off the question with a stock answer: he's keeping himself busy somehow.

The detective had tracked down Craig's father, Frank Wells, who lived in Sydney in Brighton-le-Sands. His marriage to Janice had ended ten years earlier. Despite its brutality, the story of the murder left him unmoved. His only comment was that his ex-wife had been a slut and he had no way of knowing whether Craig had been his son in the first place. Why should he care?

At a dead end and having no real evidence to present to the coroner, the detective was forced to let the case go. But it troubled him that there was seemingly nothing in existence that could have identified who Craig Wells had actually been and what he had done in the preceding three years. It seemed that somehow he must have made money. Had he been the source of the cash Janice had used for her dental treatment? If so, why kill her? Or had he been making sure that she would be identified? How to explain Craig's own teeth? If the body wasn't Craig's, how could such an identification be made, unless the substitution of Craig Wells's identity with somebody else's had started long before the murder?

The detective brought this puzzle to Harrigan, who had given him a sympathetic hearing. The cold-case team had examined the evidence but there had been nowhere to go with it. Harrigan had respected the detective's instinct but on the information available there was nothing they could do. The files had gone back to the archives.

Harrigan looked at the pictures of the murder scene: a shabby room in a rented house. Even without a body, the scene had a grimy quality, a sense of thoroughgoing despair. The amount of blood, the bone on the carpet, told a story of cruelty. In contrast to its physical savagery, the story on paper was too neat. He understood the doubts of the first investigating officer. For someone prepared to kill, it would have been possible back then to place a substitute in the front seat of the car and burn the body past recognition. After that, you could disappear and no one would come looking for you. Everything he had read indicated lengthy premeditation, careful planning.

Even if this scenario was accurate, the question still remained: what had made Craig Wells decide to kill in the first place? Other people had drunken, sluttish mothers but didn't choose to kill them. Harrigan thought, if only briefly, of how he'd not been able to fire a second bullet at his own father. Wouldn't it have been easier to walk out and never come back? And why should he think this was the same Craig Wells who had used the address of a refugee Somali family to register his car? It was too puzzling a coincidence, particularly with Eddie Grippo and his connections to the Ponticellis prowling in the background. Mohammed Ibrahim's story of his missing niece was another strange and troubling thread he could not ignore.

Harrigan put the documents back in the box and closed it. He wouldn't be able to see Toby today as he'd wanted to. It was already time to pick up Ellie.

He went home first and disarmed, locking his gun in its usual place in the safe.

When he got to Kidz Corner, he called on Kate. She met him with a smile.

'The police sent an officer around,' she said. 'A very smart young woman from the police station up at Balmain. She's my contact. If that car turns up again, I call her right away. She takes it from there. She says she'll have people down here very quickly.'

'All under control then,' he said, relieved. 'That car may not come back. We may have scared it off for good.'

'Hope so.'

He went to collect Ellie. She ran to him and he scooped her up. She laughed and put her arms around him.

'Hello, princess. Did you have a nice day? Of course you did. Come on. Daddy will take you home and Mummy will be there soon.'

After the events of the day, this was a cleaner place to be. He carried his daughter out to his car, relieved to be finished with it all.

8

Grace got home not long after they did. She walked in the door smiling, but her smile was strained and there were lines of tension around her eyes. She went and disarmed, then gave Ellie a hug.

'Hi, baby. Mummy's home early. We're going to have tea soon. How are you? Don't I love you.'

'How are you, babe?' he asked, when he kissed her.

'Oh, it's just work,' she said.

Just work. Given what she did every day, that could have covered just about anything. Something with a nasty kick had happened today, he could tell that, but it might be a long time before he found out what it was.

He kept his information to himself until after Grace had put Ellie to bed. He listened to her singing their daughter to sleep, thought how soft and almost sad her voice sounded at a distance. When she came back down, he had made coffee for her and poured whisky for himself. She smiled at him and sat down. He thought she probably wasn't aware of how quiet she'd been all night. In the last few hours she had hardly spoken two words to him. She liked to talk: about Ellie, small details of life, gossip about family or friends, particularly hers — the sorority as they called themselves, high-flying female lawyers who worked and partied hard. He had taken her away from that life. 'Are you bored?' he'd once asked her. 'Not 'yet,' she'd replied with that arch look she had. 'I'm happy,' she'd added. 'I never expected to be that.' Why did he always feel that doubt, that she might not be? All those years he'd spent on his own; the impress of that loneliness was still there and still strong.

'Is she asleep?' he asked.

'Snug as a bug,' she replied with a smile.

'I have some information for you.'

'I've some for you. Did you want to start?'

'The white Camry that was here last night. It followed me and Ellie to Kidz Corner this morning. Kate told me it'd been seen there a number of times before and she'd already got the rego. It was in the name of someone called Craig Wells. Does that name mean anything to you?'

'No, I've never heard it before. Do we need to move Ellie? She won't like it if we do.'

'Trev organised an officer to check it out today. She's on call if that car comes back. It's safe up there. I've looked it over. Don't forget Kidz Corner has its own security.'

She looked away, her face drawn with worry. 'I don't want Ellie to be bothered by this kind of thing. I just ran wild when I was young. I wish she could.'

'Me too,' he said. 'But the world's not the same. I traced the car but it took me to an address in Lakemba where they'd never heard of Craig Wells. The twist is that I once dealt with a cold case where the victim had that name, but whether there's a connection I don't know. But I did find one connection today we can't ignore. The real estate agent managing the unit is Eddie Grippo. He used to work for Tony Ponticelli senior and now he's managing their properties. We put him away for grievous bodily harm. He's just got out. It might be all these incidents have nothing to do with Newell; it's the Ponticellis looking to get their own back.'

'Why now? Wasn't your involvement with them years ago?'

'You'd have to look inside Tony Ponticelli's head to know what's really going on in there. He's got Alzheimer's; apparently he's losing it. It might be he wants to settle a few personal scores with me before he goes.'

'Like what?'

'Tony's first wife died when he was about fifty. She had cancer. He married again, this twenty-something. They had two children, a boy and a girl. She couldn't deal with the life. She left Tony and took the boy. Went into hiding to get away from him. He kept the girl, Bianca. It was before I met you and after we finished our operations against him. I don't know why but she came after me.'

'Are you saying you had an affair? Sleeping with the enemy? That's dangerous.' She smiled at him. 'Didn't it bother this woman that you were trying to put her father in gaol?'

'I think that's why she did it. She was getting at him. It was only a brief thing between us. Tony's a vain man. She was like him. She thought she was more important than she was.'

'To you?' Grace asked.

'To everything. Yeah, me as well. She was like a spoilt kid. She kept trying to attract attention to herself. The company she was keeping, she was way out of her depth. I told her that. She just laughed. No one was going to hurt her because she was Tony Ponticelli's daughter. She ended up raped and murdered. They dumped her by the Cooks River. We never found who did it. There was no information.'

'Bianca Ponticelli. I remember the case. It was when I was studying criminology, we talked about it. Does Tony Ponticelli blame you?'

'For a while he was going around saying I had a personal vendetta against him. I'd let whoever killed her get away and I was covering up for them. Then he backed off.'

'Why?'

'The tax office went after him for tax evasion. He didn't have time to think about me. It depends on what this has turned into in his head. He was always unpredictable and he's still dangerous. He can get things done if he wants to.'

'It's a potent mixture,' Grace said. 'His daughter and you undermining his business.'

It was on the tip of Harrigan's tongue to say there was one other thing as well, but he kept it to himself. He would have preferred to tell her but judged it better if he didn't. She had too much on her mind.

'Why did you do it?' she was asking him.

'She was there. She was making the offer. She was attractive. Sometimes you can spend too long alone.'

She looked at him with a half-smile. 'I've had affairs like that too.'

They were silent. Grace rubbed her forehead.

'Can we really leave Ellie at Kidz Corner? How do we know this car won't come back?'

'Where else is she going to go? If anything happens, the officer's on call and Trevor's people will be there like a shot. Kate's always got her eyes open. I'm finding out who's behind this. You can trust me. I'll protect us.'

'I do trust you. I always have.' She looked around. 'We could be happy. Why don't they just leave us alone?'

'People aren't like that.'

At that moment her face was almost disfigured with strain. 'I'm going to have to tell Orion that the Ponticellis may be behind whoever's stalking us.'

'That's okay, babe. You can do that. I don't mind.'

She was silent again. Then: 'Something's come up at work.'

'Like what?'

'I've been asked to do a covert operation. I've said I will.'

'You didn't talk to me first?'

'It's an important operation. I couldn't walk away. Clive wants to talk to you about it first thing tomorrow morning. With me there. I'm sorry about that. I hate having him involved in our lives like this but I have to.'

'What's the operation about?'

'That's what we have to talk about tomorrow.'

'How much danger is there?'

'I've been promised full backup and I have an opt-out clause if I decide I can't handle it.'

'What exactly do they want you to do?'

'Nothing I couldn't tell you about if it wasn't for the secrecy involved.'

'That's nice to know,' he said, beginning to feel angry. 'That's three questions I've asked you and not one straight answer.'

'I can't give you one, not until tomorrow's meeting. That's the condition Clive has laid down. If I break it, he'll take me off the job. You can trust me too, you know.'

'I do. But I don't trust Clive.'

'He's got his own agenda. But this is a job I want to do as well.'

'Don't forget us.'

'I never stop thinking about you or Ellie,' she said. 'You mean too much to me.'

That night, when he asked her if she wanted to make love, she said she was too tired, even though he judged she was less tired tonight than she had been last night. He felt her tense in his arms and let it go. In a matter of a few days the world had changed. They could be happy if people would leave them alone. That wasn't going to happen. But he was ready for anyone out there, and if they meant business, so did he. Tomorrow, after he'd spoken to Clive, he was going searching for a few answers. He went to sleep with some sense of security, if only because he knew his gun was in reach if he needed it.

The next day was a very early start for them both. It wasn't much after seven when Harrigan dropped Ellie off at the childcare centre. She was cranky and unhappy at having her routine upset.

'I'll come and get you this afternoon, princess. Don't you worry,' he said. 'If we can, we'll go and see your brother.'

Grace was ahead of him. She must have been at work for half an hour when he pulled up at Orion's entrance. The guard was expecting him and let him through. Harrigan had been here twice before: once for a security clearance when he and Grace had set up house together; and a second time when Clive, new to his job, had insisted on going through the process all over again. While Harrigan had dealt easily enough with the questions, he'd left wishing that Grace worked for someone else. The man was a cold-blooded manipulator, someone who played games for the kick he got out of it.

He was waiting for Harrigan in one of the rooms Orion used when they interviewed members of the public, all of which were on the perimeter of the building. Given what the meeting was about,

Harrigan wondered why Clive hadn't asked him into his office. He did have a top-secret security clearance, given to him by Clive himself.

'Where's Grace?' he asked, after he'd sat down.

'She'll be here,' Clive said. 'What has she told you about this?'

'She's been asked to undertake a covert operation. That's it.'

Clive was pleased with this. 'You're aware that this organisation can't give you any more information than that.'

'Is that what this meeting's about? For you to tell me I can't be told anything?'

'It's a dangerous operation and secrecy is paramount. I want your cooperation in every way.'

'First tell me what that actually means,' Harrigan said.

'Your partner has advised me you're being stalked. I had an email from her this morning saying the Ponticellis may be behind it.'

'I can't be absolutely certain of that but it's a possibility we shouldn't discount.'

'And you're investigating these incidents.'

'What are you getting at?'

'I want you to stop as of now. I understand you can call on the services of the New South Wales police to protect you and your daughter if you need to. I want you to do that. My people will handle the phone call and the other matters.'

Harrigan was silent for a few moments.

'What right have you got to tell me I can't protect my wife and daughter?' he asked in his neutral voice. It was the first time he'd ever called Grace his wife. He didn't know where the word had come from, but, sitting opposite Clive, he knew he meant it.

'Anything that affects your partner's identity as an operative could endanger the success of this operation and her physical safety.' Clive emphasised the word *partner*. 'Our legislation allows me to direct you not to interfere. There are penalties for ignoring that directive, up to a maximum of seven years' gaol. I've sent out a protocol to the New South Wales police. If you contact them as a result of any personal inquiries you may make, they have to notify me.'

Harrigan wanted to laugh when he heard this but suppressed it. Clive might react vengefully. He sat quietly, looking him in the eye. Eventually Clive could no longer meet his gaze and looked away.

'Why should my investigating these incidents interfere with your operation?' Harrigan asked. 'How can they possibly be connected?'

'Under the circumstances you qualify as a wild card. I'm not going to allow any possibility, however remote or unlikely, to disrupt this operation.'

'Grace still isn't here,' Harrigan said.

'She will be,' Clive replied.

'Why do you really not want me to track down whoever's stalking my wife and daughter?'

'I've told you,' Clive said.

'No, you haven't. What you've just given me is your justification, but it's not the reason. You said this mission is dangerous. Where does that leave Grace?'

'With every possible resource available to protect her. I'm also going to request that on no account are you to ask her any questions about this operation. I don't want any more pressure put on her.'

For an answer, Harrigan took out his mobile and rang her.

'Where are you?' she asked. 'I've been waiting for you.'

'I'm here in public meeting room two waiting for you, babe. Where are you?'

'What are you doing there? I thought this was going to be in Clive's office.'

Harrigan looked at Clive. 'No. Clive didn't want to see me in his office. We've been here for quite a while.'

'No one told me. Give me five, max.'

Harrigan put his mobile away, still watching Clive closely. The Orion man was angry.

'Don't take this out on Grace,' Harrigan said.

'I don't do that.'

Not much you don't.

'You don't intimidate me,' Harrigan said in a matter-of-fact voice.

Clive ignored this. 'You'd be very well advised not to discuss this meeting with your partner. If you do, she'll only worry. I've already told you. Don't put any more pressure on her.'

Harrigan's eyes said that if he could, he would have punched Clive out twice, for the two times he'd said this. The door opened and Grace walked in. Harrigan was already on his feet.

'I thought I was involved in this,' she said.

'We've already discussed everything I need to know,' Harrigan said.

'Where do I fit in?'

'We've gone over everything,' Clive said.

'See me out, babe. I'll say goodbye to you in the car park.' Harrigan turned to Clive. 'You don't mind, do you?'

'We don't have much time.'

Harrigan didn't trust himself to reply. With Grace still puzzled, and glancing behind her at Clive, they left the room together.

'What was that all about?' she asked.

'Can we go to your office?'

'Not if you haven't been given clearance to that part of the building. Why?'

'Then just listen while we walk.' He spoke softly. 'Babe, your boss told me your operation is secret and I have to accept that. It's already weighing on your mind, right? There's just one thing you have to know. You can rely on me. I'm not going to ask you any questions and we'll take it day by day. Okay?'

'Okay. But what did Clive say?'

'Nothing you probably haven't heard already.'

'I wanted to bring you into it a lot more than this.'

'He knew that,' Harrigan said 'That's why he organised the meeting the way he did. You've got to work today, right? And you want this operation to be a success.'

'Yes.'

They had reached the security perimeter. Now that they had stepped outside the building to the car park, he couldn't go back.

'Then you go and do it,' he said. 'You'll do it well, the way you always do. Don't take your boss on over this. Just concentrate on your work and come home safe and sound every day. There's only one important thing here. Nothing comes between us.'

'No,' she said. 'Nothing. We've both dealt with a lot tougher things than this.'

'Yeah, we have. I'll see you tonight.'

They kissed each other and then she was gone, stopping at the door to wave to him. He watched her slender figure slip out of sight to do whatever she had to do. It would take more than a jealous puppet master to drive a wedge into their relationship.

Harrigan drove away to his first appointment for the day, guessing that it had probably never occurred to Clive that anyone would simply ignore him. However defiant Harrigan might have appeared in the meeting, in the end Clive would still be expecting him to click his heels and salute. But he had no intention of stopping his inquiries. It just meant that, farcically, he and Grace were in the same boat: she couldn't tell him and he couldn't tell her what each of them was doing every day and what they might have found out.

In his judgement it was no way to manage someone under the kind of pressure Grace was about to feel. Whatever she was doing for Orion, he should know about it. Clive knew how much their lives were connected; yet right now he was cutting out both Harrigan and Ellie as if neither mattered to Grace. He wanted full ownership of his operatives. No divided loyalties; there could be nothing more important than the work Clive had decided they should do. No control other than his. Nothing at the centre of Grace's life other than her work and her boss.

You wait, Harrigan thought. I can play your game better than you can. You'll find that out. Meanwhile, he had things to do.

9

Frank Wells lived in a small, semi-detached brick house on Bay Street in Brighton-le-Sands. The bricks had a blue tinge to them; the atmosphere in the street, stretching from Rockdale station to the beach, was muggy in the hazy sea air. Sand from the soil had turned the footpaths gritty. The warm morning sun baked the footpath and its background of home units, parched gardens and occasional shopfronts.

The man who opened the door to Harrigan was tall, stoop-shouldered, with a heavy, fleshy face. His hair was white. He ushered Harrigan into a living room bereft of decoration; a small, dark space dominated by a flat-screen television. Beneath it was a shelf of unlabelled videos and DVDs. There were no other signs of entertainment in the room. The house had a stale odour, of old age and a place not often cleaned. Frank Wells motioned to Harrigan to sit down. He himself sat on a tiny two-seater lounge and put his hands on his knees.

'Did you bring the money?' he asked in his old man's voice, low and abrasive.

Harrigan had an account for incidentals like these. Usually his clients paid the costs but today he was working for himself. Frank Wells counted the notes slowly, then tucked them away in his wallet. It was too thick to fit back into his pocket and he put it within reach on the arm of the lounge.

'What did you want to know?' he asked.

'Anything you can tell me about your son and your wife.'

'They're both dead now, aren't they? I got this out for you.'

It came out of a cardboard box, an album housing a small, messy collection of photographs. Baby pictures of Craig were accompanied by a christening certificate with a lock of his dark hair sticky-taped next to it. There was one of him in his school uniform with a pencilled note saying it was his first day at school. He was an unsmiling, tense-looking child. There was a shot of a threesome — Janice, Frank and their son at a barbecue — and after this, occasional ones of Frank and Janice together. No one smiled much in any of these fuzzy pictures. They petered out when Craig would have been no more than seven. The last three-quarters of the album was empty.

Harrigan closed it with a slight thump. It left him with a sense of drabness, almost uselessness. The atmosphere in this room had the same negativity. In this place, you could wake up every day and wonder why you were bothering with life at all.

'How old was Craig when your wife left?' he asked.

Frank shrugged. 'I don't know if I remember. He'd been at school for a while. Eight?'

'Your wife left this album behind.'

'She didn't want it. No one wants it. You can have it if you want to pay for it.'

Harrigan had come prepared. Frank Wells forced the extra notes into his already bulging wallet like a man who is pleased to get his hands on every dollar that he can. Harrigan's gaze came back to the high-definition plasma television dominating the room. Everything else spoke of someone who probably scraped by on the old-age pension.

'Can I ask you something about yourself, Frank?'

'If you want.'

'How old are you?'

'Seventy-four.'

'You're in good shape for your age.' The old man smiled. 'When did you meet your wife?'

'It was when I came back from New Guinea. I went up there when I was younger. I was working with the police. It was good

105

money and something different to do. I was there for ten years, I suppose. I met my wife when I came back. She left her first husband for me. Then she left me and took up with someone else, then he left her. I think I was just the next one in line.'

Harrigan had the voice now. It wasn't only harshness and aggression, it was disappointment. Frank Wells was someone who had not taken much from life. There was no sign in this room that he'd spent ten years in another place so very different from this one. Harrigan thought of Grace's father, Kep Riordan. His house on the Central Coast was filled with artefacts, books and photographs from the time he and his family had spent in New Guinea. Grace herself had photographs, wall hangings and pieces of art which were now in the Birchgrove house. In this claustrophobic room, there was nothing.

'And before you went to New Guinea?' Harrigan asked.

'I worked at Gowings. Started there when I was fourteen. That's what I did when I came back too. I stayed there till I retired.'

'Did you and your ex-wife live here?'

'She kept nagging me about that. She wanted a larger house. It wasn't practical. I wasn't going to take out a mortgage.'

Whatever Janice Wells had been as a person, no one could blame her for leaving this place. Living here would have been like living in a coffin. Harrigan glanced again at the plasma television. Before he could ask another question, Frank interrupted him.

'Look, you're not from the solicitors, are you? Anything like that?'

'What solicitors?'

'My mother's maybe.'

'No, my interest in this is exactly what I've told you. Why did you think otherwise?'

'I thought when you said you were interested in my wife and Craig, it might be something else to do with my mother's will. Maybe there was some more money. You haven't really told me that much. Why are you asking about them?'

'I'm investigating the possibility that Craig may still be alive.'

At this, Frank's head drooped down. He seemed to be frowning. Then he looked up, his eyes hard and bright.

'None of this makes any sense to me,' he said, like someone feeling they're being pushed too far. 'Let me show you this.'

It came out of the same cardboard box that had held the photograph album: a letter. Dated four years back, it was written on what appeared to be a law firm's letterhead. Frank Wells was advised that according to her dying wishes, his birth mother, Dr Amelie Santos, wished to inform him of his parentage, proof of which was attached. She had died only recently and solicitors from the above-named firm were acting as executors to her will. She had left an estate valued in the millions and if he rang the above number, he would learn the exact amount of his inheritance. It was signed Ian Blackmore.

Attached to this correspondence was a photocopy of a letter from the Salvation Army to a sanatorium in the Southern Highlands of New South Wales, relating to the adoption of baby X, son of Amelie and Rafael, by a family with the surname of Wells. The letter was dated in the first half of the 1930s and gave the baby's age as two months old. The full names and addresses of the adoptive parents, in Annandale, were also recorded. It was noted that the family was now ready to receive the baby and also that he was being adopted out because the father had deserted his mother two months prior to the birth. It concluded by saying that the adoptive parents would arrange for his christening and had chosen the name Francis Martin. Also attached was an extract from a register of marriages recording the marriage of Amelie Warwick, eighteen, and Rafael Santos, thirty-five. There were eight months between the date of the wedding and the adoption of the child.

Harrigan made quick notes of these details in his notebook, including the address of the law firm. They were based in Katoomba in the Blue Mountains. He looked up. Frank was leaning forward, his eyes still sharp and bright. He was shaking, involuntarily Harrigan guessed.

'Were these your adoptive parents, Frank?' he asked. 'Is this their name and address?'

'That's them. That's where I grew up. I'd never heard of this Amelie Santos before. I rang that legal firm just like the letter said I should.' The bitterness in Frank's voice was almost too profound.

'They said they were the executors of my mother's will all right, but they'd never sent that letter and they'd never heard of the man who signed it. And they'd never heard of me. She hadn't left me a penny! When I heard that, it was a kick in the guts. That's when I went and got my own solicitor. I couldn't afford to but I was angry. I had to get something out of that woman. She wasn't going to do that to me. What she'd done already was bad enough.'

'Your adoption?'

'Throwing me away.' He sat like a rock, every bit of him radiating fury and hurt. 'I didn't care about any of this until I got that letter. But when I read that and I knew, I thought, you fucking bitch! She had fucking millions! She didn't leave me a cent.'

'Did she know who you were?'

'She could have found me. Someone did. Why not her?'

Again silence while Harrigan waited for Frank to grow calm.

'Who did she leave her estate to?' he asked.

'Some charity called Medicine International. My solicitor wrote to them and said I had a moral right to something. It took a while but she got it out of them. I've still got some money left.'

Out of an estate worth millions, perhaps not much.

'Did you know you were adopted?'

'Oh yeah, we knew. No one wanted us. That's what she used to tell us all the time.'

'Who's she?'

'My adoptive mother. When *he* was around she wasn't so bad, but when he was gone, she was nasty.'

'Your adoptive father?' Harrigan asked, avoiding an inquiry as to what the word *nasty* might cover. 'Is that who you mean by he?'

'Yeah. They were Salvos. He used to go away to meetings and things.'

'How many of you were there?'

'Five. There was even an Abo. We had to sleep with him. She had her own two kids as well. Not that it made any difference. She was just as bad to them as she was to us.'

'Do you ever see any of your adoptive family these days?'

'They're mostly dead now,' Frank said. 'Last time I saw most of them was when *she* died. That was 1970, I think. I wasn't going to go to the funeral but my wife said we should. I should have pissed on her grave. I think I just wanted to make sure she was put inside it.'

'Why have so many of you if she treated you so badly?'

'Because it was her Christian duty.' Frank mimicked what might have been the long-ago tones of his adoptive mother. 'That's what she used to tell us every bloody day anyway. There was one I got on with — Stan. He was my younger brother. Only friend I ever had.' He sounded almost wistful. He looked into the distance, shaking his head. 'She fucking broke his arm when he was twelve. Wouldn't take him to the doctor. Tried to fix it herself, bodged it up. She lied about it too. *He* came home and she said, Stan slipped and fell, he's such a clumsy boy. Fucking liar. His arm was never right after that. It fucking hurt him too.'

'Where is he now?'

'He used to be in the nursing home just down the road here. They said he had early onset dementia. I'd go and see him. Then one day he wandered off. They never found him. That was years ago, I guess he's dead by now.'

'Did your wife know you were adopted?' Harrigan asked.

'Oh yeah. She knew. And that's the thing about that fucking letter I showed you. Where this Blackmore got that information. You see, my wife kept on at me. I should find out who my real parents were. I fucking didn't want to know. I told her that. She didn't fucking listen. Then one day she says to me, I hear they're rich. Jennifer told me at the funeral. If you find them, we can get some money out of them. So what if they were rich? They didn't want me in the first place. Why would they fucking give me money? Couldn't get it into her head.'

'Jennifer?'

'My adoptive mother's niece. Nasty cow, like her aunt. She liked to big-note herself.'

'Could she have known who your real parents were?' Harrigan asked.

'Yeah. She worked in this place where the Salvos kept all their records. She told my wife. All the adoption records were there with everything else. She got to look at them.'

'You really didn't want to know who your parents were?'

109

Suddenly he looked tired almost to death. 'No, I didn't want to know. Why should I? They didn't want to know me. It just makes you feel bad inside. I couldn't get my wife to understand that. When I read that letter I showed you, I found out that my mother didn't even give me a name. I wish I'd never known that. Even with the fucking money I got now. But fucking Jennifer. She told my wife, you know, give me the money and I'll tell you, I'll give you the papers.' Frank leaned towards Harrigan, rubbing his thumb and forefinger together. 'Back then, you couldn't find out any other way. Fucking told my wife she'd already made the copies. We just had to hand over the money, she'd give them to us. I wasn't going to pay that fucking bitch for that. See her smile at me when she handed them over. My wife says, if you won't do it, I will. I'll pay her.' Suddenly he was shouting in a raw, violent voice, as if she were in the room. 'Fuck you, I said, no, you won't. I said, if you fucking do that, Jesus, there'll be hell to pay! She left after that. Took Craig with her. I didn't want him. I remember when we were having that argument, he was sitting there watching my wife shout at me. Gave me the creeps. I just wanted him to get out of there. He was always fucking staring at me.'

'Did you hit him?'

'*No!*'

You did, Harrigan thought. You hit him and you beat her up. Maybe she even thought you were going to kill her. And she left, taking him with her. Left as quickly as she could. Frank was breathing hard. Harrigan gave him time to calm down.

'What was this Jennifer's last name?' he asked.

'Shillingworth,' Frank said. 'Bitch.'

'Are you sure about that?'

'I don't know too many people with that name.'

'Do you ever see her these days?'

'Not since my wife left. Didn't want to. But that's what I don't understand. What I just showed you, that must be what she wanted to sell me all that time ago. Who the fuck is this Ian Blackmore? Why would he have it?'

He was staring at Harrigan, his look almost a plea. All Harrigan could do was shake his head.

'How did you get along with Craig when he was living here?'

Frank seemed to withdraw; his look was made up of suspicion and fear.

'Why?' he asked sharply.

'Just background information, Frank,' Harrigan said. 'I don't have any other reason for asking that question.'

'He used to tell lies about me.'

'What did he say?'

'Just lies. All the fucking time. I tried to frighten him. I hit him. Things like that. Never fucking touched him. Even my wife didn't believe him.'

'When did you last see him?'

'The day they left. I gave him my hand to shake. He twisted my finger as hard as he could.'

'And you never saw either of them again?'

'No.'

Silence.

'You said he might still be alive?' Frank asked.

'I don't know that,' Harrigan replied. 'I'm just investigating the possibility.'

Frank stared at him with an expression that spoke of strange knowledge.

'Is there something else you want to tell me?' Harrigan asked.

'No. You can go now. I thought you were going to help me more than you did. I haven't got anything else I want to tell you.'

'Okay. Thanks for your time, Frank. Are you prepared to see me if I need to talk to you again?'

'If you bring your wallet. You can see yourself out.'

Harrigan walked out of the silent, stale house and closed the door behind him.

He drove down to the beachfront and bought lunch in the local mall, then sat in the beachside park to eat it. The water was calm across Botany Bay. Planes taxied along the airport runway jutting out into the bay before powerfully skimming their massive weight upwards through the hazy air. Harrigan let the sun clear the shadows of Frank Wells's house out of his head, then checked his watch. It was early afternoon. He would give Ellie an early mark from Kidz Corner and they would both go and see Toby. His son was confined to a wheelchair but Frank Wells was locked inside his own head more inescapably than Toby's disabilities could ever have imprisoned him. Toby's mind was free; given the confines of his body, it was the best gift he could have, the one Harrigan hoped he'd given him. He tossed the remains of his lunch to the waiting seagulls and went to his car.

10

The Wongs' home at Chipping Norton was a large double-storeyed yellow-brick house in a row of similar dwellings. Camellia bushes grew in a tidy pattern in the small front garden. There were entrances for a three-car garage while a flight of steps led up to the residential storey of the house. Grace parked on the street. Several cars were parked nearby, including a van with tinted windows. Somewhere within range was a vehicle where every word spoken within her vicinity this morning would be recorded by Clive's technicians. He and Borghini were listening to it elsewhere. She got out of the car; she was in role.

The doorbell was answered by a slender man of about thirty who wasn't much taller than Grace.

'Duncan Wong? I'm Grace Riordan. I called you earlier.'

He wasn't happy to see her. He nodded without speaking and gestured for her to come inside. The house had a feel of comfort; the contoured carpets were soft underfoot, the hallway walls decorated with wallpaper showing a softly glittering pattern of graceful cranes and flowers against a silver background, probably a Florence Broadhurst print. Grace saw a god in an alcove together with a vase of gladioli and incense sticks. The living areas were spacious. In one room, two women, one middle-aged, the other elderly, sat together on the lounge watching television.

'Mum,' Duncan said from the doorway, 'the woman from the police task force is here. Do you want to talk to her?'

The middle-aged woman replied in Chinese without looking around and with a backward wave of her hand.

'Do you want to come into the kitchen?' Duncan said to Grace. 'Mum's really upset about this. She doesn't want to talk about it. Dad's not here, he's in Hong Kong, so she's got to deal with it by herself.'

'What do you do, Duncan?' she asked.

'I'm an optometrist. I've got a business in Liverpool.'

'Are you closed for the day?'

'No, my wife's there. She's an optometrist as well.'

The kitchen was large with a view out to the back garden where there was a swimming pool. Above the garden fence, Grace saw a range of red-tiled suburban roofs against a cloudless sky.

'Would you like some tea?' Duncan asked.

'No, I'm fine, thanks. How's Narelle?'

'She's okay, I guess. She wasn't working in that place, was she? I mean, she wasn't one of the girls?'

'No, she was the manager. She didn't take clients. That wasn't her role.'

He was too relieved to hide his feelings.

'I've got to tell Mum that. She's been too freaked to think about it.'

'Hasn't Narelle talked to you?'

'She won't. She's locked herself in her room and won't talk to anyone. She's been in there ever since she came home. All she does is come out for food. I hear her crying sometimes. I don't know what's going on.'

'What do your parents do, Duncan?'

'They own the Four Seas Restaurant in Liverpool. It's not just some takeaway. It's got a hat, and we got seventeen out of twenty in the *SMH Good Food Guide*.'

'What did Narelle do before she worked at Life's Pleasures?'

'She's been trying to be an actress ever since she was about fifteen. People told her that with her face, it should be a snack for her. She wanted to go to NIDA but she didn't get in. She's had bit parts now and then and she's been in commercials. Dad's spent a fortune on her. He's paid for all these lessons she said she had to have, for publicity photographs, everything. It still hasn't made anything happen. Why do you want to know?'

Maybe this was the attraction for whoever her lover was — Narelle's capacity to play a fantasy love goddess role and enjoy it. She would only have an audience of one. It might as well be virtual reality.

'I'm just trying to find out a little about her before I talk to her,' Grace replied. 'Has she had an actual job?'

Duncan smiled, bitterly. 'Not really. Nothing that's lasted. She's always been more interested in partying than anything else.'

'Where does she party?'

'She used to go to this place up at Palm Beach a lot. Sometimes she wouldn't come home for days. When she did, she was usually drunk or high on something.'

'Do you have an address for this place? Do you know who owned it?'

'No. She wouldn't tell us.'

'Did you ever visit her at Parramatta or meet anyone she worked with?'

'She didn't want us to. Mum would ring to say she was going to come over and Narelle would say that if she did, she wouldn't let her in.'

'What did you think she was doing?' Grace asked.

'She said she had a job managing a hospitality business.' He laughed enough to show how much this all hurt. 'I feel like an idiot. We never thought she'd be doing anything like this. We thought she was organising functions or something.'

'How long had she been doing this work?'

'Since February. She told us about it at Dad's birthday party. We were so relieved because she hadn't had any kind of job for almost a year. We believed everything she told us. But it was all lies. Everything she told us was a lie. And that's the point.' His face contorted with grief. 'There's nothing more important than family. Mum and Dad built everything we have up from nothing. They've worked really hard. She's treating it as if it doesn't mean a thing. It means everything.'

Grace waited a few moments.

'I need to talk to her. Can you show me her room?'

'She won't let you in,' Duncan said.

'Just let me talk to her through the door.'

As Duncan had predicted, Narelle's first response through the door was to say no.

'Go away,' came the muffled reply. 'I'm not talking to anyone. I don't care who you are.'

'Narelle,' Grace said, 'you need to talk to me. If you care about your family, that is.'

'Why?'

'You should know why. Why don't you think about it for a few moments? You should be able to put it together.'

'I don't know what you're talking about.'

'Okay. A question for you in that case. Has *he* called you? Because if he hasn't, maybe I can help you get in touch with him.'

There was silence. Narelle's mother had appeared in the hallway and had heard what was being said. She held a handkerchief crushed in her hand and her face was covered with tears. She spoke softly to her son in Chinese. He replied to her, shaking his head.

'What did you mean by that?' he asked Grace. 'Why would we be threatened?'

'If I can talk to you after I've spoken to Narelle, I'll be able to explain.'

The door was opened. Narelle stood there, her face stripped bare of make-up, her hair pulled back off her face. The exotic clothes from the brothel had been replaced by jeans and a T-shirt.

'Let's talk privately,' Grace said, and stepped inside, shutting the door behind her.

Narelle sat down on the bed and lay back on the pillows. She gestured for Grace to sit wherever she wanted to. It was a large room with an en suite, a computer, and its own flat-screen TV and sound system. A walk-in wardrobe was stuffed with clothes. The décor was fussy and girlish. Pink and blue soft toys were piled on any surface, along with Barbie dolls. One wall was covered with studio and publicity shots of Narelle in various poses. Some thousands of dollars worth, paid for by her father. Cosmetics, also expensive, littered the dressing table. There was a powerful smell of cigarette smoke in the air. Grace looked at a full ashtray and an empty packet on the bedside table. There were no books but DVDs abounded. Sentimental romances, teen flicks, and a set of *Buffy, the Vampire Slayer*. No sophisticated Art Deco fantasies here.

'Don't you have some ID?' Narelle asked, an angry, suspicious look on her face.

'I don't think you need to be interested in seeing my ID, Narelle. Not if you want me to help you.'

'Why do I need your help?'

'Don't you want to see your boyfriend again? He won't just have forgotten about you, will he?'

This hurt. Narelle's mouth opened a little. She looked like a child, angry and spoilt; wanting to answer back but unable to.

'Have you got any cigarettes? I wanted Duncan to get me some but he won't do it. Why don't you get some? Then maybe we can talk.'

She was no longer forcing her voice into its late-night up-market gloss; it had become ordinary, almost squeaky. Maybe this was why she'd never made it as an actor; she had the face but not the voice or the presence.

'He doesn't like you to smoke,' Grace said.

'What do you mean?'

'Your boyfriend. He didn't let you smoke in your own flat.'

'I don't need to when he's around. Are you going to get me some?'

'No, Narelle, you can wait for your cigarettes. Let's talk about Coco.'

'She never worked there. I don't know who she was!'

'Don't talk rubbish. Look at this. I bet you've seen this before.'

Grace handed over a photocopy of the photograph page of Jirawan's passport. Narelle looked at it once, then screwed it up and threw it on the floor.

'I don't know anything about that!'

For an answer, Grace took a miniature recording device out of her bag and pressed the start button.

'*Marie would leave the clients there, and often enough they'd come back to me and say they didn't want that. It wasn't what* they'd paid for. Then Marie started getting angry with Coco because she wouldn't cooperate. One day, madam dragged me down there and told me to sort her out. What was I supposed to do? Coco was wrapped up like this tight little ball. You could see her shaking. I lost it. I shouted at that little bitch for once. I said, you can't fucking do this! It's creating too many bad vibes. That shut her up. Anyway, after that Coco disappeared.'

'Lynette didn't like you, Narelle. She called you a nasty little cow.'

'She was just a fat, ugly, old woman. I don't know why they didn't get someone better than that.'

'She's dead now. Does that worry you?'

'Why should it?'

'Want me to play you some more of that tape? There's enough on it for me to put you in gaol. If I do, do you think your boyfriend's going to come and visit you? He wasn't there the other night. He left you to deal with the police all on your own. Sink or swim. Your problem.'

Instantly there were tears in Narelle's eyes. She bit her lip and stared at Grace with a strange, bunched expression on her face.

'Why would you want to put me in gaol?'

'You locked Coco away without thinking about it. Why shouldn't I lock you away?'

Narelle's eyes were still filled with tears. 'She didn't care. I don't think she felt it. I don't even know why the men paid. She was just this plain little thing.'

For a second, Grace wanted to take Jirawan's photograph, the one taken in Ku-ring-gai Chase National Park, out of her bag and slide it under Narelle's nose. But they had agreed she wouldn't do this. It was easy now to speak sharply.

'Narelle, there are things you don't understand. You're the fall guy in all this. That's what you were doing there, being set up to fall. Everyone else can run for cover but you can't. I can get an arrest warrant for you like that.' Grace snapped her fingers. 'Do you want me to do that? Or do you want to talk business?'

'What do you mean?'

'How much is that passport worth to you? Because I've got it in a very safe place. And if you want it back, it's going to cost you. That passport and this tape together. Just exactly how much are they worth to you?'

Narelle made a face of exaggerated rejection and shrugged her shoulders. The tears were flowing down her cheeks.

'You want to go to gaol,' Grace said in the silence, 'fine by me.'

There was a knock on the door. Narelle hadn't locked it after she had let Grace inside. It was opened and Duncan stood there. He was about to speak when Narelle sat upright and shouted at him in Chinese. He looked away but not before Grace had seen a look of deep humiliation on his face. The door was shut abruptly. Narelle nodded her head in satisfaction. She turned back to Grace.

'Where'd you get that passport?'

'Where do you think? Lynette gave it to me.'

'Aren't you with the police? What are you doing this for? It's some kind of trick, isn't it?'

'You can think what you want. You'll have plenty of time in gaol. Let's just say I'd like a bit of extra money. It would give me some excitement in my life. It gets a bit dull sometimes. Do we have a deal? That's what I want to know.'

There were more tears. Grace watched her without a shred of sympathy.

'I'd have to ask my boyfriend what he wants to do,' Narelle managed at last.

'What's he got to do with this?'

Narelle gave her a single dark look of pure suspicion. 'Why do you want to know? Don't you want to get paid?'

'Be careful, Narelle. If you want me to be nice to you, then you'd better behave yourself. You go ahead and talk to whoever you want to, but you've only got forty-eight hours to do it. Take this.' Grace handed her a card.

'What's that?'

'My private number. You can call me whenever you want. But if you don't — too bad.'

'What if I tell people you came here and said all these things?'

'Go right ahead,' Grace replied. 'Do you think anyone's going to believe you? You're still going to gaol.'

She got up to go. Narelle sat up again.

'Aren't you going to get me some cigarettes? You said you would.'

'Why don't you ask your brother again the next time he comes to see you?' Grace said with a sweet smile and let herself out.

Duncan was in the kitchen with his mother. When Grace appeared, he gestured for her to sit down. He seemed unable to speak.

'Why did you say we could be in danger?' Mrs Wong asked.

'You may not be aware of this but the young woman who was found murdered in Ku-ring-gai Chase National Park some days ago worked at the parlour where Narelle was the manager.'

'Did Narelle know that?' Duncan asked. Almost he got to his feet, his face gripped with anger. Quickly, his mother put out a hand to stop him.

'She was told the night Life's Pleasures was raided,' Grace said. 'We have reason to believe that this young woman, who went by the name of Coco, was trafficked here. Given her fate, it's very advisable for anyone who knew her to cooperate with the authorities.'

'Is my daughter in danger?'

'Not if she cooperates with the police. If you do feel worried in any way, this is a number you can ring. They will know Narelle's name and they will be able to help you.'

Mrs Wong looked at the card and began to cry.

'Was she involved in this trafficking?' she asked.

'No, we have no evidence of that. But her parlour was the last place where this young woman worked.'

'She didn't tell us any of this. I can't talk about it.'

Mrs Wong got up and walked out of the room, tears running down her face.

'Did Narelle know?' Duncan asked.

'She says she didn't.'

'Is there anything else she hasn't told us?'

'At this stage, I don't know,' Grace said. 'I do have some questions for you if you can answer them. You went and picked her up at Parramatta Police Station. Didn't she want to go back to her flat?'

'She said she wasn't working at that place any more and she wanted to come home. That was it. I could mind my own business after that. You should have seen her at the police station. She was standing there in these clothes. She looked like a — It's a part to her, you know? Nothing else.'

'Do you and your wife live here, Duncan?'

'No, we've got a house at Campbelltown.'

'One last question. Are any members of your family dual citizens?'

'All of us, my wife included and she's Australian. Mum and Dad are from Hong Kong. He goes back there on business a couple of times a year.'

'When's he coming back?'

'Tomorrow. He's probably the best person to talk to Narelle.'

'The number I gave you,' Grace said. 'If you think of anything, if you're worried about anything, it doesn't matter how trivial, ring it and ask for me by my first name.'

'There's something going on here. Narelle's putting us all in danger, isn't she?'

'No, this is just a precaution. It's also imperative that you keep this information within this house. This is an ongoing inquiry and confidentiality is very important.'

'More important than we are? Yeah, I bet it is. I'll see you out.'

Grace's next port of call was a service station on the Hume Highway. In southwest Sydney, ever since the opening of the M5 motorway had diverted the traffic, certain parts of the highway's surrounds had taken on a run-down look. Worn buildings and struggling businesses lined the road that had once been the main corridor for southern-bound traffic out of the city. Now the traffic had a local feel: intermittent cars and aging trucks farting black smoke. The grass on the nature strips was worn thin with occasional trees struggling through the drought. At least it was quieter.

Next to the service station was a motel offering cut-price accommodation. Grace parked her car out of the way and went into the motel. The receptionist directed her to a room just down the hallway. Borghini and Clive were waiting for her inside. When she walked in, Borghini got to his feet and held out his hand to shake.

'Well done,' he said. 'You were impressive.'

'Thank you,' she replied.

Clive remained seated; he was staring at her with a distant, almost absent-minded look.

'Why did you tell that girl's family they might be in danger?'

'Because they may well be and they have a right to know. They're not stupid. They could put it together themselves.'

'You were in role. You're a blackmailer who doesn't care who lives or dies so long as you get what you want. You're not supposed to be concerned for anyone's welfare.'

'In that case,' Grace replied, 'that's how I'm covering my tracks. I'm making myself appear to be something I'm not.'

'You may see it that way. Our targets may not. It's not just their safety. It's yours.'

Out of the corner of her eye, she saw Borghini watching them intently.

'Since this is your operation,' he asked, 'are these people under guard?'

'Twenty-four-seven,' Clive replied. 'As Grace is well aware.'

'Then they're not mushrooms any more, are they?' Borghini came back.

Clive gave Borghini a needle-like glance. Probably that comment would go in his notes.

'Apart from that,' he said to Grace, 'you did it well. There was some valuable information there, we have a hook to the boyfriend. There's a long afternoon ahead. Better eat something.'

There was food waiting on the table. She sat down, suddenly ravenously hungry and needing to shake her character out of her head. Clive sat down as well but didn't eat. It was unusual for him to praise anyone; the effect was almost as disturbing as his needling.

'Here's some information for you to read over before we go visiting,' Borghini said.

He handed her a brief report on the guard and the driver who had been rostered on when Jirawan had supposedly escaped.

Both had police records. The guard, Sophie Jovanov, and her husband had been involved in an insurance scam six years ago, resulting in him serving an eighteen-month gaol term while she had received a good behaviour bond. The driver, Arleen McKenzie, was a former ice addict with a record for theft and possession and who had once been convicted of malicious bodily harm.

'Who hired them to work at Villawood?' Grace asked.

'We're checking. Everything there is outsourced, including the transport. Their employer was a firm called Australian Secure Transport,' Borghini said. 'They signed their statements and got their marching orders at the same time.'

'We've asked for their financial records but it's hard to believe whoever is behind this would leave any obvious footprint,' Clive said. 'Their backgrounds mean they'll have limited credibility regardless of what they say.'

'Are you sure you're ready for another interview this afternoon?' Borghini asked Grace. 'Is your head in the right place?'

'Yeah, I can deal with it.'

She had been rolling her shoulders to relax some tension. There was too little time between these interviews. But the timeline Clive had put in place, the forty-eight hours she had given Narelle, left them with no choice. She glanced at him; he was staring at her, that same distant look on his face. It was disturbing enough for her to look away.

'Now you've both finished eating, here's something else for you to look at,' Clive said. 'Our IT people broke into Kidd's computer. He liked to take pictures of himself with the children from the orphanage. Not a smart thing to do for a man with his sexual tastes.'

Grace looked through the photographs quickly and handed them to Borghini. Once she would have been able to deal with this, her mind would have been focused on tracking down the people responsible. Now she could barely look at these pictures. The thought of the children brought her too close to her daughter. There were things she couldn't bear to have in her mind.

'Can't you cope with this?' Clive asked. He was still watching her.

'I've seen as much of them as I need to.'

He was about to say something else then stopped.

'He's a piece of shit, isn't he?' Borghini said evenly, handing them back.

'He's useful to us.' Clive's reply was matter-of-fact. 'When you talk to him, Grace, you don't want money. You want in on his scam. See if you can find out who's bleeding him.'

'How did I get hold of that information in the first place?' she asked. 'Could I have got it from the people who are blackmailing him?'

'That's a dangerous approach. We don't know who these people are or how likely that is. I think you'll have to keep him guessing. If you have to, you got these through your work, but again you're sitting on them for your own personal gain. Tell Kidd it's your decision how these pictures get used. If you choose to, you can turn him into an informant and protect him that way. That should be enough of a hook to get him onside. Right now, you'd both better get to your afternoon appointment.'

'Will it be on these women's minds that they sent a young woman to her death?' Grace asked, almost to herself.

Borghini was getting to his feet. 'I'm feeling privileged, mate,' he said sarcastically to Clive. 'You're letting me do something.'

Clive seemed to start a little. He said nothing, but in Grace's experience he wouldn't forget the comment. She and Borghini left, each taking their own car. The next act was about to begin.

11

When Grace arrived at the Jovanovs' house in Canley Heights, she saw a dark blue Audi, luxurious and expensive, parked outside. Pulling up behind Borghini, she saw him get out of his car talking on his phone.

'Registered to a Joel Griffin at Bondi Junction,' he said to Grace when she came up. 'We both know that name. He was representing Chris Newell when he got snatched.'

Grace heard the name Newell without so much as a blink. 'Looks like now he's representing the Jovanovs. He picks his cases.'

'Is he any good?'

'My information is he's very good. But if he is, why is he here? There's not much money in it by the look of things.'

'Newell wouldn't have had any money either,' Borghini said. 'Let's go find out what the deal is.'

The Jovanovs' home was a double-storeyed brick house with an untidy hedge out the front. An old Ford Falcon was parked in the driveway. Oil splatters on the pale cement suggested it leaked, badly. Like the car, the house was run-down. The lawn was unmowed and the big bins filled to overflowing. Two damaged children's bikes lay tossed on their sides near the front door. Grace knocked. The door was opened by a dark-haired man of about forty who barely spoke before ushering them inside. They followed him through to the lounge, a room with fake wood-panelled walls, grey-blue carpet and furnished with a brown velveteen lounge suite. A tall, well-dressed man got to his feet and smiled at them.

'Joel Griffin,' he said. 'My card. I'm here representing my client.'

His client had to be the woman sitting on the lounge with her hands clasped in front of her. The man who had shown them in sat down next to her. There was a large coffee table in front of them, positioned like a protective barrier.

'Your client's expecting us. We're just here to ask a few questions.' Borghini was returning Griffin's favour with his own card. 'That shouldn't cause a problem.'

'I'll be answering any questions you have on my client's behalf.'

'I'm sure Mrs Jovanov can speak for herself,' Grace said.

'Not if she doesn't want to.'

Griffin accepted her card, one that said she was with the New South Wales police, with a quick glance from the card to her. She saw him take in the scar on her neck and just prevented herself from covering it with her hand. Alone, she did sometimes touch the scar, almost against her own will. It was a reflex reaction, a private soothing of the cut she could still feel.

'If you'd like to get started with your questions. Sophie has her life to get on with as well,' Griffin said.

Even during the introductions, Sophie kept staring down at the carpet, only glancing up and nodding briefly when her name was spoken. Neither she nor her husband seemed prepared to open their mouths.

'Mrs Jovanov, Sophie,' Grace said. 'How long have you been a guard with Australian Secure Transport?'

Sophie refused to meet her eye. She was a strongly built woman with thick curly black hair. Her bulk seemed to be muscle, not fat. In uniform she would have looked intimidating. As he'd promised, Griffin spoke for her.

'Sophie was with them for nine months. If you check her record, you'll see she's had a career as a prison guard and in security generally.'

'Then you're experienced,' Grace said.

'Sophie is a very dedicated officer. My belief is that she's been treated unfairly by her former employer.'

'Are you going to undertake legal action on her behalf in that case?'

'If I receive instruction to do so, yes.'

'And what would be your advice to her?' Grace asked.

'That has nothing to do with this interview,' Griffin replied.

'You must have been very shocked, Mrs Jovanov, when you heard what had happened to your charge.' Borghini spoke in a sympathetic voice.

'Sophie was deeply shocked, going so far as to blame herself. I told her she could not be held responsible for the criminal actions of others, including those of the young woman who unlawfully escaped from her custody.'

'Why was this young woman so lightly guarded?' Borghini asked.

'The information Sophie's employer received was that the young woman was going to be moved into alternative accommodation. Neither Sophie nor the driver were expecting her to attempt an escape.'

'Sophie,' Grace said, 'I want to make it clear to you that we need to know whatever you may have to tell us. Any detail at all, however small. Because this is what we're trying track down. The person who did this. No one is blaming you for this because you couldn't know it was going to happen. But I want to find the person who did this. If you can help us, we can help you and your family, and I promise you we will.'

Grace slid the photograph of Jirawan's battered body across the coffee table. Sophie looked at it and covered her face.

'That's harassment,' Griffin said quickly.

'I don't want to be a part of this any more,' Sophie said. She had tears in her eyes. She stood up and ran out of the room.

Before anyone could speak, her husband was on his feet. He picked up the photograph and pushed it at Grace. 'You can take that back. My wife has nothing to do with any of these things. You can all get out. We don't want anything to do with any of you, including you.' He was speaking to Griffin.

'If you want me to go, I'm happy to leave,' Griffin said. 'We have each other's contact details. If I need to, I can be here at your house very quickly. One thing I'm not doing is leaving until the police go. I still have to protect your wife.'

'I'll protect her,' Jovanov said.

'You may need to,' Griffin replied.

'We're on our way,' Borghini said. 'But we may have to ask your wife to come in for questioning at some stage.'

'She's already given a written statement so she's not obliged to. And she certainly won't be there without me being present,' Griffin said, with a sharp glance at Jovanov. 'Now I think we should all leave.'

They walked out, all three, hearing the door shut hard behind them. Grace was surprised to find Griffin in step with her in the driveway. Borghini, who was ahead and already almost at his car, turned to watch the exchange.

'I met your partner the other day outside the law courts,' Griffin said.

'He told me.'

'Nice to put a real face to the name.'

'Is it?' Grace said.

'It's always interesting to see who people really are.' He seemed to be looking closely into her face. 'Your photographs don't do you justice. I hope we meet again.'

Grace stopped where she was. Close by, Borghini was listening intently.

'You were very protective of your client in there,' she said. 'Is Arleen McKenzie your client as well?'

'No, Arleen didn't want my services. If that's where you're going now, you won't be seeing me. You seemed genuinely concerned for my client's welfare in there. Are you always like that?'

'I just do my job. I guess it's goodbye now. You must have places to go and I don't think we'll be seeing each other again.'

'You just do your job,' he repeated. 'I don't know if that's true. Maybe you actually care about things. My bet is we will meet again. I'll be looking forward to it.'

And he was gone, into his car and away down the street.

Borghini came to speak to her. 'What was all that about?'

'I'm not sure,' she said. 'He seemed to want to make sure I knew who he was.'

'Are you sure you've never met him before? He was looking at you in there like he knew you.'

'This is the first time I've laid eyes on him. He doesn't know who I am.' Whatever Newell might have told him. 'I guess he's made his point, whatever it was. Time we went and saw Arleen.'

'I'll meet you there.'

Arleen McKenzie lived in Fairfield, in one side of a rented white fibro house that had been split into two self-contained halves. The house seemed a small island amongst the large blocks of units that lined the streets roundabout. Arleen's patch of ground looked half cared for. Junk mail littered the grass around the base of the mailbox while flowering red geraniums in weeded garden beds grew in a line under one of the windows. The front door was off to the side and reached through a small partially enclosed porch. Borghini knocked and then knocked again. There was no answer.

'She was expecting us,' Grace said.

He tried the door. It opened for him.

'Shit,' he said. 'I don't like this.'

He pushed the door open slowly. Grace followed him inside. They walked into a cheaply furnished lounge. There was a smell of old food and the house looked dirty.

'Anyone here?' Borghini called.

'In the kitchen,' Grace said.

Arleen was staring at them from a chair, her hands resting on the table. In front of her was a quantity of white crystals in a plastic packet and a pipe. It looked as if Arleen McKenzie had been about to smoke crystal methamphetamine when she died. There was blood on her shoulders, her clothes, the floor and the table. The back door, although closed, was directly behind her.

'Shot in the back of the head,' Grace said. 'It would have taken a half-second. In through the back door and gone again.'

'I rang her before we left the motel to confirm our appointment. Would she be smoking ice when she knew we were coming calling?'

'As soon as we were gone, maybe. But I thought she was supposed to be clean. It's more likely this is a setup.'

'Whoever it was, they're gone now,' he said. 'I'll call the troops in.'

He took out his phone and began to call the people he needed to. Grace walked out of the kitchen through the living room to the front door. A concrete path continued past the door to the back of the house. There was no way to see this path from the kitchen; the laundry blocked the view. She walked around to the back of the house, a small concreted area enclosed by a high wooden fence, and saw the back door. From where she stood, the road was thirty seconds' walk away.

She came back inside and looked around the living room. The woman's dead wide-eyed gaze seemed to follow her while Borghini talked on his phone. Whoever, whatever, she had been as a person, Arleen hadn't had much interest in house cleaning. It was fair to say the surroundings were filthy with ingrained dirt. Amongst the other odours was the smell of a dirty toilet.

Borghini had finished talking on his phone. 'Rung your boss?' he asked.

She shook her head, too filled with anger and disgust to speak.

'My guess is you'd better,' he said to her silence. 'If you don't, one of my superiors might ring him first. They don't mind a bit of one-upmanship where Orion's concerned.'

She looked at him with a half-smile and made the call. Clive's first response was silence.

'That makes your appointment with Kidd even more important,' he said. 'You'll have to come down hard on him.'

'Who's going to run with Arleen McKenzie's murder investigation?' she asked.

'The police can do the legwork. They can keep us informed. Come in when you've finished there.'

Grace turned and looked back into the kitchen. She could smell the blood now, above the other smells in the house. The pathologist, McMichael, came into her mind. Bizarrely, both for her work and the situation in which she now found herself, she was trying to get her mind around the idea of death, of not being. Death was cold, it was decay. And the dead were sticky; they held on to you, left a mark where their hands had touched you, a smell that said they'd been there. How could anyone spend their life dissecting them? What could you find amongst their remains except nothingness?

Grace couldn't mourn for a woman she had never met but she could feel that same deep burn of anger for the fact of her death that she had felt for Jirawan. She took a breath. The dirt of the house and of the dead seemed to have contaminated her clothes and her skin.

'The place hasn't been searched. They weren't looking for anything. They just wanted to shut her up,' she said.

'That's the way it looks. Maybe you'd like to come clean with me,' Borghini said. 'What's at stake here that's worth all this? I know that passport's valuable. But why go this far for it? That's two deaths, not including the one we started with. And you've brought in a lot of firepower. Would you really do that if you didn't think there was something a lot bigger in the offing? What aren't you telling me?'

Nothing, she could reply, if only because this time she didn't know herself. She was the bait but no one had told her what the prize was. She had walked open-eyed into this investigation knowing that to be the case, but she had never expected it to be this bloody.

'This is a different MO,' she said. 'This is a contract killing. It's cleaning up made to look like a drug-related murder. Lynette's death was similar. Jirawan's killing was something else.'

'Maybe this killing was already organised. Maybe Arleen was too unreliable. With Sophie, you can say keep your mouth shut or your kids get hurt. Arleen was just an ex-junkie with no connections by the look of it,' Borghini said. 'With Lynette, we turn up at Life's Pleasures and she panics. It creates a situation someone has to deal with quickly. Apart from that, you didn't answer my question.'

'You know just as much as we do. Everyone's making sure we don't get a chance to find out anything more.'

'You mean what *you* know is limited,' he said. 'But maybe your boss knows a hell of a lot more. Hope he tells us both one day.'

The sound of sirens was growing louder. Soon the house would be overrun with other police, the crime scene people and whoever else was involved. Were there any relatives to notify, any friends? Arleen McKenzie was almost as anonymous to Grace as if she'd found her lying dead on the street.

'Whatever's going on, it's vicious,' she said to Borghini.

'Hope your guard on Miss Narelle Wong and family is up to it,' he replied.

'So do I.' And to herself: hope my backup's working too.

Clive's description for what was happening was desperation. Grace was beginning to see it as ruthless efficiency. There was a limit to how long she was going to keep walking into the dark like this. A limit to what she wanted to deal with without knowing more. If she talked to Clive, he'd draw her deeper into this strange dance where he was setting the pace, deciding the music, directing her movements. Cut her off even more. For her, the only possible next step was to see out the following few hours. She followed Borghini outside to meet the police.

12

Harrigan arrived with Ellie at Cotswold House, the facility on the water's edge at Drummoyne where his son lived, mid-afternoon. Toby had no lectures that day and was in his room. Sitting in his wheelchair in front of his computer, he was using the mouse with his good hand. If Toby had been able to stand, his height might have matched Harrigan's. In his face, his father could see a reflection of his own features. But his body was twisted; sometimes he drooled because he couldn't help it. Often enough on meeting him people looked away repulsed.

Nothing about his physicality affected Ellie. Harrigan and Grace had taken her to visit Toby since she'd been born. She clambered up onto his lap where she could see the computer screen.

Hi Dad. Hi Ellie.

Toby couldn't speak easily. He was a master of one-sided conversations typed out on monitors of all descriptions. An outsider listening to them would only have heard Harrigan speaking into silence. An outsider reading Toby's written replies would have had only the detached half of what had been communicated between them.

'I don't think she can read that yet, mate,' Harrigan said.

She will. Where's Grace?

'She's fine. At work. How are you?'

I'm good. What about you?

'I've got something I want to talk to you about but it's a tough subject.'

Shoot. I can deal with it.

'It's your mother. Before you ask, she hasn't been in contact. If you don't want to talk about it, it's fine by me.'

She never will. Or when she's so old, it won't matter. I can talk about it. Why?

'It's to do with a job I'm working on. Two cases. In one, a son killed his mother. The second concerns a man who was adopted out pretty much as soon as he was born. He had a hard upbringing — his adoptive parents abused him, particularly the mother. My judgement is he turned into an abuser himself. When he found out about his real mother, it hurt him like hell. She was a rich woman who'd left him nothing.'

Did she know where he lived? If he was adopted out immediately, she might not even have known what his name was or where she could find him.

'That's true. But that hasn't made any difference to how he feels.'

Why did this other guy kill his mother?

'She was an alcoholic, she seems to have had one casual affair after the other. As far as I can tell she didn't seem to care much about her son's welfare. I think his father abused him as well. She either didn't believe her son when he told her or she didn't care.'

Is the guy who killed his mother the son of the man who was adopted out?

'Yes.'

Why do you want to talk about it?

'I'm trying to get into these people's heads. What are the drivers that would make someone do that?'

Hatred. You'd have to feel that.

'You don't.'

No. I don't hate my mother. I don't want to hurt her. I guess if I met her I'd be angry. Sometimes I am angry with her but there's too much in my life for me to think about that all the time. Do you think she thinks about me?

'I think she has to. She knows I stayed with you. And she knows you've got a good mind. She made enough enquiries to find that out. Maybe that's what she relies on to forgive herself. Whatever it is she feels.'

I don't think about her too much if that's what you're asking me. You've always been there. But there's a gap. Disappointment. That's what I feel. I wish it had been different because what my mother did, I think that was just a waste. I wish she had been here but she wasn't and there's nothing I can do about it.

It was a long way from disappointment to enough loathing to carry out a murder. Toby had always had the rest of the extended Harrigan clan to rely on as well: Harrigan's two formidable older sisters and their families, all of whom had accepted Toby as one of their own. Ellie, bored, climbed down from Toby's lap and began to explore the room. Harrigan gave her toys to play with where he could keep an eye on her.

You shouldn't worry about me, Dad. When you're like me, you've got to be practical. I know what I can do. That's what I concentrate on. My mother's like anybody else who can't handle me. They don't come near me. Why should I care? It's my body. I deal with it. With help.

It was afternoon tea time. Harrigan helped both his older and his younger child eat. Ellie would grow up to feed herself and to walk and talk easily. Unless some miracle cure was discovered, some unique stem cell therapy that could transform him, Toby would never be able to do any of these things. The coloured, flashing, electric shadows of the computer monitor were his lifeline; his good hand connected his mind to the screen and gave him a voice and the tools to be part of the world. To help him physically he had his therapist, the exercise programs that prevented muscle wastage, and the regime that washed, fed and medicated him, saw him into his wheelchair and got him to his university classes, where again he was treated as one of their own. There were worse lives; Frank Wells's for one.

Harrigan was on his way home with Ellie, tired and a little grumpy in her safety seat in the back of the car, when Grace rang.

'Hi,' she said. 'I'm going to be late. There's been a development in our operation. I probably won't be there before Ellie goes to bed.'

'That's okay, babe. I'll look after her. I guess you can't tell me what this is about.'

'No, I can't. Maybe you'd better eat without me.'

'All right. I'll see you when you get here. Are you okay?'

'Yeah, I'm fine. I'm not in any danger.'

'I hope not. Take care, okay?'

'I will. You too. See you.'

Not in any danger. He remembered what he'd said to her: We'll take it day by day, I won't ask questions. He was doing this for Grace, for the two of them, not for Clive or even Orion. He just had to keep that in mind.

Later, when Ellie was asleep, Harrigan went into his study and turned on his computer. Working in this room quietened his thoughts. He looked at the bookshelves lining one wall and saw the old pair of boxing gloves he kept on one of the shelves. Once, when he was about twenty, he'd tried to make a career as a boxer but hadn't been light enough on his feet to be successful. Then, not much more than two years later, he'd become a father, pretty much by accident. When Toby was born, his world had changed and he'd had to find regular work to support his son. He still loved boxing, still went to the fights and still worked out. These days he had more time to do it and was fitter than he used to be.

On another wall, prints of works by the Spanish artist Goya were on display. Harrigan had discovered Goya's work when he was overseas on secondment to the Australian Federal Police. He had a vivid memory of walking into the Prado in Madrid and seeing Goya's Black Paintings. Their savage and bizarre satire spoke strongly to his experiences of dealing with the lunacy people inflicted daily on themselves and each other. If asked, Harrigan would have said these surreal representations of humanity were all too exact. This was what people were like: they were as mad as this, as plagued by delusions and demons; their actions as futile, as ugly and as murderous as Goya had painted them to be. After this he had begun to collect books and reproductions of the artist's work. The paintings eased Harrigan's mind; it was a relief that someone knew as much as he did, not just about human evil, but how it actually looked when you met with it. This was its real face and it was nightmarish.

Reaching up to the shelf nearest his desk, Harrigan took down a facsimile of Goya's series of etchings *Los Caprichos*, a catalogue of human folly and vice, venality and deceit. He opened the book to the sixth print. It had the caption: *Nobody knows himself.* In the foreground, a masked man seemed to bow to a masked woman, both dressed as if they were at a masquerade ball. He seemed to want something from her, to search her face for some response; but her thoughts were unreadable. Perhaps she smiled but who knew what her smile might mean. Other shadowy figures, both grotesque and menacing, watched from the soft, dark wash of the background. *All deceive,* the text continued, *and do not know themselves.* Harrigan wondered if the print portrayed where he and Grace were themselves right now.

He left these shadows and began to search through those on the net. He sent an email to a retainer of his, a university student who found carrying out research for Harrigan a more rewarding job than waiting on tables. He had several subjects for her tonight: Amelie Santos, Ian Blackmore, Jennifer Shillingworth, Camp Sunshine charity. As an afterthought he added the name of the sanatorium in Frank Wells's letter. If the baby had been sent from there to his adoptive parents, then that must have been where the birth had taken place. Anything she could find out about any of them. Normally he would also have asked her to check out the Shillingworth Trust, but if the Ponticellis were involved, he didn't want her anywhere near them. He would do that himself.

He had just pressed 'send' when his phone announced an SMS message. When he opened it, he saw a photograph of Grace at their front gate, holding Ellie by the hand, apparently just leaving the house to go down to the park. He spent some moments looking at it. It was a recent photograph, probably taken sometime in the last fortnight. He put the phone down and got to his feet.

He glanced at the safe but decided against taking out his gun. He didn't want to be pushed into always doing that. Instead he walked through to the front of the house, stopping to listen at Ellie's door. There was only the sound of her quiet breathing. In the spare front room, he didn't turn on the light but went and stood at the dark window. Grace had put new curtains in here which were only partially closed. He stood next to the drapes and looked out. Was there anyone out there? If so, could they see him?

They could only reach into his mind if he let them. No point in physically locking them out and then letting them in by proxy. In his mind, he drew a line, pushing his stalkers to the outer edge. Then he went back to his study where he forwarded the SMS message on to Orion. The organisation had supplied a phone number for this purpose. He could only hope they would deal with it effectively.

He heard Grace arrive and went down to meet her. In the kitchen, she was standing with both hands holding the back of a chair, as if too tired to move. The sight of her face when she looked up shocked him. She was exhausted; she didn't smile and her make-up had the pallor of a death mask. He put his arms around her without speaking. She leaned against him; she was almost rigid with tension.

'Bad day,' she said. 'I have to go and shower. I feel dirty.'

'What happened?'

'I'm not supposed to tell you.'

'Just tell me. Where do you think it's going to go?'

'We found a dead woman today. Shot in the back of the head. The second woman we've found like that in a few days. I didn't tell you any of that.'

'Come on, babe. Just relax. Sit down and get it out of your head. I'll make you some coffee.'

'I'm still armed.'

'Just sit down. Ellie's asleep,' he said.

'Did she miss me?'

'Yeah, but we sorted that out.'

If she drank alcohol, he'd have got her a whisky. Instead he made coffee, strong the way she liked it. She drank it and some life seemed to come into her face. He decided he wouldn't tell her about the SMS message, or not just yet. It was the last thing she needed now.

'It's so sordid, you know,' she said. 'This woman's life looked like shit. I thought, why would you want to live like this? I know

138

people don't always get a choice but it felt like the end of the world.'

'It's her life, not yours. You can't forget that in this business. She made her own decisions, right? That's why you were there. It must have been.'

'She almost certainly took a bribe. And because she did, someone died. From the looks of how she lived, she needed the money. Then they killed her when they thought she might be a weak link.'

'Find the person who killed her and take him off the streets. That's the best you can do.'

'I'm going to put my gun away,' she said. 'I'll be back.'

When she came downstairs again, she had showered and changed, even going so far as to wash her hair. He had heated the food and set it on the table.

'I said not to wait for me.'

'I know you did. Don't worry about it.'

They sat down to eat. She took a mouthful and stopped.

'I didn't want to cut you out like that,' she said. 'Clive ambushed me.'

'Yeah, he's a bastard,' Harrigan said. 'I've worked with people like him in the past. He probably doesn't have anything else in his life.'

'I just have to stay on this tightrope,' she went on. 'If I don't separate life and work like this, I won't be able to handle it. It's my way of protecting what we have from what's out there.'

'It's a hard ask from your boss. He's asking you to treat me and Ellie like we don't matter. He should be thinking about what that's doing to you.'

'When this operation's finished, we'll still be here,' she said. 'It doesn't matter what Clive does. Nothing's going to change that.'

When they went to bed that night, Grace fell asleep almost immediately. Slept until Ellie woke her in the morning, crying. Heavy-eyed, in her nightdress, Grace hurried to her room. Ellie was lying soaked in her nappy.

'Look at you, sweetie. We'll get you dry, okay?'

How small she was. How perfect. How new and unmarked the skin. With her daughter changed, she picked her up. Ellie touched her face and Grace kissed her. How clean she smelled, after what Grace had seen yesterday. How clean and new. Her daughter had no scars. She wanted it to stay that way; for Ellie to grow with no scars on her body or her mind, whatever it cost.

13

By ten in the morning, Grace was walking in Parramatta Park near the pavilion, not far from the Macquarie Street gatehouse. It was a clear, sunny day and the light gave a yellow wash to the grass and the trees beyond. She had left her car in the parking area and seen a sleek, grey Mercedes already parked there. She knew this was Kidd's car; or more accurately these days, the finance company's. While she walked, a cyclist cruised slowly along the path in front of her. Nearby, a couple were strolling casually across the grass. They spread out a blanket and sat down, seemingly for morning tea. Her backup was in position. Then she saw Kidd, sitting on a bench waiting for her. She stopped for a few moments. *I am not myself. I want everything this man has to give because in my own head I have nothing. Whatever he says, it doesn't matter to me. Remember that.*

She went to meet him. When she sat down beside him, he didn't speak. He had his hands folded in his lap. It was an odd look.

'How are you, Jon?' she said sweetly. 'Nice of you to take some time off work to see me.'

He spoke without looking at her. 'I don't want to spend any more time than I have to talking to you. Would you get to the point?'

'What sort of person are you?'

'What sort of person am I? What sort of person are you?'

'Someone who doesn't go around organising for young women to be sent to their deaths. Particularly one as nasty as Jirawan had.'

'I don't know that name.'

'Yes, you do. This is for you. Have a good look at it.'

She handed him the same photocopy of Jirawan's passport that she had shown Narelle Wong. He looked at it for some minutes, then folded it up and very calmly gave it back to her.

'I've never seen it before and I've never heard of Jirawan Sanders.'

'You must recognise that woman.'

'Yes, of course. But this is the first time I've known her name.'

He sounded as if he was telling the truth.

'Well, Jon, that's too bad. I was about to offer you that passport back if you wanted it. And if you were generous enough, I wasn't going to go around telling people exactly how you spend your holidays when you visit those orphans in Phnom Penh and Bangkok. You know the orphanages I'm talking about. You go there every year, twice sometimes.'

'You're the one with the corrupt mind, not me. I don't have anything to hide.'

'Have a look at these before you say that.'

She handed him an envelope containing the photographs taken from his computer. His mouth seemed to grow thinner as he flicked through them. He leaned back on the bench and closed his eyes. The pictures slipped from his hand and fell to the ground. She picked them up, and put them back in her bag.

'You don't understand,' he said.

'I don't think anybody else will either.'

'I've given those children things they would never have had otherwise. They have toys, they go to school. They have good clothes and they eat every day. I'm not a monster. I'm nice to them.'

'Spare me the violins,' Grace said. 'What I want to know is, do we have a deal?'

'Where did you get those pictures?'

'Why should I tell you that?'

He looked at her so sharply and with such outright fear that, even in role, she was shocked.

'No,' he said, shaking his head. 'You got those pictures from Orion. Otherwise you'd be dead.'

'Does it matter where they came from? I've got them. It's my call what happens to them. Do you want to be a known paedophile, Jon? Do you want to be hounded out of town everywhere you go by people baying for your blood?'

He was silent. Then he leaned forward with his head in his hands, crying. She looked away. It was obscene to watch that kind of desperation. He stopped crying and stared at the ground for a few moments, then sat up. No more tears; he had the strangest smile on his face.

'If you want to play this game, then tell me what you want,' he said, in a voice that sounded oddly unconcerned. 'Money? Because I don't have any.'

Grace didn't like his tone. If this was a game, there was something disturbing about his tactics. For a few seconds she weighed up how she should handle this, then stayed with the plan she had agreed on with Clive.

'Yes, I'd like money but that's not my first priority. What I really want is in on your scam.'

'What scam?'

'Those foreign workers at Life's Pleasures. Don't tell me you don't take a cut of what they make. Bet it's a lot more than Lynette got. I'd like part of that money, thanks.'

'I don't get a cent and I don't have a cent,' he replied in a colourless voice.

'Don't talk rubbish!'

'I don't. No one pays me. You have to realise that the people who control me have pictures just like yours. I pay them and I keep paying them. I've told them there's a limit to what I have. Do they want me to sell my kidneys on the net? They just keep saying, give me more. They don't understand people. What happens when people get desperate.' He was leaning forward. Then he closed his eyes again. 'I'm so tired.'

'Who's they?' Grace asked, hiding surprise at the openness of his confession. 'These people bleeding you?'

He looked up at her. 'Why do you want to know?'

'If you won't do business with me, maybe I can deal with them.'

He laughed from somewhere deep down and closed his eyes again. He didn't move or speak; he seemed to have withdrawn completely.

After a few moments, Grace spoke again. 'Those workers don't get paid a cent, do they? Why do they do it?'

'As far as I can work it out, they're paying off the costs of a new identity. My job is to find them. I review a lot of visa applications. It's always women who will never get a visa no matter what they do, either for themselves or someone they want to bring over here.' He was staring ahead. 'After I've found them and referred them, the department never sees or hears from them again. They just disappear off the radar. What I have to do then is make sure we never follow them up. I've even destroyed files.'

'How many women?'

'Half a dozen over three years.'

'That's not very many.'

'No. I've thought that too.' He was speaking as if they were colleagues at a departmental meeting, discussing policy, not people's lives. 'Obviously I know what I'm sending these women to. I've been told that to make sure I pick the right women. But it's a lot of effort for a few people. All I can think is that they like doing this. They like breaking people down. With me, it's money. They grind it out of me. With these women, it's sex. They have to do it. They may not want to but that's just too bad.' He frowned. 'It's the kick. It can't be anything else. They like controlling people. It must be an addiction.'

'Who's they?' Grace repeated.

He smiled at her, broadly, savagely. 'The people you want to do business with.'

Again, silence.

'Where do you refer these women?' she asked.

He was still looking at her. Given the situation, and the surreal feel that seemed to have attached itself to their conversation, she couldn't judge his expression. It seemed almost businesslike. He glanced around the park. It was peaceful, domestic, with the sound of distant voices and occasional bird calls.

'There's a place in Parramatta Westfield — the Portal. An immigration self-help business. The department's been dealing with it since it opened four years ago. As far as the department knows, it's completely above board. I've sent whole families there. They help with their English, tell them how to start a business, advise on how to get citizenship. I tell these women the Portal will be able to help them and usually they're so desperate they go over there right away.'

'Who was the last woman you referred?'

'A young Somali woman. Nadifa Hasan Ibrahim. Very, very beautiful. She desperately wanted a visa for her brother. That wasn't very long ago.'

'She broke her bargain. She never turned up at Life's Pleasures.'

'Then she's probably dead,' he said in a neutral voice. 'They wouldn't tolerate someone not keeping their side of a bargain.'

'Don't you take these women over to Life's Pleasures?'

'No. The other night was the first time I'd been inside.'

'Marie Li knew you, Jon.'

'She'd met me once before, when I picked up that young Thai woman from the back door one night. The one whose passport you showed me.'

'Jirawan,' Grace said. 'How does she fit into this?'

'She wasn't one of the women I referred. I can only guess they brought her there themselves. Why, I can't tell you. They could have been punishing her for some reason. If they thought she owed them money, they might have been making her work it off. From my own experience, I'd say that's the most likely scenario. They get very upset if they don't get every cent they think is owed to them. Even the smallest amount.'

Again, the ordinariness with which he spoke was surreal.

'They put this Jirawan in the boot,' he said. 'Marie Li and her gorilla. All I could do was what I was told.'

'You didn't know her?'

'No, I was just told to go and pick her up and deliver her.'

'Deliver her where?'

'I wasn't told that. I was to receive instructions on my mobile. I didn't do it. I let her go with a train fare in her hand. It was all I

145

could do for her. I told you, I'm not a monster, I do have a conscience. That's what they don't quite get — that people have free will. They think they can squash it out of you. They were very angry with me that night. Now I'm going to have to pay for doing that. It's just how they work. It would never occur to them that I might try and get back at them somehow.' He laughed strangely.

A tall woman of indeterminate age, dressed in a tracksuit and with her hair tucked up under a cap, jogged towards them. She stopped at a bench some distance away and began stretching exercises. Kidd's eyes followed her. He stared at his feet and laughed again.

'Oh God,' he said. 'You have no idea what you're getting yourself into. They'll eat you alive and enjoy it.'

'Who are these people? How do you know them?'

'They're people I met in Thailand once. They had pictures. Since then they've had a lot of fun letting me know who they are and what they do. My own fault. I thought I could buy them off. What I finally realised was that someone must have found me for them. I was what they wanted. Someone who worked for the Department of Immigration. You see, these women aren't the only ones they sell identities to. They bring other people into the country under false IDs. Criminals. People who want to hide. But once people are here, they have to stay hidden. I smooth things over, make sure no questions get asked, that sort of thing. Warn them if I have to.'

'The way you warned them that Life's Pleasures was being raided,' Grace said. 'And that I was an agent with Orion.'

'Yes. Both those things. When you're caught in a vice, you can't see anything except what's immediately in front of you. I can't eat any more. I can't swallow, or hold any food in my stomach. At the moment, every minute I live is just the next minute I've got to get through.'

'Give me their names.'

'I don't need to,' he replied. 'The way it's working out, I think they'll find you.'

'What were they doing in Thailand?'

'Business of some kind. I got the impression they had connections with the expat community in Bangkok. I think they're probably involved in extortion, money laundering, that sort of thing. I'm certain it isn't drugs.'

'Do you know the name Peter Sanders?' she asked.

'Who's that? This Jirawan's husband? No.'

'You say you have a conscience,' Grace said, 'but you still organised Jirawan's escape from detention.'

'Yes, I told them when her medical appointment was. Every day when I wake up, it's the first thing I think about.'

He was staring into the distance, at the people walking and the slow traffic on the roads in the park. Then he looked at Grace. Oddly, for those few seconds he seemed almost relaxed.

'Either you're a cheap blackmailer or this is a sting of some kind,' he said. 'It's a sting, isn't it? You're after them.'

'No, Jon. You've got something to give and I want it. Even if it's only information. I can turn that into money if I have to. You must have a contact. Tell me who you refer these women to.'

'Sara McLeod,' he said. 'She's one of the "they". She runs the Portal. Why don't you go and introduce yourself? She's just over there, doing her exercises. Now, she's a strange woman.'

Grace prevented herself from glancing in the woman's direction. 'In what way?'

He gave her an angry and provocative stare.

'You call me a paedophile and you say I'm sick. Well, she's sick too, they both are. You should see it. She'll do anything for him, things you wouldn't believe. Meanwhile, he's off with any other woman he can get his hands on. But he can't leave her. They're always clawing at each other but they can't separate. I don't know how long they've been together but it must be a long time. I've known them for three years now. They do everything together, and I mean everything. When Jirawan was killed, she would have been part of it. That's just as sick as anything you can lay on me. But you didn't know who she was. You can't have got those pictures from them. I think that whatever you say, this is a sting. Do you know what they told me when I said I was meeting you?'

Grace shook her head.

'They wanted to know all about you. Could you be bought? I told them, yes, you could. You were just a cheap blackmailer. But

I don't think you are. I lied to them. And I'm very sure they believed me.' He laughed softly. 'They think you can be their puppet. Just like me.'

He smiled triumphantly, then got to his feet and walked quickly away down the path. She followed him. A motorbike was approaching. He saw it and began to jog towards it.

'Get away from me,' he said.

'We haven't finished, Jon.'

'Yes, we have. Get out of here. Go on! Go away! Now!'

He pushed her hard enough to wind her and knock her to the side of the path. She stumbled and almost fell. Righting herself, she saw the motorbike heading towards him. He began to run down the path as if to meet it. The bike swerved just as it reached him. There was a pillion rider on the back. Kidd stopped and flung his arms out wide. There was a popping noise, shots, and Kidd went down. The bike was gone at speed.

There was a suspension in time and then screams began to come from a distance. A man with his children rushed them in the opposite direction. Other people, including a group of middle-aged walkers, stood transfixed, gaping.

'Kidd is down, shot from a motorbike,' Grace said to her wire. 'I have to go. I need someone to think I have to run away from his murder. Tell my backup to follow the woman jogger who was exercising near us.'

She turned and looked back where she and Kidd had been sitting. Sara McLeod was walking quickly towards the gatehouse. Grace's car was parked in the same direction and she hurried towards it, passing Sara at speed. She didn't look back. In the car park, she sat in her car for a few moments, long enough to see Sara walk past to a black Porsche. Grace left it to her backup to get the registration number and drove away quickly, just as she heard police sirens in the near distance.

Adrenalin had kept her going till now. It ebbed out and left her shaking and sick. Had that been real? Had it happened or had she imagined it? It had almost been like watching a cartoon, except that someone had died. Her thoughts were caught in this circle when her phone rang. It was Clive.

'Your backup's got you in view. You're being followed by a black Porsche,' he said.

'Sara McLeod.'

'We have the name. I've got people on it now. Double back. She'll try and follow you by the looks of it. Make it look like you're covering your tracks but don't lose her. Go to Westfield at Parramatta. Find somewhere to have a cup of coffee. See what happens. She might approach you.'

'Kidd wasn't assassinated. He committed suicide,' she said.

'It was his choice.'

'He wanted to talk even before I got there. Listen to what he said. He was ready to confess. We put that final pressure on him. If we'd gone about this another way, offered him protection, he might have cooperated.'

'We have his information. That's what matters. Now go.'

As Clive had said, Sara McLeod stayed with her all the way to the Westfield shopping plaza at Parramatta. Grace parked on the second floor of the multi-storeyed centre and looked around. The black Porsche cruised in behind her, apparently looking for a parking spot. Grace left her car and walked slowly out to the concourse to find a café. Surrounded by bright lights and hurrying people, the full impact of the morning hit her. She felt giddy on her feet.

She looked around. Sara McLeod had followed her out with no attempt at disguise. As soon as Grace was sure the woman had seen her, she went into the women's toilets and was sick. They would hear that on the other end of the line. Clive would hear it. Too bad. She washed her face and refreshed her make-up. The pale mask looked back from the mirror. *This isn't who I am. This is just a skin I can peel off when I go home. I am not a cheap blackmailer. I'm not someone who wants other people to die.*

Straightening her backbone, she walked out to the concourse again and found a coffee shop with tables set outside where she could be seen. This time, she didn't see Sara. Instead, the full range of Sydney's population passed by: giggling girls in headscarves; African women in clothes whose radiant colours were even more vibrant against their black skin; men in traditional Muslim dress; Australians generally from any background, immigrant and indigenous, going about their business. She thought that here she could disappear into the crowd and feel anonymous; it would ease her mind.

She sat over her coffee until the last of it was cold in the bottom of her cup. Half an hour had passed. She got to her feet, paid and had just walked into the car park when Joel Griffin stepped out into her path. She stopped.

'Hello, Grace. You remember me. We met yesterday.'

'This is your neighbourhood, is it?' she asked.

'I have clients out here. Not just the Jovanovs.' He was a big man, tall. Standing in front of her, his bulk seemed more solid. His sharp blue eyes never seemed to leave her face. 'Have you got any time?'

'Maybe,' she said. 'Why?'

'Come and sit with me in my car for a while. We can talk privately there. I'll put my keys where you can see them if you don't trust me.'

'What have you got to say?'

'Something to our mutual benefit. Come on. I won't hurt you.'

'All right,' she said.

In the car, the dark blue Audi she'd seen outside the Jovanovs' house, he put his keys on top of the dashboard.

'You didn't have much luck with Sophie the other day,' he said. 'Why did you show her that picture?'

'I wanted to see how she'd react.'

He turned to look at her. 'You're an attractive woman. I would have said that a woman with a face like yours doesn't need to do this kind of work. Why do you do it? Is it because your partner doesn't keep you? Why don't you want to marry him? Because he's not good enough for you? Surely you could find someone with a lot more money than he's got.'

Grace suppressed profound insult behind her mask. 'What do you want?' she asked.

'I hear you've got something to sell.'

'Who told you that?'

He smiled. 'A client. But you see, I can't tally the woman I saw yesterday, the one who genuinely cares about people, with the one who wants to make a deal. One of you has to be a fake.'

'Who's your client?'

'We don't talk about my client. We talk about you. That's quite a scar Chris gave you. He told me a lot about you. Twice he almost killed you. Twice you walked away. The second time, one flick of his lighter and you wouldn't have the face you've got now. You'd be lucky to be alive.'

No, you're wrong, Grace thought. That first time, he didn't want to kill me. He wanted me to remember him and suffer. That's the only reason I'm still alive. The second time, who knew what he meant to do? Scar beyond repair? Kill? Had he even thought about it past seeing the flames?

An extraordinary fear took hold of her: that Newell was here, in the back seat. Calmly, she got out of the car and stepped away from it. The dark-tinted windows obscured whether anyone was in the back seat or not. Griffin followed, standing on the other side of the car. He leaned over the top and stared at her.

'There's no one in the back seat,' he said. 'Look.'

He walked around and opened the back door. There was no one there. She looked around. Not far away, a couple were loading groceries into their car. The man turned and wheeled the shopping trolley away. Her backup.

'He's not here,' Griffin said, still watching her.

She got back into the car but didn't speak.

'That got to you,' he said. 'You've been there and you've walked away. You know what it means to look someone in the eyes who wants to kill you. That makes you very special.'

'Do you want to talk business? Or do you just want to talk crap?'

She spoke with such anger that he recoiled slightly. Then he smiled. Even so, she caught a glimpse of something else in his face. The sense that somehow this was an unjustified insult aimed at him. She was glad she had got under his skin.

'How do I know this is business?' he said. 'I can see that maybe you think your life is a failure and this is a path you want to take.

But before my client puts himself on the line, I want you to prove yourself.'

'Tell your client that's his problem,' she said.

'No, it's yours.'

'Why is it mine?' She was angry. It was easy to act this part. 'If your client wants to deal, let him deal. If he doesn't, then Narelle goes to gaol. How long do you think she'll last faced with that prospect. Everything she knows, we'll know. Tell him that this time he's not calling the shots.'

Griffin laughed. 'What's this worth to you? What do you expect to get out of it?'

'Maybe what I'm looking for is a long-term source of income. There are deep waters here. I want to find out what's really going on. I already know enough to close Life's Pleasures down right now. Maybe there's a lot more than a passport in this for me, if I work it right. You can tell your client that too.'

He looked at her. 'Do you think we could hit it off?'

'I don't know. Maybe if you stop talking about Newell, I'll think about it,' she said.

He was silent for a while. 'Is it true what they say about you and your partner?'

'Like what?'

'You made him leave the police. He hasn't forgiven you for that. He's got a lot of enemies and he's worried they're going to come after him. Sometimes he loses it and knocks you around.'

Where did his mind live? In the garbage heap where that story belonged? Perhaps he would mistake her expression for humiliation at a truth revealed rather than for the shock and anger it was.

'Who said that?' Her tone was more dangerous than she'd intended.

'In some quarters, it's what they say,' Griffin replied.

'Don't go there,' she said. 'Don't even think about going there.'

'Does that mean he does or he doesn't?'

'It means, don't go there.'

Again he was silent.

'Give me your number,' he said. 'I'll call you in twenty-four hours. That was your deadline, wasn't it?'

'I'll be waiting.'

'Next time, maybe we can have a little down time together.'

'Maybe. If you can find something more interesting to talk about,' she said and got out. She shut the car door behind her and walked away, not looking back.

He didn't wait; he started his car and was gone before she reached hers. She got into her car and gave him time to get clear. Suddenly aware that her head was throbbing badly, she drove out of the car park. She passed the black Porsche still in its parking bay. There was no sign of Sara.

'I'm leaving now,' she said to her wire. 'Target has already left.'

Out on the road, Clive rang.

'How are you?' he asked.

'Tired,' she said.

'Did you know Newell had told Griffin about your connection to him?'

Do I lie? This time, there was no choice. It had to be the truth. 'Yes.'

'When did you find out?'

'Griffin spoke to Harrigan the day Newell escaped and told him. We thought it was an attempt at blackmail.'

'And you didn't tell me.'

'We wanted to handle it ourselves.'

'Even after yesterday when he turned up as Sophie Jovanov's lawyer?'

'It's a very personal matter,' Grace said.

'I had a right to know,' Clive said. 'The more personal, the more I need to know. That applies to anything to do with you.'

No, you don't.

'Orion does,' Grace replied. 'I don't know about you personally.'

'Yes, I do, and I think you'll find that out. We'll talk about it at the debrief. Once that's over, you can go home early. You need to recoup.' Then he was gone.

Utterly drained, she drove carefully. It was a long way from Parramatta to Mascot, a journey along busy roads, dodging trucks and avoiding drivers who seemed to have no fear for their own lives or concern for anyone else's.

There was no logic to the rumours that had surrounded her and Paul since the start of their relationship. When she first started seeing him, she had been accused of sleeping her way to the top; now she was accused of dragging him out of the police service for her own ends. But she had never before heard it said that Paul hit her. The gossip was like a poison; let it into your mind and it would destroy your happiness.

She was uncertain why Griffin had harped on about marriage. If she asked herself why she and Paul had never discussed it, she realised that on her side it had seemed too much like tempting fate. She had more happiness in her life than she had ever expected to achieve. But in the past, everything she had valued had proved fragile. She didn't want to risk losing what she had now by asking too much of fate. Take one step too many and who knew what might happen, what thunderbolts might be thrown? Leave things the way they were, they were fine just like that.

She would go home early, she would collect Ellie from childcare and they would spend what was left of the afternoon together. She needed that refreshment. Otherwise some part of her might start to atrophy; feelings like compassion or empathy might die. Small things like that.

14

Harrigan's investigations took him across the sprawling western Sydney suburbs to the foothills of the Blue Mountains, then up onto the Great Western Highway that cut across into the interior of the continent. Katoomba was the urban centre of the ribbon of small towns that clustered the length of this road, which, in parallel with the railway line, ran along the spine of the low, forest-covered mountains. He reached there late morning, and looked for parking in the steep, chaotic street near the railway station where the grand old Carrington Hotel stood and where the restaurants and coffee shops were full of holiday-makers and honeymooners.

Harrigan's appointment was at a solicitor's office, a shopfront close to the top of the town. He let himself into a neatly if modestly furnished reception area. 'Mr Lambert's waiting for you,' the receptionist said and took him through to a smallish office. Simon Lambert got to his feet to offer his hand. There was a subdued fussiness to his dress, down to the waistcoat and bow tie. Possibly he was as much as sixty. His dark curly hair was turning white.

'Thanks for making the time to see me,' Harrigan said.

'You're quite well known in this profession. I'm sure you know that. Please sit down. Where would you like to start this conversation?'

'Dr Amelie Santos. You were her solicitors.'

'We were. Why is that a concern of yours?'

'I have a client who's concerned with the affairs of Frank Wells. I've already spoken to Frank. Now I'm seeking some information from you.'

'Yes, I remember Mr Wells,' the solicitor said dryly. 'His existence was a shock to us all. I directed my staff not to deal with him after the first two phone calls. If you'll excuse my language, he told my receptionist to get fucked. I wasn't going to have us put up with that.'

'Did you have any idea that Dr Santos had a son?'

'None. In fact, until Mr Wells's solicitor sent us the proof, I didn't believe it. I thought he was trying it on. I still can't connect the man I spoke to on the phone with the woman I knew.'

'You knew nothing about her husband?'

'Nothing at all, and I certainly would never have asked her.'

'Did Dr Santos have any kind of companion in her life, even a close friend?'

'None that I knew of,' Lambert replied. 'Her work meant everything to her. I think it's fair to say it took the place of any personal relationship.'

'You seem to know her well.'

'I first met her when she was in her late sixties.' The solicitor smiled wryly. 'More than twenty years ago now, when I was a little younger myself. She was planning on retiring up here and she wanted to make her will. Her family had a long-standing connection with the area.'

'Which was?'

'Her grandfather built a holiday house at Blackheath in the 1880s. He was a very well-known Sydney barrister in his day. So was his son, Amelie's father. Apparently neither of them could stand Sydney's humidity during the summer. The family always came up to the mountains for Christmas. I remember Amelie talking about coming up by steam train. It was a very fond memory for her. She planned to live out her retirement there. As it happened, she didn't actually fully retire until she was in her seventies. She was considered a very fine doctor. She still had people consulting with her from time to time even in retirement.'

'Do you know an Ian Blackmore?' Harrigan asked.

Lambert gave a thin-lipped smile, more chagrin than anything else. 'Mr Blackmore. No, I'd never heard of him before. When I saw that letter on our letterhead, which we'd obviously never written, I didn't know what to think.' He paused. 'May I ask why you want to know all this?'

'As well as being the son of Dr Santos, Frank Wells was also the father of a boy called Craig Wells. That boy murdered his mother when he was eighteen. At the time it was believed he also committed suicide. I'm investigating the possibility he may still be alive.'

'Do you have a description of this man?'

'No.'

Lambert was silent for a few moments.

'Presumably such a man would be dangerous,' he said.

'Very dangerous. It was a brutal and premeditated murder. If he is still alive, then it means someone else died in his place.'

'Then I may have some useful information. Amelie did move up here when she retired and she did live in the house at Blackheath. It was an isolated existence for a woman of her age but she gave me to understand she valued her privacy. When she was in her eighties she was forced to accept home care. Visits from the community nurses to help her wash and dress, that sort of thing. Then early one morning one of these nurses arrived to find Amelie lying in her nightgown on her front path. This nurse was convinced it wasn't a fall. She was very sure Amelie had taken a blow to the side of the head. It left a wound that never really healed.'

'Did this nurse see anyone else at the house at the time?'

'No, but she wouldn't have been paying any attention to that. She was busy calling an ambulance. If there had been someone there, they could have easily got out through the back of the house. Amelie never recovered and she was eventually sent to Meadowbank Aged Care, which is near the Three Sisters here. By this time she was very confused. Her usually clear-headed self was quite gone. The nursing staff didn't expect her to live very long and they requested she be assessed for mental competency by the local health care service. However, shortly after she was admitted to Meadowbank she began to receive a visitor, a woman.'

'Who was this woman?'

'She gave her name as Nadine Patterson, and told the nursing staff she was a friend who had been concerned for Amelie's welfare for some time.'

'Did you meet her?' he asked.

'Only once. You see, as her solicitor, I had only a limited power of attorney over Amelie's affairs. Which meant that if Amelie was assessed as mentally competent, then she would remain in control of her assets. However, if she was declared incompetent, then she had a mechanism set up whereby all her assets would remain in trust until she died, when her will would be executed. As it happened, Amelie had left her entire estate to a medical charity, Medicine International. It was a very generous bequest.'

'Was she mentally competent?'

'No. Not in my opinion anyway. But the South Western Health Care Service in the form of one Kylie Sutcliffe disagreed.'

'With what result?'

'I was called down to Meadowbank one day to make a deed of gift. Amelie was deeding the house at Blackheath, including all its contents, and a very substantial sum of money, virtually all the readily available money she had, to the Shillingworth Trust as it was called.'

'Are you sure about that name?' Harrigan asked.

'Very. Do you know it?'

'I've come across it in my investigations before today. You agreed to do this for her?'

'In a way, that's the point I'm making. I seriously thought about challenging it. Nadine Patterson was one of the trustees. It seemed such blatant exploitation. But Amelie, who had regained a certain lucidity by this time, begged me not to. She said to please just let her make the gift and finish with it. She was so distressed that I went ahead. Then she directed the nursing staff never to let this Nadine Patterson in again. As it was, the woman never came back.'

'She'd got what she came for,' Harrigan said. 'Can you describe her?'

'I only met her once when she came to collect the legal papers. She was tall, very stylish, red hair, attractive. Very distant. Barely polite and only at first. You see, I don't want to be harsh, but the woman who made the assessment that Amelie was mentally competent, when she clearly wasn't, was a single woman who wasn't particularly young or pretty or interesting.'

'You knew her?'

'Oh yes. Kylie was a local girl. She went to school here. I knew her father very well, he was a local vet for many years. I'm a widower; my wife died eight years ago. Unusual these days, I know. Most people divorce. We always kept dogs, we used to show them. I still do. Scottie dogs.'

He glanced at two photographs on his desk; one that Harrigan guessed was of his wife, and another showing three Scottie dogs sitting on cushions, all wearing tartan ribbons around their necks.

'It was virtually the day after Amelie had signed the deed of gift. I was driving into Penrith, I had to be in court that afternoon. I realised I was beside Kylie in the traffic. I don't think she saw me. She pulled ahead and turned in to a motel. She had a passenger with her, and as I drove past I saw her getting out of the car with a man.'

'Do you have a description of this man?'

'Not really. I only saw him from the back.'

'What about the make of the car?'

'It was her car. I recognised it. Actually it was her work car. Apparently she was supposed to be working that day.'

'Your suggestion is this woman, Kylie Sutcliffe, was persuaded to make an assessment favourable to Nadine Patterson for the purposes of coercing Dr Santos into making this gift?'

'I realise it's a long bow to draw. But at the time I was angry. That anger must have shown when this Miss Patterson came to collect her papers. I told her I'd seen Kylie, and made some sarcastic comment that I hoped Kylie had been in a more serious frame of mind when she'd made her assessment of Amelie than when I saw her in Penrith carrying on with some man when she should have been at work. That woman looked at me and said, "I don't think you saw that," and walked out. I have to say I felt quite chilled. Then a day later, the following night in fact — it was winter, I got home after dark —' He stopped for some moments. 'My dogs. All three of them. They were dead. And they hadn't died very pleasantly either.'

He couldn't speak. Harrigan waited in silence.

'I have three new dogs now. That's them there — Penelope, Telemachus and Odysseus. But they're not allowed out unless I'm there to watch them. I used to have a dog flap for them. Not any more.'

'Your belief is that this Nadine Patterson killed your dogs?'

'I'm not a fanciful man. I've thought over the brief encounter I had with this Patterson woman any number of times and I'm convinced I humiliated her by what I said. That's what I saw in her face that day and, yes, I'm also convinced that she did kill my dogs and that's why.'

'You're saying that whoever Kylie Sutcliffe was with, it was possibly Nadine Patterson's lover.'

'I'm unable to reach any other conclusion. I also have to say that I can't see why anyone would be interested in Kylie if Nadine Patterson was there.' He shrugged. 'She was an arrogant woman. Arrogant and angry. And presumably vengeful.'

'Did you ever speak to Kylie Sutcliffe about any of this?'

'That's another point. Not long after I saw her that day, she resigned her job at short notice and went to London with her boyfriend. I haven't seen her in four years and neither has anyone else.'

'What about her father?'

'He's dead now, and she never got along very well with her mother. I assume she's communicating with her. I haven't heard anything one way or the other. And then, of course, there was this mysterious letter to Mr Frank Wells. I'd executed Amelie's will but I refused to act in the matter of the dispute over the probate. That was between Mr Wells and Medicine International. By then I wanted nothing to do with it.'

Harrigan glanced around the office. It was well ordered, like Lambert's desk where the papers were laid out in neat piles. Nothing about him suggested a man given to flights of fancy or paranoia. Instead, everything Harrigan had heard spoke of someone who liked stability in his life; a man who probably still grieved for his wife and was deeply attached to his dogs.

'Is this the first time you've given this information to anyone?' he asked.

'Absolutely,' Lambert replied.

'Dr Santos was a rich woman. Can I ask about the extent of her estate?'

'Certainly. She was the only child of wealthy parents, the sole heir to their estate, which was substantial. I doubt she spent much money on herself. Most of it she invested over her lifetime, very shrewdly. Including the house at Blackheath, there were three properties, two of which were still owned by her when she died. Her surgery, which was at Turramurra, and a house at Duffys Forest, which was where she lived in Sydney. Both of those properties went to Medicine International in accordance with her will. Her bequest to them was well in excess of some millions of dollars even after the deed of gift had been paid.'

'Do you know who owns those properties now?'

'No, I don't. At the time, Medicine International advised me they intended selling on both properties and realising the capital. But those sales would have occurred after probate was declared, which meant they were handled by the charity's own lawyers. I had nothing to do with it.'

'Would this Nadine Patterson have known the contents of Dr Santos's will?'

'However she found it out, yes, she very definitely did. She made a number of comments during our meeting indicating that.'

'Dr Santos seemed to live in isolated locations,' Harrigan said.

'She used to love to ride; it was her great pleasure. I think it was her only recreation. That's why she lived at Duffys Forest. She could keep her horses there.'

'What about the house at Blackheath? Is it still owned by the Shillingworth Trust?'

'So far as I know. I can tell you it's not lived in. I have that much information. The second trustee was a David Tate. You could check with him, whoever he might be. I have sometimes wondered if he was the man I saw with Kylie Sutcliffe that day.'

'Do you know who the beneficiaries were?'

'Yes, I insisted we establish that the trust was properly legally constituted, which it certainly was. It was a discretionary trust, which meant of course that the return to beneficiaries was at the discretion of the trustees. The beneficiary was a company, Cheshire Nominees. That's where I gave up. There seemed no point in pursuing the matter further. I had no idea where it might take me.'

'Could you give me the addresses of all Dr Santos's properties, including the Blackheath house?' Harrigan asked.

'I have no problem with that. Do you intend to visit them?'

'I'll take a look at them. I'm interested in knowing who owns them now and what's happened to them.'

Lambert glanced at the photograph of his dogs; then he opened a desk drawer and handed Harrigan a set of keys.

'You might need these,' he said. 'When Amelie was sent to hospital, the nurse who found her also locked up her house. When the deed of gift was made, the nursing home gave me the keys to hand on to Miss Patterson.' Lambert looked slightly embarrassed. 'I was about to give them to her when we had our verbal encounter, if I can describe it in that way. Her response so shocked me that I completely forgot to hand them over. Anyway, she'd already walked out of my office. I didn't want to meet with her again so I sent them on to her at the Shillingworth Trust. They came back undelivered. Not known at this address.'

'You didn't hand them over and she didn't ask for them,' Harrigan said.

'No. Which would suggest she already had a set. I'm sure she did. Amelie would almost certainly have had a spare set somewhere in the house.'

'An easy house to break into then?'

'It was generally said by the nurses who visited her that Amelie had no sense of security whatsoever,' Lambert replied.

'You don't think the locks have been changed since her death?' Harrigan asked.

'My information is that the house is exactly as it was when the deed of gift was made. It's been left to rot.'

'Strange thing to do after all that effort. Did Dr Santos have a peaceful death?'

'She did apparently. In her sleep. It seems that once Miss Patterson left, Amelie came back to something like her old self and was quite calm in her last weeks. We carried out the funeral according to her wishes, and right now she's buried in the Northern Suburbs Cemetery next to her parents.'

'Quite a story. Thank you for the information,' Harrigan said. 'It's been very useful.'

'It's been a relief,' the solicitor replied, feelingly. 'What I want to do now is forget about it.'

By now, it was well after one. Harrigan was on his way to his car when an SMS message arrived from Grace. She had an early mark and would collect Ellie from the childcare centre. *Talk to you later, love G.* He thought about ringing her but she was probably still at work. Better he didn't infringe on Orion's dislike of personal calls. He sent back his own message. *Ok, babe. See you at home. Lu2.* Then he made the trip further along the Great Western Highway to Blackheath.

Like much of the Blue Mountains, Blackheath had the feel of a tourist town. The gift shops, antiques centres and restaurants all invited you to come inside and spend your money in comfort. Harrigan obliged by stopping for lunch before driving out to where the edge of the town met the Blue Mountains National Park. In the 1880s Amelie's house would have been at a distance from the railway line, the village and other homes. Today, other houses had encroached on its isolation, although it was still secluded, being surrounded by a high hedge.

To Harrigan's surprise, there was a *For Sale by Auction* sign outside the front of the house. It was the perfect excuse for him to stop and look. The tall hedge was unkempt, the front gate skewed on its hinges. There was also a wide, closed wooden gate leading into the driveway. He parked a little further along the road and, letting himself in the front gate, walked down the path. There was no sign of a car in the driveway and the roller door to the garage was shut.

Once inside the hedge, the house and garden were enclosed and isolated from the street. Everything Harrigan saw spoke of abandonment. The plants that had once been grown in the garden had either gone to seed or died. The house was built of wood, with a wide veranda surrounding it on all four sides. It was some years since it had been painted. He walked up to the front door and rang the bell. He heard it chiming back into the interior of the house, followed by a deeper silence.

After another attempt, which also went unanswered, he put on a pair of disposable gloves, then took out Lambert's keys. The lock on the front door looked old enough to be an original and he soon found a key that opened it. He stepped into a hallway that ran the length of the house, hearing only the hum of silence. There was a smell of disuse rather than dirt. He took out his gun.

He went into the front room. Dust lay on the bookshelves, ornaments and pictures. The phone had clearly not been touched for years. He tried a light switch. To his surprise, there was still electricity. Back in the hallway, he opened a closed door and found himself looking into the main bedroom. The bed was unmade, the blankets and sheets lying tossed back as if someone had just got out of it. Only the dust covering everything indicated how long it must have been since the last occupant had been here. Otherwise, someone might have just got up that morning. Even the hairbrush sitting on the dressing table still had white hairs in the bristles.

Two framed photographs stood next to it. One after the other, Harrigan took them to the window to see them in the light, brushing them clean. The first had probably been taken in the mid-twenties of last century: a studio portrait of a young Amelie with her parents. The family seemed more relaxed than such poses usually allowed, each of them smiling. Her father had a hand on his young daughter's shoulder. His smile was one of pride, hers was simply happy. The second picture showed Amelie Santos on her graduation day, dated in 1942. A dark-haired young woman in academic robes, she stood against carefully arranged drapes. She held her degree but she wasn't smiling; her expression was one of sadness. Amelie Santos had had a finely made face with clear eyes. Underneath her academic gown, she was dressed in a simple, slim-fitting dress. There was nothing about her that suggested she couldn't have found someone to share her life with if she'd wanted to.

He walked through the rest of the house. There were signs where the possums had broken in and made their homes in the ceiling and where other creatures had chewed their way into the chair cushions to make nests. Spiders' webs hung from the light fittings and the corners of the room. Despite the sense of decay, the house had an air of peacefulness rather than menace.

Harrigan reached the kitchen, a room that had not been changed for at least thirty years, and looked out of the window over the sink. There was a panoramic view of the Grose Valley with its tree-covered slopes and turret-like sandstone outcrops, a sight probably unchanged in centuries. As beautiful as it was, this was a modest way of life for a woman whose personal wealth had been valued in the millions. He opened the back door and saw a pile of leaf litter balanced precariously in the air before cascading downwards. No one had opened this door for years.

Stepping over the litter, he went out onto the back veranda. A cane chair and table, now rotted and dirty, stood just near the kitchen door. The back garden was overrun with weeds and self-sown wattles. Tall, well-grown eucalypts lined either side of the boundary, stepping down the slope one after the other towards the escarpment. Forest and mountain stretched to a horizon piled with a massive accumulation of luminous clouds. Out of the deep, dark, blue-green sweep of the trees came only the sound of bird calls and the wind in the trees, giving an intense sense of peace. Perhaps this was what she had come here to find, something that could not be bought. She must have sat here and drunk it in.

Back inside, he closed and locked the back door again and then went out the way he had come, sheathing his gun. Outside, he looked at the garage. He had a key to the roller door and another one next to it that he hadn't used. He went around to the side of the house where there was a second door into the garage reached by a short path from the veranda. The key turned easily in the lock and he stepped inside.

He wasn't in the garage proper but a windowless room at the back of it. He turned on the light and found himself in a study of some kind, a room fitted with shelving. Another door led through into the main part of the garage at the front. He opened this door, which was also locked, and looked through. A small, old blue Ford was parked there, presumably from the time when Amelie Santos had stopped driving. He locked the door again and turned his attention to what was in the room. By the look of it, it was the remains of her medical practice. On one shelf was an old-fashioned doctor's bag, a stethoscope and old medical journals. There were other shelves filled with archive boxes, all labelled and dated. Tax records, financial information. One row of boxes on a middle shelf were labelled simply *Children*.

Harrigan took one box down and set it on the table in the centre of the small room. There was a chair to sit in, and on the table a reading lamp and, chillingly, a pair of reading glasses, as if Amelie Santos might walk through the door the next minute and put them on. Harrigan turned on the reading lamp, which worked perfectly, and noticed that, unlike the rest of the house and other parts of this room, there was no dust on the table. He opened the box.

He soon realised these were the medical records of children that Amelie Santos had treated throughout her career but had not been able to save. All had been filed in strict chronological order with their names and the span of their lives written across the top of the files. The records went back to the start of her practice. The children had died of accidents, cancer, inherited diseases. The information in the records made it clear that she had nursed many of them tirelessly.

As well as exhaustive medical data, in amongst the records were photographs, some just of the child, some of the family as well. In some folders there were even birth certificates. Occasionally there were letters addressed to Amelie, again sometimes from the child, sometimes from the parents. In one folder there was a small knitted toy wrapped in yellowing tissue paper. There were details of the parents' and siblings' life and health, where they were born and had lived, including overseas travel. Amelie Santos had searched hard for answers to her patients' illnesses.

The children's names reflected the changes in post-war Australia. The oldest, dating from the mid-forties, were almost completely Anglo-Celtic; then other names from other places began to appear — Greek, Italian, Eastern European, the Balkans. In the later years of Amelie's practice, the children's names were from all backgrounds: Chinese, Vietnamese, Indian, Thai, Middle Eastern,

African. Some records dated from as late as the mid-1990s. Harrigan remembered what Lambert had told him: that she'd had a reputation that had brought people to her long after her retirement. Desperate people seeking answers no one had to give, including Amelie Santos; so desperate they were prepared to place any amount of sensitive information in her hands. When put together, the records provided a comprehensive biography of the dead.

But numbers of folders were also empty with no explanation given. Then, at the end of one box, he came across a folder labelled with the name *Nadine Patterson*. He pulled it out and saw there was nothing inside. He slipped it back and opened the next box. There, almost at the front, was a folder labelled *David Tate*. He drew this one out. It was also empty. He looked at the dates of the children's births and deaths. About forty, if they'd been alive today. Working quickly, he made a list of the names on the empty files. Fourteen in all, including Tate and Patterson, boys and girls both, about half of them Asian or African.

He closed up the final box and put it back on the shelf. There was enough information in some of these folders for a person to create a new identity for themselves any time they wanted to. A very profitable item to sell on the market since the identity was effectively genuine. This was the real value of the house; not the property but these records. An identity scam, presumably run by the Shillingworth trustees, people who were already in masquerade.

What should he do now? Call his old work mates? If he did, it would get back to Orion. Talk to Lambert? It was unlikely the solicitor would want anything more to do with this. Take the files with him? What right did he have to do that? Who could be said to own these records now? Presumably they should have been returned to the families or destroyed when Amelie Santos died. But what if he secured them on the premises, in some other hiding place? Anyone coming here to use them could easily think they had been stolen.

Harrigan went back inside the house and looked around. The roof? The cellar? In the spare bedroom, he found a large linen press, the old-fashioned kind: a long, deep chest made of some dark wood, only partially filled with sheets and towels. On opening, it smelled of mothballs. Working as quickly as he could, he transferred the boxes from the garage to here, covering them with the linen already in place. The dust on the chest was disturbed when he had finished, but hopefully no one would come into this storage cum junk room to check. Then he went back outside and broke the lock on the garage's side door. Clumsy, but good enough to make it appear someone had broken in. He peeled off his disposable gloves and left the premises.

He drove to Blackheath to visit the real estate agent. A franchise of one of the major chains, they had a large office on the main street. Amelie Santos's house was listed as property of the week. *House and furnishings included. Panoramic view of the Grose Valley. Some simple repairs and a coat of paint will return this beautiful Victorian house to its former glory. Large block with excellent potential for expansion.* Harrigan went inside.

'This is quite amazing,' said the real estate agent, a conservatively dressed older woman wearing an ugly sky-blue suit, who met him with a motherly smile. 'That property only went on the market yesterday and we've already had so many enquiries. We're having an open day this Saturday so please do come along. It's a unique purchase, a piece of history really.'

Possibly she could talk prospective buyers into any sale she liked, simply because she appeared so harmless on the surface.

'Maybe you could give me an indication of what the reserve might be,' Harrigan said.

She named a figure that ensured no one who could be described as a battler would be bidding at the auction.

'Any chance of a private viewing?'

'I'm afraid not,' she said. 'The owners are going to be there over the next few days to take some things out of the house. We've been asked not to let anyone in till Saturday.'

'What sort of condition is it in?' he asked, curious to hear how she might describe it.

'It's a deceased estate and hasn't been lived in for several years now. It needs a good clean and an airing out. Structurally it's very sound, though it will need painting. We're sending some cleaners in this Friday, just to spruce it up a little.'

'Is there any reason the owners are selling right now?'

Trusts of any sort were useful tools for money laundering, another reason why Shillingworth might acquire a property then leave it to rot. Perhaps the agent had this in her mind when she answered him.

'I think they judged the market as right for the sale. Property prices are easing a little and there are more buyers around than there used to be. It's all above board. We've spoken with the trust's legal representative, a Mr Griffin.'

'Joel Griffin?'

'Yes. Do you know him?'

'I've heard of him. Thanks.'

He left to make the long drive back to Sydney. He would be late. When he was a little closer to the city, he would phone Grace and let her know when he would be home. He welcomed the drive, it gave him time to think. What was Joel Griffin doing involved in this? Why would he be a party to the sale of assets from a secretive trust? Just his name brought another dimension of threat to Harrigan's investigations.

In the mess of information he had, one name stood out: Shillingworth. Shillingworth Trust led to the Ponticellis, to Eddie Grippo at Four Square Real Estate. There, the connection became shadowy. The best he could say was that there was one. A question for Eddie: do you know Joel Griffin? If Griffin did have a connection to the Ponticellis, this was the first Harrigan had heard of it. Was his intelligence so bad? Or was the connection an occasional one, not much mentioned? And why sell Blackheath now? Forget market conditions. Whatever the reason, the trustees, Patterson and Tate, whoever they really were, had decided it was time to move on. Would other assets, such as Fairview Mansions, come up for sale? Another question for Eddie.

Then there was the line back to Frank Wells, to his adoptive mother's niece, Jennifer Shillingworth, the woman with access to Salvation Army adoption records, the one person who could have known who Frank's real parents were. A woman who, thirty-five or more years ago, hadn't been above trying on the odd scam

169

herself. In a time before changes to the adoption laws, she might well have known people who were desperate enough to buy that kind of information. If this speculation were true, then, as Frank Wells himself had said, she was the most likely source of the documents an otherwise unknown Ian Blackmore had sent to him four years ago.

Ignoring the road rules, Harrigan picked up his mobile and sent an SMS to his retainer. He had already asked her to track down the Shillingworth woman but still he texted: *Find me Jennifer Shillingworth as a first priority and forward me any information you already have ASAP.*

She's dead. The instinctive words came into Harrigan's mind even as he sent the message. It remained to be seen if his expectation was on the money. Maybe someone had eventually bought that information from her. There were only three people who could have known it was for sale in the first place, let alone want to buy it: Frank, Janice and a young Craig, watching his parents fight. Frank hadn't wanted to know and Janice was dead. Maybe after she'd left Frank, she had gone on about it to her son, the way she had to her husband. Maybe when she was drunk, banging it into his head. *If only your father had found out who his parents were, maybe we'd have some money now. We wouldn't be so broke.* It fitted with the woman he'd read and heard about.

But supposedly Craig was dead too. Harrigan smiled to himself. Death was a perfect alibi. It gave you the space to do whatever you wanted. You could coerce property out of an old and vulnerable Amelie Santos and, in some strange twist of humour, put it into a trust named after the woman who might well have led you to her in the first place. But why wait until four years ago to chase it up? What had been the catalyst? Because Amelie Santos was old and could be expected to die soon? You turn up out of nowhere and introduce yourself to her as her grandson and heir even though she's never seen you before. Would she even let you in? See you as other than a threat? And what could she be to you, other than a victim to exploit? Someone to cajole, charm, threaten and, with the help of your partner, finally terrorise?

But you couldn't announce yourself to her as Craig Wells. If you'd killed off your old identity by murdering someone else in your place, there'd be no room for you to resurrect yourself. Once Craig Wells was dead, he had to stay dead and you couldn't bring him back to life. But you wouldn't have to. Amelie Santos couldn't have known her son's name. You could give yourself any name you liked, say your father was dead to keep him out of the picture, and then try to get whatever you could out of your victim. In the way of family resemblances, maybe you even looked something like your grandfather.

Thinking this over, it occurred to Harrigan that perhaps all those years ago Jennifer Shillingworth might possibly have also approached Amelie Santos. If she had, then presumably the doctor, like her son, Frank, had sent her on her way, saying she didn't want to know. And then later, when the laws were changed and adoption records became accessible, it was only to the family members. In that case, the only recourse for someone who had expunged his existence as Craig Wells was the original one: bribery. You go back to the woman who wanted to sell the information in the first place and ask her if she still wants to make a deal. Hadn't Frank told him that Jennifer Shillingworth had already made copies of the documents? Maybe they'd been just locked away in a drawer somewhere, waiting.

Then there was the woman at the centre of this, Amelie Santos, the seemingly innocent vortex for all these connections. The strangeness of sifting through the paper remains of her patients' old lives had left Harrigan with a sense of bleakness. Amelie Santos could have kept her child. Despite the circumstances of her marriage, she had still been a married woman in a time when that had mattered. Her father had had the means to support them both. Even in those days, with his help she would have been able to become a doctor as well as raising her son. Instead, that part of her life had been obliterated, except for the pieces of paper she had kept for herself from the child patients she could not save, a lifetime's worth of grief and loss. For Amelie Santos, did pieces of paper detailing a patient's name and history replace what had been lost in the flesh? Were they like fetish objects filling a vacuum, things that were fixed in time and could not grow older? Perhaps she'd had no choice in relinquishing her son. Had her father or mother told her it had to happen, regardless? Or had the father of her child hurt her so much, she had rejected their son herself? If he had, why keep his name? No way to know now.

In all these shadows, Amelie Santos wasn't the only obsessive figure. Someone had wanted what she had so much they had tracked her to her nursing home, deceived a woman they'd had no other interest in to assist them, and then presumably threatened and frightened an aging woman to get hold of it. Had they known at the time they were also acquiring the identities of the dead? Or had there been another reason for their actions and those records were only a bonus? Were they the same people who had tried to kill Amelie Santos in the first place?

With a chill, Harrigan realised that it was only their failure to murder Amelie Santos that had allowed them to acquire the Blackheath house. Whoever had attacked her that morning must simply have wanted to kill her. If they'd succeeded, the Blackheath house would have gone to Medicine International along with the rest of her estate. Presumably the organisation would have sold it on, the way they had her other two properties. But why kill someone as harmless as a woman in her late eighties if there was no prospect of material gain? In her own way, wasn't she as much a victim in this as other people? Harrigan answered his own questions: because she wouldn't give you what you wanted. You'd have to believe you had a right to it; so much so that you hated her enough to want to kill her when she wouldn't give it to you.

It was still all speculation; nothing but shadows and guesswork. Time for home and sanctuary, Harrigan thought, negotiating the gridlock of Sydney's commuter traffic.

Grace had cooked dinner; the smell of the food greeted him when he opened the door. He kissed her and picked up Ellie. It was like walking into comfort. Then Grace slipped away from him back to the stove.

'Hungry?' she asked.

'Yeah.'

He couldn't judge her mood. She did things too carefully, put plates on the table as if they might break as she set them down. Was too quiet, too patient, with Ellie, her eyes excluding anything else as she helped her to eat, as if there was only the spoon and her daughter's mouth. Ellie's small fingers shredded still further the pieces of fish Grace gave her to eat. Grace wiped her fingers clean with a smile but still seemed distant. When she talked to him, she was trying hard to pay attention. The food was good, very good; but her mind was not there.

'What's up, babe?' he asked when Ellie was in bed and they were alone.

'Just work,' she said, the way she always did.

She turned away, got up from the table and was gone again into wherever she was in her head. He watched her clear the dishes away and tidy the kitchen. She smiled at him and went into the lounge. Soon after, music filled the room. She appeared in the doorway.

'What is it?' he asked.

'Do you want to dance? Come on. Let's dance.'

'Now?'

'Yeah. Why not?'

'Okay,' he said.

In the living room, he slipped his arms around her and they danced to the slow music. She seemed to need it, to relax against him. She was slender and her body was warm in his arms.

'What's the music?' he asked.

'Art Tatum with Benny Carter.'

She often played these musicians.

'It's good,' he said.

'It's wonderful.'

He held her a little closer.

'What do people say about us?' she asked.

'I don't know and I don't care,' he replied. 'People will say anything. It's meaningless.'

She smiled and seemed to come back to him. There was just the moment, the clean and beautiful music. In his mind, he had a fence around this space, one no one else could break through. Outside of it, everything dissolved as being neither here nor there, almost not in existence. This was the centre of things, here. Nothing else mattered.

When they went to bed that night, they made love. Later, she slept under the weight of his arm. They had always slept close together. With his other lovers, they had each tended to drift to opposite sides of the bed. Tonight, when they were both in a waiting space where the future was impossible to judge, their presence felt like a refuge for each other and they slept more deeply and peaceably than they could have expected.

15

The next morning in the meeting room, there was a third seat at the table, so far empty.

'Borghini's late,' Clive said.

'The traffic's bad,' Grace replied.

'He'd better be here when Griffin calls.'

Her mobile lay on the table. She stared at it. *I'm drowning in other people's blood and I don't know where any of this is taking me. Everywhere is a dead end.*

'I want some information,' she said.

Clive didn't speak but motioned for her to go on.

'There have been three deaths besides Jirawan's. Everyone we want to talk to gets removed. We might as well be at war —'

'We are at war.'

'I want to know what this operation is really about.'

He leaned too close towards her, the way he always did. 'Are you thinking of bailing out?'

'I didn't say that.'

'This is the crucial phase. I need to know if I can rely on you.'

'Then answer my question,' she said.

'It's very well timed because we're getting to the point where you need to know. Does the Ghost network mean anything to you?'

'No.'

'It's a name we've given to a significant financial brokerage for various criminal and terrorist organisations in the Asia–Pacific region. We don't know if this entity is run by one person or several or the identities of those people involved. They launder and shift very large amounts of funds on a regular basis. Recent investigations have identified Sydney as both a source of funds and a staging post for the network. What information we have suggests the main broker is an Australian. Three months back, we received information from the Thai police that they had established a connection between an import–export business in Bangkok run by a Peter Sanders and that network. At the time Sanders was trying to get out of the business and he approached the police with an offer of information in exchange for protection for him and his family. Shortly after this, he was found murdered and his wife, Jirawan, was missing. Our investigation indicates that his offer was leaked to his murderers. Obviously they had their informants in the police.'

'Why send Jirawan here?' Grace asked. 'Why not just kill her?'

'I think Jon Kidd gave us the answer to that yesterday. Sanders almost certainly owed the network money. They don't like leaving a debt unpaid. Not one that's owed to them.'

'Was she an innocent bystander?'

'She could well have been. There's no indication she was involved in the business. The Sanders import–export business was also associated with Angela and Robert McLeod, entrepreneurs who have done a lot of business in Asia and China over the years. They have many very significant contacts in that part of the world. Sara McLeod is their daughter, which made it very interesting when her name came up yesterday.'

'Are they suspects? Is this network some kind of cartel they're running?'

'Our finance people began checking them out once we were advised of their connection to Sanders. It's early days yet and their business interests are extensive, but our initial analysis is that the main McLeod business is legitimate. As we get more information, we may change our minds. But it may well be the source of the contacts the Ghost network has used in the past to establish itself.'

'The Ghost network is a parasite on their business?'

'Yes. Which makes Sara McLeod's connection even more interesting. She's the link.'

'What role is Griffin playing in this? He keeps talking about his client,' Grace said. 'Does this client actually exist?'

'That's something you have to find out. At the moment, he's shaping up as the central figure in this. We've already searched his unit in Bondi Junction. It's nothing more than a shell. He goes there to sleep and change his clothes probably. He's a very hard man to pin down. He seems to have almost no past and very limited means of support, despite the fact that he obviously has money. You just have to look at his car. All of which makes him a good candidate for our target. What we want now, what's central to the success of this operation, is access to the network's business records. Obviously, they're computer-based. We need to know where they are. Those records are at the centre of this and they're probably the last things we'll find. But somehow we have to get our hands on them. So far, Griffin is our best chance to do that.'

'What about Narelle Wong? Is her family connected?'

'There's no indication of that. But she's a dual citizen. Her ID could be very useful to some other member of the network who wanted to move freely around the Asia–Pacific region, including coming here. She's the perfect victim for that scenario. From what Kidd had to say, it's not the first time the network have supplied their clients with new identities.'

'Who's her boyfriend? Griffin?'

'Possibly. That's something else you have to find out.'

'You haven't told Borghini any of this,' Grace said.

'I will brief him later today, as much as he needs to know. If we can dismantle this network, it will be a significant blow to a number of very dangerous organisations that depend on it for funds.' He leaned forward again. 'I am telling you this on the understanding that you will tell no one whatsoever outside of the operation about it. That means no one.'

'I understand that.'

Briefly they were silent. Then there was a knock on the door and Borghini walked in.

'Morning. Sorry I'm late. I've been working. Check this.'

He tossed on the table a photofit of a big man, roughly dressed, with a hard face and dark hair, followed by a mug shot.

'One Mick Brasi. Standover man for the Ponticellis. You know who they are?'

'Yes, we do,' Clive replied, irritated.

'We got his description from the barmaid at the Royal Hotel. He was seen in the bar just before ten.'

'I saw him arrive,' Grace said. 'He walked in as I walked out. I didn't know him.'

'Just as well. You might have got yourself shot,' Borghini replied unsentimentally.

'Have you picked him up?' Clive asked.

'We're looking for him.'

'Don't pick him up,' Clive ordered.

Borghini sat back in his chair. 'The man's fucking dangerous.'

'Put him under surveillance instead. He may lead us to something.'

'You can get me the manpower first,' Borghini replied. 'The question is, if he did shoot Jacqueline Ryan, what are the Ponticellis doing involved in this?'

'That's what they do. They're for hire,' Grace said. 'Brasi could have shot Arleen McKenzie and Kidd as well. It's their MO.'

'We need to ask if there's more to it than that,' Borghini said to her. 'I think we should discuss it now. If you're out there on the front line, I reckon you need to be bulletproof. Especially with Kidd saying things like you're a puppet to these people. I really didn't like that.'

'Our targets probably see everyone that way.'

That was as much as she wanted to say. At the time, she'd brushed Kidd's comment aside. Think too hard about that kind of statement and she wouldn't be able to do her job.

'Grace is well protected,' Clive said quickly, then changed the subject. 'I have other information we need to discuss first. As of midday yesterday, Sara McLeod and Joel Griffin have been under twenty-four-hour surveillance. The black Porsche is registered in her name to her parents' address. She's the daughter of Angela and Robert McLeod of Palm Beach, which is where Narelle Wong used to go for parties. They're A-list. Their parties include any number of celebrities and media stars.'

'Can we tie Sara McLeod's business to Life's Pleasures?' Grace asked.

'Not without the testimony of the sex workers,' Borghini said, a little red-faced at being rebuffed. 'If they or members of their families are being offered some kind of new life in this country, they won't cooperate with us.'

Just then Grace's phone rang.

'Grace Riordan.'

'Joel here. How are you?'

'Just wonderful,' she said lightly. 'What have you got to tell me?'

'Maybe you'd like to relax a little. How about going on a picnic?'

'Where?'

'Lane Cove National Park. At one this afternoon. I'll be waiting at the Chatswood entrance.'

'Why are we meeting?' she said. 'Are we going to come to an agreement?'

'You wanted to be part of the deal. I'm going to make you an offer. We'll talk about it then.'

The conversation had been broadcast to the room. Borghini was watching her.

'You take fucking care,' he said. 'They mean business.'

Clive glanced at him angrily. 'Dress yourself up,' he said to Grace. 'Make it look like you're trying to attract him. You should be able to do that.'

'Do I need to?'

'He put the possibility forward. Give it some air. You have to be very convincing.'

'I will be.'

Lane Cove National Park was a narrow strip of land on the river of the same name, slender remains of the original forest and shrub lands now surrounded by Sydney's leafy northern suburbs. It was a heavily visited park, and most walking tracks eventually took visitors down to the water. Grace followed the blue Audi along the park's Riverside Drive. She knew before it stopped where they were going. A black Porsche was already parked where Griffin pulled up. A tall, red-haired woman in jeans and a red shirt was waiting near a picnic table. High-heeled sandals made her appear taller than she was. Grace recognised Sara McLeod out of her tracksuit and with her hair loose.

Grace glanced around before getting out of her car. There were walkers nearby, but at a discreet distance, and a cyclist slowly making his way along the road. Against her ribcage, she felt her firearm. She hadn't come here to step into the abyss.

'Who's this?' she asked Griffin.

'This is Sara. My associate. Sara, this is Grace.'

'Yes, I've heard about you,' the woman said. Her look was distant, mocking, even arrogant.

'Let's sit down,' Griffin said. 'Grace has something for sale, but more than that, she wants in.'

'Into what?' Sara said.

They sat at the picnic table where there was a basket waiting. Sara took out a thermos and poured her and Griffin coffee. Grace glanced quickly between them. What was their agenda? Why were they sitting down with her like this? Kidd had vouched for her but was that enough?

'Don't be rude, Sara,' Griffin said with a grin. 'Offer some to Grace.'

'Don't worry about it,' Grace said. 'You were there when Kidd got shot. I saw you.'

Sara laughed as she concentrated on pouring. 'You do have eyes after all.'

Laugh again. Then I'll know it was you laughing on the phone the other night.

'What were you doing there?' Grace asked.

Sara looked up slowly, raising her chin. She stared at Grace with hazel eyes. They were entirely cold, like discs of light shut off from any emotion.

'What's it got to do with you? What were you doing there?'

'I told you,' Griffin said. 'Grace has something to sell. She was trying to sell it to Jon. Weren't you?'

'He didn't want to buy. He didn't even want to talk,' Grace said. 'He just ran.'

'No spine,' Sara said.

'But we do want to talk,' Griffin said. 'And you want in.'

'What does she think "in" is?'

'Money laundering,' Grace said, to be met with silence from both Griffin and Sara. 'That's what this is all about. That's my guess.'

'Is it?' Sara muttered.

'Those sex workers at Life's Pleasures, the ones who don't get paid. Jirawan. If I got a forensic accountant on to that brothel, then that's what they'd find. Money laundering.'

'Then why don't you?' Sara threw at her.

'That depends on what I get offered, doesn't it?'

Sara looked at Grace with cold-eyed contempt, as if it was an affront to share a picnic table with her.

'You're asking a lot, Grace,' Griffin said. 'You're asking my client to trust you.'

'Who is your client? You?'

Sara snorted with contempt.

'Don't be gauche,' Griffin said. 'You don't go around asking other people who their clients are. I'm here to make sure he doesn't have to be bothered with this. If you want him to pay you, you have to respect his privacy.'

'If you're protecting his privacy, what's Sara doing here?'

'I've already told you,' he said with a friendly smile. 'She's my associate.'

'In that case, how do I know who I'm dealing with?' Grace said. 'If you're not the main man, then maybe I'm wasting my time.'

'My client will meet you and deal directly with you when you've proved yourself to him but not before.'

'Why do I need to do that?'

'Because he has no other way of knowing what your bona fides are,' Griffin said. 'It all gets back to what you want. My client can buy your passport and your tape. That's straightforward enough. But you say you want more than that. That complicates things. You have to do something for him if you want to take that next step.'

'That's right,' Sara said. 'He wants this girl. Miss Brainless.'

181

She tossed a photograph of Narelle Wong onto the table, one of the many publicity shots paid for by Mr Wong. Grace picked it up and looked up to see both Griffin and Sara staring at her. No distance in their faces this time. In its place, anticipation and greed.

'If you want this girl, it's going to cost you,' she said.

'You'll get paid,' Sara said. 'The client wants her, the passport and your tape together.'

'If I do this, where does that leave me?'

'In,' Sara said, raising her eyebrows. 'The way you wanted.'

'It's not enough.'

'What do you mean?'

'You're putting me in the position where I take all the risk. I'm the front. I've got nowhere to hide. We've talked a little about what the business is. Before I put myself on the line the way you want me to, I want some guarantees myself. I want to know more.'

Griffin was leaning forward.

'If you agree to this, then I'll do that. I'll talk to you about it myself.'

Sara glanced quickly at him, seemingly a little taken aback.

'When?' Grace said.

'After you make the arrangements and before you pick her up. Here. Tomorrow. We'll have lunch. I'll be waiting for you.' He glanced at Sara. 'Just me and Grace.'

Sara was sitting with a very straight back. Grace looked at her expression and thought she knew what it meant. He's seeing another woman. Doing it to you again.

'Okay,' she said. 'I'll be here.'

'We need to talk about money,' Sara broke in. 'That's why you're here. Because you're the kind of person who can be bought.'

'Careful, Sara,' Griffin said quietly.

'You pay me exactly what I ask for,' Grace said.

'Then tell us how much you want,' Sara replied angrily.

'I'll think about it first. I'm not going to ask for too little. You pay me half before and half afterwards. Now, how do you want this done?'

'Pick her up from her house in Chipping Norton, then drive north,' Sara said. 'There's a service centre on the Newcastle freeway

182

at Jilliby, north of Gosford. Take her there. She'll recognise the car that's going to pick her up. You just have to drop her off.'

'That's a long drive,' Grace said.

'But you're being paid.'

'How do I get her to agree to go with me?'

'She will, believe me,' Sara said. 'Just tell her Elliot wants to see her. Get her to bring her ID with her. Her passport, her credit cards, birth certificate, everything. Tell her to dress down, clothes that can't be traced. Wear something with a hood so she's not easy to recognise. She's not to bring any other clothes or personal effects with her and no mobile under any circumstances. You'll be waiting for her at an agreed location. Don't use a car that can be traced to you. If you have to, tell her you're driving her there because Elliot's going to take her to Coffs Harbour. From there, they're going to fly to Cairns and then Elliot's going to take her by yacht to Hong Kong.'

Grace laughed. 'She's really going to believe that.'

'She'll believe it.' Sara had a dangerous look in her eyes. 'If that girl had a brain cell, it wouldn't just be lonely, it'd be deranged.'

Grace turned to Griffin, remembering Kidd's words: *he goes after any woman he can.* 'Who's Elliot? You? Narelle Wong's the sort of woman you find attractive, is she? Don't you like grown-up women?'

Sara threw the remains of her coffee onto the ground. Griffin glanced quickly at her as if startled. Then he turned back to Grace.

'Why? Are you interested in knowing the sort of woman I'm attracted to?'

'Maybe. Unless you two are an item.'

Sara was looking at Griffin; waiting.

'There's always room for one more,' Griffin said. 'Sara wants what I want. She always has.'

He smiled. Sara's face was expressionless; the kind of mask you use to protect yourself, Grace thought.

'When does this pick-up happen?' she asked.

'As soon as you can organise it.' Sara stood and picked up the basket with the thermos. 'I'm going. You and Joel can work out everything else.'

She walked away, moving jerkily without looking back, got into her black Porsche and was gone quickly, too quickly for the narrow park road.

Griffin watched her go.

'You hurt her feelings,' Grace said.

'Did I?'

'You two are an item.'

He turned back to her, his eyes seeming almost a blank, without emotion. 'Why should you care?'

'Because if you are Elliot, how come Sara hasn't walked out on you?'

'She can't.' He said it matter-of-factly. 'She'll always be there.'

'Why?'

He grinned. 'We've been together since she was fifteen. She's never had sex with anyone else.'

He was boasting. Grace, feeling repulsed inside, laughed. 'You can't know that.'

'Oh, yes, I can. There'll never be anyone else. Not while I'm around.'

'Then that must be true for you as well. She must be your first girlfriend. You're the same age, aren't you?'

'It's never tied me down the way it has her.'

'Where'd you meet her?' Grace asked.

'At a camp she used to go to. As soon as I saw her and found out who she was, I made sure we got together. I knew she'd understand me and could help me.'

'But did you understand and help her?'

'I taught her how to be strong. She didn't know what strength was before she met me.'

'So why does she take it from you? Other women, I mean. I wouldn't.'

'Wouldn't you?' he said. 'Maybe you don't understand what's between us. I've shown her a whole world she would never have known about. She's done things she never would have done but for me.'

'Oh, yeah? And what are they?' she asked with a smile.

Briefly, he was angry. 'Why do you keep talking about her? Let's talk about you and me instead.' He grew calmer. 'You've turned yourself out a bit better today. Better than the nothing clothes you had on yesterday. You're attractive. You should dress better than you do.'

You'll never see me dress the way I like. That happens in my other life.

'Why don't you let your hair out?' he asked.

'Why?'

'I want to see how long it is. Maybe women with long hair attract me.'

Unwillingly, but hiding it, Grace let out her dark brown hair, which slipped onto her shoulders and then down her back. Griffin reached forward to touch it. Instinctively, she drew back.

'You don't want me to do that.'

'You've got a girlfriend. Sara. You've been with her from the beginning. You've just told me I don't know what's between you. That means you'll always go back to her.'

'I thought I'd made it clear that doesn't have anything to do with you and me.'

'Maybe it does for me. Maybe I see myself as special. I'm not the kind of person who shares.'

'You are special. I told you that yesterday. I meant it. When the time comes, it will be just you and me. But right now I want to know what you know.'

He seemed to be searching her face, much as Clive had done earlier that day, looking for something.

'What do you mean by that?' she asked. 'What is it I know?'

'Chris Newell is dead,' he said.

'What?'

'I said, Chris Newell is dead.'

She sat still, unable to speak. She did not feel shock; it was relief so powerful she almost lost her grip on her persona.

'How do you know that?'

'Just take it from me. I've got good contacts, I hear things.'

'How did he die?'

Griffin smiled. 'You don't want to know the answer to that. The best thing for him is that it's over now. Let's just say he paid a debt. I can understand that. I always expect people to pay their debts.

185

You can tell me what it was like to look him in the eyes just before he threw petrol over you. Because he's dead. He can't come after you again.'

She said nothing. Thought: I never have to be afraid of him again.

'Aren't you going to answer me?'

'I wasn't thinking about anything at the time,' she heard herself say. 'It happened too quickly.'

'No. There must be a memory in your head somewhere. Otherwise why were you so frightened of him?'

'I met you to make a deal. We've made a deal and now I'm leaving.'

'Answer my question or there's no deal,' he said.

'I made one with Sara, if not with you.'

'No,' he said. 'I'm the one who calls the shots. If I say it's not on, then that's the end of it. You don't get any cash.'

This time, she was the one searching his face, trying to work out why he was asking her this. He really did want to know. It was the first time he'd shown any genuine emotion. He leaned forward, staring at her, almost impatient, his whole body in the grip of anticipation. She didn't speak.

'Tell me. What did you see?' He was impatient.

Someone unrecognisable. Maybe you could paint those eyes but not describe them.

'Nothing,' she said. 'It was like looking into the dark.'

He sat back, watching her. Disappointment. Then detachment. All at once, she might have been a dressmaker's dummy sitting there.

'You have beautiful hair,' he said in a distant voice. 'It's your hair I'm going to remember.'

'I've got to get going. People will wonder where I am.'

He stood up. Another persona flicked into place, overlaid on the negative he had just shown her. The public Joel Griffin was back.

'I'll hear from you,' he said. 'I'll need bank account details for the payment.'

'I'll get them to you. See you.'

She walked to her car at a normal pace; glanced back to see him watching her; waved in a simple way and drove away, resisting the desire to put her foot down, to speed. She was shaking but she held on. The only thing in her mind was the process of making her way safely through the traffic; it anchored her. She realised she could not tell Paul that Newell was dead. And he was. She was convinced of the truth of Griffin's information. She had walked through a door into the strange taste of freedom, only to have it quickly replaced with the shock of her whole encounter with Griffin.

Her phone rang.

'Your backup has you in view,' Clive said. 'You're not being followed.'

'I'm on my way to the motel.'

'We'll be waiting.'

This time the motel was close to Chatswood shopping centre. Grace parked outside the room. Before she went inside, she put her hair up in a simple knot.

Borghini was waiting with a cup of coffee. 'For you. I reckon you need it. I noticed you like it strong.'

'Thanks,' she said, managing a smile and sitting down. Borghini stood watching her, his hands on his hips.

'You're a brave lady,' he said.

Clive sat in the chair beside her, putting himself between them.

'You did that very well. You held your nerve.'

'Christ,' Borghini said, taking his seat. 'That guy's a fucking murderer!'

'He can lead us to our target,' Clive said.

'And what the fuck is that? What result do you really want?'

'I've brought you into this much more than I would bring most people in. You can repay me by not asking questions like that. I'll tell you what you need to know.'

Grace's hair slipped out of its knot and fell onto her shoulders again. 'Excuse me a moment,' she said.

'You can leave it out,' Clive said.

She didn't answer or even look at him. She went into the bathroom and locked the door behind her. Standing in front of the mirror, she needed to make sure she was really there. She took out her mobile. She wanted to ring Paul. She wanted to say, 'It's me. I'm here.' Instead she put her phone away and redid her hair, then made sure her make-up was in place. The role-playing wasn't over yet. There were hours to go before she went home, when her hair could come down the way she liked it to. No one touches me or my hair but you and Ellie, she said to Paul wherever he was. Then she went outside to get on with her work.

'We have a deal with our targets,' she said, sitting back at the table. 'The question is, do I deliver Narelle Wong?'

'Yes, you do,' Clive said.

'How do we stop her ending up dead?'

'We'll be following you every step of the way.'

'After today, I'm very sure my anonymous caller the other night was Sara McLeod,' Grace said. 'That's a dual connection between this operation and whoever was stalking us. Her and the Ponticellis.'

Borghini was sitting with his arms folded, watching. He leaned forward.

'I know the boss has enemies. I know that includes the Ponticellis. With them, you're dealing with people who don't forget. I was trying to talk to you about this earlier. Is Griffin connected to them? What are his contacts? How did he know Chris Newell was dead? This whole thing smells. We're not playing them. They're playing us. They're drawing you in to delivering this woman but is that going to get us any closer to what we're trying to achieve?' He turned just to Grace. 'They trusted you, the two of them, just like that. Why? Everything Griffin says to you, it's so fucking personal. You're not stalking him. You just told us. They're stalking you.'

'Life's Pleasures,' Grace asked Clive. 'Santos Associates owns it. Have we found out anything else about that company yet?'

'We haven't been able to locate any of its office holders,' he said, 'but given that its main business is money laundering, we're very certain it's part of the Ghost network. Life's Pleasures is still operating but the building went on the market yesterday. As we know, all the income had already been moved offshore.'

'Are they selling up the farm? Leaving the country?' Borghini asked.

'That's a very likely scenario. They're removing all witnesses, liquidating assets. They may well consider Grace to be their puppet, the way Kidd said. But it's still a dangerous situation to have an organisation like Orion investigating them. Their safest course of action is to disappear overseas under assumed identities.'

'Then Mark's right.' Grace was sitting with her arms folded, looking Clive in the eye. 'They have another agenda. We're playing their game.'

'No, they're playing ours.'

'No one's told them that,' Borghini said.

'We're walking into something they've set up,' Grace said. 'We have to ask ourselves what it is. It's my safety on the line.'

'You have every resource I can put out there to rely on,' Clive said. 'The only way we can find out what they're really up to is for you to go in deeper. We will not close down this network until we know its full extent. We don't have anything like that information yet. If Griffin has a fix on you, then maybe he'll reveal his connections. You have to keep getting closer to him. You can't do anything that will make him back off.'

'It's too dangerous,' Borghini said.

'I can do it,' Grace replied.

'I didn't say you couldn't. I'm sure you can. That's not the point.'

'What we do is keep to our plan,' Clive interrupted. 'We plan Grace's next meeting with Griffin.'

'I've got some info first,' Borghini said. 'We've been checking out where Jirawan Sanders was found in Ku-ring-gai Chase. Standard police work but the results are interesting enough.'

'Send me a written report,' Clive said. 'We don't have time for that now.'

Borghini was silenced. Throughout the rest of the meeting he said almost nothing, but Grace saw him watching both her and Clive intently. She wondered if his role as the liaison officer was likely to be terminated soon. She would have kept him on but she had no authority. She reminded herself that she was here because she had made her own decisions and had her own aims in mind. But she would be sorry if Borghini was no longer there. No one else stood up to Clive the way he did. It was a pleasure to watch.

16

Harrigan sat at his desk with his computer on, his window to the net, to the world, open. Spam piled into his in-box: dross, get-rich-quick promises, miracle enhancements and pornography — all of which he erased. Nothing from his mind stalkers, either by email or by phone, which was a relief. Among the rubbish, he saw an email from his retainer with the subject line *Jennifer Shillingworth*.

Her information was that Jennifer Shillingworth was listed as a missing person. She had disappeared early in 1996 when she was seventy-one. She had been booked in for surgery at the Sydney Adventist Hospital in Wahroonga but had never arrived. Her family didn't understand this; she'd been on a waiting list for elective surgery for some time and then suddenly, from somewhere, the money she needed for private surgery had arrived. Jennifer had refused to tell them who her benefactor was and had made her own arrangements to get to the hospital. The morning she left home was the last time anyone had seen her.

Reading this, Harrigan thought how all that had been waiting for Jennifer Shillingworth had been her own death. Someone had bought her information and then removed her in case she made the connections public. Naming the property trust they'd created after her must have been their idea of a joke. The whole story read that way, as the nastiest joke in the world. The timing was interesting: a number of years before anyone had approached Amelie Santos. Probably they had been waiting until the doctor was at her most vulnerable before they acted. All of it spoke of careful, long-term planning.

His retainer had also tracked down the Camp Sunshine charity and Ian Blackmore. He had been a youth worker with the charity until it wound up in 1984. After its demise, Blackmore had worked both here and overseas before reportedly committing suicide eight years ago. His sister, one Liz Brewer, would be happy to talk to Harrigan any time he liked if he wanted to go and see her. She lived in Marsfield.

Mid-morning on a weekday, the drive up to northwest Sydney, past Macquarie University, was fairly plain sailing. The house he was seeking was on a large block where the garden was filled with native trees and shrubs. The woman who let him in was in her mid-fifties, shortish, with highlighted hair and the figure some women acquire after menopause, thickening around the middle. They sat down in a large and comfortable if untidy living room. Around him were the trappings of baby-boomer wealth and the accretions of family history. Photographs of parents, children and grandchildren covered sideboards and shelves.

'I'm very happy to talk to anyone who wants to know about Ian,' she said. 'The police were convinced he committed suicide but I didn't believe that for one moment.'

'I'm assuming there was no body,' he said.

'He walked out of his little rented flat in Cammeray one day and was never seen again.'

There were tears in her eyes.

'Did he have any kind of partner?'

'No, he'd had girlfriends but he'd never settled down. Ian was always restless. You know he was a youth worker at Camp Sunshine. The police received an anonymous complaint that he'd molested some of the boys while he'd been there. It was just rubbish! But there was a lot of detail in the complaint, a lot of names. Whoever was behind it must have been there at some stage. Ian reacted badly, got very upset. Camp Sunshine had meant a great deal to him. There was a note in his flat that said he couldn't deal with the accusations. I told the police that suicide was against everything he'd ever believed in. Apart from that, the complaint had only just been made. You wouldn't commit suicide straight off. You'd fight it. They wouldn't listen to me. They'd finished their investigation and that was that. That's us over there.'

She nodded to a photograph on the wall. An enlarged black and white picture of two broadly smiling teenagers holding a banner, *Stop killing children*, against the backdrop of a milling crowd, many carrying placards: *Stop the War*.

'The May moratorium. You know, in 1970, the protest against the Vietnam War,' she said. 'I was nineteen and Ian was seventeen. That was the most amazing day. He was so idealistic. I just can't see him killing himself.'

'Can you tell me much about Camp Sunshine?' Harrigan asked.

'I actually know quite a lot about it. I used to work there with Ian in the early years. I thought you might want to look at these. Ian kept a lot of his own records, photograph albums, that kind of thing. I got them out for you.'

She had laid out a large number of albums, boxes of documents and folders on the table for him to see; presented them to him almost eagerly.

'That's a lot of information,' Harrigan said. 'What did the camp do?'

'Offered activities to underprivileged children, boys and girls, over the summer break. They ran from 1974 to 1983 when the charity closed. Ian was very upset when it happened. One day it was business as normal, and the next day they were shutting the doors.'

'I'm really interested in just one resident. A boy called Craig Wells. He would have been there probably 1980 or '81.'

'I don't know the name. That was after I stopped going. I had my family by then, I didn't have the time any more. But the photographs are basically in chronological order. There might be a picture of him.'

Harrigan flicked through yellowing pictures of people otherwise unknown, of interest only to those who had been there with them. All were captioned in amateurish typescript with names and dates. No sign of Craig Wells. Then he came across a picture of a boy of perhaps fifteen or sixteen, sitting by himself and smiling uncertainly at the camera. The caption read: *Joel, 1980*.

'Who's this?' Harrigan asked.

'Joel,' she said, adjusting her glasses. 'Yes, I think there's a note from him to Ian. Just a moment. Here it is.'

She handed Harrigan a letter from a Joel Griffin, a single page written in almost childish handwriting. The date was December 1981, the address a unit in the inner city. A small collection of facts. He was enjoying his job working for a wholesale stationers. His mother was at a new nursing home, Avondale in Burwood, and showing signs of improvement. He was still seeing Sara. She was helping him out with getting his teeth fixed, which was making a big difference to him.

Harrigan looked back at the photograph. Under the yellowing tinge, he saw a small, slight, hunched teenager with dark eyes and light-coloured hair. His chest was thin under his T-shirt, his expression inward-looking, deeply sad. It was difficult to see him growing into the Joel Griffin he'd met.

'Is there a list of who else would have been with him at the camp?' Harrigan asked.

She was pleased to help. 'Definitely. Ian kept that sort of thing. They're in this box.'

He scanned a handwritten list of names, addresses and ages. Craig Wells was there, the Concord address beside his name. Written in red in the margin next to this were the words *Sent home*. Harrigan found Joel Griffin's name. Next to it was a pencilled note and a date from eight years back: *Parramatta Court House. Midday*. Harrigan looked up and down the list. Several of the names had similar notes beside them: a date with a time and place.

'What do these mean?' he asked.

'That's Ian,' she said with a sad smile. 'He kept up with the kids after they left the camps. A lot of them did quite well and he always felt it was the camps that had given them the edge, particularly the ones who came back each year. He always wanted to know what they were doing with themselves.'

'From this it looks like he made appointments to see them.'

'He did. He'd ring or write to ask if they wanted to go to lunch or have a drink sometime. You know, he got letters from people years after the camps finished.'

'It looks like he met Joel Griffin at Parramatta Court House. Did he talk to you about that?' Harrigan asked.

'I don't think so. I don't think he could have kept that appointment. That's when he disappeared. So I guess he never turned up.'

'Did you show these records to the police?'

She looked at him angrily, with tears in her eyes. 'They weren't interested. How could any of this Camp Sunshine stuff be relevant? Never mind about that complaint!'

'Do you know this Sara that Griffin talks about? The letter seems to indicate your brother knew her.'

'The only Sara I knew was Sara McLeod,' she replied, raising her eyebrows. 'Her parents were the main donors to the charity. They were absolutely filthy rich, they had this huge house at Palm Beach. They're the ones who pulled the plug. She used to come to the camps.'

'Why? She can't have been underprivileged.'

She shrugged, a sarcastic expression on her face. 'No, she wasn't. But when your main donor rings up and says he wants his daughter to go to the camp he's financing, you don't say no. I think her parents sent her there to get her out of their hair. They didn't seem to care what happened to her. One year when I was there, everyone else had left but her. All these underprivileged children had either been picked up or taken to the railway station. Not her. Her mother was supposed to come and get her and she'd forgotten all about it. I can still see her just sitting there, this gangly twelve-year-old looking so alone and unhappy. In the end, we drove her. I remember when we dropped her off, Ian asked her if her parents were home and she said probably not, they often went away for days. I think they just left her.'

'What kind of a girl was she?'

'A deliberate troublemaker. She'd go out of her way to spoil things for everybody else. Some of the things she did were really cruel. She told one boy once she'd heard his grandmother was dead. His grandmother was the only relative this boy had in the world. He was crying his eyes out and she was just laughing at him. Ian used to spend a lot of his time neutralising her effect. The problem was, he couldn't send her home. Her parents sent her to Camp Sunshine every year and they made it clear they didn't want her coming back until the camp was finished. I think it was because they didn't have to pay for anything. Camp Sunshine was only ever a tax deduction for them. The way I see it, she took everything out on everyone around her. She wanted everyone to be as unhappy as she was.'

'But she took up with this boy Joel, whoever he was.'

'It does seem that way. That's a bit odd, knowing the sort of girl she was.'

'Are there any pictures of her?'

'No. Ian deliberately didn't take any.'

'Do you know what colour hair she had?'

'It was red, quite striking. She was an attractive girl. It was a pity she was the way she was,' she said. 'Why?'

'Just a question. Do you have any idea why the McLeods pulled the plug on Camp Sunshine?'

'We were told they were going overseas, all of them, including Sara, and they just wouldn't be continuing.' She shrugged. 'I guess that's what they did.'

'I know you say your brother would never have committed suicide,' Harrigan said, 'but how do you explain the note he left?'

'I don't think he wrote it.'

As a police officer, Harrigan had heard this kind of denial from any number of grieving relatives or partners.

'Why do you say that?'

'It wasn't handwritten. It came off his computer, or *a* computer. That's another detail no one bothered to check. All he did was sign it.'

'That doesn't mean he didn't write it.'

'If he'd handwritten it, maybe I'd believe it. I just don't believe Ian would turn on his computer to write a note like that. He would have picked up the nearest sheet of paper. Can I show you something?'

'Sure.'

She took him outside, to a silky oak that was growing in the back garden. Attached to the trunk was a plaque with a picture of a smiling, forty-something Ian Blackmore set in it. The inscription read: *Ian. Always in our hearts, now and forever.*

'I planted this for him when the police closed the case,' Liz Brewer said. 'I'm sure he's dead, I've accepted that. I know if he was alive he would have contacted me. But I just want to know what happened to him and where he is now. I'd give him a proper burial if only I knew where he was.'

She leaned against the tree and wept. Harrigan briefly wondered if he should put his hand on her shoulder, and decided not to. Don't intrude, it's her grief. He was back to being the policeman again, watching from a distance because it was the only way to function.

'Excuse me,' she said.

'Don't worry about it. Let's go inside.'

Inside, she washed her face and then offered him coffee.

'No, thanks, I'm fine,' he said. 'Would you let me take this photograph of Joel and his letter away? I promise you, you'll get them back safe and sound.'

'Do you think you can find Ian?'

'I don't know,' he said, 'but I can try. If you've got a picture of him as well, that would help.'

'All right.' She had more tears in her eyes. 'If you can find him, that will be enough for me. It's certainly worth a couple of photographs and a letter.'

These things broke your heart, Harrigan thought. Where would a body be after eight years? Rotting in the bush somewhere? Dumped out at sea? How could he hope to find it?

The second half of his day, after a few phone calls, took him from north to south, to the inner west, Burwood, to Avondale Nursing Home. The sign outside the former late Victorian mansion announced that it was a high care and dementia care nursing home with over thirty years' experience. He walked inside to the reception desk. The air was warm, almost a little steamy. There was a smell of food and, underneath it, urine and faeces.

'Can I help?' the receptionist asked, a middle-aged woman with glasses.

'I rang earlier,' he said. 'About a Mrs Griffin. The director of nursing agreed to see me.'

'I'll just take you through.'

The director greeted him with a handshake. She was a younger, dark-haired woman.

'I'm Hilary Totaro,' she said. 'You were asking about Loretta. Would you like to tell me why?'

'As you can see from my card, I'm a consultant. If Mrs Griffin is who I think she is, my current assignment has led me to believe that her son may be dead.'

'I don't think that news will have much effect on Loretta. What was this son's name?'

'Joel.'

'I'll take you to meet her. Then you'll know what I'm talking about.'

Loretta Griffin was a tiny, birdlike woman strapped in her wheelchair. Her hair was white and thin like a child's, sparse against her pink scalp. She was being fed by a nurse's aide and looked around vacantly after each mouthful. Her hands bunched and unbunched as she ate and her feet were twisted on the wheelchair's footrests. There was a terrible scar across her head, clearly visible under her thin hair.

'Hello, Loretta. How are you today?' Hilary said.

The woman turned to her with huge staring eyes, still eating but not speaking.

'She's got a good appetite today,' said the nurse's aide, glancing at Harrigan.

'That's good. All right, Loretta. See you later now.'

They walked away.

'Can she talk?' Harrigan asked.

'A little bit. There was no point in introducing you,' Hilary said. 'She won't know who you are.'

'My information is she's been here since 1981. What happened to her?'

'That's true. She's seen out three directors of nursing and one change of ownership. Actually she's been in homes for longer than that. Her story's on the public record so it won't matter if I tell you. Her husband took an iron bar to her one night in 1977. She has irreversible brain damage. She's been like that since she was thirty-five.'

Harrigan almost said, what kind of a life is that, when he thought about his son. Toby had a mind. A mind can take you anywhere.

'I have a letter from the son dated 1981 where he says he thinks she's showing signs of improvement,' he said.

'That would have been a very vain hope even then. Do you know what this son looks like?'

'I've got one old photograph.'

She looked at it for some moments. 'I think this is him,' she said. 'We'll go to Loretta's room. It's just down here.'

It was a brightly decorated room, with soft toys on the shelves and a television set facing the bed.

'Does she watch TV?'

'She seems to. There are things she gets pleasure out of. This is her Joel.'

It was a picture taken at a Christmas party, a younger version of the same woman with her son next to her. The years had been stripped away from her in this photograph but in actuality she appeared no different from the way she was now, still strapped in her chair. A teenage boy, the same one as in Ian Blackmore's photograph, was sitting beside her and holding her hand. Seated next to him was an attractive, red-haired girl. Harrigan turned the photograph over. *Mum, me and Sara, 1981*, written in the same childish handwriting as the letter.

'Do you know the last time he visited her?' he asked, knowing the answer.

'No one I know has seen him here. Loretta hasn't had any visitors since I've been here and that's five years now. This was a long time ago. For all I know it was the last Christmas he spent with her.'

'I think it probably was,' Harrigan replied. 'Last question. Do you know her husband's name?'

'No. But apparently he was tried and convicted of attempted murder so there must be a record of it somewhere. I guess he's out of gaol by now. You'd have to say he wasn't the one who got the life sentence.'

'Thank you for your information. You've been very helpful.'

'I'm sorry to hear her son is dead. He might have been someone to visit her.'

Harrigan, used to the kinds of assumptions people made about Toby, particularly when he had been growing up, could not bring himself to make a judgement on the nature of Loretta Griffin's life. Maybe the physical comfort and care were enough for her. Who knew? It wasn't a question he wanted to answer.

He drove home, caught in his thoughts, and went up to his study. There he opened his wallet, took out Joel Griffin's card and placed it on his desk. Then he googled Griffin's name, the date of Blackmore's meeting with him eight years ago and Parramatta Court House. A courtroom was a public place; a trial was always on the public record. The information came up, not from the legal databases but on the national broadcaster, a late night program canvassing the subject of the Sydney crime world. On that date, a small-time thief associated with a particular criminal organisation was being defended by Joel Griffin on a charge of attempted murder. The trial had been complex and had gone on for a number of weeks. The man had been acquitted but later ended up dead as part of a gang war. The broadcaster had been speculating on the lines of influence operating in that same war.

These details relating to Griffin's client weren't relevant to Harrigan's current investigation. But the item did prove that Joel Griffin had been at Parramatta Court House the day Ian Blackmore had disappeared; the day Blackmore had supposedly been intending to meet him there. What if one day Blackmore had been reading the paper and spotted Griffin's name? This trial was the kind of item to make it to the newspaper, even if just in brief. According to his sister, Blackmore would have tried to get in touch with Griffin, probably immediately, to see if he was the same Joel Griffin he'd known at Camp Sunshine.

Blackmore had known both Craig Wells and the real Joel Griffin. If you were ruthless enough, it wouldn't be too hard to force a man into signing his own suicide note. One way to keep a busy police force at bay. Particularly if you had already concocted an accusation of child molestation. There was just enough time here for someone to have done that. Someone moving quickly against an unexpected threat.

Blackmore was dead, he had to be. Probably murdered the very night he'd gone missing. But someone had still put his name to the bottom of a letter to Frank Wells, just as someone had appropriated Jennifer Shillingworth's name for a property trust. Ghosts, both of them, made use of by someone with a nasty sense of humour. Just as Joel Griffin, on the basis of everything Harrigan had encountered to date, had to be a ghost as well.

Sara McLeod had been an attractive redhead. Was she also Nadine Patterson? Two ruthless people working together. That would be a formidable combination, one any person with a sense of self-preservation would avoid. Harrigan put Griffin's card away. He wasn't staying out of their way. He was coming for them. He just had to keep pushing for some more information, something that would bring some provable facts out of the shadows. Something that wasn't just his own speculation, however compelling that speculation was. So far all he had was guesswork. He locked his gun away and left to collect his daughter.

That night, the three of them had what was almost a normal evening. As always, Grace cooked; she liked to cook, it relaxed her, she said. Ellie was in a happy mood, absorbed in her own play. Harrigan felt it as someone might feel an Indian summer, that interval of warm sunshine before the weather turns bad. It was enough for the moment. In life you should take what's given to you, because you never know when you might lose it. He had learnt that lesson too often in his own life to let anything of value slip past him. Although neither could tell the other what they'd done with their day, they still seemed to understand each other past the need for words.

Tomorrow night was his book launch. He had dedicated his book to her. Until recently, his life had seemed a gift and this was his small way of acknowledging it to her. He asked if she would be there. She smiled.

'Of course I will. It's special.'

'Just a book. Just my rantings about how the system doesn't work.'

'No. It's special.'

She was asleep before he came to bed. After this quiet evening, her face was still drawn and pale. Again they slept, waiting for the next step in the dance.

17

At Chipping Norton, Duncan Wong was again the one who opened the door to Grace.

'We weren't expecting you to come back,' he said. 'Have you got any news? Narelle still won't talk to us.'

'No, I don't, I'm sorry. This is more about seeing how you've all been getting on. Has Narelle been out at all?'

'Once or twice with Dad. Mum doesn't want to talk to her.'

'Can I see her?'

'If she'll let you in.'

This time when Grace knocked on Narelle's door, it was opened almost too quickly. Narelle stood there looking pleased with herself. Her brother had already walked away.

'Yeah, I'll talk to you,' she said.

The room was as stuffy as the first time Grace had been in there. There was a carton of cigarettes on the table and a full ashtray. The smell of stale cigarette smoke had grown stronger. Narelle had freshened herself up and was wearing make-up. It made her seem more like a child in dress-up than a young woman in her early twenties. Grace recognised the look: the man you have been praying will call you has finally picked up the phone.

'How are you, Narelle?'

'I'm good.'

Grace saw she was nervous.

'Has anyone been in touch with you lately?'

'I got a message from Elliot.'

'Your boyfriend?'

'Yeah.'

Narelle smiled and took a plain white envelope out of a girlishly pretty china box. Careful about how she handled it, Grace opened it. The note inside was handwritten. *To Marie, Goddess of the Orchids. Grace is coming to see you again very soon, you can trust her. Do what she asks. Burn this. Elliot.*

'Where did you get this?'

'Someone left it at the restaurant. I got one of the waiters to take messages for me.'

A waiter who would now receive a visit from Orion. Grace hoped it wasn't someone who was having trouble with their visa.

'You didn't burn it.'

'I know I was supposed to but I wanted to keep it.'

'That was his name for you. Goddess of the Orchids.'

'He said Narelle didn't suit me, I was more exotic than that. So he got me that flat where I could be what I really was. Like the orchids.'

And you believed him.

'I'll keep this,' Grace said, tucking it away in her bag.

'No, you won't. I want that back!'

'Not if you want a lift somewhere. I'm making sure no one does the dirty on me.'

Narelle bit her lip. 'He wouldn't do that.'

'No, of course he wouldn't. I'm just being careful. The deal is this. Elliot wants to meet with you. You have to get yourself somewhere I can pick you up unnoticed. Any ideas?'

'I'll go to the restaurant. I can park under cover there. There's a shopping mall next door. I'll go through to the mall and meet you in the car park. Is he going to take me somewhere? Did he say?'

'He wants me to take you to a service centre north of Gosford. He's going to pick you up there and drive you to Coffs Harbour and then fly you to Cairns. He said he wants to go to Hong Kong with you by yacht.'

Grace almost blushed saying it. Narelle smiled with innocent delight.

'He talked about doing that. He said I could help him with his business there because I know the language.'

'I'm sure it'll be handy. Have you got a passport and money?'

'Yeah, I've got all that.'

'Bring everything you have that establishes your ID. Your passport, your birth certificate and your driver's licence. You need to dress anonymously, okay? Put on a tracksuit, something with a hood. Make sure no one can recognise you. But don't bring any clothes. Elliot will buy you everything new.'

'Okay. I'll just bring my bag with my make-up and stuff. And my mobile.'

'No, don't bring any of that either. Especially the phone.'

'I need my phone.'

'If you bring it, people might trace you on it,' Grace said.

Narelle nodded. 'He'll buy me a new phone anyway. Something really nice. I am so looking forward to this.'

This was as much as Grace could deal with.

'Tell me about Elliot,' she said. 'What does he look like?'

Narelle smiled and shook her head. 'Oh, no,' she said. 'He told me never to talk about that to anyone. Never tell anyone his last name or anything about him. He has to protect his identity.'

'Then I won't ask. I have to go now. Let's make a time for when I'm going to pick you up. Whatever happens, you have to be there.'

The girl laughed. 'Nothing's going to stop me.'

'You do realise you won't be coming back? Your family will be worried about you and they'll call the police. You realise that as well?'

She shrugged. 'How are they going to find me? They won't be looking for me with you.'

'I guess not. Okay. Tomorrow afternoon at three.'

'I'll be there. This is going to be the longest day in my whole life.'

Grace made the time to talk to Duncan before she left.

'How's it been?'

'She's been locked in her room most of the time. She won't talk to me. Mum won't talk to her. Sometimes she talks to Dad. Then he gets upset and argues with Mum about her. It's horrible being in the house. Is anything going to happen now? It's like we're living in no-man's-land.'

'We're waiting on the results of our investigations. I honestly can't say more than that.'

'If Narelle's not going to be charged with anything, can't we just know that and get on with our lives? Get her to snap out of this?'

'I can't tell you one way or the other what's going to happen. But our first concern in this is for you, your family and your sister. As soon as we can, we'll advise you what the next step is.'

'When hell freezes over.'

'Whether you believe it or not, it's true.'

He only shrugged. 'It'll get worse before it gets better.'

When she drove away from the house, Narelle stayed in her mind like some monstrous, innocent child about to run happily to her own murder. In the present, she had her own encounter with Griffin to go to. Less dangerous than tomorrow's — she hoped — but still unappealing in the extreme.

This time in the Lane Cove National Park there was no black Porsche, just the blue Audi waiting for her. It was a clear autumn day, warm, the sky cloudless. If it hadn't been for whom she had to meet here, it might have been just another day in paradise. Griffin was waiting for her at the picnic table. She had dressed carefully for this meeting, not over the top. She had her hair out; something she hadn't wanted to do but Clive had insisted on it.

Griffin didn't get up; his solidly built figure took up space on the bench. He was dressed casually without a tie and had brought along an *al fresco* meal. Cheese, olives, cold meats, dips, bread and champagne. He poured her a glass when she sat down.

'Have a drink.'

'I don't drink,' she said.

'You can drink just one glass with me.'

'I can't even handle the smell of it.'

'Chris said you used to drink a lot. Is that why you don't drink now?'

'Yes,' she said, seeing no point in any other answer. Then she realised that hearing Newell's name had not affected her. He was a ghost already losing its potency. 'Narelle's all ready to go as planned.'

He brushed this aside. 'I don't want to talk about her. You look very nice. Tasteful. I don't like it when women dress like sluts. I got you this,' he said and handed her an envelope, as if it were a present.

It was a picture of her at nineteen when there was no scar on her neck. She'd had her hair cut short then. Her emotions seemed so close to the surface, her eyes almost raw with feeling. Had she ever been that young? Even though she was laughing, her eyes were so sad. Back then, the only way to deal with grief had been to live constantly in the present. Once this scrap of paper had been part of a photograph of the band, but someone had cut the other musicians away, leaving only her.

'I like the way you look in that photograph. You look very beautiful.'

'There's only one place you could have got this,' she said.

'I took it off Chris. He wasn't going to need it.'

Before or after he died? And why did you need it?

She put the picture back in the envelope and laid it on the table. Griffin picked it up and put it in his pocket. He was staring at her.

'I'm still glad your hair is longer now. Eat something.'

'After you.'

With his eyes still on her, he took a piece of bread and dipped it. She did likewise. He smiled.

'Breaking bread,' he said, still looking at her. 'I wanted us to do that together.'

She ate. Under his gaze, she barely tasted the food. She was trying to pin down the way he was looking at her. His cold blue eyes were staring and intense, they never seemed to leave her face. They frightened her, badly. She might be a professional, an agent who was working, but there was no way around that feeling. *You*, that expression said. An intent aimed very specifically at her.

'We were going to talk business,' she said.

He looked at her with a friendly expression. 'Let's say you've accurately described what this business is. What do you think you can do for us?'

'Don't you think someone in my position could help you out quite a bit?'

'An accountant would be more useful. Law enforcement agencies aren't that hard to avoid if you're careful.'

'You're one step ahead of them, are you?'

'Yes, always. Now if what you're trying is blackmail, that could be very dangerous for you.'

'We're partners already, aren't we?' she said. 'I'm putting my safety on the line for you.'

'And you're being paid for it. I can't use you in the money side of things, you don't have the skills. But I can use you for what you're doing now.'

'What does that mean?'

'Will you trust me?' he asked.

'Why?'

'I will pay you double what you've asked me for, which is a lot of money, if after you pick up Marie tomorrow, you do what I ask you to.'

'Which is?'

'You have to wait until tomorrow to find out. But it'll tell me whether you're genuine or not.'

'I thought you were going to give me more information about the business. That's why I came.'

'And I've asked you to trust me. That's what you have to do first. Now let's talk about something else. I want to know about you. Tell me about your daughter. She's in childcare, isn't she?'

Slowly Grace shook her head.

'No, tell me.'

'Off limits.'

He stopped eating to look at her. 'I want to know.'

'Off limits,' she repeated.

He went back to eating. He was angry by the look of it, although the anger was contained. Grace watched him in silence for some moments.

'What is this meeting really about? Because you keep changing the rules on me.'

'No, Grace. You're the one who keeps changing on me. You're going to become a part of my work. If I can rely on you, you're going to help me fulfil obligations. I wanted to spend a little time with you to work out what sort of person you are.'

'What have you decided?'

'You're very hard to reach. Most people I can persuade to talk about themselves. But not you. That makes you a challenge and I like that, I suppose.' With this, he managed to look up and smile. 'Let's try again. Your daughter. Did you really want to have her or did your partner make you?'

'Why do you want to know?'

'I just want to know if she's important to you.'

Grace decided this question was beyond what could be expected of her. She stopped eating. 'I can't stay. I have to be back at work. People will notice if I'm not on duty.'

She moved away from the table; he followed her and took her arm.

'Why does that offend you so much? Because you don't care about her?'

She pulled away from him. He tightened his grip.

'Let me go,' she said.

He was holding her arm, staring at her. Then, very reluctantly, he loosened his grip.

'Let me kiss you,' he said.

'No.'

'Why not?'

'It's what I told you yesterday. You've already got a girlfriend and I don't share.'

'You will one day. And you'll talk about yourself as well. One day you'll tell me everything I want to know about you.'

'Not today.'

'No, not today. But you will. Maybe tomorrow. You'll see.'

She went to her car without looking back.

Once again she went to the motel at Chatswood. Expecting to find both Clive and Borghini waiting for her, she was surprised to see only Clive.

'He'll be here soon,' he said. 'You handled that well but there are a few things I think you should have done differently. That's why I wanted a word with you in private. Sit down.'

Grace was still feeling the impact of the meeting with Griffin. What she needed was strong coffee and some encouragement, the kind Borghini usually gave her. All at once the room seemed small, even claustrophobic. She took a chair at the table. Clive sat opposite. She felt a creepiness up her backbone.

'There are one or two things.' He was looking at her with an odd expression in those usually expressionless eyes. 'You should have kept Griffin talking for longer than you did and gone a little further. You should have talked about your daughter when he asked you to.'

'I couldn't. Least of all about her.'

'The job requires you to get over that. And if he wanted you to kiss him, I think you should have done that.'

Grace looked him in the eyes. 'I'm not doing this job at the expense of myself,' she said. 'When I'm at work, I'm at work. And when I'm home, that's somewhere else altogether. To me, that's how we handle this. I can't mix the two like that.'

'You need to be able to put your home into a compartment and leave it there. I've decided you have a future with this organisation but that's still something you're going to have to work at.'

Before she could answer, Borghini walked in, slamming the door behind him. He had been part of the backup. He was clearly very angry.

'I'm going to get straight to the point,' he said, sitting down and speaking directly to Clive. 'You're putting too much pressure on Grace. It's all her. You shouldn't be running the operation that way. You should be sharing the load.'

'There are other people involved,' Clive replied angrily. 'There's surveillance, there's finance, there's IT. The police. And there's you.'

'But not on the front line. I don't say Grace doesn't handle it well. She does. But why go to that meeting in the first place?' He turned to Grace. 'I thought that yesterday. It's exposing you too much. You met him on his turf. You shouldn't have done that.

You're the one with the perfect bargaining chip. He wants Narelle. Get him to meet you on your turf. Demand more of him than he's giving you. Let's get back to basics. What's his motive? What is this thing he wants you to do? Shoot Narelle Wong dead for him? We're letting him manipulate us, not the other way around.'

'I haven't asked for your opinion. But now that you've given it, this is a good time to make an announcement,' Clive said to Borghini. 'There's been a change of arrangements. I've asked for you to be replaced as the police liaison officer. You won't be required for this meeting.'

Borghini looked poleaxed. 'Why?'

'I'm finding you obstructive and difficult to deal with. It's my decision who works on this investigation. You can leave. Now.'

Borghini threw up his hands, acknowledging there was no point in arguing, and stood up.

'No.' Grace spoke sharply. 'We need a liaison officer. There's no one here to replace Mark. He can stay until his replacement takes over.'

'I have the authority here,' Clive said.

'Our agreement says it's ultimately my call how I handle the undercover operation within the broad ambit of your directions. He stays until his replacement turns up or I execute my rights under the opt-out clause as of now.'

Clive was expressionless, staring at her. After a few moments, he gestured to Borghini, who sat down at the table again.

'I guess I stay in that case.'

'For now,' Clive said. His cheeks were red and he took a few moments to regain his equilibrium. 'This operation is in the balance. Tomorrow, when you deliver Narelle Wong, we'll have people watching to see who she meets and where she's taken. There'll also be people ready to move in immediately. Now let's have that note you took from her.'

Grace placed the note on the table and watched Clive pick it up. She was wondering what had really been in his mind when he had spoken to her earlier or even if she wanted to know. She knew she didn't want to be in the same room with him by herself. She thought back over other operatives who had worked closely with him. Orion's secrecy meant those operations couldn't be discussed. Small comments, the occasional raised eyebrow, were all she had to go on. Strange vibes and impossible demands were the last thing she wanted to deal with now; the operation was dangerous enough as it was. She was in the balance as well; she hoped Clive had the sense to realise that.

She left the motel with enough time to get home and collect Ellie before they both went to Paul's book launch. Borghini followed her out.

'Thanks for sticking up for me in there,' he said.

'No problem,' she said with a tired smile.

'I've got to say this to you. Your boss has lost sight of what this is really about. You know what he's doing? He's watching you. I don't know why but he's fixed on you and he's putting you in danger. The first rule for any operation like this is that you protect your undercover officers as much as you can. But he's putting you and this Griffin together and he's watching you. I think he's getting a kick out of it.'

Grace didn't want to think about this.

'The way things are set up I don't see how I can back out now,' she said. 'Not until after tomorrow.'

Borghini looked back at the motel room, frowning. 'After today, I'm not supposed to be involved any more. Jesus.' He looked down at his feet. Grace couldn't quite understand what was in his mind. 'Give the boss my regards,' he said. 'He's a decent man. He's always done the right thing by me.'

Then he was gone, driving away into the afternoon traffic.

Grace got into her car. She held on to the fact that no one could stop her from walking away if she chose to. With a bit of luck, this would all be done with in twenty-four hours. Or she would have done all she could do and would have no choice but to bail out. Assuming nothing happened to her first.

18

Harrigan's retainer had emailed him a cache of information regarding Amelie Santos. She had found the private sanatorium in the Southern Highlands where Frank Wells had been born. Now closed, it had been famous, or infamous, in its day as a place where those who could afford it sent their daughters to have their illegitimate children out of anyone's way. It had also offered a nursemaid service that cared for the babies until they were adopted out. The sanatorium had become a private psychiatric clinic in the 1970s and then gone out of business in the early '80s. When the building was sold, the records had been sent to a social research archive in Canberra. While the hospital's medical information had been destroyed long ago, its administrative records were available to researchers and a number of articles had been written about its history.

The dates of Amelie Santos's admittance and discharge had been recorded in one of the hospital's registers. She had arrived on a Monday morning and left four days later. A note next to her discharge read: *By taxi to station 11 am. Parents will meet at Central.* Harrigan's research assistant had added the information that Amelie was most likely shielded during the birth. According to the testimony of several women who had given birth there — now mostly in their sixties or seventies, one in her eighties — a screen had been placed in front of their faces, and one remembered being blindfolded. Amelie Santos might never have seen Frank, let alone held him. Only heard him before he was taken away.

Harrigan emailed back the name Loretta Griffin and the date 1977. A brutal attempted murder, the husband convicted and gaoled. There'd been a son by the name of Joel, by the look of it an only child. Any information she could find on any of them.

In the meantime, he'd been doing his own research into the Shillingworth Trust. The details were much as Lambert had already told him: a discretionary property trust with Tate and Patterson as its trustees and the beneficiary an otherwise unrelated company called Cheshire Nominees. The names of the company's office holders were unknown to him, and he suspected that if he investigated them they would prove to be untraceable. The contents of the trust's property portfolio were also no surprise. Among a number of commercial and residential properties, it included Fairview Mansions, the Blackheath house and Amelie Santos's two other former properties at Duffys Forest and North Turramurra. Many of the properties were in less desirable parts of the city, leading Harrigan to speculate that the portfolio was a dump for dirty money. Distribute the management of properties among a range of agents and who would bother putting the pieces together?

Valuable information but still nothing to link his investigations to Joel Griffin or Sara McLeod. Shillingworth Trust must have bought the latter two properties when Medicine International sold them on. But why? What was so special about owning them that you'd go to all that trouble? If the trustees had a use for them, then he needed to find out what it was.

He checked the time and closed down his laptop. It was getting on and he had a long drive in front of him.

Duffys Forest, on the northern edge of the metropolis, was a part of Sydney Harrigan rarely visited. His travels north usually took him in a direction more to the west, on the freeway across the Hawkesbury River to the Central Coast, where Grace's father lived in retirement and her brother and his wife ran a restaurant. This far-flung piece of Sydney suburbia, like its next-door neighbour Terrey Hills, was a peninsula in the bush, surrounded on three sides by the Ku-ring-gai Chase National Park. It was almost rural, a home to riding schools and properties offering stabling and agistment for the much-loved horses of teenage girls. The blocks of land were large and still partially bush-covered; trees and scrub lined the narrow roads. He passed plant nurseries, a golf club, Buddhist temples, private schools and a gun club.

Like the house at Blackheath, the property he was seeking had a *For Sale* sign out the front. Inspections by appointment; price on application. The house was on the southwestern edge of the suburb at a lower level than the street, and apparently reached by a long driveway. A thick line of trees on the boundary, surrounded by a cyclone-wire fence, isolated it from the road. Entrance to the driveway was through a high, locked Colorbond gate. The other houses roundabout were not much different, with the occupiers clearly valuing their privacy. Ignoring your neighbours would be easy in this place.

Harrigan decided to risk it. He parked at a distance past the driveway where he would be out of sight of anyone arriving at the house. As well as being armed, he had brought along a few tools in case he needed to do some breaking and entering. He tossed his backpack over his shoulder and made his way towards the house, approaching it from the side via the next-door neighbour's block of land. Their only front fence was a low wooden affair, while their house, which was built on higher ground, was some distance away and also surrounded by trees.

He followed the cyclone fence down a slope to the park boundary where the fencing stopped and the trees merged into the national park. He pushed through the scrub to the edge of an open grassy area at the back of the house. It was an older brick building, possibly dating back to the 1950s, and sprawled over the grounds. The grass near the back door had been kept mowed but the rest of the garden had been left to itself. Rusted white garden furniture was scattered among areas of taller grass and shrubs. A pair of brightly coloured crimson rosellas was bathing in an ancient stone birdbath filled after recent rain. It could not have been more peaceful.

Beside the house was a large garage of the same vintage. Readying for a stint of housebreaking, Harrigan pulled on a pair of

214

disposable gloves. He didn't approach the house directly but stayed out of sight, moving through the trees on the boundary till he was close to the back of the garage where there was a door. He tried it and it opened. Inside there was space for at least two cars but at present none were there. Most likely, no one was home. Life without a car would be impossible out here.

There was no way into the house through the garage and Harrigan went out the way he had come in. Between the house and the garage was a cement pathway which had been kept reasonably clear. A high gate between the garage and the front corner of the house blocked the view to the road. He opened the gate and looked up the length of the empty gravel driveway to the locked gate. Again, there was no sign of anyone being here.

He went to the back door. It was secured by a deadlock, newer and much stronger than the old lock on the house at Blackheath. He didn't attempt to break it, but walked along the back of the house, turning a corner, until he was looking at a small high window. It was the kind that winds open outwards and was just large enough to let him into the house. He dragged over one of the garden chairs and stood on it, finding himself looking into the laundry. There was a window lock on the inside, but the wooden window frame was rotten, the white paint peeling away. Whoever owned this house now wasn't concerned with maintenance. He took a jemmy out of his backpack and began to force the window open. The rotten wood tore away, the glass cracked. All that was left was a section of the window frame, still secured in place by the window lock.

Harrigan lowered the barely intact, broken window to the ground. Soon he was letting himself down into dry, old-fashioned, twin laundry tubs. By the look of the room, no one had washed any clothes in here for a long time. The door was shut. He took out his gun and tried the handle cautiously. It was locked but the lock was old-fashioned and easy enough to pick. Soon he stepped into a small hallway leading to the back door. The house was completely silent. He walked through into the kitchen.

Unlike the house at Blackheath, this place was both liveable and lived in. It looked and smelled clean, although nothing appeared to have been upgraded from Amelie Santos's time. The fridge was old enough to date back to the 1960s. He opened it and saw some basic food and a bottle of wine stored inside. Washed dishes, including two wine glasses, stood in the dish rack on the draining board. They were dry and had been for some time.

Listening for every sound, Harrigan moved from the kitchen into a dining room. There was no sign of anyone using this room. He opened a top drawer in the sideboard. Tablecloths, linen serviettes, place mats. In the next drawer, silver cutlery. Someone was using the house, but all they had done was move in on top of what was already here without changing anything. They ate and possibly worked and slept here, but it was no home.

He went through to the living room, where the windows looked out onto the front garden. Thickish, good-quality net curtains, now grey with dust, covered these windows. The room was shadowed but not so dark that it was difficult to see. In here, there was an atmosphere of complete abandonment. On a cabinet stood a photograph of Amelie Santos, probably from when she was in her early forties. She was dressed to ride, her cheek pressed up against her horse's. Her smile was one of real happiness. Scrawled across the picture were the words *Buster and me*. It was covered in dust. Placed here more than fifty years ago, now meaningless to anyone and presumably ignored by whoever still came here.

Moving carefully, Harrigan walked down a hallway past several bedrooms. A quick glance into one of them told him that two people slept in one bed. It had been left unmade, the doona tossed back, the sheets disordered. A change of clothes for both a man and a woman were thrown over a chair. On the end of the bed there was a compact bundle of women's clothes, a dress and underwear, all carefully folded.

Something about them caught his attention and he walked in to look at them more closely. He realised they were new, still folded as if they had just come out of their package. Waiting for someone to put them on for the first time. He found himself thinking of the woman who might wear them. The sight of them disturbed him, but why he couldn't say. He looked around the bedroom. It had a stale smell. He left the clothes where they were and walked out.

The bathroom, like the rest of the house, was clean and useable. The make-up and the electric razor on the vanity unit showed that both a man and a woman had washed there, although perhaps not that morning. He went back outside. There was a set of double doors next to the bathroom. He opened them and found himself looking into a large linen cupboard, an old-fashioned one, the kind you could step inside. The sheets and towels must have dated back to Amelie Santos's time. He glanced up. There was a manhole cover above his head. He closed the doors and moved on.

Then he smelled something: bleach. A little further past the bathroom was what appeared to be the fourth bedroom. There was an outside lock on the door and fittings for a padlock. He opened it. The room was shadowed and it was only possible to see by the light that came through the doorway. It was a small, bare room with white-tiled walls. There had once been a window but it was boarded over. There was nothing in there except a cheap two-litre plastic container of hospital-grade bleach against one wall. It was a secure room. The whole house was built of double brick and the door was thick wood. A place to wait until someone came for you.

He stepped inside to look more carefully. The room had a foul atmosphere. He looked down at the floor, which was bare wood. The boards were stained with patches of liquid discoloration. He squatted down to look at them more closely. You'd need a chemical analysis to know what had caused those markings.

Harrigan was staring at the floor when he saw a hairline cut in one of the boards close to the door. At the threshold to the room, he saw a notch in the same floorboard, just large enough for someone to get their finger into. You could only reach it when the door was open. Glanced at quickly, it looked like a natural flaw in one of the boards.

He levered it up and found himself looking into a cavity under the floor. He took his torch out of his backpack and shone it into the hole. There was a black bag inside, the kind used for carrying a laptop computer. He reached in and pulled it out. Beneath it was a briefcase. Harrigan took this out as well. Then he replaced the floorboard and carried both back into the living room where he placed them on the coffee table.

There were two main compartments to the black bag, each holding a slender laptop. Other smaller compartments had a range of portable hard drives and a number of flash drives. He took them out and looked them over. Each was labelled with a letter but there was no sign of any written records. He opened one of the laptops and turned it on. It asked for a password. Harrigan sat thinking. He typed in *Griffin* but the system responded with the message *Details unknown*. He turned the laptop off and closed it.

The briefcase was locked and there was no way he could guess the combination. He forced it open, pretty much destroying it in the process, to find it packed with neat bricks of American dollar bills. He took them out one by one and counted them. Used hundreds and fifties. Quite a nest egg. You could live very well anywhere in the world on this, for quite some time.

Harrigan suddenly realised that he was so absorbed in looking at these things, anyone could have walked up to him unnoticed. He looked up quickly but there was no one there. The room was empty. What to do with what he'd found? He put the laptops and portable drives back into the black bag and closed the briefcase again as best he could. He had already disturbed the chain of evidence. Assuming he was prepared to admit that he'd broken in here, it could be argued by a defence counsel that he'd compromised what was there, even planted these things. If he took them with him, it was theft.

He thought for a few moments and got to his feet. Collecting a chair from the dining room, he took it down to the linen cupboard where he stood on it and pushed open the manhole cover. Then, one after the other, he pushed the black bag and the briefcase as far into the roof cavity as possible. Let them wonder where they were.

He had closed the cupboard doors and was standing with the chair in his hand when he realised that he'd left the door to the white-tiled room open. He went to close it, stopping to look at the empty room in front of him. People had almost certainly died in there. Killers kept souvenirs. Who knew what else there was in this house? It was getting to the point where he would have to take his information to the police, regardless of what Orion would do.

He closed and was able to relock the laundry door. Once

outside, he wedged the broken window back into place as best he could. Then he returned the chair to its place in the overgrown garden. Judging by the length of the grass, nobody came out here very much. Probably they wouldn't notice that the chair had been moved. Not until they discovered what was missing and began to look around.

The sun was warm and the overgrown garden, with its sounds of bird calls and a soft wind in the trees, seemed dreamlike in its peaceful, bright greenness. Shillingworth Trust was using this house as a bolt hole. It was a good place to be if you didn't want anyone looking over your shoulder. Or if there was someone in the white-tiled room you wanted to attend to. Given the amount of money in that briefcase, someone would be back here for it soon enough. The best outcome would be if the police were waiting for them when they got here.

There was one last place for him to go: the surgery at Turramurra. He would do that tomorrow morning. Then he would call the police, regardless of Orion's protocol. Would twenty-four hours make much difference? He could only hope it wouldn't.

Now he had to get back home himself. He had his book launch to go to.

He was driving down Mona Vale Road when his mobile rang.

'Harrigan? It's Eddie.'

Good, Harrigan thought. Contacting Eddie Grippo had been next on his list of things to do.

'What's the word?'

'That place you were asking about the other day, Fairview Mansions. It's being sold. Went on the market yesterday.'

'Who are you dealing with?'

'Some lawyer called Joel Griffin.'

'Do you know him?' Harrigan asked.

'He's done work for the family in the past. That's all I know about him.'

'Any other news?'

'No, that's it.'

'I want to see you,' Harrigan said.

'Shit, mate. If anyone sees me with you, I'm fucking dead.'

'Tomorrow morning at nine. There's a hotel in Tempe, the Royal Exchange. I'll be waiting for you in the back room. Don't worry, it's private. No one will see you there.'

'I've got to work.'

'I've got things to do too, mate. Be there. I'll be waiting.'

By the time he got home, Grace was there with Ellie, changed and ready to go. His daughter ran to him as usual and he swung her up in his arms.

'She's had her dinner,' Grace said, 'and Kidz Corner made sure she had an extra nap this afternoon. We'll see how she goes tonight. I've got her dressed in her party frock. Doesn't she look pretty?'

Grace looked tired but the smile was real. She had on a light dusting of make-up and her hair was brushed out. She had dressed herself as she did whenever they went out, with a touch of style, colours that showed the delicacy of her skin.

'*You* look lovely,' he said.

'It's a special night.'

They arrived a little later than he had expected. When they walked into the Police Museum, the room was already crowded. Toby was there with his therapist and two friends from university. Harrigan went to speak to him. *Hi Dad*. Silent words as usual but words nonetheless. His friends, two young women, smilingly shook Harrigan's hand.

'Tobes has told us so much about you,' one of them said.

Tobes. He hadn't known his son had this nickname.

'I didn't know he talked about me.'

'Oh, yeah. All the time.'

Grace kissed Toby on the cheek and stayed to talk while Harrigan had to mingle. He looked back at them through the crowd. Ellie was in her mother's arms while Grace stood chatting with Toby and his friends. There was a burst of laughter over something. Don't ever let anything happen to any of you.

The crowd grew larger. Drinks and finger food were being handed around. Representatives from the publishers and the media mingled with Harrigan's friends and former colleagues. Then the speeches got under way. First the Director of Public Prosecutions, who was launching the book, then Harrigan himself.

'In the years I served in the New South Wales Police Service, I often left the courtroom feeling as disappointed as the victims or their relatives, and sometimes as disappointed as the accused when they were sentenced. The apparently disproportionate nature of sentencing doesn't only apply to those who have been the victims of the crime. But equally as bad, if not worse, is the bureaucratic maze you have to walk through even to get to that trial and the delay of years that process has built into it. And then there's the trial itself. I can't tell you how often a witness or a victim has come up to me afterwards and said: "That trial had nothing to do with what happened to me or what I saw. They left out so many facts that were relevant, seemed to know nothing and to care even less about what really happened. What was going on?" Then you have to tell people that trials aren't necessarily concerned with truth and justice or even facts; only the law and, often, the prejudice of its practitioners.

'Why does this seem so unfair? Because the law is a blunt instrument? Or an instrument that, as it is administered today, operates mainly to serve itself, not the people it is supposed to protect or deal with fairly? Why is it that in a courtroom you can so often encounter what seems to be a caricature of the truth, of yourself and your actions? Where the idea of justice seems to be the last consideration in anyone's mind? These are the questions I address in my book.'

The speeches were well received. Sales were brisk, the queues to the table where Harrigan was signing books were lengthy. The launch went on longer than expected. People stayed on to talk. Ellie was tired and rubbing her eyes. Harrigan saw Grace sit down with her in a chair a short distance from the table. Ellie fell asleep in her arms. In a period of quietness, he found himself in an intense discussion with two friends, an SC and a journalist. The SC, a man, thought he had been too critical of the administration of the law; the journalist, a woman, thought he had been more than fair and could have gone further. Toby wheeled himself over to listen. Both people knew him and greeted him.

Then Harrigan looked past them all to the entrance to the room and saw Tony Ponticelli senior walking towards him, his grandson, Joe, by his side. Without even seeming to notice them, Ponticelli pushed between Harrigan's two friends and threw a copy of the book down on the table. Toby, his head leaning back against his chair's headrest, was watching the scene. He was a sharp observer, Harrigan knew; years of sitting watching, often enough ignored, had left him with the skill of reading people shrewdly.

It had been years since Harrigan had seen Tony senior. He had aged to a skeleton of himself, thin and stooped, shockingly old. His eyes were too bright; they ranged over everything without seeming to take much in.

'Tony,' Harrigan said in a neutral voice. 'How are you? I haven't heard much about you for a while now. You brought your grandson with you, young Joe.'

The old man stared at him. Both the journalist and the SC stepped back.

'He's a better son to me than my real one,' he said. 'Paul Harrigan. I've come to buy your book.'

His grandson had supplied him with a chair. He sat down as if he were planning on staying for a while.

'Is that your partner over there?' he said, looking across at Grace. 'Is that your daughter?'

'Why do you want to know, mate?'

'I hear she doesn't stay home. She goes out to work. I wouldn't let any wife of mine do that. Is this any good?' He pushed the book forward.

'You'll have to read it to find out.'

'I'm here to tell you something. When you leave tonight, you think about Bee. You think about what she looked like when they found her. You think back to when you were all so fucking useless you never found out who did that to her. You write this fancy new book and you can't protect a twenty-five-year-old girl. You didn't want to. Don't think I'm ever going to forget that. That's what I wanted to tell you.' He looked around for his grandson. 'Joe. Home.'

Joe helped him to his feet.

'Paul Harrigan.' Tony senior smiled. 'You never got me in a courtroom.'

He looked around as if trying to make sure he knew where he was. He was about to head for the door, his grandson guiding him, when he almost walked into Joel Griffin who had come up behind him out of the crowd. Griffin stopped, excused himself and walked around him. The old man turned to stare after him. Surprised, Harrigan waited to see if any word or sign of recognition would pass between them. The old man's mouth was working without speaking. Joe took him by the arm and steered him around, back towards the door. Tony senior saw Grace again and stared at her, seemingly half-comprehending, angry and resentful.

'I do things my way,' he said. 'I don't fucking let anyone tell me what to do. You'll find out.'

Then, to the obvious relief of the bystanders, he walked out, leaning on his minder's arm.

Griffin didn't seem to see anyone much except Harrigan. He was carrying a copy of his book. 'I've come for something of yours,' he said. 'Can I get your signature on this?'

Harrigan scrawled his usual sprawling signature across the title page of the book. 'Enjoy,' he said, a slight edge in his voice.

'I will,' Griffin replied. 'Because this is you. A signature is personal however often you give it out.'

As Griffin turned to leave, he saw Grace. He stared at her for a few seconds, then walked the short distance over to her.

'Is this your little girl?' he said, without otherwise greeting her. 'Does she look anything like you? Show me. I can't see.'

Grace held Ellie a little closer.

'You don't need to see. You'll wake her up and then she could start to cry. It's better that doesn't happen.'

'I've never seen you look like this. Even your make-up's different. You didn't dress like that for me today.'

He reached out and touched Grace's hair. She jerked her head out of the way. Then Harrigan was standing in front of him.

'It's time you left, mate.'

Griffin turned, his blue eyes looking directly into Harrigan's own, meeting his gaze without embarrassment. It was a detached stare. As a police officer, Harrigan had interviewed people with that look in their eyes; they were invulnerable to anything you said, to any emotion expressed. What are you seeing? he wondered. Me? As what? Whatever it was, Griffin didn't answer him.

'I said you should go,' Harrigan repeated to his silence. 'You've got your book.'

Griffin looked at Grace and Ellie, then at Harrigan again, and turned and walked out without a glance at anyone else.

Suddenly Harrigan's publisher was there, smiling and professional. 'The editor of the *New South Wales Law Journal* wants to talk to you,' she said. 'Do you have the time?'

'Just give me a few moments,' Harrigan replied. He spoke to Grace. 'Are you okay?'

'We're okay. He's gone. That's all that matters.'

Later, when almost everyone else had gone, Harrigan went up to Toby, who was about to leave as well.

'Sorry, mate. I didn't get much time to talk to you.'

You were busy. Those two men, the old man knew the other one. I don't think he liked him.

'I don't think Tony cares for anyone much except himself.'

What's going on, Dad? Why are they interested in Grace?

Harrigan glanced back at Grace who was getting to her feet, still holding a sleeping Ellie in her arms. He saw her look in their direction.

'I don't know what's going on. But I know something is. I can't say more than that.'

You've got to take care. I don't want anything to happen to Grace.

By then, she was with them. 'What are you two talking about?' she asked.

'It's a pity those two arseholes turned up and had to bother you the way they did.'

'They're gone now. Let's forget about them. That's all they deserve.'

They saw Toby into the Cotswold House van, waved goodbye to his friends and left. Harrigan had declined the publisher's offer of dinner, wanting to take his daughter home. It was with some relief that he was finally able to pour himself a whisky and sit down to talk to Grace over something to eat.

'Griffin knows you,' he said. 'Is he your target? He's a dangerous man. You do know that.'

For once she answered directly. 'Yes, we know that. I'm not treating him lightly.'

'Have you got him under surveillance?'

'What do you think?'

'What are you doing?' he asked after a short silence. 'Stinging him in some way? I hope your backup's out there.'

'They are.'

'You're not going to tell me what you know about him or who he is.'

'I can't.'

'Babe, does he believe you're genuine? Can you just tell me that?'

'Yes, he does. He's responding to me in that way.'

'I don't like the way he looked at you. Have any of your inquiries turned over the Ponticellis?' Harrigan asked. 'Are they involved?'

'I can't answer that question. I can only say everything's under control.'

'When's this going to be over?'

'This time tomorrow night, I hope. I'm going to be late but I will be here.'

'Jesus, I hope so,' Harrigan said.

There was silence.

'Clive fired Borghini today,' she said.

'What did he do? Stand up to him?'

'All the time. There was no need for it. You don't chase people like Borghini away. You work out how to handle them.'

'It was a stupid thing to do,' Harrigan said. 'Mark's very smart. Who's going to take his place?'

'Knowing Clive, a lapdog.'

'And you're telling me everything's under control?'

'Twenty-four hours and it'll be over. I promise. After that I'm bailing out. I've made up my mind on that.'

'I'll be glad, babe. It'll almost be back to normal.' As much as Grace's life could be described as normal, given the nature of her work. 'But I wish Mark was still there.'

That night when Harrigan lay in bed staring at the ceiling, he tossed around the question of Griffin being under Orion's surveillance. So far in his work he had turned over a trail of shadows, ghosts and missing people, something he'd made sense of only through constant speculation. Plenty of personal tragedy, any number of possible scenarios, but few facts. Joel Griffin was connected to his investigation through the Shillingworth Trust, if only because he was acting for the trust in the sale of two of their properties. But what if Orion had found other connections, ones Harrigan knew nothing about or had only guessed at? They had means of surveillance and investigation far beyond his capacities. Had he managed to walk into their surveillance? If he had, what would they do? Gaol him? No one had stopped him yet. He would keep going. The end was almost in sight.

He turned over to go to sleep, thinking that at least no one seemed to be stalking them any more. The last he'd heard from his tormentors was the SMS they'd sent. The thought stopped him there. People stop doing things when they've got what they want. Harrigan didn't believe their stalkers had just gone away. Had they got what they wanted? Which was what?

He suddenly felt they were closer than they should be, that somehow they'd found a way into his house. It was a jolt of paranoia unlike any he'd felt. He pulled himself together but his thoughts returned to Griffin, how he'd acted tonight. As if he were the organiser, the one with a mission.

If you let them panic you, then they've won. Don't lose your nerve. Take the next step. See what it tells you.

He willed himself to sleep. Tomorrow he would need all the strength he had.

19

Harrigan just had time to check his email before he left the house the next morning. His retainer had found Loretta Griffin's husband, one Elliot Griffin. Both had been English migrants who had arrived here in the late 1960s and seemed to have failed to make a go of it. A drunk Elliot Griffin, just fired from his job, had attacked his wife with an iron bar in 1977 and been charged with attempted murder. In the end, he had served nine years for what the judge had described as a brutal crime. If alive today, he would be close to seventy. They'd had one child, Joel, as Harrigan had expected. Did Harrigan want her to keep searching for father and son? He sent her a message to start with missing persons.

He still arrived early at the Royal Exchange in Tempe. Eddie was already in the back room, nervously working his way through a beer. The room was near the entrance to both the beer garden and the toilets and on a quiet day it was possible to get in and out without being seen. Harrigan, who came in through the beer garden via an alleyway, found it as empty as he'd hoped it would be. He wondered why anyone would want to sit out there in the first place. It smelled of the toilets, which were old and hardly ever cleaned, and the ashtrays on the tables were always full.

The hotel opened early and the regular drinkers would be in the bar, in all likelihood smoking in there even if it was illegal. This was a pub where people came to drink seriously all day and no one was much interested in government regulations. The Royal Exchange dated back to the nineteenth century. The back room was a small closed-in space with stale carpet on the floor and a fireplace. Probably it had once been the ladies' lounge or, as people had used to call it, the sows' parlour. Harrigan had an arrangement with the licensee, also the barman, who would set it aside for him for meetings like this.

When Harrigan walked in, Eddie almost jumped out of his skin.

'Jesus,' he said. 'You got here fucking soon enough. Don't do that to me. Does that barman out there know how to keep his mouth shut?'

'Just stay calm. With him, it's see nothing, hear nothing. Now, Joel Griffin. What work does he do for the family?'

Eddie looked around, as if expecting someone to be standing behind him.

'I think he shifts money,' he said very quietly. 'Been doing it for years. For both Tonys.'

'What do they give him?'

'Well, he gets his cut. Other than that, muscle. If he wants something done, Mick'll front up. Apparently there's a couple of things that went down not too long ago.'

'Does Griffin often need things done?'

'Now and again. No, not that often.'

'What about you?' Harrigan asked. 'Do you do things for him?'

Eddie shrugged. 'It was work. Years ago. Not since before I was in the slammer.'

'He's managed to stay off everyone's radar.'

'He comes and goes. Spends a lot of time out of the country. Keeps himself quiet. Just real careful, you know. No one hardly ever sees him.'

'What did you do for him way back when?'

'A bit of snatching now and again. That's all really.'

'Where did these people end up?'

'In the boot of his car. Still alive. What he did after that I don't know. Don't know any names either. Never asked.'

Eight years ago Eddie was in gaol. Ten years ago he wasn't.

'This doesn't go past me,' Harrigan said. 'Do you remember an older woman, maybe seventy? Just before you went away.'

Eddie worked his mouth a bit, swallowing the beer. 'Just between you and me?' Harrigan nodded. 'Picked her up at Wahroonga station. She was expecting a lift. Thought she was going to hospital.'

Finally, Harrigan had testimony to tie Griffin to at least one of the missing persons. Where was Jennifer Shillingworth now? If he found her, would he find Ian Blackmore?

'Where'd you take her?' he asked.

'Ku-ring-gai National Park. We met Griffin there. I don't know where he went after that. There's something else about him.' Eddie spoke like he was making his run. 'He sells information.'

'What information?'

'He's a fucking barrister, isn't he. He talks to the people he's defending. Like he talked to Chris Newell.'

'Did he?'

'Yeah, mate. And everything Newell told him, he sold to the family.'

'What did he tell them?'

Eddie was thinking. There was something else besides fear at work. Cunning was sliding into his face. Searching for an advantage, whatever that might be.

'Harrigan, you fucking told me to be here, even though if I'm seen with you, I'm dead. I don't want to have to drop everything every time you want something. I know you've quit. But you still know everyone. You can pull strings.'

'What do you want?'

'It's what you said, isn't it? I reckon when Tony senior carks it — and that's not going to be too long — I'm out on the street. Tony junior won't give a shit. What am I going to do then?'

'You tell me, mate,' Harrigan said. 'What are you going to do?'

Eddie took a long drink. His beer was almost finished.

'I want protection,' he said. 'Twenty-four fucking hours a day so I can sleep at night.'

'It's not me that makes those decisions any more.'

'Come on. You can still fucking ring people. I know you can.'

'It depends on what else you've got. It had better be good.'

'I reckon what I've given you is pretty good, but I've got even better than that. Something you'd know a bit about. Bianca. You'd remember her.' Eddie grinned dirtily.

Harrigan, expecting to be told that Griffin had sold Newell's information about Grace, was surprised to hear her name.

'What about her?'

'Newell killed her.' Eddie finished his beer and pushed the empty glass away. 'That's what he told Griffin anyway. His brains were fried, I know that. Fucking didn't know what planet he was on half the time. But he knew enough. From what he said, he did it all right.'

'Are you telling me Tony senior was responsible for that shoot-out on Oxford Street?'

'You bet he was. He wanted Newell. Griffin was supposed to get him off and out of gaol and then Tony could get him. He wanted to do it himself, you see. But Newell just kept digging the hole he was in. In the end, Tony says, fuck it, I'm not waiting any longer. I'm going to go in and get him. And he did. Is that worth protection?'

'I don't know yet, mate,' Harrigan said. 'You know a lot about what went on. If my old work mates go in, what's the family going to tell them about you?'

'I work for 'em, mate. What was I supposed to do?'

'What did you do?'

'I rang Newell. Told him the day it was going down. I said, you act up in court about eleven in the morning. Get yourself hauled out of there. He thought he was being sprung.'

The Judas kiss. It didn't look as if it had kept Eddie awake at night. But Newell was dead, and that meant Grace was free of him.

'I've got it all,' Eddie went on. 'Names, who did the shooting, everything. Tell you who was driving the van. Joe Ponticelli. He's his granddad's man. Mad like him. Okay? Let's do a deal.'

'You've got more information in there besides that, haven't you?'

Eddie shook his head. 'What else is there?'

'Tony senior talking about Bianca. Anyone else's name come up? Like mine? You want your protection. You fucking tell me now.'

'You want to know? He hates your guts.'

'I know that. And?'

'That's enough, isn't it? Look ...' Eddie glanced around. 'Tony junior, he just wants to move on. He didn't want this mess. He's going to tell you he had nothing to do with it. He said if Newell goes back to gaol, so what? Do it there. What does it matter who does it? Tony senior, he set that whole fucking thing up. What's he got to lose? He's mad and he's dying.' There was a twist of contempt in Eddie's face. 'The family's not what it used to be. He doesn't like that. He still wants to prove he's king shit.'

'It's not enough, mate. There's more, right?'

Eddie picked up his glass. 'I need another beer.'

Harrigan grabbed his arm. 'No, mate. You're not going anywhere. What else is there?'

'Fucking let go of me, Harrigan. Don't you touch me!'

Eddie yanked his arm away, looking towards the door with a sick expression on his face.

'Who are you expecting? Have you set me up? You have, haven't you?'

Harrigan was on his feet, his gun out, getting out of the line of the doorway to where he could fire.

'No, I wouldn't —'

The door was kicked open but the two gunmen who stood there didn't come inside. One shot from the doorway directly at Eddie. Eddie, on his feet, took the bullets with a gasp, no scream. 'You fucking —' he said, then staggered forwards to the floor. The other gunman, apparently expecting to find Harrigan also at the table, jerked his head in shock toward where Harrigan stood with his own gun out. 'Drop your fucking gun,' he shouted but it was too late. Harrigan had already fired twice from close range immediately the first gunman had shot at Eddie. His bullets cracked into the second gunman's shoulder almost as he spoke, breaking the bone. The gunman staggered back, then tried to turn and leg it, crashing out the back door into the beer garden. In those brief moments, Harrigan recognised Mick Brasi. There were shouts from outside in the beer garden. The first gunman didn't wait. He turned and ran out through the front of the hotel. Seconds later, two men were running after him shouting, 'Police. Stop.'

Harrigan went to Eddie's aid, kneeling down to feel his pulse. He was still alive but bleeding heavily, his breathing painful. His eyes opened. He stared at Harrigan but didn't speak.

'I'm getting you an ambulance, mate,' Harrigan said. 'You were spinning me a line, weren't you? Keeping me talking.'

'Fuck you, Harrigan,' Eddie said. 'It was all true. I still want my protection.'

He passed out.

The barman appeared in the doorway, ashen-faced. '*Fuck!*'

'I'm calling an ambulance,' Harrigan said. 'He's still alive.'

The two men who had chased the other gunman out through the hotel reappeared behind the barman. Both were armed.

'No, you're not,' one of them said. 'We'll call an ambulance. Put your phone away.'

'What the fuck's going on?' the barman asked in a panicky voice.

'You're closed for the day. As of now, no one leaves. Keep everyone out of this back room and don't let anyone in the beer garden. Come on, we'll close up together. And in regard to what's happened in here, you saw nothing and you say nothing. Is that clear?'

Silenced, the barman was led away back to the bar. The second man had been speaking on the phone. He hung up and turned to Harrigan.

'Ambulance is on its way. Outside now.'

'What about Eddie?'

'You can't do anything for him. Out.'

Harrigan walked out. A third unknown man was holding a gun over Mick Brasi who was lying face down in the beer garden. Blood was pouring out onto the cement and he was gasping in pain.

'We couldn't shoot to stop the other one,' said the man accompanying Harrigan. 'Too many people in the bar. He got away.'

'You were a bit late getting here, boys,' Harrigan said. 'Have you got any ID?'

'Have you?' the man with the gun asked.

'I'll show you mine if you show me yours,' Harrigan replied dryly, one eye on Mick Brasi on the concrete. He was caught by the cold-bloodedness of this conversation while the man lay there in agony.

'We don't have to show ID.'

'You're from Orion,' Harrigan said. 'My partner's got a standard-issue firearm just like that one.'

'Did you shoot this man?'

'I did. It was self-defence. If Eddie Grippo ever wakes up, he'll tell you that.'

'Was he going to kill you?'

'My belief at the time was that he was,' Harrigan replied. 'They have motive and I can't think of any other reason why they'd go to all this trouble.'

'You'd better take a seat,' the third man said, the one pointing the gun. 'We've got someone who wants to talk to you.'

Two ambulances arrived seconds ahead of the authorities. Harrigan watched Brasi being stretchered out under police guard, followed by Eddie. It wasn't just the police who arrived. In the phalanx of plain-clothes and uniformed officers that swarmed over the Royal Exchange, Harrigan saw Clive coming towards him.

'What are you doing here?' he asked Harrigan.

'Maybe I should ask you the same thing.'

'Were you able to get any information from Eddie Grippo before he was shot?'

'Yes, quite a lot. I was going to pass it on to the police.'

'We'll do that jointly.'

Harrigan glanced around. 'Where's my wife?'

'Your partner's working,' Clive replied. 'Let's hear what you've got to say.'

They sat in the hotel's dirty kitchen. It took time, giving his statement, working through all the information Eddie had given him. He knew one of the two police officers interviewing him. He started by calling him boss but quickly went to Mr Harrigan. The meeting was strangely subdued. Both Clive and the third gunman were present. From time to time, the police officers glanced in their direction. Making sure they were doing what they were supposed to do.

'Eddie set me up,' Harrigan said.

'If they were coming after you, why shoot him?'

'I guess he'd proved he was unreliable. Probably it was two birds with one stone.'

'Why were you meeting Eddie Grippo in the first place?' Clive asked.

'He's an informant. I'd asked him to keep his ear to the ground for me. I wanted to know if any of the Ponticellis were coming after me or my family. He rang to say he had some information and we set up a meet.'

'Did they really want to kill you?' one of the police officers asked. 'Why not shoot straightaway, the way they did Eddie?'

'It happened pretty quickly,' Harrigan said. 'It's true they didn't fire at me immediately. But I wasn't where they were expecting me to be and I had my gun out. Maybe this was a snatch, I don't know. I certainly think they'd planned on killing me in the long run.'

'Why did you have your gun out?'

'Eddie lost his nerve. I knew something was going down. I'd only just taken it out.'

The two police officers glanced at each other, then Clive, and kept on. Harrigan knew that they needed to act on this intelligence as soon as possible. The gunman who'd got away would already have told the Ponticellis that the hit had failed. Eddie had been sent to keep him talking until the boys turned up. They already knew Eddie was unreliable and good at playing both sides against each other. If there was any chance he'd spilled his guts to Harrigan, they wouldn't wait around. They'd go undercover as soon as possible. Yet there was nothing in this police interview that suggested any kind of urgency. The opposite: there was frustration in the officers' expressions; suppressed anger and tension between them and Orion. Harrigan decided it was time to talk about Griffin some more.

'He's a player, an important one. You need to investigate him at depth.'

There was no response, just a nod, a quick glance between the interviewing officers, then onto another subject.

'I think we should talk about him some more,' Harrigan persisted.

'Later,' Clive said from the sidelines.

'No, he's important.'

'No one will say another word about Joel Griffin as of now,' Clive ordered.

Stymied, all three of them. The hands-off order Clive had slapped on him was in play for the police as well. In the past, Harrigan had encountered these directives himself. There was nothing you could do but wait until they were lifted.

At least the police thanked him for what he had to tell them. Once they'd finished, Clive cleared the room of everyone except himself and the third man who still hadn't told Harrigan his name.

'What were you doing here today?' Clive asked.

'You just heard me tell those two officers. Why were you here?'

'Our operatives were following Mick Brasi. They weren't expecting to find you here. I've already told you, I don't want a wild card involving himself in a very delicately balanced operation.'

'Why would I have any reason to believe that my meeting with Eddie Grippo could have anything to do with your operation?' Harrigan asked.

'I thought I'd given you the message loud and clear. Whatever private investigations you're involved in, you are to stop immediately.'

'I asked you before. Where's my wife?'

'I've told you. Working. What has she told you about this?'

'Nothing,' Harrigan said, and, on seeing the unguarded satisfaction on Clive's face, successfully hid the intense anger he felt. Years of practice came to his aid.

'I'm asking you to go home and wait until she comes home this evening. If you don't do that, I'll arrest you.'

'For what?'

'Obstructing an Orion operation. If pursued, it carries a maximum sentence of seven years.'

'You could tell me what's going on so I know Grace is safe,' Harrigan said. 'What about doing that? Wouldn't that solve a lot of problems? It would take a lot of pressure off her.'

'You're not in a position to be told classified information.'

'I've got a top-secret security clearance. You gave it to me. If I, my wife or my daughter or my son are in any danger, then don't we have a right to information that could assist us in protecting ourselves?'

'*We're* protecting you. You don't need to do anything.'

'You've just told the police the same thing, haven't you? You've told them not to act on the information I've given them until you give the all clear. Why? What are you waiting for? That directive could seriously undermine *their* operation.'

'If you say another word, I'll arrest you. This interview is over.'

Harrigan looked him in the eyes. *You cheap little tyrant.* Hopefully the message got across unspoken.

'See you, mate,' he said, and walked out without looking back.

Outside in his car, he asked himself what he was doing. Would it make things worse or better if he went ahead with his check of Amelie Santos's surgery? He didn't trust Clive. It was too powerful a feeling to be ignored. He didn't trust Clive and he didn't trust him with Grace's safety. His instinct told him to rely on himself. He couldn't sit home and wait, wondering what might be happening to her; if he did, he would go mad. He'd always had to know the worst of what was on offer. Find it out, look it in the face. It was the only way to deal with it.

He drove away, too deep in his thoughts to do more than pay just enough attention to the traffic, making the long trip to northern Sydney.

20

Narelle had a better gift for subterfuge than Grace had expected. Perhaps it excited her. Dressed in a dark blue, mass market tracksuit with the hood up, she appeared anonymously from the entrance to the mall and slipped into the passenger seat beside Grace.

'Leave your hood up,' Grace said, and pulled away quickly.

Narelle fastened her seatbelt. She was carrying a small leather bag. She took a packet of cigarettes out of it and lit one.

'Put that out!'

Narelle ignored her, an expression of untroubled bliss on her face as she stared straight ahead. Grace brought the car to a halt, reached over, snatched the cigarette out of her mouth and threw it away.

'Keep smoking and you can get out and walk! Do you understand that?'

With a sudden violence, Narelle opened the door and threw her cigarettes out, then slammed the door shut again, hard and angrily. Grace restarted the car and drove on.

'What did you tell your parents about what you were doing?' she asked.

Narelle didn't reply. She was sulking.

'You have to answer my question, Narelle. I need to know what you've told your parents.'

Narelle shrugged and curled up in her seat, staring out of the window.

'A question you really have to answer. Did you bring your ID with you?'

'It's in the bag.'

'What about your phone?'

'I left it behind! Like you wanted. I brought my iPod.'

'Fine.' At least they wouldn't have to talk to each other.

They drove in silence. Grace took them out onto the feeder roads heading north across the western part of Sydney. She was under a communications blackout but every word spoken in the car was being listened to. The phone was for emergency use only. After a while, Narelle pushed her hood back and shook out her glossy black hair. She had made up her face, again replicating the look of Gong Li. Grace wondered if she'd put on special underwear before she'd dressed herself in her tracksuit. She thought about asking her to put her hood back up and decided not to bother.

'When are we going to get there?' Narelle asked.

'I'm aiming for six. That's when they're expecting us.'

'Can't you go faster than that?'

'Not if we don't want to attract attention,' Grace said. 'Now tell me. What did you tell your parents?'

'I just told Dad I was going shopping.'

'What about your mother?'

'I didn't talk to her. She's been horrible to me lately.'

Goodbye, Mum and Dad. Lucky what's supposed to happen to you isn't going to. She glanced quickly at Narelle who was staring ahead with a dreamy look in her eyes. *Are you really that naïve? Or am I the one who's been blinded?*

'Did it bother you, what you were doing to Jirawan?' she asked. 'Sending her down to get raped every day. Or did you get a kick out of it?'

'What are you talking about? It was just something she had to do. I didn't know that was her name. What are you talking about her for? She's dead. I can't do anything.'

Grace said nothing.

238

'If she'd just done what she was told, she'd have been all right,' Narelle said angrily after a short silence. 'Elliot said she owed him money. It was her own fault she was there.'

'You think it's as straightforward as that, do you?' Grace asked.

'She had to pay her debt. It was his money. He was really upset about it. She owed him.'

'For what?'

'He looked after her husband's business for them and they wouldn't pay him for it. It was a lot of money.'

Protection money. Give and you just keep giving. Like Kidd.

'Who do you think killed her?'

'I don't know! Why should I?'

'What about Lynette?'

'None of that's got anything to do with me. They did the wrong thing by Elliot. I never have and I never will. He knows that.'

'Every time you look into those amazing blue eyes, you melt, do you, Narelle?' Grace said. She remembered Griffin staring at her yesterday in Lane Cove National Park. Blue eyes whose only effect on her had been to chill her through and through. Narelle looked at her sideways with a smile.

'You don't know what's between us, what we feel for each other. It's so real. What do you know about that?'

'What about the guy who helped you guard Jirawan? Did you like having him around?'

'He stank! I don't think he ever washed. I said I could take care of her, she was only little. But Elliot said I needed him.'

'Including the night you took her down to Jon Kidd's car and put her in the boot.'

'That nasty little man? Elliot said he was weak.'

'Did you know where Jirawan was going?' Grace asked.

'No. I don't know if he did. He was weird. He said all these weird things.'

'Like what?'

'Nasty things, like he was probably taking her to hell. Why say something stupid like that? And if that's what he thought, why did he do it? It's got nothing to do with me. I don't want to talk about it any more.'

She took her iPod out of her bag and put on her earphones. Soon she was in her own world, bopping away to her chosen music.

I let Jirawan go with her train fare. Given what Kidd had known about the people he was dealing with, he'd been brave at least once in his life. Twice when you counted Parramatta Park. Narelle was the last of the witnesses. Griffin had no ties; he could, with the right passport, leave any time he wanted. There were any number of ways to leave the country without going near an airport. He wasn't taking Narelle with him. Presumably he was taking Sara, if only because she'd always been there.

They drove on in silence until Grace reached the Sydney–Newcastle freeway, heading north to the Hawkesbury River. She was ahead of the worst of the traffic. Her phone rang. It was Griffin, speaking to her through her earpiece.

'There's been a change of plan,' he said. 'Drive to Brooklyn and go to the public jetty.'

'Why? What's happened?'

'Should you care? It's a shorter drive for you. Sara will be there.'

'Where are you?' she asked.

'Somewhere,' he said. 'You want to get paid. Do what I ask.'

Narelle had unplugged herself.

'Who's that?'

'Elliot,' Grace said.

'You're stupid! Let me talk to him!'

She reached to grab Grace's earpiece; Grace batted her down.

'Too late, he's gone. Change of plan,' Grace said. 'We're going to Brooklyn. You know Brooklyn, don't you?'

'What's there?'

'A public jetty.'

'Oh, his yacht! He said one day we'd sail away.'

Are you listening, Clive? Get your people down there. Get someone on the river. Do it now.

She was close to Berowra, where she would have to turn off the freeway onto the old Pacific Highway for the run to Brooklyn, a small fishing village on the Hawkesbury River some fifty kilometres north of Sydney, best known for its marinas and oyster farms.

Griffin had rung at too opportune a time for her liking. Someone was telling him where she was.

She had reached the turn-off. The old road was a single-lane highway left to deteriorate, its surface cracked and cheaply repaired. It twisted over the hilly, tree-covered ground leading up to the high ridge overlooking the river, much of which was national park or nature reserve.

'He knows where we are. We're being followed,' she said, speaking not to Narelle but to the listeners on the end of her wire.

'What are you talking about?' Narelle asked. 'You're weird.'

Grace's phone rang again. This time it was her backup.

'There's a motorcycle with a pillion passenger behind you. They've been with you for a while. They're moving faster and getting closer. You're going to need to take evasive action.'

'Where are you?'

'In range. Moving up behind them. Keep the line open.'

'What was that about?' Narelle asked.

'Put your hood up and get down in your seat.'

'Why?'

'Just do it!'

Grace put her foot down, speeding up a winding hill towards a communications tower on the summit. She looked in the rear-view mirror. A motorcyclist with a pillion was speeding up to come alongside her on her right. Narelle hadn't moved. She sat there looking sullen.

'Get down now!' Grace shouted at her.

'What's happening?'

'Down!'

Grace swung out onto the wrong side of the road as the motorbike drew level with her, almost knocking the bike over. The rider swerved to avoid a collision, almost went off the road, drew back, and then followed her back to the left lane and was again trying to draw level. Grace saw her backup behind them.

'What's going on?' Narelle's voice was almost a shriek.

'Keep quiet and don't panic!'

The rider was accelerating to come alongside, only to find the backup car on his tail trying to nudge his back wheel. Then Grace's back window and windscreen shattered almost instantaneously. The pillion on the bike behind her had fired. Narelle began to scream, curling into a ball in her seat. The on-coming air hit Grace like a wall. She hung on to the car, fighting to keep it under control and on the road.

On a tight bend, she came close to swerving onto the wrong side of the twisting road, almost colliding head on with an approaching vehicle, but managed to drag the car back. The car's horn blared as she sped past it. Then there was a crash.

The bike had still been there, swinging away from her backup to come alongside on the left, beside Narelle. Pushed by the backup car behind, it had collided with Grace side on as she swerved back to her side of the road. She had hit it at full speed. Gripping the wheel, she dragged the car away from the bike up onto the shoulder, where she brought it to a stop. Then she radioed in.

'We've had an incident. The pick-up is aborted. We may have two deaths as well.'

Clive was on the end of the line. 'I'll have an ambulance and police on the way ASAP. Expect me also.'

Narelle had got out of the car and was running along the road. Grace ran her down and dragged her back.

'Let go of me,' Narelle shouted, struggling.

Grace pushed her hard against the car. 'Keep quiet. You will sit in this car and you won't move.'

Narelle was quiet for a few moments, then made to run again. Grace was holding the girl's wrists in a tight grip when a member of her backup arrived, carrying a pair of handcuffs.

'Just sit still,' he said, and cuffed Narelle to the steering wheel. Grace took the car keys.

'Don't do this to me,' Narelle shouted. 'What have I done?'

'Sit in the car and be quiet,' Grace snapped. 'If it wasn't for us, you'd be ending up dead. So count your lucky stars.'

'What are you talking about? Elliot wouldn't hurt me!'

Grace didn't bother to answer. The car she had almost collided with head on had come back and pulled to a stop on the shoulder just near the bike. Its driver, a man, was hurrying towards the rider and the pillion passenger where they lay sprawled on the road.

Behind them, another car had come to a halt and a small line was beginning to form. One car started pulling out to drive around the smashed bike; a concerned driver got out of another.

'I'll deal with the traffic,' one of the backup team said, and went to move the cars on. The other backup was standing over the rider and pillion, pointing a gun at them. The pillion rider's gun lay where it had finished up on the dirt. Grace reached the injured men at the same time as the driver from the first car.

'Stop there,' the Orion operative ordered him.

The driver stopped, white-faced, staring at the operative's gun. 'Who are you?' he asked.

'We're with the police. Who are you?'

'I'm a nurse,' the man said.

'Let him look at them,' Grace said.

The operative stepped back, gun still at the ready. The nurse was calm, if pale.

'I think your pillion rider's probably dead,' he said.

'Can you help the other one?' Grace asked.

'Can I take his helmet off?'

'Do it.'

The nurse removed the helmet and used his own coat as a cushion for the rider's head. He was moving in and out of consciousness. Grace recognised Joe Ponticelli from Harrigan's launch.

'Probably internal bleeding,' the nurse said. 'Probably quite severe. We need an ambulance.'

'It's on its way.'

The nurse checked the other man, also taking off his helmet. This man was unknown to her.

'Very dead. Probably almost instantly. His neck's broken.'

Despite her years of training and experience, Grace swayed on her feet, feeling cold and sick. Briefly she closed her eyes.

'Are you all right?' the nurse asked.

She nodded. Glancing sideways, she saw the other operative looking at her speculatively.

'I saw it happening when you almost ran into me,' the nurse said. 'I don't think it was your fault. They ran into you.'

You can expect it in a business like this where the people who make the rules are murderers. She had heard this from a speaker during her induction course all those years ago. It had never been more real. She nodded her thanks to the nurse but couldn't speak.

First on the scene was Clive, with the police and ambulance following. The injured man was taken away first; the dead man waited his turn under a cover on the road.

'Where's Narelle Wong?' Clive asked.

'We had to handcuff her to the car. She kept trying to make a run for it.'

'Let's have a look at her.'

They walked over to where Narelle was sitting in the passenger seat.

'This hurts!' she said. 'It's cutting off my circulation!'

'You were on your way to meet someone,' Clive said. 'Do you want to tell me who that person is?'

'None of your business.'

'I think you'll find it is. Is it this man?' Clive showed her a surveillance photograph of Joel Griffin.

'I don't know. Take this thing off me!'

'You are aware you're implicated in Jirawan Sanders's murder? Certainly as an accessory before the fact.'

'I didn't know anything about that. I still don't.'

'We have testimony that she worked under duress at Life's Pleasures and was under your control. That's deprivation of liberty. Did you know that? You were also involved in the intended sale of her passport. These are serious offences.'

Narelle was dissolving into tears. 'What would I know about any of that? My arm hurts!'

'Get it unlocked,' Grace said to the operative with the key, who was standing beside her.

'Would you come with us, Miss Wong?' Clive said. 'This gentleman here will show you to a car. We'd like to speak to you.'

'You haven't told me who you are. Are you the police?'

Clive reached for a small wallet, which he flicked open for her. She stared at it uncomprehendingly.

'This is my identification. I'm advising you that under our legislation we can hold you incommunicado without charge for fourteen days and I intend to do so. This man will look after you. Go with him, please.'

'This is her ID,' Grace said, handing the operative Narelle's leather bag.

'No, I'll take that,' Clive said.

Narelle turned to Grace. 'You lied to me.'

'Just this way, Miss Wong, with this gentleman here,' Clive said. 'We'll get you in the car.'

'I hope he kills *you* for it,' Narelle lashed back at Grace one last time.

A tow truck arrived and removed Grace's car. The smashed bike was also being readied to be removed. The traffic on the highway was crawling just enough. Someone handed her a cup of coffee. Clive, who had been overseeing the cleanup, came over.

'You kept the media away,' Grace said.

'I want this under wraps. You handled it well. You kept your head under very difficult circumstances.'

One person dead, one person critical. Murderers both. Whatever they were, she wasn't a killer. She hadn't wanted to be responsible for anyone's death.

'I've missed my rendezvous,' she said. 'Do we know what's happening down at Brooklyn?'

'Sara McLeod is still down there. She's moored a small yacht at the public jetty. I want you to stay in role. I have a surveillance team down there now and I'm organising a boat as well. They'll be there as soon as they can. I've got you another car. I want you to go down there and tell her Narelle is dead.'

'Then how come I'm alive?'

'They were aiming for you and got her. You ran them off the road, killed one of them and left the other there. Then you took a side road into the bush and dumped Narelle's body. As well as Jirawan Sanders's passport, you have Narelle's ID and you want to be paid for it the same as if you had delivered her in person.'

'For them to believe that, the car has to be shot up in some way.'

'No, you abandoned it. The one you're driving is stolen.'

'What am I trying to achieve?' she asked.

Clive didn't blink. 'Griffin has given us the slip. We don't know where he is. He's definitely not down at the marina. I want to see if Sara McLeod will take you to him.'

'How did that happen?'

'He went back to his apartment building at Bondi Junction last night after he left your partner's book launch. He never arrived at his unit in that building. Sometime since then he left without us seeing him. We think he must have a second unit in the building under another name and also had another car ready to go. He was probably driven out by someone else.'

'Well, he's made fools of us, hasn't he?'

'Give me your opinion. Does he know this is a sting?'

'Whatever he thinks, he's playing his own game,' she replied. 'And whatever we're doing, it's not relevant to him. We're just something he has to deal with. Probably keeping his activities very secret is something he does regardless of whether he thinks he's being watched or not.'

'We have to take the initiative. Take the car, keep the rendezvous. You're wearing your wire. It has a GPS in it. Whatever happens, we can track you. Don't let him take your firearm.'

'You want me to go now?'

'Yes. We'll be listening to everything you say but I want you to maintain the blackout. But if at any time you want to pull out, say "Time to go" and we'll be there.'

Grace finished her coffee. 'I'd better go then. But there's one thing I want you to do for me. Ring Harrigan and tell him I'm okay, and ask him to tell Ellie I'll be home soon.'

'I'll do that,' he replied. 'Here's Narelle's ID. Don't worry. We're with you every step of the way.'

She prepared by scrubbing off her make-up and slicking back her hair as if she'd washed her face recently. Then she drove away along the Pacific Highway in the growing dusk, making the descent to the river. She had thought the operation would be over by now but it felt like it was just starting. She wanted to ring Harrigan herself and talk to him, wanted to hear his voice, wanted to know how Ellie was. At least they were home, safe.

21

The route to Turramurra on Sydney's upper north shore took Harrigan to another boundary of the Ku-ring-gai Chase National Park, to the west of Duffys Forest. He drove north along Bobbin Head Road into the suburb, a landscape of private hospitals and private schools. The streets were lined with well-grown trees giving shelter to expensive houses on large blocks. There was very little traffic; no one was behind him. The dwelling he was looking for was on the eastern side of Bobbin Head Road, in a cul-de-sac on the edge of the national park with a view over an expanse of bushland. There was no *For Sale* sign out the front. Maybe they hadn't got here yet.

Harrigan reached for his backpack with its selection of tools and got out of his car. There was a high cyclone-wire fence identical to the one surrounding the Duffys Forest house. Again, trees and shrubs crowded against the fence and there was a Colorbond gate across the driveway, also locked. Harrigan looked through a gap between the fence and the gate, down the driveway to a house in the style of a suburban Spanish hacienda. The garden appeared overgrown and the property was enclosed by both the street trees and those growing on the block. Nearby was a mailbox combined with a doctor's lantern, the red glass now largely broken. Despite this being a suburban street, there was a sense of isolation about the place. There was silence except for the sound of bird calls and the quiet hum of the day's heat.

As far as he could tell, the fence surrounded the whole block. He was wondering where to start when a man in his sixties appeared in the opposite driveway and walked quickly across the road towards him.

'Are you a real estate agent?' he asked.

'No, I'm not. Can you tell me who you are?'

'My card. I came to ask you what you were doing here.'

He was a short man, a little overweight, bright-eyed and balding, casually dressed in expensive clothes.

'Pleased to meet you, Adrian,' Harrigan said, reading from the card that announced the bearer, an Adrian Mellish, to be a financial consultant. He offered his own card. 'Paul Harrigan. Can I ask you why you have an interest in this place?'

'Your name's familiar,' Mellish replied. 'Weren't you once a policeman? I seem to remember reading in the newspapers … Aren't you a private investigator now?'

'Not exactly. I'm a security consultant. If you want to know more about me, you can check my website. You didn't answer my question.'

'Our interest is that we live across the road,' Mellish said. 'We've been wishing ever since Amelie retired that this property would be sold and someone would do something with it. It's been empty for at least fifteen years. One or two people have been looking at it lately. We were hoping that something might actually be happening.'

'Do you know who these people were?'

'No, not at all. You're the first one I've spoken to.'

'This was Dr Amelie Santos's surgery, wasn't it?'

'Yes. Did you know her?'

'Only by reputation,' Harrigan said. 'It seems an out of the way place for a doctor's surgery. Can you tell me anything about her?'

'Actually Amelie was very successful. People trusted her and they came to her. We used to go to her and take our children. She was quite wonderful with children. But she was a very private woman. We always invited her over for Christmas drinks but she didn't always come. I know she died about four years ago. There was an obituary in the paper. But still nothing's happened.'

'You've been here for a while,' Harrigan said.

'Helen and I moved into this street when we were first married. Best thing we ever did.'

'How long has the fence been here?'

'A long time. It went up when Amelie retired.'

'She put the fence up?'

'Oh, yes. She came and saw us. Apologised for the inconvenience, that sort of thing. At the time, she said it was just temporary. She didn't want the place vandalised while it was empty. But once she retired, she never came back here. I don't think she could bear to sell it. She'd spent so much of her life here. She left it in limbo and it's been that way ever since.'

'Addie.'

Across the road, Harrigan saw a thin middle-aged woman dressed in white. She was waving to her husband.

'Have to go,' he said. 'A grandchild's birthday party.'

'Have a nice time,' Harrigan said.

Mellish hesitated. 'What *are* you doing here?'

'Just looking the place over.'

He glanced at the backpack Harrigan had over his shoulder. 'You know, Helen and I … we've lived here for a long time. It's a lovely suburb, really.'

'Yes.'

'But once or twice we've wondered if there've been people over here. At night.'

'Did you ever report anything?' Harrigan asked.

'I did once. Just a month ago. We heard a scream, or we thought we did. I suppose it could have been in the park. I rang the police the next day but they just sent their community liaison officer around to patronise us.' He looked at Harrigan, an odd expression on his face. 'We've both really grown to wish this building wasn't here. Most of the time, we ignore it. I don't think anything would make *me* go inside. But if I were to, I'd look along the back boundary. There's a gate. I've certainly never seen anyone go in through the front. Bye, now.'

Harrigan watched them back out of the driveway in a Volvo. Mellish leaned out of the window to call to him. 'We'll be gone for a while. You can park your car in our driveway if you like. Get you off the street.' They both gave him a wave and drove away.

Harrigan decided he would move his car, and parked it in the Mellishes' lengthy driveway, which was overhung with exotic trees, their leaves turning gold in the autumn. A pervasive sense of solitude settled on the street. He walked down to the furthest end of the cyclone fence and saw a track leading into the national park. He followed it down to the park boundary and looked along the line of the fence. Judging by the state of the vegetation, few people walked along here. About halfway along, he found what Mellish had sent him to find: a makeshift if secure gate cut into the fence. He took bolt cutters out of his backpack and went to work.

Eventually, he had the gate open. When he left he could put it back in place without it appearing to have been damaged. Before he went inside, he turned to look at what was behind him. There was no path as such down into the national park, just a curtain of trees. Looking in the direction of the road, the house stood as a barrier. No one would see what was going on down here from up there.

He climbed through the gateway and walked around to the front of the house, startling two white-cheeked eastern rosellas that flew up out of the long grass. The exterior was a dirty white stucco with columns on either side of the front door. The windows were dirty and cracked, the window frames rotten. The paint on the front door was peeling. Although the lock was broken, the door itself seemed secure. He shook it; most likely it had been nailed shut on the inside.

There was a separate garage facing a concreted parking area where the grass had grown up through the cracks. The roller door opened for him but there was nothing inside other than the usual rubbish found in most abandoned garages. He looked up at the road. The trees surrounding the property provided a screen from the other houses in the street. This and the fall of the land deepened his sense of isolation.

He walked around to the back of the house again. The building was more compact than it had first appeared. Two rusted metal rubbish bins stood by the back door. He checked them and found they were empty. He was still armed; he took his gun out of its holster and looked behind him. No one was there. He tried the back door. It was locked. He looked around in the intense quiet and then shot out the lock. The cracks brought a deeper silence, a cessation of bird calls. They would echo across the suburb and those who heard them would wonder where they had come from. Let's see if they bring anyone here.

He pushed the door open. It wedged at an angle against the floor. He stood on the threshold, looking both forward and back. Outside, there was no one but him; looking inside, the room was dark. He took his torch out of his backpack, illuminating what had once been a simple kitchen. The floor and all the surfaces were thickly covered with dirt, the ceiling corners heavy with cobwebs. There was no sign that anyone was there. He stepped inside. It was warm and the air smelled strongly of mould and decay. Following the powerful beam of his torch, he walked past rooms that opened on either side of the hallway. One had been a bathroom, another possibly a dispensary. The floorboards were shaky under his feet and there were signs of water damage where the rain had got in. In any number of places, the plaster had fallen from the ceiling to the floor to lie in heaps on rotting carpet. The whole house was derelict.

He reached what had been the waiting room, revealed under his torch beam. Chairs sat in a line in front of a window covered by net curtains so thick with dirt they were black. Insect nests appeared as dark clumps in the rotting fabric. In the bright afternoon sun, the room was in darkness. His eyes were growing used to his surroundings but in the mass of shadows, he still needed the torch to see the detail of what was around him. The sound of something scrabbling startled him. He looked around quickly but the torchlight revealed only a possum. In what was otherwise silence, he felt certain there was no other living person here besides himself.

On the opposite wall the torch beam showed a long, narrow, aged photographic print that might have come from Amelie Santos's long-ago university days: *Spinal Medulla or Cord*. Like a top-heavy jellyfish, the dual hemispheres of the human brain were shown suspended above its long, trailing propellants. Harrigan read the labels attached to these floating threads, some of which were thicker than others: *spinal nerve roots* and *dorsal root ganglia*.

Familiar descriptions. When Toby was born, Harrigan had studied the brain and spinal cord seeking to understand his son's disabilities, forcing himself to accept there was no cure. Since then Toby had lived with permanent damage to the very same spine and nervous system that hung on the wall. This is all we are; these filaments, those hemispheres, the two reflecting mirrors in the brain. Instruments of delusion and cruelty as much as anything else. Glitch them and the person was deformed or dead.

Harrigan turned and his torch raked across the dark to the reception desk. Then he saw it, sitting in the centre of the desk, quietly waiting. An axe with a black stone head protruding from its handle at an oblique angle. The thick, club-like handle was almost a metre long. It had been set down on a carpet square, presumably to protect it.

Harrigan moved forward to scrutinise it. The head was clean and polished. With both hands on the handle, it would be a powerful weapon. He recognised it for what it was: a stone axe from somewhere in the highlands of New Guinea. Grace's father had several in his keeping, including one not unlike this from West Papua, all stored under lock and key at his home in Point Frederick. As an artefact, it was valuable and it looked old. Old enough to have been brought back in the 1960s by Frank Wells. Why choose this weapon? Unless it had meaning for you. Perhaps it was a weapon once brandished threateningly against you, now turned against others. Frank Wells would know the answer, if he was prepared to admit it.

Harrigan put his torch down and picked up the axe. It was heavy enough to need both hands to lift it. This was the heart of it. The smash. Some fundamental breaking out of every piece of brutality, causal or intentional, that had gone into making Craig Wells or Griffin, whoever he was, whatever he was. But it wasn't just the violence. What is it you want, that using this can give you? Something beyond words. Some force you decide to let go without any intention to control it. Adrenalin. Just a chemical. Things like the pleasure of manipulation were secondary, they just built you up to this point. But you had to take that step to kill, you had to want to. Something in you had to want to smash that energy outwards and you had to choose this way of letting it happen, knowing what it would do. What the person would look like when you'd finished.

Maybe once you could lose it. You could go mad. But nothing in the history Harrigan had uncovered suggested any set of circumstances like that. If his beliefs were correct and Janice Wells had been the first victim, then that murder had been planned; planned for years by someone still in their teens. What had come first? This weapon stolen from his father or the intent to kill? Or had they both gelled after this weapon had first come into his hands? *I can use this.* A few simple words. Meeting a boy whose father had taken that step already. *Did he hit her? How?* The first realisation that this was possible, breaching the membrane that restrained you, to be followed by the act that confirmed: yes, you can kill. Either way it had been a deliberate choice. He could have said, *I don't have to do this.* There were always other possibilities. If Harrigan was right and Wells had created his own new persona out of the death of the real Joel Griffin, why not choose to create a new life for himself some other way? Because he wanted this. He wanted what it gave him.

Harrigan set the axe down where it had been, stepped back from what felt like the edge of nowhere. He had to get out of here soon. It was a terrifying place.

His torch beam touched on the net curtains. The blackness impregnating the material wasn't only dirt, it was old blood. This was the epicentre. While you were waiting to see the doctor. He glanced in a line from the reception desk to a door, now shut. The consulting room.

He opened the door slowly. The smell of mould throughout the building had grown to be almost overpowering; in this room it was the stink of death. Harrigan took out his handkerchief and put it over his mouth and nose.

It was a large room with an old desk facing the door. A high-backed chair stood behind the desk, giving the impression that someone had just this minute got up from it and walked out of the room. Behind the chair and along one wall to his left, overgrown plants pressed against bare windows, crowding the cracked glass like silent onlookers.

Harrigan walked inside. The silence felt loud, like someone shrieking for his attention. He looked at the empty walls, the bare wooden floor. In the far corner, the floor had caved in. He walked forward and looked down into the space between the broken boards. Pale in the shadows, the bones he saw were all too real. There were two of them. Lying on their sides in the dankness, bodies that had decayed to skeletons, looking as if they were about to be absorbed into the ground. Thin locks of dark hair still clung about their skulls, their teeth were scattered like seeds. One had its hand just in front of its face, the way children lie sometimes when they're sleeping. Indifferently, efficiently, the insects had cleaned their bones and built their nests around their shreds of clothing. Whoever they were, these people had been here for a long time. They couldn't be the source of the stench he smelled now.

In the torchlight he saw a line of ants near his feet. The busy column had cut a path through the muck on the floor towards the opposite corner of the room. He shone his torch on the column and followed it. A line visible through the dirt and leading past the windows that looked out of the front of the surgery. There were crude, broken marks on the floor where the boards had been roughly taken up and then laid back down again. He counted them as he walked. Four, making six with the two in the corner. One set of marks was newer than the others. Here the ants were disappearing into a crack in the floor, busily at work.

Someone had died here recently. Someone had stood out there in the waiting room facing the unimaginable before finding release in their own permanent silence. Harrigan stood over these makeshift graves and looked down with an instinctive respect for the dead. The silence no longer jammed in his ears. I've found you, he thought. You can lie quietly now.

Harrigan reached the other side of the fence with deep relief. The sunshine on his back, the sight of colour, the sounds of birds, brought him to life. He breathed clean air into his lungs. His phone was in one hand, his gun in the other. He was thinking, seeing a map of the suburbs roundabout in his mind. You could walk through the park from Duffys Forest to here. Probably there were tracks you could take. If you knew what you were doing, knew the terrain well enough, you could make your own tracks. Make your own and choose your time. No one would see you. Make your victims walk from the white-tiled room there to here, both of you knowing what you were going to. From bolt hole to graveyard, it was a ritual carried out six times over the last ten or so years. Not so infrequent. An addiction.

He was weighing up the question of who to ring. Borghini was with the local command. It was his turf, he knew what he was doing and he wasn't likely to be put off from doing his job.

Before walking up to the road, Harrigan sheathed his gun. The Mellishes still weren't back from their birthday party; there was no sign of a Volvo deprived of its usual parking spot. But there was another car a little further up the street that he hadn't seen before. He stopped just at the entrance to the Mellishes' driveway and looked at it. Then he stepped away from the avenue of trees that sheltered the driveway from the rest of the street. Trees that would have hidden him from view if he had walked along there to get to his own car.

They came at him anyway, three of them, too quickly for him to avoid them or reach for his gun. He still had his phone, he had already punched in Borghini's number. He hit the call button as they reached him. Ponticellis' thugs. His phone was knocked out of his hands, skidding away. He fought them hard, dragging them further out onto the street where they had to be seen. He thought he heard a shout from someone else, not them, but by then he was face down on the ground. He felt the savage jab of a hypodermic needle in his thigh and then the world went black.

22

Grace drove through the quiet streets of Brooklyn feeling the eeriness of knowing that somewhere Clive's surveillance teams were watching like patrons at a theatre where the action was real. The town was laid out in a long, narrow line along an inlet. It wasn't much more than houses clustered along a single dog's-leg road that eventually reached its dead end at a public jetty looking out at the main channel of the Hawkesbury River. By the time Grace reached the parking area close to the bay, it was getting dark and the place was almost deserted.

Sara was waiting, solitary in the dusk. She was dressed in jeans and a jacket and had her hands in her pockets. The bush-covered hills behind her tall figure were a hard, massive shape against the softening sky. On the water, the last of the light had taken on an iridescent, diamond-shaped patterning, rocking with the movement of the waves. Boats, small and large, were moored some distance out. Was Clive's boat out there? He had said that it would be.

Grace walked up to Sara. She was pacing restlessly up and down.

'You're hours late. Where's Narelle?' she asked.

'Did you set that up?'

'What are you talking about?'

'Joe Ponticelli. Did you set him on me?'

'I said I don't know what you're talking about!'

'First you change things. I'm told to come here to Brooklyn. And when I do, a motorbike with a pillion comes up behind me. In fact, it looks just like how Kidd got shot. They shoot through the passenger window. But they don't get me, they get Narelle. I ran them off the road. I had a look. Joe Ponticelli's dead. I wasn't sure about the other one. If he wasn't then, he probably is now.'

'Where's Narelle?'

'Sleeping in the bush. She's not going to wake up again. I had to go and wash as well.'

'What about your car?'

'I had to get rid of it. The one I'm driving now belongs to someone else.'

'Then why bring it here? It'll be traced. Did anyone see you?'

'No! I'm more careful than that. Let's get down to business. I've got the passport, the tape and I've got Narelle's ID. I want to be paid.'

Sara looked at her and then around her into the dark, but there was no obvious sign of movement.

'Is that her ID you're carrying in that bag?' she asked.

'Yes.'

'Let's see it.'

'No. Later. I'm owed a lot for this.'

Sara smiled arrogantly at her. 'You'll be paid in full, don't worry about that. But that wasn't supposed to happen. You never know who's going to turn out to be unreliable, do you?' She laughed softly.

'What are you talking about?'

'They were watching you all the way from Liverpool. Joel might have trusted you. I wasn't sure I did.'

It was only when Grace had to deal with them that her backup had told her they were there. Clive's directions.

'Why did they go after me? I was delivering Narelle. What's the point of sabotaging that?'

Sara didn't reply. She stared at Grace with an almost frightened expression on her face. Then she shrugged.

'I don't know. I just told them to watch you. And you killed him! God.'

'It was a stupid thing to do,' Grace said contemptuously. 'Next time you want backup, pick someone who's not a lunatic.'

Sara looked away. 'We don't have time to talk about this. Let's go.'

'Wait a moment. Where's Joel?'

'Out there somewhere.'

'That's not good enough.'

'It will just have to be,' Sara snapped.

'No, it won't. Where's Joel and where are we going?'

'For a boat ride. What else?'

'I'm not getting on any boat until I know where I'm going.'

'*Keep your voice down.*'

There was silence as Sara looked around. Her face was barely visible in the dark, her expression unseen. She stepped forward.

'I'll tell you where we're going,' she said in a whispered voice. 'But no way am I telling you where Joel is right now. Do we trust each other or don't we?'

'Where are we going?' Grace asked.

'Cottage Point. It's not far. Now let's get a move on. We've wasted too much time.'

What if she took out her gun and arrested Sara now? But she still didn't know where Griffin was. The surveillance teams would have heard everything that had been said. They could get to Cottage Point if they had to. *Are you going to follow me up the river, Clive? Fish me out?*

'How do I get back from wherever we're going?'

'Joel will drive you. It's all organised.'

'All right,' Grace said. 'Let's go.'

The sailing boat, named *Cottage Days*, was waiting at the pontoon. It was smaller and neater than Grace had expected.

'Is it only you?' she asked.

'I know what I'm doing. This is what I do to relax. I sail. I know this boat, I've had it for years. I know the river. I love it here.' Sara's sense of relief was obvious in her voice. 'You can just be yourself here. Get in, and do me a favour: don't talk.'

Grace sat in silence while Sara cast off and, using the motor, guided the boat past the other vessels and out into the channel.

Stars covered the sky. This far from the city, it was possible to see out to other worlds. Sara turned off the motor and began to pilot the boat under sail. Then she started to laugh.

'You killed Joe Ponticelli. Life has its twists and turns. Oh, what a joke that is.'

'Why?'

'You'll find out.'

There was malice in her voice, almost childishly so.

'Why didn't you want me to talk?' Grace asked.

'Because I may not get to sail down this river again for a while after tonight and I want to enjoy it.'

'Why? Are you leaving? Where are you going? I thought we were setting up a deal.'

'Maybe you'll be our Australian connection,' she said mockingly.

They sailed on in silence for a short while. There was only the sound of the river, the presence of the forested hillsides and the soft, starlit sky. Sara had withdrawn, she was silent.

'How long have you been sailing?' Grace asked.

'Since I was a kid. Don't talk to me. I want to enjoy this.'

'Why shouldn't I talk to you?'

'Because most people are fucking idiots and I'm not sure you're not one of them!'

Grace waited. Sara was where no one could touch her, lost in the simple self-directed pleasure of what she was doing. Grace spoke, deliberately puncturing the emotion.

'If you're leaving, you'll miss all this when you go, won't you? There can't be anywhere else in the world like this for you. Why do you have to go? Why can't you stay here?'

Sara looked back at Grace, her expression shadowed.

'It's just the way things have to be,' she said.

'Is Cottage Point where you were going to bring Narelle?'

'Do you think that would have been difficult? Elliot's waiting for you at Cottage Point, Marie. Oh boy, let's go. I want to see him as soon as I can.'

Sara imitated Narelle with too much savagery for Grace to laugh.

'You just called her Marie.'

'That's her name when she's with Joel.'

There was silence. Sara was staring out at the water.

'You and Joel are an item,' Grace said after a while. 'Did it bother you when he spent time with Narelle?'

'No,' Sara replied. 'Any more than it would bother me if he spent time with you. That's what you want, isn't it? It's not just the money. You want him.'

Grace wondered why she found this so offensive when it had been part of Clive's strategy from the beginning. She had met it before; situations where other women assumed you were chasing after their partners when you had no interest in them at all. It had worked for her; it had helped persuade Sara she was genuine.

Sara laughed. 'I knew it. He thought you were too standoffish. I told him you were just playing hard to get. You thought you were better than he was. I told him, just wait. She'll be there for you. Like all the others.'

She. I'm sitting here in person. Why should you think I find him as compelling as you do? But if she said she found him repellent her cover was gone. *All the others.* How many of them had there been? She kept silent. Sara smiled at her, scornfully.

'Where did he meet Narelle?' Grace asked.

'At my parents' place. Her and all the other wannabe actresses seeing who they can have sex with to get a part. Didn't have a hope.'

And you just watched while he chatted up this little self-serving user, Grace thought, seduced her in your own parents' house, and set her up as a gaoler and a fantasy pastime in a brothel you probably both owned. And you didn't care. Not much.

'Joel told me he'd known you since you were fifteen,' Grace said.

'Why do you want to know?'

'He was your first boyfriend. That's all.'

Your first boyfriend and you never shook him off. Some women don't. Sara was staring at her with hard-eyed condescension.

'We understand each other. Something you can only see from the outside. You'll never get anywhere near it.'

Grace thought how at that moment Sara sounded strangely like Narelle.

'Where'd you meet him?'

'At a camp I used to have to go to when I was a teenager. He was different. He saw things from the outside, the way I did. He was smarter than anyone else. We got talking and we knew we understood things other people didn't.'

'You still think that.'

'I know it,' Sara said.

'Why'd you have to go to camp?'

'Because my parents didn't give a shit if I was alive or dead!'

Grace waited till the air cleared.

'Do you get on better with them now?' she asked bravely.

'They're useful.' Sara spoke with a sense of superiority. 'Joel taught me that. Use them. He told me, if they don't care about you, just use them. From everything they've got, take what *you* want. Drain everything you want out of them. We did just that.'

Again, Grace waited.

'You've never had sex with anyone else,' she said.

'I don't want to.'

'What if you did?'

'No! Why would that happen? You really don't know Joel. You don't know what he is.'

Why would I want to know what you know?

'Do you take him sailing?'

'He doesn't like the water.'

'Does he mind if you go sailing? Or does he think you shouldn't do things he doesn't like you doing?'

'Sailing is just something I do,' Sara said, angrily.

'You're rich.'

'Isn't that what you want?'

'You had money, but Joel taught you other ways to make more money. So you went and did it. Whatever he wants you to do, you go and do it. Except this. Sailing. But now you have to leave that behind as well.'

Sara's head jerked back in a dangerous way. 'You don't know anything about us. I've learned from him all my life. The first years we were together, they were amazing. He taught me what you can do if you want to.' She smiled in the strangest way, barely visible in the light. 'I'd never had a high like that before. No one else would have shown me those things. You just don't know. Compared to him, you're just like Narelle. A nothing. Now you can just shut up.'

Grace felt her gun against her ribcage, glad it was there. *Did you hear that, Clive? I'm walking into a meeting with two very dangerous people. You'd better be there.*

They turned into Cowan Water. The steep waterside hills of Ku-ring-gai Chase National Park closed in on them. Then the lights of the tiny suburb were in view. Situated on the banks of Cowan Creek and surrounded by bush in the heart of the national park, it was an isolated, if beautiful, place. From here, the lights of Sydney were a pale glow in the night sky. Soon the boat slid quietly up to a mooring place. There was a dinghy moored nearby. They got into it and Sara rowed them to the private jetty of a three-storeyed house, the last in the short line of buildings on the water's edge.

There was a light shining dully over a door not far from the jetty; otherwise the house was in darkness. Before they went inside, Sara turned and looked around at the water, the hills surrounding them, and the sky.

'What are you doing?' Grace said. 'Saying goodbye to *Cottage Days*? We're not coming back here then.'

'Just keep quiet,' Sara hissed, an edge of tears in her voice. 'Sound carries.'

She let them both in, switching on the lights to a spacious rumpus room. The décor, from the '70s, looked old and kitsch. Under other circumstances, the house would have had a comfortable, holiday feel, the kind of place where you could kick your shoes off. There was no sign of Griffin.

'Is this where you were bringing Narelle?'

'Check that room over there.'

Grace walked up to a door with a lock on the outside. She looked back over her shoulder but Sara hadn't moved.

'Don't worry,' she said. 'I'm not coming after you.'

It was a small room with one window, too small to get out of and too high to reach. The walls were brick, the door solid wood. Once you were locked in here, there would be no way out until someone opened the door.

'What was going to happen to her in there?'

'You were going to shoot her.'

'I was?' Grace said.

'I was going to strip her and then I was going to watch. She was going to cry and beg for mercy and I'd say, too bad, Elliot doesn't love you any more. But she's already dead. We don't have to do that.'

'Where's the gun?'

'It's the one you're carrying. You are carrying one, aren't you?'

'Why me?'

'Proving yourself to Joel. Oh, he thinks you're genuine and I'm beginning to think you are too. But that's what you were going to do to prove it.'

No, I would have had to arrest you and take you in. The operation would have been aborted. Grace shut the door and once again felt the security of her gun against her ribs.

'There's no Narelle. What are we doing here now?' she asked.

'Just wait.'

Sara took a mobile out of a drawer, turned it on, sent a quick message, then turned the phone off again and put it in her pocket.

'All right. We're moving on. You're finally going to get what you came for.' She held up a set of car keys. 'The garage is two levels up. Let's go.'

'This is your parents' house, isn't it?'

'It's basically mine,' she replied with a shrug. 'We've had it for years but they never come here. I'm the only one who's ever used it.'

'You came here to go sailing. When you were a kid. This is where you learned to sail.'

'So what?' Sara replied, a little puzzled. 'Why do you want to know?'

'It was before you met Joel. Before you found out about all those things he taught you. You came here and you were happy.'

Before you let him turn you into a murderer.

'What are you talking about? What are you getting at?'

Sara's tall and slender figure was shaking. She stared at Grace, almost crying.

'Nothing.'

'Then stop talking rubbish and let's go.'

'Where to?'

'Mona Vale Road. We have to hurry. We're late.'

The car was a Mazda Grace hadn't seen before. 'Where's your black Porsche?' she asked.

'Do you want to ride? Or do you want to walk?'

'Why drive some cheap little blue Mazda when you can drive a Porsche?'

To her surprise, this comment, which was only intended to tell her listeners which car to look out for, had clearly hurt Sara's feelings.

'It'll be good enough to get you where you're going,' she said, a crack in her voice. 'That's all that matters.'

'Don't tell me you've had to say goodbye to your car as well as everything else?' Grace said as mockingly and mercilessly as Sara could have done.

'Get in! We have to go!'

Sara drove in silence, staring at the road ahead, pushing the car. Her face was set; had she been walking, she would have had her head down and been powering through anything that got in her way. They climbed the steep slope up from Cowan Creek, through the national park, then too fast along the ridge out of the park to the main road. It was getting late. Grace allowed herself to think about Ellie and Harrigan. *You'll see me*, she told them. Then Sara turned off Mona Vale Road into Terrey Hills.

'What are we doing here?' Grace asked.

'Going where you want to go.'

'Terrey Hills? Duffys Forest? What's here?'

'Wait.'

She drove deep into the heart of the rural suburb of Duffys Forest. The roads were dark and Grace couldn't see any street signs. Finally she caught sight of one illuminated in the car lights.

'We're out in the sticks,' she said. 'The Bush Fire Brigade is just down there.'

'But we're not going there, are we?' Sara replied with a razor-edged smile.

There was a car a short distance in front of them along the road. Its lights were turned off. It drove for a little longer, then turned into a driveway. Grace watched a man get out and open the gate. Griffin. He cut his engine and coasted down the driveway. Sara had already turned off her car lights and followed him. When they turned into the driveway, Grace could just make out a *For Sale* sign out the front of the house.

'Is this your house?' she asked. 'Or is it empty because it's for sale and you're just using it?'

'Quiet!'

They coasted down the driveway into a garage with a light on overhead. Griffin had already pulled up in a white Toyota Camry. Sara stopped behind him. Grace recognised the numberplate: the car that had stalked Harrigan and Ellie to Kidz Corner.

'Get out,' Sara said.

Grace did so. She had her gun, they knew she did. Would it be enough to protect her from the two of them? This was enough. Time to bail out.

'Why are we here?' she asked Sara, who was standing by the open door of her car. 'Why come here? It's time to go.'

'Not yet,' Sara said.

Griffin came over. Grace stood where she could see both of them. Griffin didn't even look at her.

'Why are you so late?' he asked Sara. 'I've been waiting for your SMS for hours.'

'She killed Joe Ponticelli.'

'What?' He turned to Grace, seeming to see her for the first time. 'Why did you do that?'

'Because he tried to kill me. The same way Kidd got gunned down. I ran them off the road. They got Narelle. She's in the bush.'

'He wasn't after you, he couldn't have been. Unless —' He stopped. 'It doesn't matter one way or the other now. Did you get Marie's ID?'

'Yes.'

'Okay. We've no time now. Coopes won't be with us tonight.'

'Oh, why not?' Sara asked, not hiding her disappointment.

'Who's Coopes?' Grace asked.

'An old friend,' Griffin replied dismissively. 'He can't be involved. There's no time.'

'I wanted to see him. It's the last time,' Sara said.

'Who is Coopes?' Grace repeated.

Griffin looked at her in the weak light, a friendly, apparently candid expression on his face. 'Coopes was going to help me pay you, but we don't have time to take you to him now. It doesn't matter. I have money inside the house.'

'Are we still meeting at Halfway Hut?' Sara asked.

He stepped forward, a finger in the air, shaking it at her as if it might transform itself into a blow. 'Don't. You should know — no —' He left whatever he was going to say unfinished. 'You should leave now. Make sure the gates stay open. And whatever you do, no games till I get there. Okay? Don't underestimate anything. It's too dangerous.' He spoke harshly, angrily.

'I know what I'm doing,' she said. 'I'll see you there.'

'Wait!' He stopped her as she turned away. 'Give me your mobile.'

'What if I need it?'

'You won't. Give it to me.'

She handed it over, smiled angrily at Grace, then got into her car and drove up the driveway out of sight. Grace felt the chill of the smile. Then she asked herself: they're an item, lovers supposedly. Why didn't they kiss? Do they touch? Does he always talk to her like that?

'What's going on?' she asked. 'How do I get out of here?'

'I drive you. Don't worry.' He stopped, listening. 'Did you hear a car?'

'Sara?'

'No. After her.'

Grace listened but heard nothing.

'There's no one there,' she said, with a touch of despair.

Where are you, Clive? You must have heard the pull-out signal. Are you here at all? You can find me. I'm wearing my wire.

'Is that Marie's ID?' Griffin was asking.

'Yes.'

'Give it to me.'

She did, having no choice.

'What about the passport and the tape?'

She handed them over. She watched him open the Camry's door and put all these things in the glovebox, along with Sara's mobile.

'We're taking all that with us, are we?' she asked.

'Come inside,' he replied, ignoring what she'd said. 'I have some things I have to get before we leave.'

She followed him but stayed back. If she took out her gun, she'd have to use it; probably to kill. Kill or wound. Wounds that incapacitated often did so permanently and sometimes killed. If she only had herself to rely on, she would have no choice. They reached the back door where he turned on an outside light.

'Is this your house?' she asked.

'I should have inherited it,' he replied. 'But in the end I had to buy it.'

'Why did you want this particular house?'

'Not your business,' he said.

He unlocked the door, switched on the inside light, and they walked into an old-fashioned kitchen. There were jerry cans of petrol on the table.

'What are they doing here?' she asked.

'I'm cleaning this house away. But first I have some things to get.'

'You're going to burn this place down?'

'Not me. Some people will do it for me later on tonight. By then we'll all be long gone.'

'The house is for sale.'

'It's already been sold by private treaty. I have the money. I have another house for sale. As soon as I sell that, it'll go up as well.'

'Why?'

'Because that's what I've done all my life. Clean away shit. Turn it into something useful instead. When this goes up in flames, that'll be the last of it wiped out. I'll have got what I wanted from it. It'll be money in the bank instead.'

Still keeping a distance behind him, she followed him while he switched on the lights first in a dining room and then the hallway. They passed a bedroom. Grace looked at the disordered sheets. She had a perception of bodies wrestling with brutal movements. You couldn't tell whether it was love or a beating. A small pile of women's clothes, including underwear, had been placed on the end of the unmade bed. She glanced at them, then jerked her head back. Who were they waiting for? Not Sara.

'Why didn't you wait for us inside the house?' she asked. 'Then you could have got what you wanted and we could just have got in the car and gone.'

'People might have seen the lights and realised someone was here. Only do what you have to do when you have to do it. I don't want anyone knowing I'm here.'

He walked past a bathroom to a door at the end of the hallway. He pushed it open onto a small white-tiled room. This one smelled of bleach and the wooden floor was stained.

'Let's not waste any time,' Grace said. 'It's time to go.'

'I won't be long,' Griffin replied.

He knelt, levered up a floorboard and reached down into the cavity below. Grace stepped back and took out her gun.

'They're gone.' He sat up straight on his knees. 'That's not possible.'

'What's missing?' she asked.

'Everything. I put them there just two days ago.'

'Put what there?'

'My business records. Money. I have to have those records. I can't leave without them.'

He stood up and turned around on this last question, saw her gun and stared.

'Lie down on the floor,' she said. 'If you try to do anything else, I'll kill you.'

He shook his head. His friendly expression was back. 'You're not the type to kill. I can tell.'

'I'm counting to three. One, two —'

She would have fired at him if someone hadn't taken hold of her from behind. She fired anyway but the bullet went wild, burying itself in the door frame. The man who was pushing her to the floor was too strong for her. He twisted her gun out of her hand, almost breaking her wrist. Then he ripped her phone out of the pocket of her jacket. All she could see were Griffin's feet, the open cavity and the stained wooden floor.

'You wouldn't have killed me,' Griffin said.

Yes, I would have.

'Give me that,' he said to whoever was holding her. 'It's a powerful gun. Standard Orion issue, I suppose. Better than mine. Yes, I'll use this. You can stand up.'

She did, and looked at who was behind her. A man she didn't know, probably a Ponticelli goon. Griffin was holding her gun. The man who'd tackled her had his own.

'Where was he?' Grace asked.

'He's been waiting here for hours. In the dark. I always take precautions.'

'What do you want to do?' the muscle man asked Griffin.

'Someone came here and took some things I own,' Griffin said to Grace. 'Computers. Portable hard drives. Do you know where they are?'

'I've never heard about any of those things before. Don't you have backup records somewhere else?'

'I'd have to go and get them, which complicates things. You and I have somewhere else to be and we're alrcady late.' He looked past her to the man holding her. 'Who's been here? Do you know?'

'I don't know. I didn't get here till late this arvo. I just dumped the petrol on the table and waited.'

Griffin looked around the white-tiled room, searching for something invisible.

'Would Sara do this? She can be so bitchy when she's angry with me —' He stopped. 'Something like this happened at my other house in Blackheath. Is someone stalking me or is —' Again he stopped.

'Doesn't Sara want to leave with you?' Grace asked.

'We both want the same things. We always have,' he said with the strange and apparently candid look.

He stood there silent in the hallway, thinking.

'Mate,' the muscle man said, 'she drew a gun on you. I reckon she'd have used it. You say she's from Orion. She's got to be wired.'

'Are you?' Griffin asked.

Grace's wire, a sophisticated piece of miniature wireless technology, was neatly twisted in the underwiring of her bra and finished in the decoration set in lace between the cups.

'I came here to get paid,' she said. 'That's all. Then you double-crossed me. That's why I drew my gun. Your money's gone. Maybe it was never there in the first place. It's time to go. Let's just do that. Forget all this.'

'It'll be in her clothes.' The muscle man giggled. 'We can get her to take them off.'

To Grace's surprise, a look of powerful distaste crossed Griffin's face.

'I've already got some clothes I want her to wear,' he said. 'Sara bought them the other day. They're in the bedroom.'

Soon he was back, offering her the compact bundle. 'Put these on. You can dress the way *I* want now. With your hair out.'

'What for?'

'It's the way I want to remember you. I told you, you have beautiful hair.'

You're sick. Don't say it. Don't make him lash out.

'I'm not changing in front of this ape.'

'You can change in there.' Griffin nodded to the white-tiled room. Then he was staring at her with a total lack of expression. 'If you won't change, I'll kill you now. Your brains will be all over those tiles. I don't want to have to do that but I will. It's up to you. I'll be waiting in the kitchen.'

'Get going,' the ape said, pushing her inside. 'Take everything off and give it to me.'

'Get out,' she said.

He grinned and pulled the door not quite closed. She felt his eye on the crack. There was nothing she could do. Shaking, she changed, keeping her back to the door. The dress was blue, waisted, coming to the knee, a glittering little-girl thing. Nothing like her taste. At least the clothes were new and clean. He had chosen her size well; he'd looked her over carefully every time they'd met, the way lovers do, not murderers. It was an odd look, as if he'd tried to make her a child.

She'd just finished when the door opened and the ape was there. He motioned to her to come out. When she did, he tossed her own clothes back inside the room and shut the door. Her wire was sensitive, but left in that room it wasn't going to pick up anything.

In the kitchen, Griffin looked her over. He was still holding her gun.

'Take your shoes off,' he said.

'Why?'

'You don't need shoes for this.'

She kicked them off.

'Hands,' he said, and the ape tied her arms behind her with plastic rope.

'Good,' Griffin said. 'You look much better.' He stared at her. 'You're very cool. All the other women I've had were sobbing by now. They all beg. *I couldn't do it because of my family, you must understand that. I couldn't do that kind of work*, or *No, I won't tell anyone. You can trust me.* The men are no different. They cry too. You're trained, but you're human. Why aren't you crying?'

My backup are coming for me. They must be.

'Maybe I don't believe this is real,' she said.

'Oh, it's real,' Griffin said. 'What have you got for me?'

The ape handed Griffin two items, one after the other. He held them up for her.

'Watch. I have a Rolex. I don't need this.' He tossed it on the floor. 'Photograph. This is different. It's unique.'

The photo showed Grace with Ellie in her arms, immediately after she was born. Her exhausted face. Everything that followed. All that love. Grace looked it at, her mouth closed against the uprush of emotion. Tears were in her eyes. *I can still feel myself holding you. If only I was with you. Who will look after you if I'm not there?*

'You can cry,' Griffin said. 'Talk to me.'

'Where's Paul?'

'Waiting for you,' the ape said with a cackle.

Griffin put the photograph in his trouser pocket. 'I'll keep this. I'll take your hair too, before I finish. They'll be my keepsakes. Whenever I think of you, I'll go and look at your hair.'

I've dealt with people like you before. In the end you're all the same. I'm not crying for you. You are not touching what matters most to me.

'Where's Paul?'

'You know what people are going to think?' Griffin said. 'He murdered you and committed suicide.'

'No one's going to believe that. Not our families, not the police, no one.'

'Your partner wrote a letter and signed it. It'll be posted on his website tonight. I'll show you. I spent most of last night matching his signature. I think I've done it pretty well.'

He reached into his inside jacket pocket and took out an envelope. It was addressed to Toby care of the University of New South Wales. The information that Toby was a student there was on Paul's website. Griffin held up the letter for her to read. The words jumbled in her mind. *Know she's been cheating just not sure who. Never been sure. Made me leave my job.*

'No one will believe that rubbish.'

'People believe what they want to believe. There are enough rumours out there for people to wonder if maybe it is true. And it's his signature. Who can argue with that? People will say, who knows what he was thinking? He was always a private man. It'll muddy the waters enough for people never to be sure.'

'*Where is he?*'

The anger came out of her, a frustrated force. He stepped back a little, then laughed.

'You won't be like that soon. You'll get down on your knees and you'll beg and crawl like all the others. Enough talk. Everyone outside.'

'In that little white Camry? The police have its registration. Did you know that? Anyway, where are we going?'

He stepped forward, looking her over.

'The police aren't here. There's no one out there. You need to understand the situation. Everybody begs. I told you you'd kiss me. You will. You'll do more than that, much more. You wait.' He searched her face, looking for a fault line. She saw him look at her scar. 'I know how to do it.'

Nothing will make me do anything for you.

'Where are we going?' she asked.

'Wait till we get there. Remember, I'll kill you if you do anything stupid,' he said.

'I'll get going,' the ape said.

'Where's his car?' Grace asked.

'Where you wouldn't see it. I told you, I always take precautions.' He turned to the ape. 'Give me her shoes. I want to take them with me.'

'Sure.'

'Before you go, I've got a message for Tony senior. I've kept my side of the bargain throughout.'

'I'll tell him.'

'No, you won't. Because he's double-crossed me.'

Grace's shoes in his spare hand, Griffin shot the man dead. His body lay on the kitchen floor.

'Why did you do that?' she said.

'The only people who know about my houses are the Ponticellis. They must have stolen my records and my money. If the old man sent Joe after you today when we had an agreement that I'd kill you myself, then he's broken our bargain. If he thinks he can get me to pay him for those records, this is a message for him. He'll be dead first.'

He pushed her out in front of him. There was no way to run. At the garage, he motioned her to sit in the Camry's front seat. He tossed her shoes in the back, then fastened her seatbelt. She was pressed back uncomfortably in the seat, her hands losing circulation. He drove up the driveway and out onto the street. Sara had left the gate open.

'Where are we going?' she asked.

'Back the way you came.'

'Who's Coopes?'

'Coopes is a thing, not a person.'

'What is it then?'

He took one hand off the wheel, took out his wallet and placed it on his lap. He flicked it open and eased out a photograph, which he then held up to her.

'That's Coopes,' he said.

She recognised it immediately. A stone axe from New Guinea. Her father had one not unlike it.

'Why do you call it Coopes?'

'Mr Coopes,' Griffin said. 'The headmaster at the last school I went to. He said I could achieve anything I wanted to if I just tried. Every time I use Coopes, I think, yes, this is something I've wanted and I've achieved it. He wanted to be nice to me. It was insulting. I didn't need his pity.'

The resentment in his voice was genuine. More than twenty-five years ago and he still thought about it.

'Did you use it on him?'

'No, I don't know where he went. He was due to retire. He's probably dead by now.'

Silence.

'I kept my bargain,' Grace said. 'You didn't keep yours.'

'That's not true. As far as I was concerned, we had no deal. I made my deal with Tony senior. And he broke it,' Griffin said.

'What was the deal?'

'A personal contract for the old man. We've worked together on and off for years now. He wanted to get back at your partner before he died and he asked me to do something special. I was pleased when he named you. Chris had already told me all about you and I liked the look of you. Chris may not have been able to have you, but I can. Then Kidd told me you were with Orion. And then Marie said you had something to sell. I didn't have to chase you any more. You walked into my hands.'

'Why choose me?'

'Tony wanted your partner to suffer the way he did when his daughter was killed. He wanted you and your daughter. But we couldn't get to her so I decided to get you and your partner together instead. Tony would have liked it. We're giving him a bit extra. Now I'm doing it for me. And Sara. It'll be a buzz.'

Grace felt relief so powerful it made every bone in her body ache. You're safe, she said to Ellie. But was she really going to die? Was she really never going to see her daughter again? She had to protect her. Somehow she had to see Ellie and Paul —

Griffin had said they'd die together. That meant Paul was alive now.

'Sara likes these occasions, does she?' she said. 'Gets a kick out of them?'

That same look of distaste appeared on his face.

'Say anything else about Sara and I'll break your jaw. What she does is up to her. At times like this, she can do anything she wants. It's almost the one time she can. I let her go and then I take over. And then everything's sweet.'

After this, they drove in silence. He was so matter-of-fact. Could this be real? They were out of Duffys Forest and back to Mona Vale Road by now, turning north again and then into the park. They passed the park's gatehouse, closed and dark. Not far in he turned off the road onto a fire trail usually closed to public access by a low boom gate. The gate was open. He drove downhill. Occasional kangaroos leaped along the side of the trail, none into their path. She wished one of them would; it would stop the car.

He drove down the narrow track, then turned off his car lights and made a sharp turn onto another trail. They drove along it for some time, going deeper into the forest. He turned off the engine and coasted the car downhill. No one could know whose death they were driving to.

23

Harrigan came back to consciousness, unable to see. The noisy, then fading sound of a vehicle driving away had woken him. He didn't move immediately but instead tried to work out whether he could think, what he could hear, if he felt any pain. Whether anyone was here with him, watching.

At first there was only silence, and then, distantly, the harsh bark of a wattlebird calling. He was trussed up and blindfolded, the elastic of the blindfold pulled tight about the back of his head. His hands were behind his back, numbed and at the same time made painful by the bite of whatever they had used to tie them. Don't straighten your legs, his mind told him, but there was no rope around his neck. Very slowly and carefully he stretched out and found he was able to move his feet a short distance away from each other. It felt like he'd been hobbled. He realised he was barefoot.

He was lying on his side on what seemed to be a thin and rank mattress. He swung his legs to the ground and managed to lever himself to his feet. In the blackness, he got his balance and took a few deep breaths. He swayed with nausea from whatever drug they had administered, taking some minutes to let his head clear. Wherever he was, it wasn't in a house. The floor beneath his feet was packed dirt and the place had the feel of some kind of shed. The air smelled of piss and rubbish, like a place where derelicts might sleep. It was too quiet to be in the city; the sound of the bird calls was too close. There was no sound of there being anyone else here with him.

Harrigan took a small step forward. He had been hobbled, but he was able to move with very short and awkward steps. Probably he was supposed to be able to walk, barefoot and blinded, into whatever had been lined up for him. His bonds made him lean forward, as if he was being forced to bow his head to his captors. Carefully he moved, one step at a time, occasionally finding sharp rocks on the floor. Then his foot hit a wall. He turned side on, leaned on it, and followed it around. Soon enough he came to a door. He pushed at it with his foot. It was metal, rattled on its hinges, and sounded like it was secured from the outside by a chain.

As best he could, he tried to trace out its width. It seemed to have a metal strut across the middle and a lip where it met the door frame. He encountered the hinges on the inside, standing out from the metal frame like dog's balls. He leaned his cheek against the set closest to him. They were large and felt rough-edged around the pin. Old, bulky, possibly steel hinges, probably poor craftsmanship. He touched the door's lip. It hard a thick, hard edge, rough enough probably to have torn the skin on his cheek.

His legs had been tied at the knee as well as the ankle. He sat down on the dirt and drew his knees up as close as he could to his chin. He leaned his head forward to find out by feel what kind of rope they had used to tie him up with, brushing his cheeks against it. It felt like plastic and had been tied to allow the circulation to flow in his legs. He was definitely meant to be able to walk. It was too uncomfortable to stay in that position any longer than was necessary and he leaned back. He tried to feel what was tying his hands. Not plastic rope, more like electrical wire. Malleable plastic coating, soft copper wire inside, pulled tight enough to bite into his wrists and break into the flesh. *Fuck you*, he thought.

He stood up and manoeuvred himself into an awkward position that allowed him to press the bonds tying his hands together against the door's lip. Then he began to saw, pressing hard. You rub something softer against something harder and rougher for long enough and attrition will work; it has to, even on a bluntish edge. The question was whether or not he had enough time. Stamina wasn't an issue. The certainty that he would die if he didn't free himself was all the motivation he'd ever need.

His hands were both numb and aching blocks of ice hanging uselessly at the ends of his arms. They hadn't stinted in the amount of wire they'd wound around his wrists. He stopped thinking about what he was doing and concentrated on something more pleasant: Grace; how they made love. Then he realised he was afraid for her and changed his thoughts. Where was Ellie right now? With his oldest sister, who was first on the list of emergency contacts? Kidz Corner would raise the alarm if neither he nor Grace turned up to collect her; they would ring the contact number at police headquarters he'd given them. But no one would ever find him here. He put that thought to the side and remembered days fishing at Green Cape. Watching the whales swim past in the distance. Stay there. It'll keep you going.

Once he slipped sideways and grazed his arm badly against the hinges. Later, he slid down to a crouch, to give relief to his back. His legs began to ache instead. As he stood up, he felt the wires around his right wrist begin to loosen. He pulled the bonds apart but the wire hadn't quite given way. He went back to it and kept going, losing track of time. Then, at last, the wire slipped away from his right hand altogether.

Blood flowed painfully back into his hand and he had to wait until he could use it. Then he slid to the dirt floor and pulled the blindfold from his eyes. It was a black mask. Being able to see felt like liberation in itself, even if he was still in a dark place. Turning his head to the side, he saw thin cracks of daylight marking the outline of the closed door, the thickest band of light being at the foot. Otherwise there was no source of light in this place at all.

The door was old and battered and, while there was a lock, there was no handle on the inside. As he'd thought, it had been chained on the outside; there was no way he could open it. He peered out through a crack at the fading daylight. They had picked him up mid-afternoon and he'd heard them driving away. He had spent a lot of time freeing his hand. They couldn't have taken him far. Judging by what he could see, he was in some kind of hut in the national park, with a bare space between the door and the surrounding trees.

He looked at his left hand, bringing it close to his face. The wire was knotted too tightly for him to unpick it with his right hand. He went back to rubbing the wire against the door lip, this time facing the door. I look like I'm jerking myself off, he thought. Strangely, freeing this hand seemed just as uncomfortable, almost harder than when both hands had been behind his back. Between rubbing it and pulling at it, the wire finally gave way and he pulled the last of it off. It had cut deeply into both his wrists, bruising them and making him bleed. He had cut himself further while sawing through the wire, and his arm was raw where he'd torn his skin away against the hinges earlier. But his hands were free and he could use them. Again he waited while his left hand stung itself back into life.

He looked around, his eyes adjusting to the shadows. The light from the doorway was too weak to give him anything other than an indistinct view of the hut he was locked in. It was circular and seemed to have been built on the slope of a hill. A few feet away he saw a lumpy mattress, stinking of rot. He checked himself. His belt was gone as well as his shoes. His watch and wallet too. He had been left with nothing except the clothes he stood up in.

He checked the rope that hobbled him. It had been threaded through a loop around his knees and then tied at his feet. With his back against the wall and his knees pulled up as close to his chest as possible, he could still barely reach the knot. He sat on his side, with his feet side on against the door, and reached for it that way. It was probably the best stretching exercise he'd had all year. He worked at it, took breaks, and finally pulled the rope away. By the time he had got himself free, it was so dark he was working by feel.

Despite the blackness, he began to explore by touch the small cell he was locked in. The roof was low, barely more than a few inches above his head. Lifting up his hands, he could reach it easily. It seemed to be made of cement. He followed the wall around; like the roof, it was made of cement. Then his foot knocked against something lying on the floor near the mattress, in line with where his head had been. It skidded against the wall. He searched and picked it up. It was a book, a hardback. He moved closer to the door where there was a little more light. Even here, it was too dark to see what it was but he was fairly certain it was a copy of his own book, *Justice Under the Law*. What would be the point of leaving any other book here? He tried to see if the title page had been signed but it was too dark. He put the book back on the floor, there being nowhere else for it.

He had left the rope near the door and went back to it. Could he use it for anything? Fix it so that whoever was coming to get him could be tripped when they opened the door? As far as he could tell in the dark, there was nothing to which he could tie the rope to make it work as a tripwire. He did have one advantage. They would be expecting him to be lying on the mattress like a chicken waiting to be slaughtered. He would be waiting for them instead. As best he could in the dark, he moved the cut wires and the rope to where they couldn't be seen if the door was opened in any kind of a light. Make it appear there was no one in here just to throw them as much as possible. Then he sat down on the mattress to think.

Time lost definition when you waited in the dark. He was hungry and thirsty but put those things to the side. Feeling he had arrived at nowhere, he leaned against the wall and worked through the possibilities. Killing him could not have been part of his captors' brief or he would already be in the afterlife, assuming it existed. Someone else must be on their way here to do that. Someone had left a copy of his book here to be part of the action. It was a logic all their own.

He thought about Grace. Whatever reason he was here, she was working. She would have her backup; they'd better be doing their job and protecting her. He thought of his daughter and his son. Toby was old enough to take care of his own life, but either himself or Grace had to come out of this alive for Ellie's sake.

He was so deep in these thoughts that when the sound of a car coming to a stop outside broke the night silence, he was startled. Whoever it was, they hadn't had their headlights on. Someone got out of the vehicle, and shut the door quietly but audibly behind them. Quickly, Harrigan got to his feet and stood to the side of the door. If anyone opened it, he could get them with a blow to the side of the head.

He listened. In the night silence, he heard soft footsteps approaching the door.

'Are you in there?'

Harrigan drew in a breath. The last thing he'd expected to hear was a woman's voice.

'You must be awake by now,' she went on. 'You just wait. There are other people coming. Grace is one of them. We're going to have fun tonight. Grace is going to watch you burn. Then she's going to burn herself. You just sit there and think about that.' She laughed.

Is that right? Harrigan thought. Well, fuck you, whoever you are. He had never hit a woman in his life. His father had sometimes hit his mother when he was drunk, until Harrigan had been big enough to stop him. Watching his father do this, and then, maudlin, beg for forgiveness in the morning, had left Harrigan with a contempt for anyone who did the same. But this wasn't a woman. This was a murderer who happened to be female.

'Are you going to talk to me? You can talk. I know you can.'

There was an odd hint of hysteria in the woman's voice. She was building up her excitement. There was some other edge too. Tears. Why tears?

'I thought someone was following me tonight. But I got rid of them. No one's coming to save you. You might as well talk to me. You're not dying alone. Grace will be with you. And if we can, we'll get your daughter too. We've got something that'll turn her head to pulp.'

Keep talking, whoever you are. I'm waiting for you. Everything you say makes it easier.

'Are you going to answer me? Open your fucking mouth. You can still talk.' Hysteria again, this time wound up to a greater intensity. Strange anger, resentment. 'Go on. Cry. That's what you'll do in the end. Everybody does. They cry and they shit themselves. They all say please when it's too fucking late. When we open the door, you'll come crawling out saying please. When you do, she'll be watching you and it'll be too fucking late. Then she'll crawl in the dirt too. Everyone does.'

There was silence again. Still Harrigan waited.

'You're going to burn in your own car. We've done that before. The first time we ever did anything. I can't wait to see what it looks like again, what you sound like. What do you think?'

Come in and ask me if you want to know so badly.

'Joel will be here soon. Maybe fifteen, twenty minutes. That's all the time you've got left. I'm going to piss on your face. You can lie there and drink it. I'll turn on the lights, I'll take your blindfold off. You can look up at me before you die.'

You are sick. You are so sick.

Suddenly the bright lights of a car glared through the cracks around the door. Harrigan heard her unlocking the padlock, then removing the chain. Maybe when you'd done this so often before you got arrogant. You didn't see your victims as anything other than creatures waiting for slaughter, crying for mercy you didn't have to give.

A key turned in a lock, then the door swung open. The glaring headlights lit up the interior of the hut, revealing only the empty mattress. The woman stopped in the doorway, startled. 'Where are you?' she shrieked even as Harrigan came out of the dark and hit her on the side of her head as hard as he could bring himself to hit a woman.

She went down, not quite unconscious. She didn't seem to be armed. He got hold of the rope they'd used to tie his legs and began to tie her up. She tried to fight and bite him but she was too groggy and had no strength to match his. A stream of obscenities came out of her mouth, barely comprehensible. He still had his handkerchief. He took it out of his pocket and pushed it into her mouth. Then he picked her up and put her on the mattress. She was still making noise and began to wriggle, trying for the door. He looked around. There was nothing to tie her to to keep her in one place. Then she collapsed back, breathing hard. Her eyes rolled up and closed. He pressed her eye, a common test for pain, to see if she was awake. She didn't respond.

He took the time to look at her. An attractive redhead probably just over forty. Sara McLeod? Nadine Patterson? What name would she answer to? He searched her, found her car keys in her jeans pocket and took them. She had no weapon of any kind and no mobile. He stood up. In the car lights, he saw the book near her head and picked it up. It was *Justice Under the Law*. He flicked it open to the title page and saw his signature. Bought last night at his launch by Joel Griffin, who was supposedly on his way here right now. It was his MO: everything planned to the last detail.

Carrying the book, Harrigan went outside into the free air, shutting the door behind him. It locked on closure. The key was still in the lock. He took it, then re-chained and re-padlocked the door. The lights of the car were glaring in his eyes and he walked around to the side of the vehicle, cursing whenever his bare feet trod on something sharp. The car was a blue Mazda he hadn't seen before.

He looked around to see where he was. As he'd guessed, the national park. He'd been locked in a small, squat building situated on a low slope. Probably it had been put here during World War II, some home-defence facility close to the coast where equipment might have been stored or the home guard were expected to fight invaders. Darkened forest surrounded the open area it stood in, at that moment illuminated by the lights of the Mazda. At this time of night, it was a good place for a murder.

He searched the car. There was no gun and no mobile telephone. He opened the boot. A digital video camera and jerry cans of petrol. He closed it and looked up the way it must have come in. A fire trail cut through the bush up a steep slope, presumably towards the nearest ridge. Parked to the side of this trail a short distance up the slope, gleaming palely and pointing downwards to the open space, was Harrigan's car.

Painfully, he limped up to it. The keys had to be somewhere here. How else was anyone going to turn it into a murder weapon? Then he saw rocks wedged against the front wheels. He tried the door. It opened. This was simple. Turn the whole thing into a missile. Who needs to start the engine? Just set it up so it rolls forward over whatever escarpment is below.

Harrigan was a careful man. He had a spare key concealed on the outside of his car for emergencies. He tossed his book on the front seat and set about checking for it; it was still there. Once he'd retrieved it, he began searching the car. They had taken his mobile, his gun, his backpack with its handy collection of tools. He had no weapon and he couldn't call for help. How much time did he have? Time to drive out of here and get help? Griffin was coming, Grace with him. Griffin was supposed to be her target not the other way around. They'd be here very soon, if the woman in the hut knew what she was talking about.

Someone had been following her, she said, but she'd got rid of them. Did that mean Grace's people were out there, tracking her? They had the means to do that. If so, why hadn't they acted? Or had they already stopped Griffin's car? He couldn't know. He did know he didn't trust Clive. If he drove out now, would he meet Griffin coming in? Where would that leave Grace if she was with him? No, he would wait. He couldn't leave her alone in this place. There would only be Griffin, one man. She had to be armed as well. That was a point in their favour. And if no one came, then he would leave.

What he most wanted were shoes, but there were none, not even the pair of old thongs he usually tossed in the boot when he was going fishing. There were some rags. He tied them around his feet but they were almost useless. They had left his car tool kit behind. He searched through it and selected the heaviest spanner he could find. There was also the torch he always carried in his car, which was powerful. He took that as well. He made sure the handbrake was on, locked the car and took the keys. Then he went back to the Mazda, turned off the lights and locked that as well.

After this he followed in the direction his car was pointed. A breeze coming up from distant water ruffled his hair. Again wishing he had shoes, he reached the edge of an escarpment and looked down. A short, steepish fall onto rocks, young trees and ferns growing below. Soak the car in petrol and send it down here. Both of them burned to ashes, still alive when the fire was started. These were the people he was dealing with. No point in being sentimental about them.

A small arc of trees extended out from the forest towards the hut, coming closest to it on the far side near the back. He walked into the trees as quickly as he could, crouching down where he could stay hidden. It was a clear starlit night; extinguishing the headlights had brought a sense of peace to the scene. The silence around him deepened; he turned off his torch. In the quiet, he heard the calls of the night birds and rustling in the bush around him. Just the wildlife going about its usual business.

He had been there only a few moments when he became aware of a car making its way down the trail. No engine, no headlights. It was time for something to happen. In the darkness, Harrigan waited. He was supposed to be marked as a dead man, but this time the dead would bite back.

24

Grace could see the rounded shape of a hut at the end of the fire trail, a pale gleam of cement in the starlight. They passed Harrigan's car on their right and came to a halt beside the blue Mazda. There was no sign of anyone.

'Where is she?' Griffin said. 'She should be waiting in the car.'

'She didn't do what you wanted.'

He leaned forward to look into her face. 'You keep quiet. Save your voice till later.'

He turned the lights on low beam. The hut's door lit up dully as a dirty green. The clear ground about the hut itself became a lighter grey. The colours of the end of the world. Grace checked both sides of the hut as best she could. There was no one in sight. *Why didn't you come, Clive? Three times I called you. Why didn't you come?*

Carrying her gun, Griffin got out of the car and walked up to the Mazda, tried the doors. It was locked. He stood there looking around. Grace tried to move but she was pinned in her seat.

'Where are you?' he called out. 'Why did you lock the car? I told you, we have no time. We can't play any games.' He turned on the spot. 'Sara? If you're here, come out. Stop playing these fucking games! There's no time!'

There was no answer, only the silence of the night.

'Are you there?' Griffin called, anger in his voice. 'Come out! Don't do this to me!'

Again, nothing. He walked to Grace's side of the car and opened the door. He reached across to unfasten her seatbelt and it struck her, the terror he'd said she would feel. *I am here, this is real, there's no way out.* It took complete possession of her.

He stood back. 'Get out.'

She couldn't move. He laughed.

'I knew it would happen,' he said. 'It always does.'

The laughter gave her something to hang on to, some residual stubbornness. She got out. *I have nothing to lose now.* Her body seemed to be flashing hot and cold; she felt she would lose control of it. *Hold on. Don't let them turn you into a thing they want you to be.*

Griffin had her by the hair. 'This way.' Pulled her to just in front of the hut. The stars seemed to wheel overhead.

I want to see my daughter. I want to see Paul. I may not see them again.

'Kneel.'

She knelt. He had put his gun away somewhere, a pocket perhaps, and produced a knife instead. He put it to her neck. She felt the bite of steel on her skin. He had nicked her.

'Move and this knife will find the vein. I'm not like Chris. I know what I'm doing.'

She began to shake uncontrollably. She did not know how to stop it. There were tears in her eyes. He wasn't looking at her.

'Sara? Where are you?' Again the only reply was silence. 'There can't be anyone else here. She must be here.'

'What about the people who left our car?' Grace was surprised to hear herself speak. Her voice was shaking.

'They're gone. You see, I told you. You're starting to come apart now. I knew it when I saw how you reacted to Chris's name that day in Westfield. This is the way to you. A knife and a can of petrol.'

'You aren't him,' she said, some strange calmness coming out of nowhere.

'What did you say?'

She stayed silent.

'You're not as frightened of me, is that what you mean? Feel that? You will be.' He cut her again, a little deeper. 'Stand up.'

She stood. In the car headlights, he looked at her neck.

'You see — you're bleeding a little. Everyone starts somewhere.'

He called out again. 'Sara. I don't want to wait. Where are you?'

A thumping came from inside the hut, a rattling of the chain on the door.

'Oh, no, she didn't,' Griffin said. 'I told her not to.'

The thumping continued.

'*I told you not to!*'

Another bang, then more thumping, frantic. Holding Grace in a grip that twisted her down to the ground, Griffin looked around at the trees.

'If you're out there, Harrigan, you can watch me cut your partner's throat. Sara! Stop that racket!'

The noise got worse, a constant drumming. Suddenly, Grace felt her bonds cut through, the rope fall away and the blood run stinging into her hands. He pulled her upright. She turned swiftly. He was there with her gun.

'Do anything and I'll shoot you. I won't kill you but I'll make you hurt. Anyone out there listening — hear what I just said. You take these.' He threw a set of keys in the dust.

She picked them up, dropped them, picked them up again and dropped them from her still stinging hands. Finally she grasped them.

'What am I supposed to do with them?'

'Open the hut. I want to see what's inside and I don't want to open it myself. No one's going to come up behind me.'

Grace put the key in, fumbled, dropped it, picked it up, dropped it again. This time she was stalling. If Harrigan was out there, she had to give him time. With his spare hand, Griffin hit her hard across the side of her face. She fell forward, stunned.

'Stop wasting time. Open it.'

Shaking, she got to her feet. The padlock and the chain came into focus. You could use that chain for something. It was thick and heavy. Griffin was edgy, constantly looking around behind his back, waiting for whoever might try to come up behind him out of the dark. She put the key in the padlock, unlocked it, let the chain slide to the ground with a thud. She unlocked the door. It swung inwards. Griffin grabbed her by the collar and pulled her back and then sideways. Sara came rolling out, staggered to her feet, making noises behind the handkerchief in her mouth. Griffin looked at her and laughed. He pushed Grace forward.

'Get that handkerchief out.'

She reached and pulled it out quickly, jerking her hand back. Sara spat. There was dirt on her face and in her hair.

'He hit me!' she shouted.

'Why did you open the hut?' Griffin shouted back simultaneously.

'Just get these ropes off me.'

Griffin pushed Grace to the ground till she lay face down in the dirt, pointing the gun at her. Sara suddenly kicked her in the stomach. She gasped but kept her eyes open. From where she lay, she could see the chain on the ground. Keep your eyes on it. Don't let it slip away.

'Turn around,' Griffin said to Sara. With the knife in one hand and the gun in the other, he cut the ropes.

Sara turned and directed a few more kicks into Grace where she lay on the ground. She gasped but didn't call out and kept her eyes open. Have a baby; be in labour for twelve hours before you're rushed into an emergency Caesarean — it teaches you about pain.

Griffin had put the knife back in his pocket. 'Go check his car,' he said.

Sara sprinted up the slope to the car.

'It's locked,' she called back, almost shrieking. 'He's out there. Just shoot her. Let's go.'

Griffin turned towards her, away from Grace in the dirt. Grace pulled herself up on all fours, pretending to retch, edging a little away.

'I didn't want to just shoot her. Fuck you, why did you have to open the hut? I told you not to!' he shouted.

Grace snatched at the chain and was on her feet. He turned and, with both hands, she smashed it across his face with all the strength she had coupled with her desperation. He fell back and she hit his hand, cracking the bone. The gun fell to the ground. Before she could reach for it, Sara was coming for her, screaming. Griffin stumbled back, shouting in pain, one hand on his face. Blood began streaming from his nose. Grace met Sara full on and knocked her back. In this grip, they twisted like mad dancers. In the mêlée, the gun got kicked away into the dark past the two cars. Grace thought she heard it hit something. Sara struggled like someone possessed but Grace got her on her pressure points, holding her between herself and Griffin.

'Make her let me go. She's hurting me,' Sara wailed.

Griffin had his knife. He was holding it in his left hand, not his right. His mouth was open. Blood was pouring down his face and shirt.

'Are you going to come at me with that knife?' Grace shouted at him. 'Or will you put it in Sara first? I think you would if you wanted to. You make her do everything else. Why not make her die for you?'

'He's behind you,' Sara shrieked as Harrigan came out of the dark, spanner raised to bring it down on Griffin's head.

Griffin leaped sideways, feinted with the knife, then stumbled backward off balance, falling and twisting one leg. The spanner missed.

Sara tore herself out of Grace's grip with enough strength to knock her backward. She leaped onto Harrigan's back and began to claw at his eyes. Griffin got to his feet, scrabbling for his knife. Harrigan dragged at Sara with one hand, pulling her hair, swinging around. She clung on. Then he swung away, falling back heavily against the car, knocking the breath out of her. She lay in the dirt, gasping.

Harrigan still had the spanner. Griffin had the knife. They circled each other, Harrigan with one eye on Sara. He was between Griffin and the car.

Grace had picked herself up. Find the gun. It's over here somewhere. Find it.

'You always put her in the front line, don't you,' Harrigan said, contempt in his voice. 'You get women to do your dirty work. What does that make you? A pimp.'

Sara was dragging herself to her feet. Grace scrambled in the dark. Griffin said nothing.

'You want to get to your car, don't you?' Harrigan said. 'That's why you're coming at me. You want to make a run for it. That's you. You're a coward.'

Griffin's face was dead. There was no reaction in it to any of Harrigan's taunts. He was choking on blood in his nose and trying to breathe through his mouth at the same time. Suddenly he took out his car keys and threw them to Sara. Still shaken, she missed catching them and they landed in the dirt.

'Get them! Start the car,' he shouted, but Harrigan ran between her and the keys, still holding the spanner.

'We can get him,' Griffin said. 'You and me. We can.'

Both of them moved towards Harrigan as if to come at him from each side.

'Get the keys!' Griffin shouted at Sara.

'Come near me and I'll use this spanner on you,' Harrigan said.

She hesitated, her mouth open.

'He won't.'

'Yes, I will. What are you doing sending a woman to do your work? Face up to it yourself. Put your knife down and fight me man to man. You don't want to do that, do you? You wouldn't have an advantage.'

Sara jumped forward, stopped. Harrigan laughed at her.

'Always in the front line. People see you but not him. He hides where no one can see him. What a cheap piece of shit he is.'

She ran at him again, just a little, stopped. Griffin suddenly raced for the keys. A bullet cracked in front of him. Everybody froze. Grace walked forward carrying her gun.

'Kneel down,' she said. 'Both of you. Get down in the dirt. Now.'

Her voice was unrecognisable with anger.

'She won't fire,' Griffin said, but his voice was shaking.

'Oh yes, I will. Get down!'

They knelt.

'This isn't happening,' Sara said, and began to cry.

Harrigan walked over to Grace, always keeping an eye on the two people kneeling on the ground. There was a quick glance between them, small emotional electricity communicated.

'Are you all right, babe?'

'I'm okay. What happened to your shoes?'

'Gone.'

'Like mine.'

Other than the one quick glance, she hadn't taken her eyes off Griffin and Sara.

'He's got a mobile. It's in the Camry's glovebox,' she said.

'I'll get it.' He turned to walk to the car.

'Eat dirt,' Grace said. 'Both of you. Eat it!'

Harrigan stopped and turned. 'Babe —'

She wasn't listening. 'If there was shit, I'd get you to eat shit. But there's only dirt. Now eat it!'

'No,' Sara said.

'Why not? You've done much worse things than that. Eat it!'

Harrigan spoke softly in Grace's ear. 'Just keep them under control, babe. That's all you need to do. Do this and you'll lose control.'

'He's made me kneel in the dirt. He wanted to cut my throat and burn us alive. He said that people always crawl, they always cry. Well, now you can eat some dirt!'

Griffin reached down, scooped up a handful of dirt and began to eat it, his face expressionless. Sara put her hands over her eyes.

'Eat it,' Griffin said to her, his voice a monotone.

'I got my one last sail in,' she said. And then: 'I'm not eating dirt for you.'

With a single fluid movement she was on her feet and running screaming at Grace, her face distorted into the Medusa's mask. She leaped forward into the air. Grace fired but at the same time a second crack resounded in the night, both bullets catching Sara as she fell forward into nothing, a long resounding scream closing behind her into silence. Then she lay on the ground, dead.

There was a shout. 'Police! Don't move!'

Harrigan turned to look up the fire trail. Groups of uniformed and plain-clothes officers were hurrying down the slope towards them.

'Don't move,' he heard Grace say and turned to look. Griffin had tried to get to his feet. The blood had stopped flowing from his nose and had stained his clothes. He looked from Sara to the police and then sat back on his heels. He said nothing. The police surrounded him.

Grace dropped her gun down, then disarmed it in one movement.

'I didn't need to do that,' she said. 'They just needed to sit there.'

The same thought was in Harrigan's mind but he didn't give voice to it. He looked at the blood on her neck.

'You're only human, babe,' he said.

Mark Borghini appeared out of the dark and walked up to them. 'Boss, Grace. You okay? Sorry we didn't get here sooner.'

'We're alive. That'll do. Thanks, mate,' Harrigan said, and they shook hands.

'If you're here,' Grace said, 'where's my backup?'

'Behind us. We've been with you since Duffys Forest but we lost you coming down here. Lucky we saw the car lights.'

Still holding her gun, Grace walked over to the prone figure of Sara McLeod.

'Which bullet was it? Yours or mine?' she said.

'Our marksman shot one. I know you shot another. The autopsy will tell us. Don't worry about it.' Borghini was dismissive. 'She was a mad dog. I don't have a problem with it. I'll see if I can get the two of you some shoes. You look like you need them.'

'Mine are in his car,' Grace said. 'In the back.'

She was still staring down at Sara McLeod. The bullets had hit her body. Her face was intact but there was no peace in it, even in death. Had she killed her? She did have a problem with it.

Harrigan was with her. 'She was running at you. She wanted you to kill her,' he said.

'But I didn't want to do it. They got me to do what they wanted. They brought me down.'

'No, they didn't.'

'You were very brave. Congratulations.'

They both turned to see Clive standing close by. They hadn't noticed him approaching.

'Where were you?' Grace said. 'I called you three times to get me out.'

'We're here now. You should have trusted us. We've got our fish and he's still alive. We can interrogate him. It's been a very successful operation.'

He was looking over to where Griffin was still kneeling on the ground, the police around him. Someone tapped him on the shoulder and he stood up. As he was led away, he didn't once glance towards Sara on the ground.

'What we have to do now,' Clive said, 'is find his records and his money.'

'Check in the roof cavity at Duffys Forest. There's a manhole in the linen cupboard,' Harrigan said, watching Clive with barely controlled anger.

'How do you know that?'

'I put them there.'

'That building's due to go up in smoke. It could be burning by now,' Grace said.

'We moved in and secured it as soon as you left.'

'You were there,' she said. 'You let Griffin drive away with me. Why didn't you intervene at the house? I gave the call.'

'The job wasn't finished. He might have led us to those records, which we're now told are still in the house.'

'I gave the call for you to get me out. When we left, I had no wire. You couldn't hear me, you couldn't know what was going on. We were flying blind.'

'We knew he was going to take you somewhere else. We needed to know where. I told you, you should have trusted us. We were there, we're here now, and we've got you out. We weren't going to let you die. I'll be in touch about a debrief.'

As he turned away, he stopped to look at Harrigan. 'Your partner's a very brave woman.'

'I could have told you that years ago.'

'Take my gun,' Grace said. 'I don't want it. It's needed for ballistics anyway.'

Clive took the firearm and walked away.

'He didn't keep his side of the bargain,' Grace said. 'He left me there just in case I gave him something more. I'll never trust him again.'

A uniformed officer walked up to them carrying two pairs of shoes.

'The DS sent these over. These are yours, miss. And for you, boss — a pair of thongs. Sorry. That's all we've got.'

'They'll be fine. Thanks.'

With some relief, they put the shoes on.

'Do we have to stay?' Grace said. 'Can we go? We shouldn't be needed tonight. I want to see Ellie.'

'They might need to photograph your neck,' Harrigan replied. 'I'll ask. We won't be able to take our car, but there may be someone here who can give us a lift.'

They turned to each other. She gave an exhausted half-smile and he put his arms around her. They hugged, hard and long. Harrigan looked over her shoulder and saw Clive watching them. Then the spymaster turned away into the night.

'Come on,' he said, and they walked away. They walked past the car where Griffin sat, but he was staring ahead. If he saw them, their existence didn't seem to register. His face was completely empty, as if there was nothing in him, no thought, no emotion.

'He's got your picture,' Grace said. 'The one you took of me when Ellie was born. It's in his pocket.'

'Does he now?'

Harrigan walked away and found Borghini. A little later, Borghini and two uniformed officers went over to the car.

'Could you just step out, Mr Griffin? Just for a moment, thanks. We need to check your pockets.'

Griffin did. After a short search, one of the uniformed officers handed Borghini a photograph. He nodded, walked back to Harrigan, who had returned to Grace, and handed it to him.

'There you go,' he said, and walked away.

Much later, a police car took them to Harrigan's older sister's house where Ellie was sleeping. They had called Ronnie earlier and she was waiting for them.

'She took some settling down but she's asleep now. I told her Mummy and Daddy would be here soon. She seemed okay with that. So, big little brother,' the diminutive woman said, giving

Harrigan a sharp-eyed glance, 'what have you been up to?'

'Later,' he said. 'We just want to go home.'

Grace picked Ellie up from the bed. The little girl rubbed her sleepy eyes and put her arms around her mother's neck.

'Hello, chicken. Mummy and Daddy are here. We're going home. How's that?'

I have you back, Harrigan thought. Safe at last.

25

Borghini asked Grace and Harrigan if they wanted to watch when his people interviewed Griffin. The interview they attended was one of a series. Grace went as a private individual, not as an official representative; Orion's protocols excluded her from any questioning they would do. She went not out of curiosity but to try to diminish his ghost in her own mind, to convince herself that he was where he could do them no harm.

In all, a small group of about five people, including an official observer from Orion, were watching when Griffin was brought into the interview room with its one-way glass wall. Borghini was also there, as an observer. He had passed this interview over to a trained interviewer from headquarters and a profiler. Griffin was accompanied by his lawyer, a well-known, highly skilled and expensive practitioner. Harrigan, remembering Griffin's skill as a barrister, wondered what directions he had given his counsel. He was dressed in prison overalls and sat with his arms folded, seemingly detached from the situation. His business as a criminal banker was still under investigation by Orion and there was only limited information available on that side of his activities. Six bodies had been found at the Turramurra house. Two were at least ten years old. Some were men, some women.

'My client wishes to advise you that he will be conducting this interview and his defence under the name of Joel Griffin,' Griffin's lawyer said.

The statement was made at the start of every interview.

The police interviewer began the process. 'We do have irrefutable DNA evidence that your client was born Craig Wells, son of Frank and Janice Wells.'

'Be that as it may, it's been many years since he adopted the name Joel Griffin. That's what he calls himself now.'

'All right, Joel. Just for context, let's go over the chronology of your life after your mother was killed. You left the country as Joel Griffin almost immediately and went to Asia with Sara McLeod and her parents. During your time in Asia you worked in the McLeods' import–export business. After several years, you went with Sara McLeod to Britain. You didn't return to Australia until the mid-1990s. Is that correct?'

'Joel has already acknowledged he spent that time out of the country,' the lawyer said.

'During that time in Britain you attended the University of London where you completed a law degree. Is that correct?'

'Yes, my client admits to that.'

'The murders we're investigating began to occur once you returned to Australia.'

'My client denies any knowledge of those murders.'

'Our investigations have found six bodies in the surgery at Turramurra previously owned by a Dr Amelie Santos. We believe her to be your natural grandmother. Is that correct?'

The lawyer glanced at his client.

'The evidence has established that so I think we can move on,' he said when there was no acknowledgement from Griffin.

'With Sara McLeod, you owned that building as trustees of the Shillingworth Trust, under the names of Nadine Patterson and David Tate.'

'Joel has made no admission on that.'

'We have a positive identification of Sara McLeod as Nadine Patterson, and we have in our possession passports in those names showing photographs of Sara McLeod and your client.'

'Joel still wishes to make no admissions on that subject.'

'We've established the identities of the victims. Placing them in order of their deaths so far as we can tell, they are: Jennifer Shillingworth, Stan Wells, Ian Blackmore, Elliot Griffin, father of the actual Joel Griffin, Kylie Sutcliffe and Nadifa Hasan Ibrahim. Can your client confirm that for us?'

'My client has no information to give on that subject. He's made that very clear. He denies any part in their murders.'

'Joel, you're aware that we've searched all properties associated with the Shillingworth Trust and also the McLeods' residences at Palm Beach and Cottage Point. We've located numbers of items belonging to the victims and also photographs and videos of you and Sara that were taken at the time of the murders.' The police interviewer's voice was calm. 'The photographs place you both as present and active in all these murders. There's also sufficient evidence to identify you and Sara McLeod as the murderers of Jirawan Sanders.'

'My client still denies all knowledge.'

'Does Joel want to speak for himself?'

Griffin shook his head. The profiler spoke next.

'Joel, let's talk about your grandmother, Dr Amelie Santos. When did you first find out about her?'

Griffin looked at her and spoke for the first time. 'Amelie Santos was a woman who owed me money.'

'Why did she owe you money?'

'The point is, if you owe someone money, you should pay them. If you don't, then you're at fault.'

'She was at fault,' the profiler repeated. 'Did you tell her that? Did you go and see her at her house in Blackheath?'

'She knew she owed me money,' Griffin said.

'How did she know she owed you money?'

Griffin looked at his lawyer.

'I'm doing this under instruction from my client,' the lawyer said and took an envelope out of his briefcase. It was old and yellowing. From it the lawyer took and placed on the table a copy of the letter from the Salvation Army identifying Frank Martin Wells as the son of Amelie and Rafael Santos.

'She already had that,' Griffin said. 'She'd had it for years. I had to pay for it.'

'Presumably Amelie Santos had to pay for it as well,' the police interviewer said. 'This is the information you bought from Jennifer Shillingworth. Am I correct?'

'If you check the envelope, you'll see the stamps are from the late 1960s, early '70s,' Griffin's lawyer said. 'Dr Santos must have obtained that information illegally and then declined to act on it.'

Watching, Harrigan thought that of all the people involved in this, the one with the most clear-sighted understanding of Dr Amelie Santos had been her son, Frank. *She didn't want me. She didn't even give me a name.* Just this once, all those years ago, she seemed to have made a tentative step towards finding him, but had then, for whatever reason, drawn back.

'Joel, are you saying that your grandmother knew all along who her son was?' the profiler asked.

'She had that letter. She must have done.'

'But how could she know who you were? You were Joel Griffin by then, not Craig Wells.'

'She knew she owed me money as soon as she opened the door.'

'You went and saw her in the house at Blackheath. She recognised you. Did she let you in?'

'She came outside. She said, *I don't want to see you.* She wouldn't even talk to me.'

'Did you ever go into the house?'

'When they took her away.'

'She later gave it to you,' the profiler said.

'She knew she owed it to me.'

This seemed to be as close as Griffin could get to admitting he was her grandson. The depth of resentment in his voice reminded Harrigan of Frank Wells. *The bitch! She left me nothing!* Resentment decades old. The one point on which father and son were in agreement.

'Joel,' the police interviewer said, 'you started burying people at Dr Santos's surgery in Turramurra years before you first visited her. That was before she told you she didn't want to know you. You were using her surgery while she was still alive, still its owner. Why?'

Silence. Griffin looked down at the table. He was almost smiling.

'There's no point in that question,' his lawyer said. 'Joel has no admissions to make.'

'As soon as you got back to this country, Joel, your grandmother was already in your mind,' the profiler said. 'You started to do things that were associated with her in a very negative way.'

'As I've said, there's no point in those questions. Joel has nothing to say.'

'Why did you wait four years before you went and saw her? Why not see her as soon as you came back to Australia? That's when you found out who she was.'

'I wanted to see her before she died. She was getting old.'

'You wanted to make sure she put you in her will before she died. Were you watching her?' the profiler asked.

'No. I do things in my own time,' he replied.

'After your mother, Janice Wells, Jennifer Shillingworth was your second victim. Whose decision was it to kill her? Yours or Sara's?'

'There's no proof that Joel killed his mother,' the lawyer said.

'Jennifer Shillingworth was your first victim when you came back. Why did you kill her?'

'When I do business with someone,' Griffin said after a few moments, 'I always stick to the deal I've made. Once I've settled on a price, I never ask for more money.'

'Jennifer Shillingworth wanted more money. Is that what you're saying?'

Silence.

'Why did you use her name for the property trust you set up? Because she led you to your grandmother? Or because she tried to get money out of you? Was this your way of putting her in her place?'

Silence.

'Your next victim after you came back to Australia was Stan Wells. He was your father's brother. Why did you kill him?'

Silence.

'The first thing you do when you come back to Australia after years away is find out who your grandmother is, and then carry out a killing that will cause your real father genuine grief,' the profiler said. 'Those are things Craig Wells would do, aren't they? Not Joel Griffin.'

'I'm not Craig Wells.'

'For all your killings you used an axe you stole from your father. Everything you do seems to lead back to your real family. Have you ever really left home, Joel? You've travelled the world, but aren't you still back in that little house on Bay Street?'

'You don't know the places I've been,' he replied.

'You never killed your father.'

Griffin looked down at the table and this time he did smile. 'Isn't he already dead?'

'You made your grandmother the centre of this,' the profiler said. 'You buried your victims in her surgery. The young women who worked for you at Life's Pleasures said they were there to work for Amelie. You used her home as a base for your murders. You called your property trust after the woman who found her for you and whom you then killed. Why?'

Silence.

'You and Sara met at Camp Sunshine,' the profiler said. 'You were both fifteen.'

'Joel has already agreed with that statement,' the lawyer said.

'You planned the real Joel Griffin's death from that time, didn't you? Sara started seeing him. She paid for him to get his teeth fixed but he didn't know it was under your name.'

'That allegation is pure speculation,' the lawyer said.

'No, there's sufficient evidence to support it,' the police interviewer replied. 'We also have Joel's own dental records. They date back to when he was fifteen. Given that DNA testing has established his identity as Craig Wells, we can state that he was using Joel Griffin's identity while the real Joel was still alive.'

'Sara knew from the start what you were planning,' the profiler said. 'You planned it together.'

'She liked being with me. She said it was exciting. She said there was only us in the world.'

'She was in love with you.'

'I guess so.'

'You're fascinated by identity, aren't you?' the profiler said. 'You used the medical records you found in Amelie Santos's garage to sell new identities to other people. You used them for yourselves. You even used them when you were extorting Amelie Santos's Blackheath house from her. It was like having a second self you could draw on whenever you needed to do something. Like being invisible. And you sold several of those IDs to women who then worked *gratis* at Life's Pleasures in payment. You even murdered one of them who refused to keep her side of the bargain. You used the names of your victims. It seemed to be almost a way of keeping them alive. You even brought Craig back to life. Or is that your way of keeping your victims prisoner? A way of going back to what you did to them? You bring them back to life. You murder them again.'

Silence.

'Why did you kill Elliot Griffin, Joel?' the police interviewer asked. 'Did he believe you were his son and try to seek you out? Did he want money? Why not just tell him he'd made a mistake? How could he connect you to his son?'

Silence.

'Or did he remind you that you weren't who you said you were?' the profiler asked. 'You were killing your old self all over again when you killed him. Because you really aren't Joel Griffin. You're Craig Wells.'

Griffin looked her directly in the eyes. Watching, Harrigan thought he saw her flinch.

'This is who I am,' he said. 'If someone comes to you and says, you're not who you say you are, then, whether they want money from you or not, they're drinking your blood. I don't put up with that from anyone no matter who they are.'

'Are you making a threat, Joel?' the police interviewer asked quietly.

'No.'

'Elliot Griffin found you and wanted money,' the interviewer continued after a pause. 'That's what you're saying. And because of that you killed him.'

Silence.

'Are you obsessed with the past, Joel?' the profiler said. 'You seem to have to keep worrying at it. Punishing it. You keep trying to obliterate it and then you keep bringing it back to life. Isn't that like being on a treadmill?'

'I was finished here,' Griffin said. 'I was leaving. I wasn't coming back.'

'Don't you like Sydney? This is where you were born. Why come back after all those years if it hooked you back into the past?'

'I never wanted to come back here. That was Sara's idea.'

'Why did she want to come back?'

'She was homesick. She didn't like the weather in London. She wanted to go sailing again.'

'So you came home.'

'She was going to get on a plane without me. It meant I had to move the whole business here.'

'Are you the main driver of the business, Joel?' the police interviewer asked.

'Yes.'

'You're a very skilled financier.'

'I'm good with money. I know how to make it work.'

'Money's important to you.'

'Money is real. When everything else is finished, there's always money,' Griffin said.

'Financial analysis has identified the companies Santos Associates and Cheshire Nominees as ultimately owned by you and Sara McLeod. Everything you own, you own jointly with her. You both shared your money. That's a statement of commitment, isn't it?' the profiler said. 'You owned in common. You killed people if they wanted money from you or didn't pay you. But you and Sara shared every cent you had.'

Silence.

'So when she wanted to get on a plane home, you couldn't let her do that. You couldn't kill her either. You had to go with her.'

Silence.

'You couldn't leave her. She knew everything about you.' The profiler spoke almost gently. 'Knew you as Craig and Joel. Was your lover as Craig and Joel. Helped you kill your mother and Joel

Griffin. The first police on the scene that night passed a motorbike coming towards them with a rider and a pillion. That was the two of you, wasn't it? How were you feeling? Exhilarated? You were only eighteen, the both of you.'

'It was a long time ago,' Griffin replied.

'It's almost like you both stayed back there, when you were eighteen. You kept doing it over and over again. But it began to wear out. And you started fighting with each other.'

'She's dead,' Griffin said. 'If she's dead, then the past doesn't matter. It's finished. It was finished anyway.'

'Are you grieving for her?'

Harrigan leaned forward. Griffin looked completely detached.

'Everyone dies,' he said. 'Don't you know that?'

'You needed her because she was the other half of you as a murderer and you can't get rid of that self. You like to kill. It eases your mind in some way, doesn't it? What's left now she's gone? The money?'

'There's no point in questions like that or these speculations,' the lawyer said. 'My client has already said he has no admissions to make on any of these subjects.'

'There's always money.' Griffin spoke simultaneously with his lawyer, then turned his head away from his questioners towards the one-way glass.

He couldn't know it but he was looking directly at Harrigan and Grace. His eyes seemed empty of expression, his face dead. Grace looked away and stood up.

Harrigan glanced at Borghini and all three of them left the viewing area.

'Every time we talk to him, it's like that,' Borghini said. They'd gone to a nearby shopping centre to have coffee. 'I've sat opposite him, and sometimes before the interview starts he's normal. He'll talk to you. As soon as we start, he's gone. It's like he's turned off a switch in his head. After that, nothing reaches him. He hasn't said a word about Sara McLeod. Unless you ask him directly, he won't talk about her. They were together for how long? Since she was fifteen. She was forty-three when she died. Nothing. Not even goodbye.'

'He's a sick man,' Grace said. 'There's nothing else to say.'

'How did you know to be at Duffys Forest?' Harrigan asked.

'Police work. I tried to tell your boss but he wouldn't listen,' Borghini said, looking to Grace. 'When we found Jirawan Sanders, we checked for any possible related incidents in that locality. A neighbour, Adrian Mellish, had reported hearing a scream from the surgery about a month ago. We checked the ownership of the building. It belonged to Shillingworth. We checked further, found the house at Duffys Forest. If you track where Jirawan Sanders was found, it's on a path between the two. We were working to get a search warrant for the Turramurra building when I got your call, boss. Except that when I answered it you weren't there. Then we get another call a couple of minutes later saying a man's been kidnapped. When we get there, we find your phone and Mellish tells us you were there looking at the house. We go in and find this graveyard. I didn't know where they'd taken you so I thought, okay, I'll put a team at Duffys Forest just in case. Lucky I did.'

'Did you tell Orion any of this?' Grace asked.

'Oh yeah. I called them in straightaway.'

'When did they get to Duffys Forest?'

'We went there together, which was about half an hour before Griffin arrived. They were calling the shots, saying when we should and shouldn't move. We moved too late in my opinion. They stayed too far back.'

Grace said nothing.

'I think that squares things, mate,' Harrigan said. 'You don't owe me any favours.'

'Not a problem, boss. Just doing my job.'

Grace was silent for some time while they were driving home.

'What did you mean when you told Mark he didn't owe you any favours?' she asked.

'Do you know who he is?'

'I guess you'll tell me.'

'His birth name's Vincenzo Ponticelli. He's Bianca's brother.'

'Did she tell you?'

'Yeah. I don't think she could have told anybody else because otherwise he'd probably be dead by now. They see him as a traitor. He's got no loyalty to any of the family. He saw old man Ponticelli beat up his mother and worse. When she ran, she went to Perth and married again. Mark took his stepfather's name and grew up there, a long way from any of them. He came back here about five years ago when he married a Sydney girl. I went and saw him, wanted to know if he was straight or bent. But he's as straight as they come.'

'No one's put the faces together? Him and his father?'

'Apparently, he looks more like his mother. I don't think they'll stay here. It's too close for comfort for him.'

'Does anyone else know?'

'Just you. It was the best thing about this operation for me. Knowing he was there for you to rely on.'

'I almost wish I hadn't sat in on that interview,' she said. 'I don't think I found out anything. He didn't answer any questions. It was their words; they did all the talking.'

'He'll never tell us anything. He'll just live in his head till he dies. Lucky him.'

'Whatever else I do, I'm going to forget about him,' Grace said. 'Once this is all over, it's going to be like he never existed. I'm promising myself that.'

Proving she was nothing if not thorough and reliable, Harrigan's retainer sent him one last piece of information by email. She had found a picture of Rafael Santos in a newspaper from the early 1930s. He had made it to the society pages, attending a debutante ball somewhere in the eastern suburbs.

> Mr Rafael Santos is visiting our shores from far-away Argentina where he is in the cattle business. 'I am hoping we can establish commercial ties between our two great nations,' he told our journalist. 'In the meantime, I am enjoying your wonderful hospitality and your beautiful harbour. And the ball, of course.'

Harrigan studied the photograph. A handsome man who looked more like his grandson than his son. He looked at the date. A little less than ten months before Frank Wells had been born. Did Rafael Santos meet Amelie Warwick at the debutante ball, ask her to dance? Did she think she was in love? Did he care for her? Or was he just someone with an eye for the main chance? Did he panic when he realised what he'd got himself into? Or did he meet with such hostility from her parents that he ran anyway, rather than live like that? Or was he just a conman, someone who'd never been anywhere near Argentina, a chancer living on his wits who did what he had to do before making a run for it?

Nothing in this photograph could answer any of Harrigan's questions. He didn't even save it. He deleted it and sent his retainer a request for her invoice. Time to let the past go. It had done enough damage.

Meanwhile, it was time to collect Ellie from Kidz Corner. He left the house, pleased to be doing something ordinary.

The quiet room hadn't changed since the last time Grace had sat in there. The debriefs were finished, the reports had been made, the evidence collated. Clive had asked her to see him today. This suited her; she was ready to talk to him now. He smiled at her when she sat down, his papers in front of him. She was also carrying a folder.

'I want to congratulate you again,' he said. 'Griffin's arrest is a very important development. We now have a map of most of his network. He was very skilled with finance. He ran a slick and effective operation.'

'He has a good mind,' Grace said. 'Pity he used it the way he did.'

'I'm authorising you to be paid a bonus and I'm also giving you a pay rise. You've earned it.'

He smiled. She didn't smile back.

'Thank you.'

'I have another offer as well.'

'Yes?'

'I'm looking to recruit a number of people to be my 2ICs. I'd like you to consider taking up one of those positions. I can't do this job forever and someone has to take over when I go. This is your chance to put your hat in the ring.'

'What would that involve?' she asked. 'Me working closely with you on a regular basis? Long hours?'

'The hours would be more demanding, but you've got your partner to look after your daughter for you. Yes, you would be working closely with me. That's the point. But it is a step forward in your career.'

'I shot a woman that night.'

'The autopsy showed that it was the police marksman's bullet that killed Sara McLeod, not yours.'

'I still shot her. I'm not sure I ever want to do that again.'

'In this position, you won't have to,' Clive said.

'Someone else does the dirty work.'

'You handled that situation very well. Whatever you think, you have a great deal of potential. Maybe you'd like time to think this over.'

'No, I've already done my thinking,' she said, and, opening the folder she'd brought with her, took out an envelope. 'This is my resignation. I'll complete any outstanding tasks, I'll be available for debriefings and court appearances as required, but I want to leave by the end of the month.'

'Why?' Clive asked, suddenly angry, suppressing it quickly.

'It's all in there.'

'I don't think the real reason will be there. People don't put those things on paper.'

'That night there were two things you didn't do. I asked you to ring Harrigan. You didn't.'

'I didn't have the time. To point out the obvious, he wasn't able to answer his phone.'

'You should have tried to call him. I was going into a situation where my life was in danger. He had a right to know. You also told me you would pull me out as soon as I asked you to. You didn't.'

'If your partner hadn't gone in there and interfered with Griffin's information in the first place, we would have come in.'

'I gave you the pull-out signal before we knew those records were missing. Then I called you twice more when I was in great danger. You said you would come in and you didn't.'

'I've handled this whole affair with great discretion. Your partner's investigations could have derailed this operation. I could have charged him if I wanted to, but I haven't. I think you should consider that.'

'His being there probably saved my life. Why didn't you come in?'

Grace's question was greeted with silence.

'Why leave me there?' she asked again. 'They took my wire. You couldn't even hear what was happening.'

'I told you that Griffin's business records were our main prize. I needed to find out whether he would go and get them when he left Duffys Forest. I've been through your notes in detail. They're as good as listening in. We know who our man is and we have him. He'll never see the outside of a prison wall again.'

'He didn't go and get those records. And you were almost too late to stop him killing the both of us.'

There was silence. Clive closed his folder and sat there staring at her.

'All right. Consider your resignation accepted. You can leave as soon as you've finished anything that's outstanding. Today, if possible. Don't worry, you'll still get your bonus.'

'Then I'll say goodbye.'

He didn't speak.

She got to her feet and walked to the door. She glanced back to say goodbye one more time but he was staring down at the table. She walked out, closing the door behind her silently. Later, she'd think that he hadn't been able to break her to fit the mould he'd wanted and she would always be one of his failures. At the time, she only wanted to clear her desk and go.

'What will you do?' Harrigan asked.

They were sitting in the kitchen, drinking coffee. Ellie was alternately playing and demanding their attention.

'I don't know,' she replied, taking Ellie up onto her lap.

'Go back to the police?'

'No. It was too much like a snake pit the last time I was there.'

'Work with me.'

310

She smiled, shaking her head. 'Too close.'

'Then let's have a party,' he said.

'Why?'

'To celebrate our non-marriage.'

She laughed. 'Why do we need to do that?'

'Because it must be safe to do it. No one can touch us now, babe. We've been through it all. Call it a break with the old world. A chance to get rid of the past. We can be normal.'

'We could have a party,' she said. 'Invite everybody. Play lots of music. Dance all night. Ellie, here's your chance to be at your parents' non-wedding. You can embarrass your first boyfriend's family by telling them all about it.'

'Is that a yes?'

'Yes. But I still have to work out what to do for a living.'

'Think of the world as your oyster,' he said.

'Maybe I will.'